THE BRAMBLE HEDGE

By
D. J. Lane

PublishAmerica
Baltimore

© 2005 by D.J. Lane.
All rights reserved. No part of this book may be reproduced, stored in a retrieval system or transmitted in any form or by any means without the prior written permission of the publishers, except by a reviewer who may quote brief passages in a review to be printed in a newspaper, magazine or journal.

First printing

All characters appearing in this work are fictitious. Any resemblance to real persons, living or dead, is purely coincidental.

ISBN: 1-4241-0604-4
PUBLISHED BY PUBLISHAMERICA, LLLP
www.publishamerica.com
Baltimore

Printed in the United States of America

Dedicated to Sharon, my sister.
My husband Frank.
My nieces and nephew, Renee, Rachelle, Charisse and Chris.
My son Joe and daughter-in-law Yvonne
My granddaughter Barbara and my two great-grandchildren Ethan and Jordan

A huge thanks to Tammy and Dave Muczynski, who helped get this book to the printer.

Chapter One

The young child came running into the cottage so excited she could barely manage to take a breath. Her mother was standing at the table kneading dough for the day's bread making. "Slow down, little one, before you fall and break your neck. What is all this excitement about?" Sera was so used to her eldest daughter bringing her newfound treasures for examination that she didn't turn to see what the object was. Of the four girls, Fila was the most curious, daring and imaginative. She had collected a large assortment of items found during her forays into and around their forest home. There was one place Fila had been forbidden to enter, an eerie, massive, bramble-edged land area that abutted their property and seemed to have no end. Strange lights and mysterious rumblings sometimes occurred that were unexplainable. Sera had an unaccountable dread not knowing who or what inhabited the place. If she had known where Fila had found her new treasure, she would have been furious.

Finally, finishing the kneading, she rolled the dough into a ball, thinly coated it with a film of melted fat, and placed it in a sunny window for its first rise. Dusting her hands lightly on her apron, she turned to her daughter and motioned her forward. Fila extended her hand to her mother, a curious brown figurine clasped tightly in her fingers. It was such a weird-looking figurine that Sera didn't really want to touch it. "Where in the world did you find this, Fila? It's not very pretty. Why ever would you want to keep it?"

Fila held the small image close to her chest, a stubborn look beginning to form on her face, a look her mother was very familiar with. "Mother, I like it. And it likes me too. Can I keep it? I'll put it away in my treasure chest. You'll get to like it after you get used to seeing it." Fila waited for her mother's nod of assent, then pulled a chair to the wall shelf, climbed up to reach the pretty chest her father had made for her, and deposited the little icon within.

Sera thought it the ugliest carving she had ever laid eyes on, but Fila was such an odd child. She had always been the adventurous one. Exploring the woods, climbing trees so tall that Sera had almost fainted when she had spotted her daughter swaying in the top of a towering evergreen, laughing at the fun she was having being swirled about by the wind, ever the daredevil trying new antics. It was unusual for Fila to take an interest in a toy. "Oh! Well! What harm in keeping her newfound treasure?" The girl was never one to ask for things like her siblings did. Fila never cared what items were purchased at the trading post. Always willing to give her sisters anything they wanted, generous to a fault with a very loving heart.

Sera smiled at Fila's pleased expression knowing her daughter couldn't wait to tell her sisters about what she had hidden in her treasure chest. They surely wouldn't be as excited as their sister but, to please her, would exclaim over the little carving as though it were made of gold.

Sera went back to her bread making, kneading the dough again then dividing it into four loaves that would rise again before being baked. One loaf would be eaten hot from the oven with fresh-churned butter. The others, once cooled, would be wrapped in oiled cloth to be kept fresh.

As for Fila, all she could do was think about her new friend and how she had been led to find it. She wasn't one to misbehave but something had happened to her that she couldn't explain. When her father returned she would tell everyone about her experience. Until then, something told her to keep silent, and that's exactly what she was going to do.

There would not be many more nice days this late in autumn. The four sisters sat outside in the warm sunshine playing cross and daggers. They could see their mother, Sera, through the kitchen window, busily finishing the making of meat pies for their dinner. She had already milked their cow, Bell, who supplied them with enough milk and cream to make butter, cheese, and buttermilk. Though days were always busy, life was gentle.

Their home was situated on a large fifty-acre parcel of land in the midst of a great forest. Many years ago Aaron, the man who would become their father, happened on the area while hunting. He had collected many seeds during his travels, some berries, some fruit trees. These he had planted. Now, years later, during summer and fall, everyone ate their fill of a wide variety of fruits. Sera was clever at preserving and drying foodstuffs for winter consumption and had finished the last of that work yesterday.

Their chickens and a small flock of sheep provided eggs, meat and wool for the making of Sera's beautifully woven items that Aaron used for trade goods. The spring wool had been prepared for just such a day as this. It had been washed and well dried, ready to be carded, finely separated, and spun into filaments which could then be made into clothing or other household goods. Once Sera had wound the first wool filaments on the spindle, her spinning could begin when she noticed it was lunchtime.

Rising from her stool she stepped to the window and called. She watched as the four came laughing and tumbling through the doorway. They quickly washed and dried their hands at the washbowl, then settled themselves at the long wooden table. Sera placed portions of yesterday's stew in each of their dishes and poured fresh milk into their tin cups, serving herself and finally sitting at the table's head. The girls—Fila, Alea, Mina and Nia—and their mother, Sera, began to eat their lunch, light conversation and teasing between the girls made Sera laugh.

When finished, they cleaned the utensils, neatly replacing everything back on the shelves. Although they had planned to go back outside a light rain had begun to fall. "What shall we do now?" Fila asked, trying to think of something that would amuse her younger siblings, her eyes traveling the room looking for something to do. It was then her eyes alit on her treasure chest, a perfect way to pass some time by sorting through her collections.

Fila pulled over a stool to reach the shelf. The girls gathered excitedly as the chest was placed upon the table and the lid opened. The old relic Fila had placed within lay amid an array of articles she had collected over the years, all made of various substances. A golden key attached to a slender gold chain attracted Fila's eye immediately. She had not put it there. Turning to her mother she asked, "Did you or the girls put anything in my chest?" Receiving a negative reply from both her mother and sisters, Fila turned again to the chest's contents.

Reaching for the necklace she also picked up the small image she had been so intrigued with. Somehow, it felt as though the two belonged together although she couldn't imagine why. They were so different, the key and chain delicately made, whereas the image was rather roughly carved and, she had to agree with her mother, a bit ugly. But there was something about it that drew deeply from her inner nature a feeling of care and concern for the safekeeping of the little image. Without a second thought she slipped the necklace over her head, the little key resting snugly upon her young bosom. She could feel warmth beginning to generate from both the necklace and the relic until the warm paths wended their way toward each other and connected near her heart.

She could plainly hear the Relic's voice in her mind giving instructions and admonitions. "You must take this key, Fila. It will unlock the panel in a hidden portal where I will be kept safe. Afterward, you must wear the chain and key always until I decide when it will no longer be necessary. Attend to what I say, it is most important you obey. Eventually, all will become clear to you. Until then fear not, be strong. When your father returns, ask him to take you to the Winter Forest, I will guide you." Fila sat quietly as she listened to the voice in her mind while the family examined the various items she had collected. The array was quite extensive, some very pretty and others looked quite ordinary. There was a silver-handled mirror, a slender golden arrow that seemed almost ready to fly away, a dainty tin cup with foreign-looking words written along its edge, a small, black iron-bound book about the length of a large man's hand which was impossible to open but had looked so interesting that Fila felt compelled to keep it. At last, everything had been examined minutely and replaced within the chest, which was returned once again to the top shelf.

Suddenly, the quiet was broken by the echoing notes from a ram's horn. With one motion all arose from their seats. The four girls raced out the door, while Sera quickly swung the cooking pot back over the fire. She set the table with bread, cheese, fruit and a jug of cider. Soon four excited voices could be heard, along with the deeper baritone of a man. Aaron was home at last. It had seemed much too long a trek. Usually he was home within four months, this trip had taken almost six.

When she heard his step at the door Sera threw herself into his arms. Luckily, he had already dropped his huge pack or her enthusiastic welcome-home embrace would have knocked him from his feet. He picked her up and swung her around in a wide circle, happy to be home once again. It was always this way on his return. His restlessness satisfied by the travels, he was content for a while until the urge plagued him once again. Setting her down, he gave a satisfied grin, and turned to pick up his pack and set it aside.

Right now, he was famished. A good meal and the welcome companionship of his family was all he was interested in. They sat at their places hoping to hear some of their father's stories. Sera remembered to get the smoked venison strips from the larder, adding the newly hard-boiled eggs and freshly churned butter. Lastly, she placed a bowl of stew for him. The joy of being together lent excitement to their noisy conversations.

Finally replete, the table cleared, Aaron retrieved his pack and opened its flap. Removing items one by one he placed some on the table, others he arranged on a large deerskin spread upon the floor. The vast array of goods was a picturesque bouquet of colors. Sera and the girls crowded around excitedly trying to contain their curiosity. There were three beaver coverlets, a small bundle of deerskins, six pair of beaded moccasins, silver neck bands, bracelets and hair ornaments. There were pouches of herbs, dried lemongrass and sassafras root. He had several nicely made bone combs, six bone needles, and two bone spoons.

The best he saved for last. Reaching deep within the pack he withdrew a soft, quilled and beaded leather sheath, and from its opening a smooth, black obsidian blade which lay gleaming on the outstretched palm of his hand. The curve of the carved handle and blade was one breathtaking piece of workmanship. This was a prize worth all others combined. So rare that most men never had the opportunity to see obsidian, let alone own it. He turned to Sera with a pleased grin on his sun-browned face. Sera looked at the object, curiosity making her brow furrow in puzzlement. She was so accustomed to the usual metal cutlery that something created from another element was too unusual to accept at face value. "What sort of knife is this?" she asked, not feeling comfortable with something so strange looking, so drastically different. Just looking at it she knew it would be a bit unwieldy and awkward, however Aaron was so pleased with his find she didn't want to hurt his feelings. She gave a sidewise glance at his face, knew that this was something he had brought to her with pride and pleasure to please her. Leaning forward she kissed him. "It's beautiful," she said smiling at him, knowing it was the right thing to do when a wide grin split his face.

"I thought of you the moment I saw it. The blade is so sharp you must be careful to not cut yourself. This should last a lifetime as long as we're careful to keep it away from hard objects which could break or damage it." Aaron extended his hand to Sera offering her the magnificent gift. As she lifted the slim blade from his hand, a thin line of red appeared to follow its path. With a cry of alarm Sera dropped the knife, which fell harmlessly onto the deerskin bundle. At the same time, Aaron looked in surprise at the rivulet of blood dripping onto the fallen blade. It had been a painless cut. If not for the blood he would never have noticed it.

Sera quickly stepped to the shelf and selected a clean white cloth. She hurriedly tore the fabric, dipped one of the pieces into the urns cold water, and then cleaned his cut. She wrapped the remaining piece tightly around Aaron's hand and tied the ends.

They both looked down at the blood-stained blade resting on the deerskin. It had all happened so quickly. The jet-black obsidian now seemed to have a small flame burning deep within its burnished surface. It had been marked as though at a ceremony. Sera carefully cleaned the blood from the blade's surface, inserting the knife into the leather sheath that had been specially made to protect the precious object. At least she now had a strong respect for the sharpness of its cutting edge and would always handle it very cautiously. However she had no intentions of using it after what had just happened.

Aaron's hand didn't seem to be causing him any problem. He was systematically stashing some of the trade goods in the attic storage chests. Finally, everything at last sorted and put away, everyone could relax, get comfortable, and listen to the stories Aaron would relate about his travels.

THE BRAMBLE HEDGE

This was the best time of all. The girls settled themselves on their stools while Sera and their father rested in the two chairs near the fireplace.

Aaron cleared his throat, paused for a moment sorting through his memories then began. "When I left here last spring, I decided to travel north and look for a different route than I usually take. The forests were just beginning to show their leaves, the earth dry from lack of rain so traveling was easy. Within three days, after entering the great forest, I came upon a tribe of Indians. They were friendly when they saw I was a trader and very anxious to swap when they saw Sera's woven wool. That's where I bargained for the deerskins. They told me of a large lake, far to the northwest, where I could find a guide. When our trading ended I followed their directions arriving at the new encampment.

"The guide took me by canoe along a wide deep river that flowed in a westerly direction. I visited many scattered villages along that waterway and was joyously welcomed. Pleasure in trading also gave them a reason to celebrate a break in their everyday routine. Some of the items I received in trade I swapped with other tribes for things that took my interest, such as a large turtle shell that had been scraped clean inside, given a smooth surface by sand rubbing, then polished to a high gloss with beeswax. I had every intention of bringing it home, at least until I saw the obsidian knives, then it seemed I couldn't deny the obsession that overcame me. The chief owned two. I could see he was quite taken with the turtle shell, which in fact was very beautiful. I didn't want to appear too anxious, knowing if I did he would drive a much harder bargain. I ended up staying there almost a week. Thankfully that was near the end of the trade route. Finally, toward the end, the chief relented and accepted the shell in return for the smaller of the knives. It had been a matter of who could hold out the longest and I was determined to get that obsidian knife. It's something we can pass down to our first grandchild someday. Everyone had finished trading by the time we two had reached a final agreement. We were both satisfied. Thinking we had made the best of the deal we parted as friends. It was time to start my journey home."

Aaron continued. "The guide was anxious to get back to his family. We managed to make better time returning upriver than I had expected. The many months of trading had gone quickly. The weather was turning much colder at night. It wouldn't be long before frost. We both wanted to get home to ready for winter. The guide said he had hunting parties waiting for him. They needed to supply their wives with more meat to cure, to take them through the winter months. When we arrived back at his camp we said our goodbyes and I hurried home as quickly as possible."

    Aaron fell silent, it felt comfortable resting before the fire feet propped up on one of the stools. He began to doze, the warmth and contentment easing the stress of his travels. Soon Sera heard a gentle snore. The girls were still sitting on their stools, not wanting to disturb their father's nap, she felt it was time to send the girls off to bed. Rising quietly, she motioned to them. All four rose and tiptoed to the attic stairs climbing, one by one, until they disappeared from view.

    Sera heard their nightly preparations until finally all fell silent. She brushed the crumbs from the table and wrapped the cheese. The few remaining chores could be left undone until morning. She glanced fondly at her husband's relaxed face; he looked so young and vulnerable when he was at rest. He could never imagine how very much she loved him. Needing to awaken him she tugged on his sleeve until he stirred from his slumbers and opened his eyes. Giving a shake to his shoulders, he arose from the chair and followed her to bed. She helped him undress and then into bed where he slept soundly until the morning sun, streaming through the window, awoke him from the first good night's sleep he had enjoyed in months.

    Aaron gave a great stretch of his muscles before sitting upright and swinging his feet to the cold floor. He saw that Sera had placed a pair of woolen slippers for him to use, he pulled them on gratefully. Stepping to the nearby chair, reaching for his clothes, he was dressed and ready to dig in to the breakfast he could smell cooking. It was nice to be home again. He had missed Sera and the girls very much. The one thing he took pleasure in was bringing back items he knew they would use and treasure. He recalled the smiles on their faces when they had seen the bone combs and needles, how intently they had inspected the fine workmanship of each. Sera smiled at Aaron's serious expression. She could see he was deep in thought and wondered what could be causing his reverie. She placed the bowls of hot cornmeal mush on the table along with the bread, butter, applesauce, and jug of cider. She also reached for the honey jar. This was one of his favorite breakfasts he had looked forward to. The girls came scrambling down the steps late, knowing their mother would not be angry this morning because she enjoyed those few extra moments alone with their father. It was always this way on the first morning after he had returned home. He gave a tousle to their sleep-mussed hair knowing they had been waiting expectantly for his morning teasing they had missed so much while he had been gone.

Once everyone had taken their places breakfast began with happy smiles and the welcome chatter of young voices. Aaron has missed this very much. He could never explain how all these little things made life so full and worthwhile.

He noticed Fila watching him. He tried to analyze the expression on her face but for the life of him he couldn't figure out what could be causing the anxious look she was giving him. He glanced at Sera and caught her nod toward Fila, the signal when one of the girls had something to discuss with him.

When breakfast was finished, everything cleaned and put away, Aaron pulled Fila aside and asked if she had something she wanted to talk to him about. She gave him a tentative smile, pausing for a moment to call her sisters to join the conversation.

She pulled the stool over to the shelf, lifted her treasure chest down and carried it to the table, placing it in front of her father. As she stood quietly for a moment trying to decide what to do next, Aaron raised the lid and began examining the articles within. He noticed the little brown figurine. It was such an odd carving. Dark wood which seemed unusually hard, an almost indiscernible face with deeply carved eyes, a roughly shaped head and a jagged gash where the mouth should be. He could not figure out what the figure represented, man or animal. Nothing was prominent that could tell the nature of the article. He looked quizzically at Fila wondering where she had acquired the little statue. Finally he spoke. "Fila, where did you find this?"

He watched as the color drained from her face. She sat quickly, as though she had felt a moment of weakness. "Father, please don't be angry with me. Something happened which I had no control over. The urge that overcame me seemed to take over my every action and thought. I was at the edge of our compound near where the woods begin. I had walked that way many times looking for wildflowers. For the first time I noticed a faint path that led into the forest and I was drawn to follow it. Later I came upon a wicked-looking briar barrier. The path continued along the obstacle for a short distance then just stopped. That's when I noticed an opening that could have been easily overlooked. It seemed large enough for me to crawl through so I did. The path continued on the other side and I followed until I arrived at a cave in the mountainside. I was drawn to look inside, I felt I had been led there. I saw a long table containing a multitude of objects where my eyes were drawn to this statue. With no volition on my part, my hand reached to pluck it from midst the other images. I turned, hurried from the cave and back to the safety of our own property."

Fila paused for breath, stepped to the water urn to get a sip of water to moisten her dry lips and then continued. "Father, it is a magical charm or something of that nature. It spoke to me, not exactly in words, and said that you must take me to the Winter Forest."

Fila fell silent, waiting for her father to speak. She didn't know why this was so important but a sense of emergency seemed to be associated with the mental message that had been conveyed to her.

Fila adored adventure. Whatever had drawn her to the cave had given her a strong feeling that life was going to be much more exciting in the future. There was even a hint of danger surrounding the little image.

Aaron was still holding the statue loosely in his hand. There was a certain aura about the thing that stirred his curiosity. An attraction that seemed to draw a deep feeling of awe, as though he held a precious object of prehistoric art. It seemed associated with the exceptionally crude craftsmanship of the image which was undeniably ugly. Whoever had carved the thing had not tried to pretty it up. The oddly sunken eyes and voracious mouth made his skin crawl. At first he had thought Fila was just making up stories because she had such a vivid imagination. There was, however, something that confirmed her tale, a feeling that grew stronger the longer he held the image. He was drawn to gaze into its eyes. It was like looking into a pool of black water. He peered down into them seeming to see something moving deep within. As he drew closer to the darkened orbs he felt himself being pulled into their depths, found he was standing at the edge of the legendary Winter Forest where a light snow was falling. He heard Fila telling him they must hurry to reach the hidden portal. She reached for his hand and pulled him into the woods, seeming to follow an invisible path that led them onward. At long last they reached a clearing that seemed to be ringed with a silvery curtain of mist. In the very center stood a great oak tree which must have been centuries old. With a glad cry of discovery she hurried to the tree, and then turned to her father with a grin. "Now we are ready," she said.

The words were still echoing in Aaron's ears when he felt a shock sting his fingers. He became aware he was sitting at his table, in his cottage, with his family surrounding him. He saw concerned looks on their faces and noticed the little statue was no longer in his hand but standing upright on the table facing him. He turned to Fila, who had been watching his facial expressions while he appeared to be in deep concentration.

"Fila, I do believe there is something to the tale you have told us. This image seems to have a strong magnetic force that sends a warning to follow its instructions. Although I'm not one to believe in magical things, I feel impelled to follow its wishes. We must ready ourselves for our journey."

Sera found a pack for Fila and began to fill it with provisions, Fila made sure her Relic was safely inside, Aaron was ready and waiting. With hurried goodbyes they stepped out the cottage door.

They exited the property near the mountain's base. Aaron knew there was a good trail above if he had been alone, but he could not chance it with Fila. Some of the chasms were too wide a leap for her shorter legs. Best they follow the base trail, it was well defined and much easier, although it would take longer.

The morning passed quickly. When the sun reached its zenith, Aaron called a halt. They found a small clearing where they could rest and eat the lunch Sera had packed. A clear deep spring gave them refreshingly cool water to drink.

Fila felt herself dozing off, sleepy from a restless night when her thoughts had spun like a twirling maple-tree seed in the wind. She was at the edge of complete slumber when she heard a familiar voice deep with her consciousness.

"Fila, child. Hear me, there is danger lying in wait for you. He who once had possession of me has planned my return. You must heed my instructions—come, child, arise. There isn't much time."

Fila, unaware of her surroundings, rose unsteadily. The whisper continued, "You must retrieve my image from your pack." The instant her fingers closed about the image she felt a stinging sensation that was almost painful, although she tried to release the icon it was solidly bonded to her hand. She felt herself guided toward the woods at the edge of the spring where a dense growth of underbrush looked impassable. However, a few steps within and she found herself at the mouth of a tunnel. She stepped inside, disappearing from view.

When Aaron awoke from his doze, disturbed by something that had disrupted his dreams, he ran his fingers through his hair, gave a stretch, and then turned to wake Fila from her nap. She was nowhere in sight, her pack lying in the same place. He assumed she had stepped into the woods for a moment but not a leaf stirred.

Aaron began a thorough search of the area, even checking the pond. The water was so clear he could see the bottom and thankfully Fila was not within. After calling loudly he thrashed through the trees and shrubbery until exhausted. Finally, head in his hands, he wondered what he should do, where she could have disappeared. He leaned against his pack, eyelids becoming so heavy he could not keep them open.

In a moment he could see Fila standing at the oak tree. "You must return home, Father," he heard her say. "I will be spending the winter here, there are things I must do that cannot wait. I'm not exactly sure what happened. I was in grave danger." Fila's voice faded away as Aaron awoke.

Almost ill with worry he retrieved Fila's pack, slung it over his shoulder along with his own, and hurried back home. He was unaware of the figure that stood hidden in the forest's shadows. A cape disguising and blending the image amidst leaves and branches so even if Aaron had passed close enough to touch, he would not have seen Luther's angry features. Pure rage distorted his features until it was unrecognizable as even being human.

Once Aaron was beyond hearing distance a hoarse growl emerged from Luther's throat which then turned into a howl of frustrated fury. He promised himself he would have his treasure back where it belonged and next time he would take precautions to keep it safe. How that brat managed to gain access to his property was a mystery, the Hedge should have prevented it.

Years ago when the man had begun to build on the property so near to his own, he had been uneasy. He wanted to be as far away from other people as possible, however he already had everything arranged exactly as he liked. When there had been no intrusions by the new family he had relaxed, the years had passed pleasantly. Who would have guessed that a bratty young girl would walk into his home and take his most prized possession? His rage unbound, Luther was clenching his teeth so tightly his jaw was beginning to ache. The invasion of his privacy stung him to the quick. It had been so close. He had almost captured the thief and recovered his Relic, the most prized of all he possessed.

Years ago he had heard of an image that could impart great power. He had scoffed at the idea, too ridiculous to even imagine, just old wive's tales. However, many times the story was repeated, over and over, until he had to find out for himself. Tracking the rumor from one part of the country to another he slowly focused on the area where all the tales seemed to originate from.

He traveled to the small village of Umer where, according to the latest information, there lived an old man named Calis. Luther had disguised himself to look like a poor cooper smith. With his mule and rickety cart filled with extra staves he was an unimposing figure. The worn clothes, shaggy hair and calloused-looking hands made the fantasy complete. He took the side trail to avoid going through the village knowing he would be unable to actually do repair work.

Finally he neared the old man's small abode. It was a two-room cottage handsomely constructed of fieldstone with a good solid roof and sturdy plank door completing the scene.

As he drew closer he noticed a small brown dog sleeping on the cottage path. Cautiously, he stepped over the animal and entered the doorway. Not a soul in sight. He surveyed the room searching for anything that could hold the item he had heard so many tales about.

Seeing nothing of interest, he edged into the smaller rear section.

The old man was lying on his cot seemingly in a deep heavy slumber. Luther glanced about the room, then at the articles on a shelf. As he turned his head he spotted a small leather pouch hanging from a peg in the wall. A searing flash of knowledge lit his eyes as he reached greedily for the treasure. As his fingers closed around it a set of needle-sharp teeth clamped upon his ankle. A high screech burst forth from his lips as he thumped the creature on its head with the leather pouch. The small dog backed away.

Luther looked toward the cot, expecting the old man to arise from his sleep and try to protect his treasure. Not a twitch. It was then Luther realized the old man had passed beyond.

Tucking the pouch into his cape he lost no time exiting the house to make his way home, the unseen little brown dog following closely. Smiling to himself at how easily he had attained the Icon, he had almost burst into song as he strode through the village, not caring if anyone saw him or not. He had succeeded and didn't give a fig what anybody thought. He could hardly wait to get home and set the Artifact on his large collection table where all his prized antiquities were on display for his pleasure. There had been many wild goose chases. Whenever he became distraught after a fruitless quest he had only to gaze upon his collection to boost his morale and continue his search for just one more collectable.

What need of family did he have? Not a whit, he had no need of companionship. All the way home he had clasped the wooden image close to his chest, almost caressing it. The memory of that intense pleasure made a smile crease his face.

Luther shook himself free from his reveries, all this searching to find his stolen Relic and all for naught. He knew Fila had been at the spring, had pictured her as clear as his inner eye could see. How she had disappeared was a mystery. Her father had been fast asleep in one of the little spells Luther was adept at conjuring. It came in handy when he wanted to do a little searching of premises.

Now he must return to his private hideaway, away from prying people who would love to steal more of his treasures. He had amassed many small, magical Icons and Potions that gave him power, more power than he could use in his lifetime.

Luther slipped quietly into the trees hurrying along the almost invisible trail. He would be home before nightfall. Plenty of time to use his sorcery to find Fila, she couldn't be very far. He would feel more secure when the Icon was back in his possession. Curses, why did he feel so nervous, as though unseen eyes were watching his every move? He glanced about edgily hoping to discover the reason. There was nothing that should disturb his consciousness. Finally, closing his mind to the unknown disturbance he hastened on his way, lengthening his stride then finally breaking into a mile-covering lope. As he disappeared from view a pair of sharp brown eyes kept track of his location.

Familiar scenery came into view as Luther trod well-known paths. In a short time he arrived at the barrier that surrounded his private world. Walking along the hedge he stopped at a section that looked identical except for a round gray rock resting at the edge of the thorny barrier. Pressing his foot upon it, a narrow passage opened. He entered, not bothering to see it close behind him; he was home at last.

Once inside his cavern dwelling he relaxed a little but still couldn't dismiss the question of how Fila had managed to escape. He had a feeling there was more to the entire scenario than met the eye. A probable explanation, she had the Icon with her and had been warned of his approach. Too bad he couldn't have snatched her, now he'd have to make other plans.

Tomorrow would be a good time to take a look at the family homestead. See who lived there and what their daily habits were. He should have paid more attention, should have expected the possibility of trouble and had a plan to put into effect. There was always the chance of nabbing one of the family and holding them until his property was returned, but then, with that trader home, maybe not a good idea at the present, something to keep in mind though.

Luther's nerves were drawn taut as a bowstring. It seemed the more he dwelt on his problem, the more upset he became. This would be a perfect time for one of his home remedies. Wandering along the shelves in the room where he kept his potions, herbs and homemade mixtures he selected a small green jar. Holding it to the candle he carried, he felt confident it was what he was searching for, at the same time realizing for safety, he should sort and rearrange all the concoctions into a semblance of order. He promised himself that was exactly what he would do when he found the time.

Swinging the kettle over the fire, he sat to wait for the water to boil. He couldn't stop himself from wondering how Fila had disappeared and managed to escape his grasp.

For a moment Fila stood in darkness waiting for her eyes to adjust, then the craggy ceiling came into focus. She let her gaze travel around the stony walls that encompassed her. At one end of the cave she could see outside into sun-brightened greenery that hid the cave's entrance, the other side meandered off into darkness. With a flash of awareness, she realized she still had the small carved image grasped tightly in her hand. "What in the world is happening," she mumbled to herself, gazing intently at the tiny image. "One minute I was dozing off almost asleep, the next I'm standing in a strange cave."

She placed the little carving upright on the ledge next to her and stared at it, hoping for an explanation. The words it conveyed were expressed in a mental monologue that held Fila entranced. "You were in grave peril," the image said. "It was necessary that immediate action be taken to protect you, and therefore myself. It was important that we leave for the Winter Forest at once. I sent your father home using your image in a dream to help convince him and calm his fears. He is content that all will be well with you. Come, child, we must be on our way, but before we begin I have a gift for you. On the ledge over your shoulder there is a garment for you to wear. It is rather cool in these subterranean hallways, it will keep you warm."

Reaching upward she pulled a soft cape down from the shelf. Surprisingly it felt as light as a feather yet the bulk of it looked quite heavy. Slipping it over her shoulders it felt so luxurious she couldn't help but give a spin to see the way it belled out from her body then fell back into soft folds draping around her form. She couldn't imagine what it had been made from. Of all the fur pelts her father had brought home from his trading journeys she had never in her life seen anything like it. She wanted so much to ask the little Artifact about it but she felt a little intimidated. This was all quite strange to her and truthfully even a bit odd.

"It is time, child. On the inside of your cape you will find a special pocket, place my image therein." Fila hurried to comply, then following the voice's instructions went to the far end of the cave and stepped into the opening that appeared before her. She felt a slight twinge of unease, nervousness making her mouth feel dry. However, having the little image in her pocket seemed to build her feeling of confidence. Eventually, making her way through the strange underground tunnel, she began to feel only excitement and anticipation of what new experience might be around the next bend in the walkway.

The tunnel was lit with an eerie green glow that seemed to emanate from some type of fungus that grew everywhere. The rough walls were studded with a multitude of tiny twinkling flecks that reflected and enhanced the glow. It was quite beautiful. The path she trod was so even, it looked as though years of flowing water had carved and sanded it to a smooth level surface. She inhaled a deep breath of the cool, fresh-smelling air. It felt invigorating, making her feel she could walk forever and not tire.

She set a steady pace, trying to cover as much distance as possible. She would continue to travel this way the entire time. After a short rest she would again rise and press onward. Occasionally, deep sleep drifted over her consciousness after eating the fungi which the Relic had told her would help keep up her strength. Truthfully, Fila was a strong girl; however, the pace she was keeping could only be attributed to the tangy, sweet, glowing growth that enhanced the beauty of the underground path. Also, if there had been a mirror or reflective pool she would have been pleased with how her image had seemed so much more refined. Now, nearing the end of her journey, she became aware there was a different look and feel to the tunnel. At first she couldn't quite place what that difference was, then she realized the light was no longer a soft green but a more golden color. As Fila followed the curve of the walkway, sunlight cast such a dazzling brightness it was almost blinding. She quickly closed her eyes, squinting a bit until they adjusted to the light. When at last she finally emerged into the fresh cold air, she found herself standing at the edge of the Winter Forest.

She glanced around, noticed that the tunnel opening was not even visible, evergreen boughs covered the entryway making it undetectable. She made a mental note of its location in case a hurried escape was ever necessary.

Turning to the forest's perimeter she peered through the overhanging branches, feeling sure she would come upon an old deer trail or other manageable passageway. She must have searched at least a mile before finding an opening. Pulling her cloak closely about her body, she stepped onto the shadowed trail. The sunlight was so heavily filtered it looked more like twilight at the end of day rather than high noon. Hopefully, she would reach her destination before nightfall.

It seemed she walked for hours. Sometimes brambles caught at her cloak, other times she stumbled over fallen limbs or dry twisted tree roots. Little by little, she began to tire as the daylight dwindled. If she didn't reach a place of safety soon, she would have to curl up at the base of one of the trees and spend the night. She was too spent to notice that the trees had started to thin a bit and the evening sky glowed with the multihued colors of sunset. If she had lifted her head she would have seen the edge of a clearing just ahead and the cedar-shingled roof of a log cabin just beyond. As she stumbled along she finally became aware that the wall of trees pressing in on her had disappeared. Numbly, she raised her head expecting an impasse or barrier she would have to navigate around. What she beheld was a large clearing midst the forest. Generous in size and having at its center the tallest, oldest oak tree she had ever seen. It seemed to soar to the heavens, spreading immense limbs above most of the glade. Nestled at the outer edge of its expanse sat a roomy looking log cabin.

She lengthened her stride, hurrying to reach the welcome sanctuary, almost tripping in her eagerness. She reached the wooden door and lifted the latch. Stepping inside, closing the door, she turned to examine the interior, so exhausted she took only a quick glance at the surroundings. Her eyes focused on the wooden bed in the far corner of the room. Dragging herself to its edge she collapsed onto the feather coverlet and within moments was sound asleep cradled warmly in her cloak. She slept soundly until morning.

"Time now to awaken from your slumbers," the Relic sent his insistent demand. The distant voice wormed its way into her consciousness, driving her dreams away and bringing her into the sunlit room. She stretched lazily, feeling so warm and comfortable she was loath to stir. She lay a moment letting her eyes drift around her new dwelling. It was indeed, a snug haven that seemed to have everything she would require for her extended stay. Sitting upright, she placed her feet on the floor, at the same time pulling her cloak a bit more closely about her shoulders. It was quite chilly, a perfect day to have a warm blaze in the fireplace heating the room. The bright sunlight gave lie to the golden glow that seemed to suggest warmth. At last, rising lazily, she walked to the near window. The view that greeted her at once stunned and caused her to gasp in surprise. In the long night that she had slept so soundly winter had arrived in all its sparkling beauty. It dazzled her eyes to the point of blindness, the sun so reflective on the snow it was almost painful to gaze upon. Turning from the window it took a moment for her eyes to adjust to the dimmer interior of the cabin. As the room slowly came into focus she saw that the fireplace was already generating heat, the fire almost dancing as it greedily consumed the well-laid logs. For a moment she was startled at its mysterious appearance then she remembered the little figurine in her cloak and all the magic it seemed capable of. She began to search anxiously through the various folds for the hidden pocket where she had placed the Relic. It was not there. Terrified that she had lost it when stumbling through the woods, she was ready to leave when her eyes happened to alight on the fireplace mantle. There, highlighted by a ray of the morning sun, the Relic was illuminated.

"Come, Fila, we have much to discuss. You are the recipient of my power until my desire has been attained. Your goodness dictates that you must be wise in the choices you make so you do not cause unintentional harm. We have all the time we need here in the Winter Forest. Go, prepare some breakfast and then make yourself comfortable. You are the first in many eons whose goodness can help bring an end to the destructive behavior of an individual who is bent on creating havoc with his mania to accumulate that which is not meant to be hoarded. Hurry, child. I have waited many years for a time such as this. I am impatient to begin."

After Fila had satisfied her hunger and prepared a cup of tea to sip, she waited for Relic to continue. "Look now to your family, see how they fare since you disappeared. Mentally see what is happening at your home. If there is something you deem important, place your suggestion in the mind of the person of your choosing." Fila closed her eyes, letting herself see and sense images and thoughts. In a moment she was outside the family door watching her father approach, it was soon after she had disappeared. She watched as he hesitated before entering the cottage, knew he was trying to formulate the words to explain Fila's disappearance.

He couldn't think of a single logical explanation. Pushing open the door he saw Sera and the girls waiting, an expectant look on their faces. They looked for Fila, not understanding why she was nowhere in sight. They knew something was amiss. He would not let Fila travel alone to the Winter Forest. Where was she? Sera looked questioningly at him, not wanting to frighten the girls if something had gone wrong. "Girls, get the bread and the cheese, go to the springhouse and bring a jug of cider."

Once they were out of hearing Sera turned to Aaron and, while removing his cape, asked the question he dreaded trying to explain. "Where's Fila?" Sera hung the cape on its peg and turned to her husband, watching the motions play across his face as he tried to decide how to relate the mystery to her. Aaron wasn't sure where to begin, the events seemed so strange, so he just began at their arrival at the spring, how they had stopped to rest and he had fallen asleep. When he awoke there was not one sign of where or how Fila had disappeared. He reached the part where he had fallen into a doze and seen Fila in a dream telling him not to worry. He had felt confident she was safe and unharmed although there was no logical reason for him to believe so. He turned to Sera, hoping she would accept his explanation and not feel he had neglected his parental duties. It was then that a feeling of complete confidence seemed to descend upon them. Fila hovered near for only a moment, until she was confident they had sensed she was safe and unharmed.

When the three girls returned with the cider Sera was already setting the table for lunch. She had a deep feeling that the Relic would be Fila's Protector. She was also aware of how much her daughter had changed since first finding the Relic.

After lunch had been consumed and the table cleared, Sera made a quick decision that seemed quite logical. "Aaron, you must take Alea to the Winter Forest, Fila shouldn't be alone. There is still time to get there before hard winter sets in. You must also bring Fila her treasure chest." Aaron, seeing Sera's serious face, knew she was right in her decision. Everyone began to help gather the items Aaron and Alea would need. Food parcels of bread, cheese, dried fruit and meat were wrapped, divided and placed into the two backpacks. Aaron's would be the heavier although Alea's would also be balanced according to how much she could comfortably carry. It was time to set off and cover as many miles as possible. With last-minute hugs, the door was opened and the two were on their way.

In minutes they were passing the tree line at their compound's edge, turning left and following the deer trail that led northward. Once they passed the mysterious territory where Fila had found the figurine their passage would be easier. At noon they stopped for a rest at the same place where Fila had disappeared. Aaron pointed out the places he had searched without success. Alea went to look, hoping to discover where her sister had vanished, but could see nothing unusual. She turned away in disappointment, the mystery unsolved. No matter, she would be happy to see her sister again. It would be fun staying the winter with her, just the two of them alone for the very first time. Hefting their packs to their shoulders they continued on their way.

By evening they had bypassed the stony mountain trail and just beyond, they camped for the night. There was frost in the air but swathed as they were in their fur capes, they were kept warm and comfortable all night long. The next two evenings were much like the first, only slightly colder. They made good time. Aaron was pleased and very pleasantly surprised at the stamina Alea had shown. The trip was going much better than he had expected. If the weather held, they would reach the Winter Forest in a few more days.

The following morning they arose at early dawn. When Aaron noticed the sky's distant haze of red he worried about the possible weather change. "Today, Alea, you must try to keep up. There may be a heavy storm closing in on us, we have to make as many miles as possible. The closer we are to our destination, the less chance of being stranded out here in a blizzard." Alea wasn't worried one whit, she was with her father who could manage anything. Following him, seeing his strong back and easy strides put her in a good traveling mood.

Hurriedly eating a cold breakfast they were packed up and on their way. Aaron kept his eyes on the horizon where the forefront of the storm would give him enough warning to make a secure camp. He had hopes that the worst would pass them by.

Alea was determined to keep up with her father, make him proud of her stamina. Luckily she had inherited his long legs, it wasn't difficult. She tried to match him stride for stride, but it made her laugh when she overstepped and tripped. Now she understood why he loved his trading voyages so much.

The day passed quietly, and when at last they settled down for the evening both were tired but looking forward to reaching their destination on the morrow. They curled up in their furs and fell into a deep restful sleep. Alea wasn't aware that a small figure looked her over with friendly brown eyes before nosing his way under the fur and curling up next to her warmth.

The next morning Alea awoke slowly, finally managing to pull her arms from under her fur and sit upright. She had slept well except for a small disturbance in the night. She had no memory of what had occurred. Looking over at her father she saw he was just beginning to stir. He would be up and about before she was ready to exit her warm covering.

Sure enough, he was already rising, pulling his cloak around his shoulders, delving into his backpack for their morning breakfast. He glanced over at her, extending his hand offering her a red apple and wedge of cheese. Hungrily she accepted and sat comfortably in her furs consuming the repast. It was at this point she felt something move under her covers, she leapt from her bed and as she flipped the cloak away from the moving mound, ready to let loose with a loud yell, she actually froze in surprise when she saw a small bundle of fur staring up, ready to race away at the slightest movement. The rather thin, scruffy little dog with his small pointed ears, large brown eyes and busy black nose seemed to taking a huge interest in the piece of cheese she had dropped during all the excitement. She stepped back not wanting to frighten him away.

Dropping to her knees she picked up the cheese and extended it toward the twitching nose. Cautiously, the mutt leaned over taking the treat between his teeth and darted out of reach. Moments later, his wagging tail gave proof that more would be welcomed.

By this time Aaron and Alea were captivated. Alea coaxed and fed until she was rewarded with friendly kisses on her fingertips, and lastly on her chin after she picked him up to cuddle and pet. Aaron was so enthralled by the tender scene he knew his heart was also lost.

"Come, Alea, time to get moving. We must reach Fila before nightfall. Give me your new friend. He can ride inside my cloak." Aaron tucked the fury bundle within the opening where the little face could peer out to observe the passing scenery. They were on their way.

They didn't stop for lunch. Heavy snow clouds were looming on the horizon; they needed to reach Fila before the storm arrived.

When they finally found the woodland deer trail, they hurried along the path as speedily as possible. Snow had already started to fall as they struggled through the dimming light. When they finally emerged from the forest's depth, night was upon them. In the distance they could see the glow of a candlelit window beckoning them onward.

Fila threw open the door; she could see her father and Alea struggling through the deepening snow. Slowly they progressed until they at last reached the landing and Fila. The excitement of having them arrive was almost more than she could bear. Endearing words of love, warm embraces, the cabin filled with joy and laughter. Even the little dog danced, feeling secure that he was once again where fate wanted him to be. It was a celebration. Aaron and the girls settled themselves at the table that had been set and ready for their arrival. Fila had prepared stew which she ladled into their bowls, also setting out the freshly made bread. Their joy at being together once again was evident in warm smiles and animated conversation. When dinner was finished and chairs were pushed back from the table, contended sighs echoed from the pleasure of a good meal.

Alea scraped any remaining food from the dishes, preparing leftovers for the hungry little dog. His tail was wagging furiously when he saw what she was doing, how she kept looking at him. Nose twitching, he wasted not a second when the dish was placed on the floor. He was a neat eater and not a morsel of food went anywhere but into his mouth. When he finished, a container of fresh water was set for him. Gratefully he took a long drink, giving a wag of his tail in thanks.

"What a friendly little mutt," Alea mused as she picked him up and began stroking his fur. He wasn't intimidated by her gaze, he was in fact returning the visual examination with the same intensity. Speaking aloud Alea murmured, "I name you Friend, for that is what you seem to be." Placing him again on the floor, she went to find a suitable box which she lined with a soft mat which Fila was happy to put to good use. Friend curled comfortably within and was soon asleep.

On the mantle the Relic observed the goings-on, satisfied that Friend had managed to find his way. The little animal had been chosen as guardian. Relic had never been out of Friend's sight, except during Fila's journey through the tunnel to escape Luther.

Everything was progressing well. Relic was satisfied. It had almost been too late for his plans until he had been able to entice Fila into making her foray into Luther's cave. Now there were events that must be prepared for, some that could be quite dangerous. For now they had time to enjoy themselves, take pleasure in each other's company. Strong families had strong defenses. All would come to fruition with the passing of time.

Everyone was ready to settle down for the night. Alea let Friend outside while sleeping arrangements were made for the new arrivals. At the slight scratch at the door, Friend was let in, returning to his cozy box. Aaron curled up on the corner bed taking pleasure in stretching out to his full length. Fila and Alea climbed the steps to the upper sleeping area where they nestled under fur covers atop deerskin-padded straw mattresses. Soon, only a few gentle snores sounded throughout the cabin. The long day had come to an end.

Relic set in the silence watching, waiting. Knowing there would be some unpleasant occurrences unfolding in the future. A trial for some of the family, but the time not yet come. He would be ready, and unknowingly, so would they.

The night dissolved into the predawn hours. The storm passed, the sky beginning to lighten in the east, slowly dimming the heavenly glitter until only the bright morning star was left to greet the rising sun.

Relic did not sleep. He needed neither sleep, happiness, anger, sadness, hunger, nor any of the earthly pleasures or woes that mortals suffered during their lifetime. Mortal time to Relic was just mere minimal moments. He could not imagine existing in such a short span of years. He, of course, counted in millennia, which to the class of objects he held sway over would exist forever.

"Girls, time to rise, I'm starving. Which of you will make breakfast this morning?" Aaron's voice echoed throughout the cabin.

There was not a chance of sleeping longer. Fila and Alea both awoke at the same instant. They donned their dresses, throwing warm wraps around their shoulders. Wool stockings and leather moccasins would keep their feet warm. They shared the use of a bone comb to make themselves presentable. Fila was first to reach the steps, Alea close behind. It would be a race to see who would have the honor of making breakfast. Although Fila was first to reach the steps, Alea was quickest to reach the cupboard and begin selecting items for the morning meal. "Where did all this come from?" Alea exclaimed as she picked up a small basket of eggs, a slab of bacon, and tucked a heavy loaf of brown bread under her arm. "I have never seen so much food in one place at one time."

Fila, standing nearby, picked up the covered butter tub, plates, utensils and a jug of buttermilk. "This is a gift from our friend, the Relic. He has promised to provide when conditions prevent us from doing for ourselves." She placed the items on the table while Alea stoked the fire and readied the old iron skillet to accept the bacon she had sliced. Soon the tantalizing aroma had everyone's mouth watering.

When everyone was seated, golden-crowned eggs gleaming on their plates with bacon, thick slices of the brown bread spread with butter, mugs of buttermilk sitting ready, they bowed their heads for a moment in silent thanks. Even Friend lay quietly in his bed, knowing he would also partake of the feast.

Eventually, breakfast over and everyone comfortably replete, conversation began with Aaron's question to his daughters. "So, girls, what are the plans you have in mind? Will you be staying here for a short time then heading for home, or shall I remain here until you have taken care of the Relic's requirements and then bring you home with me?"

Aaron waited silently for a response from either daughter. It seemed neither was in a hurry to answer, both gazing at each other, wondering how to tell their father that they would not be returning home. They would remain here at the Winter Forest until bade otherwise. Nervously, Fila revealed their decision to Aaron, knowing full well he would be very upset and displeased, even quite angry since he felt they were far too young to be on their own.

"Father, something has happened since I found the Relic, it changed the direction of all our lives. I realize that we seem too young to be on our own, but in only a few years we will be old enough to meet and marry some young man who comes courting. It's only that we are becoming independent a little earlier than you and mother had planned. We will be completely safe and snug here. Please, Father, you know in your heart this is the right thing for us to do." Fila waited with bated breath, hoping her father would understand the dilemma she was in.

Aaron searched his daughter's face in disbelief. He understood her desire to remain, but on a permanent basis? Not possible. How would he explain it to Sera? What logical reason could he give? He could see the resolve Fila displayed, knew there was no way he could sway her decision. The impasse was making him feel ill. Aaron turned toward the window looking out at the snow-covered glen, the dense forest pressing in. Was this a safe enough place for his precious brood? Turning again to face the two girls he knew whatever he said would make no difference. Whether they stayed or not, it had been a done deal before he and Alea had even arrived. Aaron thought he knew what to expect when he arrived back home to face Sera and tell her about the girls' decision.

Aaron watched his daughters' faces as they, in turn watched him. All were very uncomfortable with what was happening. This was a sensitive issue. Feelings could be permanently hurt if the wrong words were blurted out with no regard for consequences. As a father, Aaron would never take the chance of estranging his loved ones from the family only because of stubbornness on his part. With a final reevaluation of the only choice he had, he at last voiced his concerns.

"Girls—or maybe I should say young ladies, for that's how you make me feel—I realize destiny seems to have taken your future from my hands and this makes me unhappy. At the same time I realize neither you nor I have any influence on what is occurring, it seems there's no choice for either of us. At least when I explain to your mother, she'll know I'm speaking the truth. We'll miss having you home, and your sisters will be terribly disappointed. As far as I'm concerned, there is nothing more to be said on this subject. It seems everything has been prearranged and out of both our hands. You have my love, always."

Collectively, they breathed a sigh of relief, glad they wouldn't have to contend with any resentment or damaged egos that would need mending. Fila and Alea started talking and laughing at the same time. They adored their father and had been worried about hurting his feelings.

"Father," Alea paused until she had Aaron's attention. "Will you be able to stay a few days until the snowstorms ease, or must you leave immediately?" Alea hoped he could remain. "We would love to have you. It will be a long time until we see each other again." Alea waited hopefully.

Aaron knew it would be spring when he next journeyed this way on his trading trek. It seemed too long a time not seeing his daughters. It would be pleasant visiting here a few more days, watching how grown-up the girls had become, how well they seemed to approach adulthood. Thoughtfully, he looked about the pleasant room, so bright from the reflected sunshine. It was a snug, cheerful room in the well-built cabin. Through the window he could see several cords of firewood stacked neatly nearby. He saw their advantage of having the water pump inside anchored to the metal sink stand. The wooden outhouse sat back from the rear door of the cabin, a heavy rope strung from building to building to use during blizzards. There was a small barn attached to a paddock. Everything solidly built and near to hand. Aaron would enjoy staying awhile, visiting here for a few more days. Making that decision, he told the girls of it.

From that time they filled each of the following days with pleasure in each other's company. . Even Friend seemed to realize that time was precious. He romped and played in the snow, watching snowball fights, bounding through deep drifts, disappearing from sight then springing up with a joyous bark of greeting to the searchers. When they came back inside, rosy cheeked and breathless from play, they ate heartily then slept long and well.

The few days turned into a week. It was time for Aaron to return home. This had been a worthwhile stay for all. There would be times in years to come, when these days would be brought to mind and treasured. Aaron was packed and ready to leave the next morning. The weather had cleared, his trek home would be relatively easy. With a final kiss and wave, he was on his way.

Chapter Two

Sera and the two girls, Mina and Nia, sat closely around the fireplace. It was well into evening, dinner had been eaten, everything cleared and put away. The chill in the room had brought them together to discuss what they would do tomorrow. More firewood had to be brought to the shed to be handy for any extra needs. Sera wanted them to learn everything about cooking and baking. However, they would make their own choices on what to prepare.

It would be a busy and entertaining day far Sera, watching how the girls would accomplish their meal plans. Usually she gave them the instructions then left them to their own initiatives. It usually ended with laughter, flour-dusted faces, and sometimes barely edible products, but most of the time Sera was delightedly surprised.

She had recognized this as the best way for the girls to learn. They weren't restricted to a rigid list of ingredients and could incorporate their own ideas into the homemade items. Sometimes they enjoyed biscuits containing diced peaches or even shredded cheese, which had been a tasty surprise. It was necessary that a good homemaker be able to prepare a meal with anything at hand, thus tomorrow would be an interesting day for all.

Mina and Nia were discussing what they would attempt, Mina opting for a tasteful meat pie, while Nia wanted to make potato and cheese pasties. Their two heads were close together choosing vegetables, spices, deciding to have gravy or not. It had been a major decision on which recipe to create. Finally however, the selection was made, pasties it would be. The hour late, it was time for bed. The two girls raced for the steps. Sera banked the fire and doused the oil lamp. After hanging up her dress she donned her flannel nightgown, slipped off her woolen slippers and settled into bed. Calling a final "goodnight" to her daughters, she heard their sleepy-sounding, muffled replies. In a few moments, she had drifted off into slumber.

"What is this strange place?" she asked herself. She was sitting near a long table covered with an assortment of various and colorful collections. Tiny statues, brilliant jewel-like gems in odd shapes, dark wooden rods, marbled stones, so many unusually shaped articles that teased her imagination.

The surrounding walls were indistinguishable, almost as though a dark curtain hid them from view. Sera looked for someone, anyone. However, the place seemed uninhabited. She felt the first twinges of intimidation. "Hello, is anyone here?" Her voice echoed, as though through a cave. She thought she heard a faint whisper. Turning her head she tried to focus where the sound was coming from.

"Hello, please, can you hear me?" Again, the breath of a whisper, closer this time. She could almost distinguish distinct words. Then, the whisper seemed at her ear.

"Hello, Sera, I've watched you for a very long time. Our meeting has occurred sooner than I expected, it was fated to happen. You have something that belongs to me, I want it returned. Until it is in my possession, you will be a guest here. I promise to not mistreat you; however, you shall have no contact with your family until my property is in my hands. I have left a message for your daughters on the kitchen table."

Sera was terrified, she had no idea who or what the invisible creature could be. If she knew what it was referring to, possibly she could strike an agreement, find out what she supposedly possessed.

"Who are you, what are you referring to? I have never taken anything from anyone. At least tell me what you've lost and why you presume I took it." For a time there was silence, Sera thought she was once more alone until a whisper sounded right next to her ear, startling her.

"I want my Relic returned to me. I didn't spend all those years searching for it, only to have that nosy daughter of yours take it right out from under my nose."

Sera realized what the voice was referring to and recalled Fila's excitement when she returned home with the little image, remembered Fila had been impelled to take the object, had been led directly to the table on which the Relic resided. It seemed there was a being more powerful than the shadowy image of the whisperer, though how it would help her find a way out of this quandary was a mystery.

Sera drew her powers of concentration into focus, trying to make a mental connection with one of her daughters, form a picture of herself in distress and then place that image into their mind. The power of suggestion was sometimes remarkable and she felt confident that one of her daughters would feel the danger their mother was in and find a way to help.

Luther couldn't bear going through this ridiculous charade. What difference did it make if she saw him? There was nothing she could do to harm him, he was the most powerful magician in centuries and once he had his Relic back, he would just release her.

Making a spur-of-the-moment decision, he began to slowly emerge. First his boots, then calves, hips, shoulders and lastly his head, he stood complete. If it were not for the darkness of his eyes and the fire therein, he would have seemed a normal human. Rather tall, black haired, swarthy complexion and on the slim side. He grimaced at Sera with what was intended as a smile; he had never felt it necessary to learn the niceties of ordinary courtesy. After all, when had he ever felt the need to consort with ordinary people?

When he began to take shape, Sera felt uneasiness settle upon her. She would much rather have the Whisperer, than the intimidating black-clad man glowering at her. He looked frightening, emitting an undercurrent of power and mysticism. She closed her mind to the mental probing she felt, knowing he was searching for information about the Relic that Fila had been drawn to possess. Calming herself, withdrawing into a silent void where she tried to block off all connections from Luther, she began to experience a slight dizziness. Disturbing images began to take shape, so distracting she found it difficult to concentrate. She firmed her resolve.

The challenges continued, each trying to gain the upper hand. Eventually, Sera began to tire just as Luther knew she would. He was enjoying this little game immensely. Seldom did he have the chance to make use of his exceptional cleverness. Too bad no one else was here to admire his tricks of distraction. Luther now began a monologue that he knew would hypnotize his captive into telling all she knew. Sera felt the stress, tried to repel the feeling that was overwhelming her, she focused on her daughters.

Nothing that Mina or Nia tried would awaken their mother and they were becoming frightened, not knowing what could be wrong. Shake and prod though they may, nothing brought her back to consciousness. For the first time in their life, they were alone and left to use their own initiatives. It was a very scary feeling. Closely, they examined their mother's features, watching the play of ever-changing expressions. Sometimes a frown pulled her mouth downward, other times her lips were pressed firmly together as though in stubborn resistance. The emotions they witnessed, from anger to fear, kept them in a state of turmoil. It seemed as though Sera was in the grasp of a terrifying nightmare, but nothing they did eased her dreams or stopped her unrest. The only thing they could do was make sure she was kept warm. Always, one of them held her hand to try and convey physical support and comfort.

When Nia approached the kitchen table she noticed a folded note tucked under the saltcellar. She didn't remember seeing it last evening, though it is possible it was from her mother. The brown paper looked old and she didn't remember ever seeing anything of its like anywhere about the cabin. Curiosity getting the best of her, she unfolded the note and read its contents:

YOUR MOTHER IS UNDER MY POWER UNTIL THE RELIC IS RETURNED TO ME. YOU WILL NOT BE ABLE TO COMMUNICATE WITH HER. IF TOO MUCH TIME PASSES SHE WILL GROW PROGRESSIVELY WEAKER AND DIE. PLACE THE RELIC NEXT TO THE GRAY ROCK AT THE EDGE OF THE BRAMBLE HEDGE. THE LITTLE THIEF FILA KNOWS WHERE IT IS.

LUTHER

Nia's face turned white as the outside snow. She stepped to Mina's side and held the paper out for her to read. By the time Mina had finished she was squeezing her mother's hand so tightly that Sera let out a low moan. Hastily Mina relaxed her grip.

"What are we to do?" Nia was so agitated she couldn't stand still. She paced around the room, wringing her hands in distress over the situation. Mina wasn't much better off except she still held her mother's hand, not letting go for any reason. They were in a quandary.

Nia stopped dead in her tracks. The strong urge to go into the attic was so compelling she couldn't resist. "Wait, Mina, something has just occurred to me, I'll be right back." With that, Nia raced up the steps into the storage area. She didn't know what she was looking for, just knew that when she saw it, the choice would be correct. Slowly, she passed her hand over the containers until the urge told her this was the one she needed. Untying the leather skins she withdrew the ornately decorated sheath. Holding it tightly to her breast, she hurried down the steps and back to her mother's bedside. Carefully withdrawing the obsidian blade from its protective cover, she placed the hilt in Sera's hand, firmly pressing her mother's fingers around it. Then both daughters stepped away to watch what the outcome would be.

Sera lay still as stone, not a quiver of expression passed over her countenance. Then she drew a huge breath of air and a wild shout of triumph echoed through the cabin. A look of pure contempt leapt from her features for a single moment, and a gleeful laugh of victory. She was free.

Sera opened her eyes, flushed with the thrill of Luther's defeat, she lay quietly for a moment trying to orient herself to her surroundings while savoring her defeat of Luther. It had happened so easily, almost as though she had no control over what had happened. She saw her daughters' pale faces, wondered why they looked so frightened, then realized she held something in her hand. Looking down she saw something black clasped tightly in her fingers. Peering more closely she realized it was the obsidian knife.

Swinging her legs from the cot Sera sat upright and laid the blade carefully on the blanket's edge. She remembered how razor sharp it was, remembered the cut Aaron had sustained. It was a dangerous weapon to keep around the house but she was very glad to have had its use.

Rising to her feet, Sera walked to the fireplace and swung the kettle over the heat. What she needed was a hot cup of chamomile tea and something to eat. Glancing at the still-immobile girls, she asked what they would like to eat and drink. Receiving no reply, she continued to set out cups, bread and butter, and a plate of leftover chicken.

Returning to where the girls continued to stand, she retrieved the sheath from Nia, and the blade from the blanket. Re-inserting the knife into its leather holder she stepped to the mantle and placed the object thereon. From now on, it would be kept close to hand.

"Come, girls, let's have lunch. After we finish I will tell you of my adventure but right now I am famished, as you must be also." Sera sliced the bread, poured hot water into the teapot with a generous amount of the herb, and placed everything on the table. Her daughters were more interested in their mother's story than in eating, however, since they were hungry, they knew it would be much more interesting to hear with a full stomach. They took their seats and joined Sera in the welcome repast. When finished, everything except their tea was speedily picked up, washed, and put away. Bringing their teacups to the fireplace, they took their seats and made themselves comfortable.

Sera began her story. "When I went to bed last night nothing unusual happened, at least when I first closed my eyes. As soon as I dozed off however, I found myself in a strange room. There was a table nearby holding such an array of unusual objects I was intrigued. After a time, with not a soul there, I became frightened, especially when I heard a threatening-sounding voice whispering in my ear which said I was a prisoner, a note had been left for you on the kitchen table. By then I knew his name was Luther. It was draining too much of his energy being invisible so he regained his human form. It gave him more strength to overcome my resistance. He had a multitude of tricks to distract me and as more time passed, I began to feel very weak. I knew if this happened, it could mean grave danger for me and the entire family. It seemed an endless time passed while I tried to thwart his mental prying. Slowly he began to diminish my defenses. Suddenly I felt something cold being placed into my hand. I couldn't believe it, the obsidian knife was firmly clasped in my fingers and it was pointing at Luther. The blade started changing colors from black to fiery red. For a moment it frightened me, then a thin streak of blue light shot from its tip and entered Luther's eyes. They turned completely opaque. He let out a scream of fear, thinking he had been blinded. I wasn't there to see what happened next, I only knew he had been defeated and I laughed." Sera looked at her daughters, glad her tale was finally told. They were all safe, at least, for now.

She was just picking up the cups to wash when she heard footsteps at the door. With a quick turn she flung open the door and threw her arms around Aaron.

He dropped his pack and returned her bear hug with enthusiasm. It seemed such a long time since he had left with Alea for the cabin at Winter Forest. The girls crowded around, trying to extend their arms about both parents. Sera stepped back, letting the girls greet their father. He lifted them, one in each arm, and stepped through the doorway, kicking it closed behind him. He was so glad to finally be home. Releasing them, he removed his cloak and unlaced his boots, placing both near the hearth to dry.

He walked to his chair near the fire and sat, stretching his legs out, dropping his head back to rest. He felt exhausted. The snow had been deep making his travel difficult. A new storm was brewing, he had sensed it, knew he must push himself to make it home before it struck. It would be a nasty blizzard, at least he had made it in time. Turning his head, he mentioned his concern to Sera. "I think you should have the girls make sure the animals are fed, gather the eggs and also bring extra provisions from the smoke house. We are in for a bad storm and must have everything we'll need brought in now. The storm will hit before evening. I'll get more firewood as soon as I rest a bit. Hurry, girls, we won't want to chance being outside afterward."

Sera fixed a cup of tea for Aaron and one for her. She would keep him company while he warmed himself. They could catch up on all the news after they were snuggled down and ready for the storm. Sipping the hot liquid carefully, she looked at her husband, gauging his emotions, and seeing that he looked calm and contented. Apparently, things had gone well at the Winter Forest cabin.

She was satisfied Fila and Alea would do well together. They had always been closer than just sisters. They knew how to run a household and care for themselves. It just seemed odd not to have all four girls here together. It seemed too soon to have two of them off on their own. Now, however, was not the time to worry.

Aaron finished his tea and passed the empty cup to Sera. He replaced his boots and put on his cloak, cap and gloves. Pausing for a moment at the door, he asked, "Is there anything else you want me to bring besides the wood?"

Sera thought a moment. "Bring a fresh-killed chicken, and a smoked ham. The girls can manage the rest." Aaron nodded, stepped out, and pulled the door closed behind him. Arriving at the stacked cord-wood he began piling the limbs into his arms, making as many trips as necessary to finally have sufficient wood to last the duration of the storm. It was tiresome, the snow deep and the pathway had been tough to manage, at least until the snow had been packed down to make the going easier. At last when enough wood was stacked, he brought his freshly slain poultry and picked up the ham from the smokehouse. He saw the two girls emerging from the barn. They called to him that the sheep, pig and chickens had been fed. They had brought a dozen eggs, and a head of cabbage. Potatoes and apples from the root cellar completed their selections. Aaron waited for them to catch up and they all proceeded to the cottage.

Sera helped them off with their outerwear hanging them on pegs near the door, their boots placed near the fire to dry. Now she could start the supper preparations. She was anxious to tell Aaron everything that had happened. She also wanted to hear the news about Fila and Alea. With so much to catch up on it would take most of the evening to relate; she could hardly wait. The kettle was swung over the hot fire. As soon as the water started to boil she added potatoes, cabbage, onions, and small chunks of ham. The chicken was hung in the cold pantry. It would be part of tomorrow's dinner.

THE BRAMBLE HEDGE

The aroma of the stew made everyone impatient; they were famished. At last, all the chores had been taken care of before the storm hit. There was something satisfying about knowing nothing had been left undone, having the scent of a good meal rounding out the end of a busy day. Pure contentment put everyone in a good mood.

Aaron smiled at the serene expression on Sera's face. He felt so lucky to have her as his wife. Her father, Lucas, had been very unhappy about her choice of a husband. Lucas had worried knowing Sera was being taken to a wilderness cabin, far from family and friends. However, everything had turned out just fine. Each time Aaron went on his trading trips he always stopped at his in-laws' whenever his destination drew him near their homestead. It was handy swapping letters, keeping both Sera and her parents happy and content with all the latest news.

Sera had the girls set the table while she sliced the bread and set out a pitcher of milk. "Aaron, come, everything is ready." She ladled out the stew as each brought their bowl to the simmering kettle, Sera prepared hers and then took her seat at the end of the table. Bowing their heads, they said a silent prayer of thanks.

Supper commenced with so many questions that Sera told everyone to wait until the meal was over. It was the wrong thing to say, everyone finished so quickly, anxious to hear all the news, that within a very short time they were gathered near the fire.

Sera began by telling Aaron about her experience with Luther and how the obsidian blade had saved her. By the time she had finished relating the story, Aaron was in a rage. "Who is he to think he can trifle with my family? If it were not for the storm, I would be at his door, face to face, and get this matter settled once and for all." Aaron's face was so flushed, it looked as though he was ready to explode. Sera couldn't remember a time she had seen him this angry. The girls sat silently intimidated by the rage their father displayed.

Aaron fumed until he noticed the effect it was having on his family. This he could not abide. He loved them too much to see them upset by his actions. Getting a grip on his emotions, taking a moment to stifle his anger, he finally let a smile crease his face. Sera and the girls, not realizing they had been holding their breath, released a collective sigh of relief that the crisis was over, at least for the time being. His rage banked for the present, Aaron told them the latest news about Fila, Alea, and the little brown companion named "Friend" who had accompanied them on the way to the Winter Forest. He felt comfortable knowing Fila would no longer be alone. He told about the cozy cabin in the clearing, how happy the two sisters were to be together. And lastly, how they had insisted it was important they remain there for the present.

Discussions over, silence gathered about the family, everyone lost in reveries. The day's activities weighed on tired shoulders while sleepiness gathered behind heavy-lidded eyes. The girls struggled to their feet, heading to their upstairs sanctuary.

Sera folded down the blankets on the bed. Undressing, she slipped into her flannel nightgown. Aaron took off his outer garments leaving his long johns on as sleepwear. Soon, the only sounds that could be heard were soft snores and the blowing snowstorm. Sera felt the comfort of her home surround her, a deep feeling of contentment at being tucked into bed beside her sleeping husband while listening to the cold gusting wind. At last, curling against Aaron's warmth she fell asleep.

Luther was in misery, his eyelids sore, and his eyes red and weepy. Tears constantly streamed down his face. Whatever had occurred yesterday had happened so quickly, he didn't really remember. The only other time he recalled a similar incident, was in his youth when he had been concocting a new potion. Something had gone amiss and the mixture had exploded in his face. If he could only recall the remedy he had used to cool the burns. Drat! His memory was failing and he couldn't see to check his potion ledger. Where had he put those herbs? At least the liquid tea would ease the burn when applied with a soft cloth.

Clumsily, he groped through the various jars and pouches on the shelves in his work room. A whiff or two and he could differentiate the ingredients of the pouches. Jars had to be opened and carefully investigated; he didn't want to sniff one of his lethal liquids and end up deceased. Slowly, he worked his way around the room's various storage areas. It was taking forever. He should have had everything in alphabetical order instead of this haphazard mess. At last his fingers closed around a familiar pouch. He had smelled so many scents that his nose was getting desensitized with overuse. He was sure this was the herb he was searching for.

With a snap of his fingers the fire ignited and he pushed the kettle over the flames. Feeling along the mantle for his favorite cup his hand brushed against its edge and he picked it up. He also found a small bowl along with a folded piece of cloth; this would be perfect, the cup for the tea and the bowl for the solution. As soon as he heard the water boil, he dropped a generous scoop into the bubbling liquid. A few minutes to let it steep, there, that should be perfect. Carefully he ladled some of the liquid into each receptacle and dropped the cloth into the bowl. Holding the objects so as not to spill any, he stepped to his favorite chair and sat.

Sipping his tea, waiting for the solution to cool before applying it to his eyes, he eased his head back and relaxed. A few more sips of his tea and it was finished. He squeezed the excess liquid from the cloth and placed it over his closed eyes. It felt so soothing he could feel the pain abate, the burning sensation disappear. His mind seemed to be drifting away. He was actually floating, gently rocked by the sound of soft murmurs, though where it came it from he didn't care. A curtain of mist surrounded him. He could see nothing except an indistinct shadow shifting behind the shimmering veil. Was this someone he had known? Something felt familiar but he couldn't quite place where it had been. No matter, he felt himself being drawn into a deep peaceful sleep. It had been years since he had rested this well, some nights he was lucky to get four or five hours of release. Now, he reached a plateau where every muscle and nerve in his body was completely eased of tension. The shimmering veil folded him into its voluminous shadows. At last, Luther was in a deep slumber that would not release him for a number of hours.

Luther had been so sure of the herb he had selected because it was one of his own creations, a potion meant to disable his enemies and allow him to search their premises for as long as he desired.

Before first light Aaron was first to awaken. Hurriedly dressing, he grabbed a hunk of bread and dabbed it with butter. He hoped to be out the door and on his way before Sera awoke and tried to stop him. His anger still fulminating, he just couldn't put aside his determination to face Luther. Nothing was going to stop him.

Sera felt the cold creep against the side that was normally warmed by her husband's comfortable presence. Sliding her hand over, she felt the chilly emptiness where Aaron should have been resting. Sitting bolt upright, she saw he was already donning his coat, preparing to exit the cabin. "Aaron, where are you off to this early in the morning? I don't recall you mentioning anything about traveling somewhere in this snowstorm."

She watched the play of emotions across his countenance—guilt, anger, and determination. She knew his moods so well it was almost impossible for him to hide anything. He was planning on confronting Luther. Dread seemed to well up within her; Luther was not someone to trifle with. He had a fearsome aura that surrounded his entire being, a warning to those who would dare confront him or threaten his person in any way. She rose from the bed and hurried to her husband's side throwing her arms about his neck. "Please, my dear, don't jeopardize our entire family by letting your anger lead you into peril. Luther is a very dangerous man, you may only bring harm to yourself."

Aaron's expression softened at the look of fear on Sera's face. It hurt him to know it was placed there by him. He would do anything for her, except this—he intended to face Luther. That person must know, once and for all, that he could not endanger Aaron's wife or children ever. Somehow, he would teach that cretin a lesson he would not soon forget. Gently, he kissed Sera and put her away from him. "No, Sera, this is something I must take care of, I promise to use the utmost caution." Turning away, opening the door, he felt a moment of regret at leaving Sera to her fears. With a backward glance at her worried face, he tugged the door closed behind him.

The snow was very deep but at least for the present, the flakes had stopped falling and the wind had abated a bit. Without the blowing snow to blind him, he made decent time crossing to the tree line and finding the trail. It was a little easier within the forest, the snow minimal in some areas. Several hours later he was closer to Luther's property, at least close enough to make out the barrier hedge that surrounded it. He remembered

Fila telling about the opening she had crawled through. He searched carefully along the high, forbidding-looking barricade. At last he spotted the low tunnel-shaped access. Carefully, to prevent shredding his clothing on the needle-sharp thorns, he crawled to its end. When he at last stood within Luther's compound, he could see the cave opening in the near distance. Moving as quickly as the deep snow would allow, he arrived at the entrance and stepped inside. Ahead there was a wooden door. Giving a hard push, he entered Luther's domain.

The first thing he noticed was the long table Fila had described laden with all manner of articles. Then he saw Luther sitting in his chair sound asleep. Aaron stepped to Luther's side and gave him a hearty shake—not a twitch. Grasping Luther by the shoulders, Aaron lifted and shook him roughly. When no sign of wakefulness was evident, he dropped Luther back onto his chair. He noticed the cup sitting on the end table stone cold, the dregs starting to dry out. Whatever its content it had given him the opportunity to visit retaliation upon the culprit who had taken his wife captive in order to discover where Fila could be found. Aaron's curiosity could not be curtailed. This was a perfect chance to take a good look around Luther's domain. When first stepping through the doorway he had assumed it to be just a cavernous space set up as living quarters. Now that he had a chance to examine the surroundings, it was quite impressive. A trio of caves melded into one large edifice, like three globes grouped together.

The largest, where he stood, was a combined cooking-sitting room. There were several chairs, a mammoth bookcase with many dog-eared editions resting on shelves in haphazard disarray. Nearby sat two oaken rockers and a deerskin-covered settee. Close to the fireplace various-sized pots were hanging from iron hooks imbedded in the stone wall. A heavy oak table held an assortment of bowls, jars, a large chunk of beeswax and numerous ladles and funnels.

Aaron entered the next section on the right. He could see light filtering down from a hidden opening somewhere above. It lit the multitude of shelves lining all the walls. There were too many items to even count, probably tens of hundreds. Pouches, jugs, jars, tubes, hollowed antlers filled and sealed with wax, hanging dried herbs—it was an apothecary.

Unnameable things that at once roused fear, yet also excitement at what remedies could be concocted. Aaron exited the room, not willing to bide there longer. As he entered the last part of Luther's home he couldn't help but realize what an empty existence the man led. Not a single person to care what happened to him. Not even a pet waiting to greet him at his door, or lie at his feet in close comfort. What kind of life was that for a person to live? Aaron felt a stab of sympathy but quickly smothered it. What was he even thinking? This was the creature that put a spell on his wife, kept her in a trance, and threatened her. This last room was only for sleeping and storage anyway, he could see nothing interesting. Aaron turned to leave, he had already stepped from the room when he heard a faint faraway voice. Turning, he re-entered the room and stood silently listening, trying to locate the source.

He heard the voice again, "Come closer, look to your left, halfway up the stone wall. Can you see the ledge, the glass globe resting there? Reach up and carefully take it down. Please, do not drop me." Aaron followed the instructions, finally holding the fragile orb gently. Searching the colorful depths of its interior, he was fascinated with the odd swirling creations displayed by the sinuous mists. He was almost drawn into a deep reverie when the faint voice spoke again, "You have found a receptacle deemed payment for the ills Luther has caused you and your family. Now you must leave immediately. He will awaken shortly and you must be gone from here before he stirs. Hurry! Time is short. I can feel his inner self rising from his slumber. Now! Now! No time to dawdle."

Aaron tucked the globe into his coat and tied it snugly in place. He could feel a change in the atmosphere, as though some dark image was stirring, ready to awaken with a torrent of wrath. He ran for the door, almost bursting through it, slamming it closed behind him. He felt his feet had wings. Racing for the briar tunnel, sliding through easily, then up on his feet again running for the protection of the forest. His breath came in gasps and he could feel a stitch starting in his side but he dare not slow. He could hear the voice in his mind telling him once he reached the tree line he would be safe, then at last, he was.

When Aaron reached his cabin door and pushed it open, his breathing was again normal. Sera was waiting for him tense and nervous, wondering what could have happened. Aaron removed the globe from his coat and handed it to Sera. She was fascinated with the delicate gold scrollwork around the base and the beautiful blue radiating from the thin glass that enclosed a misty haze. She could almost make out shapes in the vapor. A tiny figure appeared, then a small animal, and then another figure. The shapes shifted so quickly she had trouble recognizing what they were. She thought it could be a child's toy, something for amusement on a rainy day. Whatever it was, she couldn't seem to withdraw her gaze from it. It enthralled her, captivated her entire attention. Everything around her seemed to disappear until there was only her and the vision she was almost able to see.

Aaron, after hanging up his coat and removing his boots, became concerned when he noticed how absorbed Sera had become. He moved to her side placing his hands over hers, careful that she wouldn't become startled and drop the fragile object when he spoke to her. "Sera, give me the globe, we wouldn't want to have anything happen to this, would we?"

For a moment Sera stood in mute stillness, at first so distracted by what she thought she had seen that she didn't comprehend the words. She handed the Globe to Aaron, who after placing it safely on the table drew her closely into his arms. She released a huge sigh, reveling in the comfort. It hadn't been fear or insecurity that had taken hold of her while looking into the mist. She tried to analyze the emotion and at last voiced her speculations. "I believe the sphere has knowledge about what is happening in places elsewhere. I kept thinking I could see familiar people moving around but I couldn't distinguish anything clearly. I felt the harder I tried, the better I would see but I only got drawn deeper and deeper until I became lost in it. I felt I was within and wandering through a fog."

Aaron stepped back to see Sera's face. She looked calm, her eyes the clear gray that had always captivated him, and not a trace of the concern she had felt remained. She was his mainstay in life, he would do anything to keep her safe. If he thought for a moment there was any danger to her from the object he had found, he would not hesitate to destroy it. Just the thought of possible harm to her made him angry and he shot a ferocious look at the globe, his anger building.

The small voice echoed through the room, "Do not fear me, I will bring no harm to you or your family. There is much I can do for you. Place me on the shelf near the steps, the same place Fila's treasure chest stood. There I can view the room and you can view me. In time you will become curious and want to learn my mysteries but until then, learn to see me as part of your life and family. When you are so used to my presence that you accept me as a fixture belonging in your household, I will know it is time for us to get acquainted, you'll learn my secrets and how to use them to your advantage. Come, place me on the shelf."

Aaron crossed to the table, picked up the globe and placed it where it would be safe from breakage. He felt comfortable now, not having sensed even a hint of danger. "For the good of the entire family," seemed to echo in his ears. He glanced at Sera as he turned away from the shelf, wondered if she had also heard the message.

She was still standing where he had left her, except now she had a smile on her face and a gleam of adventurous excitement in her eyes. He wondered what she had seen when she had been so absorbed in the mysteries of the mists. There were so many strange things happening lately, changes that occurred soon after Fila brought that artifact home. He wondered if it was just coincidence or something to attribute to the little wooden icon.

Aaron was surprised it was still so early in the day; it seemed hours since he had risen and made his way to confront Luther. He could hear his daughters playing upstairs. Sera put the kettle over the fire to prepare lunch while he was enjoying a second cup of tea. He felt well satisfied with the morning.

In a moment the girls came scrambling down the stairs laughing at some private joke. They were always so exuberant when their father was home. His exciting stories were their greatest pleasure. Each evening after dinner, anticipation was rampant until they were all comfortably seated and the tales began.

Mina sliced bread while Nia poured the glasses of milk. Hot soup was ladled into the bowls and the butter tub was set out. Everything ready, they sat and began their meal. Nia was just about to take her first spoonful when her eyes were attracted by a golden flash of light emanating from the highest shelf in the corner. She watched in amazement as a spiral of colors flashed and spun in a dizzying rainbow hue, making her feel faint. She dropped her spoon into her bowl with a clatter, causing everyone to look at her. Sera stepped to her daughter's side. "Nia, what's wrong? You look quite pale, do you feel ill?"

Nia withdrew her gaze from the swirling light to focus on her mother's face. "I'm sorry, Mother, I didn't mean to upset you. I happened to notice the bright object atop the shelf. It seemed to be spinning so fast I began to feel dizzy. Where did it come from? I never noticed it before." Nia returned her gaze to the mystery sitting on the shelf, nothing was happening now. It looked to be only a beautifully decorated globe, however, the longer she looked at it, the more her mind seemed to become entranced. She forced herself to look away. Maybe once she was used to seeing it she wouldn't feel so lightheaded. She decided to ignore the thing. Sera could see that Nia was feeling herself again so she returned to her lunch. Everyone finished eating as though nothing out of the ordinary had happened. It would take a while for everyone to get used to the new object. Until then curious glances would often be cast in its direction. Within a week's span it would be completely forgotten.

Once the table had been cleared and articles washed and put away, Mina and Nia pulled on their boots and donned their coats. They would feed the animals and milk Bell the cow. Then they could spend time playing while their father cleaned out the stable. The animals were always happy with the attention they received. They liked to brush Bell; she seemed to give more milk when they gave her special care.

Back in the cottage, Sera was getting ready to begin spinning some of the clean carded wool into skeins of yarn; she was getting low on supplies. The items she made during winter were used by Aaron for trading. She totally enjoyed making her creations and took pride helping provide for the family.

Finally she found the comfortable speed and motion and settled into the repetitive routine. Time passed, the wool batting diminished and the yarn spindle grew fat. Contentment washed over Sera like a warm cloud, her mind drifting off into daydreams, while the whirr of the spinning wheel droned its two-toned melody. Sera continued her spinning unaware of the passing time.

Aaron and the girls had finished their chores and were now engaged in a game of checkers, the girls' strategy against Aaron's prowess. Occasional groans or gleeful laughter broke the silence. The morning dwindled into noontime. Sera was still so absorbed she was unaware it was time to prepare lunch.

When hunger pangs could no longer be ignored, Aaron spoke out. "Sera... SERA... are you ready to take a rest and have something to eat? You've been at this for several hours." Aaron looked to his wife for a response, none forthcoming as she continued her repetitive motions. Stepping to her side, resting his palm lightly on the turning wheel, he applied pressure until it came to a stop. Sera had been so deeply in her daydream she had completely lost track of time.

"Girls, put the kettle over the fire. Why in the world didn't you tell me you wanted something to eat? You know how I am when I start spinning, it's my best time for making plans for your future. It won't be long you'll want pretty dresses to wear when we go to the Trading Post. Sometimes I'm amazed at how quickly the years have passed, it doesn't seem that long ago you were making mud pies and chasing fireflies." Sera sipped at the cup of tea Aaron had handed her. Sometimes he surprised her with his thoughtfulness.

Sera prepared lunch. Scrambled eggs with bits of ham, placed between thick slices of bread. Thinly sliced apples sautéed in butter and brown sugar, warm from the pan was dessert. As soon as the meal was finished the girls cleaned up while Sera started the vegetable soup they would have for supper. Once the pot was placed over the fire she returned to her spinning, wanting to do as much as possible so everything would be ready when she started knitting and crocheting items for Aaron's trading treks.

That evening after the supper and the table cleared they again took their seats. Sera asked Aaron to bring the globe and set it on the table. Placing a hand on each side of the shining orb, Sera softly intoned, "Show the pictures clear and bright, which appear within my sight." The mist slowly began to swirl and thicken. "Let me see Fila and Alea at the Winter Forest." For a moment nothing seemed to be happening, then with a bright flash the haze began to thin and shadowy images began to take shape. Mina and Nia gave a gasp as their sisters appeared as clear as though looking at them through a glass window. Fila and Alea could hear them.

Standing at their table stood Sera's two homesick daughters. A voice could be heard faintly in the background which caused Fila to hurry to her treasure chest. When she turned, she held a round silver-handled mirror. Gazing into it she could see her family clearly. For a moment her breath caught in her throat at the sudden pang of loneliness seeing her parents and sisters again. It only took a short time for the family to accustom themselves to using the globe and mirror for communication. She wasn't sure why they had been given this gift but something important was happening, almost as though the Fates were drawing their pawns into line and preparing to launch their frivolous Games.

Fila replaced the mirror in her treasure chest smiling with pleasure. The visit had been wonderful. She and Alea had been getting so homesick they had been on the brink of planning a trip home. Now they were contented knowing everyone was well, it had been the next best thing to actually being at home. Alea finished clearing off the table. When everything was neatly in place the sisters sat to enjoy a hot cup of tea. They would plan what duties would be completed during that day and discuss ideas for the morrow. It seemed there was always something to accomplish. Mending or crocheting with the yarn and needles they had found stored in the attic. Friend wagged his tail hoping they would pay some attention to him, for the sisters always made time for play. They had crocheted a yarn ball and stuffed it with remnants. He adored his toy and even brought it into his bed with him at night.

Fila thought she heard the Relic call her name and glanced toward the mantle. Not one word had she heard after he had finished instructing her, other than the advice to use the mirror.

She stepped to the mantle and reached for the little image, finding that it felt quite warm to her touch. She turned it several times, examining the roughly carved surface and the deep-set eye sockets. She was so used to seeing it each day it no longer looked strange to her. It seemed almost like an old favorite wooden doll, something she treasured and loved.

"Good morning, Fila, and you too, Alea! Today is the end, and also the beginning of a new phase. Put on your cloaks and boots, it's time for me to be interred in my resting place, at least for a time."

Fila replaced the icon on the mantle while she and Alea dressed for the chill overcast weather then she again reached for the image and asked, "Where do we go and what do I do?" The icon replied, "Have your golden key ready to use. Go to the northern side of the old oak tree where the burled knot is set into the tree bark, tap on it with the key and a keyhole will be revealed, insert the key and turn it three times. When the niche appears, place me inside. Once I am within, it will automatically reseal itself. Remember, Fila, always wear the key, you will have need of it again. And Alea, you are an important part of this, you must keep this a secret always for your own protection." Fila and Alea followed the instructions to the letter. When the panel was closed and hidden once more, Fila felt a sharp sense of loss, as though her best friend had passed away. She was surprised and a bit dismayed at the unexpected emotion. She also had the sensation of a guardian angel hovering just out of sight. It was a very comforting feeling.

Chapter Three

Gideon stood silently in the empty cottage. He had just returned from burying his grandfather, Calis, who had raised Gideon from the age of six when both mother and grandmother had died in the great flood. Shortly after that sad event, life had changed drastically.

Gaddy, as the old man had been called by the young boy, had found a curious Relic while searching for the two lost and drowned women. He had thrust it into his pocket, planning to give it to his grandson as a toy. With all the burial preparations and friends from the village who had stopped in to offer condolences, it had been forgotten.

Many months after the funerals, Calis found it tucked into his old, worn coat pocket. It was such a curious, intimidating-looking object that Calis was loath giving it to his young grandson. He sensed somehow, it was not something to toy with. Calis searched for something to keep the icon safe and out of reach of young curious hands. He recalled the small case his wife, Nola, had kept her miscellaneous keepsakes in. Where in the world had she put it? Searching through the hope chest she had brought with her at their wedding, he found it at the very bottom tucked under her embroidered linens.

The case held only a dainty tin cup, a black book, a round blue stone, and a miniature filigreed golden arrow. Calis didn't remember ever seeing these items. They must have been something his wife had treasured. Thoughtfully, he laid the curious icon amidst the collection and closed the lid, placing the case once again in the cedar chest beneath the linens where it would stay for a decade.

    The years passed. Gideon was taught his letters, numbers, and proper courtesy. What Gaddy wasn't able to teach, knowledgeable neighbors or friends became willing instructors. He grew into a sturdy handsome lad. He earned extra money doing chores and helping on several farms. By the time he turned twelve, he had saved enough to purchase a newly weaned colt. It was pitch black and shiny from the brushing he gave it every day. He named him Night. Night's friend, a mutt Gideon called Buddy, was a constant companion inseparable from the frisky colt.

    Over time, Calis had given almost all of the fancy linens away as payment for lessons Gideon had received. The few items remaining, he wrapped carefully in waxed paper and tied with twine. This, in turn was sealed in oiled cloth in order to waterproof it. He tucked the package into the small keepsake case and set it up on the corner shelf. He also placed thereon the miscellaneous collections that had occupied the case, the little icon among them. After a time, however, the sight of the image became so unsettling he dropped it into a leather pouch and hung it on a wall peg; this seemed to set his mind at ease.

    The years were kind to Calis. Young Gideon now did most of the work around their cottage, his grampa being in ill health and suffering dizzy spells. He rode Night every day, traveling to his various work places, and then hurrying home to prepare supper and visit with the old man. Buddy had been at Gaddy's side since the old man's health began to fail.

    Today, however, was the saddest day in Gideon's life. He must be on his way. There was no longer anything to keep him here. He would start packing the items he wanted to keep. He wondered what had happened to Buddy. Probably just as well, it would have been difficult for him to keep up with Night's pace.

    Gideon put the thought of the missing dog out of his mind, turning instead to selecting things he would pack for his journey. Gideon lifted his granny's keepsake case down from the shelf. The leather would be a good carryall. When he opened it and saw the oilcloth-wrapped package within, he decided it was something his grandfather wanted him to keep, so he placed it at the bottom of his pack. Next, he considered the small tin cup and a small black book resting next to it on the shelf.

The cup was a delicate little thing with fancy scrollwork engraved around its drinking edge, a nice memento to keep. As he reached for the cup, his fingers closing about it, a clear image of the old woman took shape in his mind. "Take the cup and my book," she seemed to be saying. "Keep them close to you always. You may drink from the cup. DO NOT open the book." He felt suspended in time for a moment as the image faded from his mind. He could almost catch the scent of sage that permeated her clothing. It had always created a comforting feeling in him whenever she was near. He felt that comfort even now.

Placing the cup and book deep within the pack he felt his hand brush against an object he hadn't noticed. Grasping it he pulled it out and saw he was holding a small blue-dyed suede pouch with tiny embroidered words running around its circumference. Peering closely at the message he located its beginning. "When in need reach within my well. Do not drink too deeply." Gideon was puzzled, the message didn't make any sense. He was tempted to put it aside. Some instinct, however, told him it might be important to keep handy. He stuffed it into his shirtwaist planning to examine its contents later.

Finally satisfied he had packed everything he could possibly need, he thrust Granny's keepsake case into his travel pack, which then was tied securely to the saddle. With a last look around he pulled shut the cottage door. He wondered if he would ever return.

The sun was at its zenith. Gideon felt the first pangs of hunger and decided to stop at the small cabin he saw in the distance. There were bursts of color surrounding its stone walls, all very neat and well cared for.

Night was anxious, scenting water and the sure expectation of a few oats to chomp. As Gideon neared the abode, a young woman stepped from the doorway and walked to the well that stood only a few paces away. She lowered a wooden bucket, attached to a spindle, into the depths then proceeded to crank the handle and raise its dripping contents to the well's stony edge. A tin ladle was attached by a leather thong to the wooden frame that held the turn screw. She dipped the ladle into the bucket. By the time Gideon had ridden up to the cabin door and dismounted, she was extending the filled ladle to him. He took it gratefully from her hands and drank his fill. He removed a metal pot from the burlap sack tied to the pommel and filled it for Night, who seemed as thirsty as he.

When he turned to thank the woman she had returned to the cabin, soon emerging with a bowl of stew and a thick slice of bread. She motioned for Gideon to sit on the wooden stump near the well. He could use the well's rim as a table. This he did, eating with enthusiasm. He hadn't realized how hungry he had been and then remembered he had not eaten that morning. The inner pain of loss returned. The woman saw sadness lower like a curtain over his face. Ah! She knew exactly the deep pain he felt. She had lost her husband only a year ago. Sometimes forgetting, she still reached out for his warmth when waking from a deep sleep. She wondered if the emptiness would ever be filled again. She silently wished the young man good fortune in his travels. He seemed much too young to be on his own.

Finishing his meal, Gideon thanked the woman and offered pay. She refused, saying that his company had been payment enough. "Life, when living alone, seems to drift away day by day, the same chores, same scenery and walls for me to notice all the little imperfections. This has been a wonderful change to my daily routine."

Gideon felt embarrassed, the red flush that bloomed across his cheeks spoke volumes. At his impressionable age he was not entirely comfortable being the focus of a stranger's attention. The woman extended bread and cheese she had wrapped in a linen cloth, wishing him a safe journey. With a hurried goodbye and an over-the-shoulder thank you, he mounted his horse and continued on his way.

He had spent more time than he should with the young woman. The morning had passed too quickly. Now he would have to hurry to make camp at the stream marked on his grandfather's map before nightfall. He gave a nudge to Night, who began an easy gallop, a ground-eating pace that would devour the miles and get them there before dusk.

Twice he stopped to rest Night and also ease the ache in his own thighs. He could see clouds looming on the horizon, hopefully the storm would pass and allow him a dry camp. A kick with his heels at Night's flanks sent him into a run.

He could see a line of greenery in the far distance. It could only be marking the path of the stream. The gentle curve of the earth bending toward it appeared in sight. Black clouds were boiling closer. He must cross to the other side before rain torrents made the crossing too dangerous, they were racing against time. Arriving at the downward slope he could see that, back along the stream's path, a heavy ridge of water was tumbling swiftly toward his crossing spot. He urged Night onward and plunged into the rapidly rising water. It was icy cold.

Gideon held tightly to his pack while trying to keep hold of the reins. They were drifting downstream too rapidly. The distance to the opposite shore seemed to lengthen with every increase of the rushing water. The struggle was taking too much time and strength, sapping both their energy. Finally, he looped the pack securely across his shoulders and slipped backward along Night's flanks grasping his tail as he slid into the heaving water, easier for his horse to swim without the excess weight.

Night slowly began to draw closer to the shoreline, even as his master was dragged back by the pull of the water. Gideon could feel his strength beginning to ebb as the shoreline came closer. Silently he begged help from any being or god who could assist.

Suddenly Night gave a mighty heave of his body. He had found footing on the edge of the embankment. Climbing slowly, he was able to drag Gideon into the shallows, and then he stood head down, flanks trembling with exhaustion.

Gideon lay half submerged in the shallows. Feeling the cold beginning to dull his senses, he struggled to his feet, pulling himself upright by grabbing the stirrup. He looped his pack on the pommel and shrugged off his water-soaked coat, draping it over the saddle. Hanging on tightly, he urged Night up to level ground above flood danger.

He was totally exhausted. He needed to build a fire to dry out but knew he didn't have the strength. He leaned his head against Night's still-quivering side trying to find the will to move. As he shifted his position to keep from falling, he felt the warmth of the suede pouch still inside his shirt, curious that it was warm. As he reached into his shirtwaist he could feel it was also dry. Impossible, every stitch on him was soaked. He pulled out the pouch, loosening the leather thong threaded through the suede edge. As he poked his fingers into the pouch opening, he felt a sharp sting that traveled all the way up his arm.

He jerked his hand back so quickly that Night became startled and skittered sideways, almost causing Gideon to fall. With a quick grab at the stirrup he again settled himself against Night's side, this time making sure he had a firm grasp. Finding that it was too awkward trying to hold the stirrup and the pouch, he wrapped the leather stirrup around his bicep and held his arm snugged against his side. Although he didn't have full movement of his arm he had full use of both hands. He peered into the pouch opening. Pitch black and nothing visible therein. He thought maybe a pin or needle had stuck him. Hesitantly, he edged two fingers into the opening, hoping to grasp the hidden hazard. A warning "ZZinnng" along with a flash of light, he almost dropped the pouch. "What in the world is going on?" he puzzled aloud. "If I can't take anything out, nor put anything in, what use is this oddity? I may as well throw it away for all the good it's doing me but it does feel nice and warm and that's exactly what I could use right now, the warmth of a nice fire."

The words were barely out of Gideon's mouth when a miniature bolt of light flashed from the pouch just missing his fingers, and shot into a nearby grove of birch trees disappearing from view. "Great," he thought sarcastically. "I'm cold, hungry, half drowned and not in the mood for games." He shoved the pouch back into his shirtwaist. Unwinding the stirrup from his arm, he held to the pommel and guided Night into the glade.

He had no idea what he would do. The rain was still falling, though not quite as hard. At least he was absorbing some of the heat Night was emitting. It helped a little. "Well, the birch grove is as good as any, might as well try to find a dry spot under some thick branches." Gideon continued to mumble to himself as he wended his way deeper into the trees searching for a more protected area. A few more steps and he nearly stumbled onto a cheerfully burning fire which was well protected from the rain. He noticed the thick overhead boughs that looked almost laced together. Not a drop of rain was admitted. Nor was there a sign of any person. He hung his coat and the burlap sack on a nearby branch, removed the saddle and brushed Night dry with a handful of grass, turning him loose to graze in the shelter. He placed the saddle near enough to the fire that he could rest against it and begin to dry. At last, he reached into his pack and retrieved the package the woman had given him at her cottage. The bread was ruined, but the generous slab of cheese inside was unharmed. He bit off a hearty piece and closed his eyes in pleasure as the flavor burst in his mouth. It was pure heaven. He replaced the other half of the cheese in his pack. Maybe tomorrow it would be needed. For now, Gideon was contented.

He removed everything from his pack and arrayed it around the fire to dry. Night was dozing nearby after having eaten his fill of the greenery. Gideon was just about to curl up near the heat and go to sleep when he remembered the pouch still within his shirtwaist. He tugged it out, intending to toss it to the side when something told him to keep it near. Somehow it was important. It was also something that had belonged to Granny. Just out of curiosity he decided to take a look inside; he could still feel the sting he had received when he had stuck his fingers into the pouch. Slowly, he pulled open the top trying to see inside. He was amazed at the sight. It was a miniature scene of a man and his horse arrayed around a cheerful fire. The horse looked just like Night. He felt a jolt of fear when he realized the man looked exactly like him, even to be holding something that resembled the blue suede pouch.

The image faded from sight even as Gideon was staring at it. All that remained was a dark empty void. He felt a shiver go down his spine at the eerie sight he had seen. Now he could understand the warning embroidered on its edge. "Do not drink too deeply." He would be very careful about making a wish when the pouch was open. Although he had needed a fire desperately, this was for emergency use only. He tucked the pouch back into his shirtwaist. When everything had dried out he would place it in the little case with the other items from his grandmother.

Time now to sleep. He rested his head on the saddle, which was placed just right for him to feel the heat generated from the fire. He took a last look at Night, who stood dozing nearby. Soon his eyes flickered closed and he was deep in slumber.

He found himself wandering through a great forest, the pathway just a faint trail meandering through the deep woods. It was so dark he assumed it was evening, but because of the overhead branches he could see neither moon nor stars. This was a strange place he had never seen before. Still, the urge to continue pushed him onward to an unknown destination. Each step he took was magnified tenfold so it seemed he was walking through huge boulders and tree limbs. This caused him to place each foot carefully so as not to fall or injure himself. He could see nothing past his immediate surroundings.

The hours dragged by as he walked further and further, past the point of exhaustion to danger of total collapse. When he dropped to the ground unconscious, stillness settled over the entire area. Not the twitter of a sleeping bird nor hoot of an owl broke the silence. From a distance, the bark of a small dog could be heard. In his quiet state Gideon took note of the sound he heard, something so familiar to his ear, it brought an ache to his heart, an echo of feelings from his past reflected loss and sorrow. Unknown to his recumbent self, tears had gathered in his eyes.

Gideon awoke with a start. The rain had stopped and morning had arrived. Slowly, he sat up feeling the stiffness from sleeping in an awkward position. He brushed moisture from his eyes, gave his face a vigorous scrub with his hands to chase some of his sleepiness away; he was still bone weary. Night was busy nibbling at clover, contented with having a rest. As for himself, he considered staying an extra day to recover his strength and also make sure all of his pack contents were completely dried. There was plenty of firewood.

Making the decision, he gathered more wood and stoked the fire. Soon a cheerful blaze was emitting welcome warmth. Items that had dried were replaced in his pack. Others, still damp, were rearranged and put closer to the heat. The burlap sack was half dry, so it was turned and moved to a closer branch after Gideon located the canister containing dried oats and bran. He went to the stream and dipped a pan of water, then set it on a rock next to the fire. He added a scoop of the mixture to the boiling water. When it finished cooking, he thought it the most delicious he had ever eaten.

Relaxing for the rest of the day, sorting his possessions and repacking dried items, it was a peaceful time for both Gideon and Night. They recouped their strength.

The following morning dawned clear and sunny. The pack finally filled with everything now dried and smelling sweetly of fresh air, Gideon saddled Night, took a last look around at the pleasant campsite he had made such good use of, and turned Night's head to the opposite edge of the birch glade. There was an exit trail they could follow. Once clear of the trees, finding open range, he kneed Night to a comfortable gallop. It was a beautiful day for travel. Gideon was heading north.

In the distance to the east he could see mountains rearing their stony heads, some areas of them covered in thick evergreens. Further northward, they looked to be just a rough tumble of boulders and hazardous rock falls.

Back home in Umer, snow would have been gone and spring on the way. Here in the more northern climate it was a chilly day and thin patches of snow lay in shaded areas. His mind drifted back to his grandfather. About now, if he had lived, he would have been planting a vegetable garden. Not an overly large one, but big enough to provide them with fresh produce for soups and stews. Dried beans put aside for winter, a few herbs to dry hanging in the rafters, waiting to be used for flavor in roast chicken or other meats.

Gideon had slowed his horse to a walk, not paying heed to where he was going. Night had set a course that nothing could deter him from. His keen scent was leading him to a nearby destination, past the beginning of a thick pine forest to a faint foot trail leading into the woods. Night turned into the pathway.

By the time Gideon stirred from his reveries, they had exited the woodland and emerged into a large homestead surrounded by forest. He had no idea how he had arrived here. The pleasant time he had spent in memory had lost him the sense of direction ingrained in him.

He pulled Night to a halt, inspecting the premises for possible danger before calling out a greeting to anyone within hearing distance. In a loud voice he called, "HELLO, IS ANYBODY HERE?" The cottage door was swung open and a tall, dark-haired man stepped out, pulling the door closed behind him.

"Hello to you, stranger. What brings you here and how did you find this place?" Aaron was cautious. Disturbed with the fact that they had never had uninvited visitors. He waited for the stranger to approach to get a better look and inspection of the man.

Gideon kneed Night forward and dismounted. Holding his horse's reins, he led Night nearer then he stood quietly, trying to decide how to explain to the man that he had no idea how he had arrived there. Truth would be the best action to take. Clearing his throat nervously, he blurted out, "I'm not really sure if I fell asleep or just got lost in memories. We were just riding along. I was remembering my grandfather and our home before he passed away, and how much I miss him." Gideon stood quietly embarrassed in front of the stranger. He was ready to mount Night and ride away.

Aaron could see the uncertainty and shame on the young man's face. He felt sorry for the youngster. He didn't look much older than his daughter Fila and he had a good feeling about the nice-looking, open-faced kid.

"Come along to the barn. You can unsaddle your horse, brush him down and give him some feed. After that's finished, come up to the house with me." Aaron took Night's reins and set off for the barn, Gideon close on his heels.

The barn was clean and smelled of dried alfalfa and the warm scent of animals. A cow gave a "moo" of greeting. Through the rear opening Gideon could see an attached paddock, in a farther field some sheep grazed on new spring greenery.

By the time he had unsaddled, brushed and fed Night, he had regained his composure and was ready to carry on a sensible conversation. Side by side they walked back to the cottage, Aaron talking about his family and daughters. When they walked through the door, Gideon's nose almost twitched from the delicious smell that emanated from the cooking pot. He was afraid they could hear the rumble of his empty stomach.

Sera had a smile on her face as Aaron introduced them. She took an instant liking to the pale-faced young man. This would be a very interesting day.

Sera set the table and called the girls. Mina and Nia scurried down the steps, unaware that a stranger was there. When Mina turned and saw the handsome young man, she froze. She knew her hair looked a mess, she also was wearing one of her oldest dresses. She could feel her face redden with embarrassment. Without a word, she turned and hurried back up the steps, not to return until she was presentable. When she finally descended, her parents were surprised at how pretty she looked. It had been ages since they had seen her dressed up. The last time had been on their visit to see Sera's ill mother, several years ago.

Everyone was seated. Sera had ladled stew into the bowls. Fresh bread, cut into thick generous slices, was piled on a serving plate. A tub of butter, jug of milk and a homemade apple pie were arrayed on the table. Gideon was almost dizzy from the delicious aroma but waited politely for Aaron to begin. Aaron took notice of Gideon's good manners and was impressed. Well-brought-up young men were few and seldom encountered. He thought about his eldest daughter, Fila, almost at a marriageable age. He would see what Sera had to say about the possibility.

Lunch was enjoyed by all. When a second helping was pressed upon Gideon, he accepted with pleasure. It had been ages since he had eaten such a wonderful meal, and it would probably be ages before he could indulge in another. When he had finished, he picked up his plate and helped clear the table. This was just like the days when he had lived with his grandfather, sharing chores to make life easier for everyone. It was second nature to him now after all the years of Gaddy's teaching. He missed the old man so much.

After everything was cleared and put away, they sat at the table getting acquainted. Aaron was first to speak, directing his question at Gideon. "Is there a special destination you are heading to, someone you are going to visit? If not, you are welcome to stay here for a while. There is a storage room in the barn where you will be comfortable. We have extra blankets you can use and if the weather turns colder, a small woodstove will keep you warm. There is a cot that only needs fresh straw to make a suitable bed. We have always used the place when freezing spring storms arrive and newborn ewes need protection, we also welcome your company. It's seldom we get visitors."

Gideon was happy with the invitation, he hadn't realized how lonely he had been. This was the first time in his life he had been without family. His existence since leaving Umer was like an empty void. No warmth or laughter, nobody to know or care if he lived or died. He had almost reached the point of numbness by blocking any emotion from his mind. He couldn't hide his feelings one bit. Gideon replied, "Thank you, I would like to stay if it will not inconvenience you. There's no destination I have in mind, nor any person anywhere who is expecting me. I guess it would be a good idea for me to tell you about myself. My grandfather raised me to be honest. I welcome the chance to have you get to know me." With those words he told the family all there was to tell. When the life tale ended, everyone sat in silence for a moment. Sera's heart was touched by the sadness Gideon had endured. His mother and grandmother both drowned so terribly in the flood. The love his grandfather had given him, and the deep loss he must now be feeling.

Sera made up her mind. This young man would not be turned away from having a home. Something about him reached a core deep within her heart. She had always wanted a son. If he was agreeable, he could make his home with them. Aaron could teach him about trading—it would be a good livelihood and provide a good living for him. As far as she was concerned, it was settled. She looked to Aaron. What would he have to say about this?

Whatever his opposition would be, Sera was bound and determined to make him see her side of the discussion. The young man deserved a break. She was so upset about the possible disagreement with Aaron that she had trouble keeping tears from welling up.

Aaron was well aware of Sera's quandary. Her tears were so near to the point of spilling that the only reason he didn't take her in his arms was the embarrassment it would cause her. He excused himself from the table and stepped to Sera's side. "Come, my dear, I have a few things I would like to discuss and would like your opinion. Please, girls, apportion the apple pie and pour the milk. We will return in a few moments." With that, he guided Sera to the door.

Mina and Nia were happy to oblige. They carried on a cheerful one-sided conversation with the cute young man. Telling him about their other two sisters, Fila and Alea, who were at the Winter Forest. How much they missed them. Gideon sat in silence listening to their animated chatter. He liked them. Wished he had had sisters when he was growing up. They were very pretty and their beautifully clear gray eyes were spellbinding. A person could get lost just looking into them.

At the sound of the door opening, they all turned. Sera and Aaron were holding hands. The smiles on their faces and their pleased expressions caused the gathering at the table to smile in return.

Aaron spoke first. "Gideon, we have something to ask you and it's not necessary you give us the answer this very moment. Sleep on it tonight, give it your best consideration. Tomorrow morning at breakfast you can give us your decision. Would this be agreeable to you?"

Gideon saw the serious look on both Aaron's and Sera's faces. He couldn't imagine what could be so important, but since it seemed to mean so much to the both of them, he readily agreed.

Aaron nodded to Sera. This was something they both had a part in, now it was up to her to make the request. Nervously, she cleared her throat, trying to formulate the words and sentiment she wanted to express to this homeless youth.

"Gideon, we can see you have been well brought up, your grandfather must have been very proud of you. I think if he were alive, the last thing he would want would be for you to be out in the world alone without family or friends. We, of course, have every confidence that you are capable of making it on your own. We would wish, however, that you will consider making your home with us. You would be well treated like part of the family. Don't answer now. This is a serious decision for you to make. We want you to be absolutely positive."

Gideon sat mutely, too surprised to even think of a reply at the moment. He recalled the teachings his grandfather had impressed upon him. One of them had been to never make a hasty decision. As much as he desired to answer immediately, he knew he should delay. He had wanted to roam the world. See new sights, meet new people. It had seemed an exciting prospect. He also remembered the rain, getting hungry and cold. Being on his own was not as wonderful as he had thought it would be. Still, he would follow his grandfather's wise admonitions and wait until the morrow to give his answer. The silence seemed to stretch interminably as everyone sat waiting for a response.

"I promise, tomorrow morning I will give you my decision. Thank you for not pressing me for an answer now. I'll feel more confident after a longer time to think it over. This is a very kind offer you are making and I will not take it lightly."

The discussion concluded, everyone set to eating their pie and sipping their milk. Small chatter from the girls filled the passing minutes, dispersing the edgy anticipation each was feeling. It would be a long semi-sleepless night for Aaron and Sera. Possibly for Gideon too.

Dessert finished, Aaron and Gideon went out to the barn to ready the sleeping area and make it comfortable for its new tenant. Sera, in the attic, searched for the warmest blankets and a spare pillow. She found a bowl and pitcher to hold water, a towel, soap and cloth for wash-ups. She sent the girls back downstairs with the items while she dug through the chests looking for something that could be used as a throw rug. She spotted the deerskin bundle, remembering the reason for the small bloodstain on it. Removing its contents, it would serve as a perfect rug next to the cot in the barn. She found a large piece of material from a flour sack she had tucked away for some future project. She knew a perfect use for it, also reaching for a length of rawhide that lay nearby. Arms full, she called to the girls for assistance and divided the assortment between them asking them to wait until she was finished searching before all three went to the barn.

Meanwhile the two men were removing some tools and other items from an old chest, placing them on several high shelves that lined the back end of the barn. Aaron emptied the drawers and tipped them upside-down to disperse dust and small refuse. Giving a good whack on their bottom, he replaced them. The three drawers would comfortably hold any clothes or miscellaneous trappings Gideon had been toting. With a last look around, it looked presentable enough to serve as a bedroom. Anything else to be done would be taken care of by Sera and the girls if Gideon decided to stay. They were pleased with what they had accomplished working side by side. Both filled with a feeling of camaraderie and mutual admiration. As the two exited the barn, Sera and the girls were on their way, arms filled with a large assortment of miscellanies. Aaron and Gideon exchange smiles, sometimes it was great being a guy not having to mess with little stuff.

Sera looked at the dusty mess, this would not do. She sent Mina for a bucket of water, a brush and broom. Nia was sent to find the chunk of beeswax and a leather chamois. Soon Mina was swiping the walls down with the broom, while Nia washed the window. Sera was using elbow grease to polish the old chest until it glowed. When Mina was finished she started on the floor, vigorously scrubbing the dirt and dust away. She made several trips for fresh water. The old wood floor now had the nice clean scent of soap. An old lattice-backed chair was brought from the barn stall where the cow, Bell, rested. A stool would be used for future milking. The chair was cleaned and waxed. At the last, Sera stretched the strip of rawhide across the top edge of the window and draped the pretty flour-sack material over it, making a suitable curtain. When Sera stepped back to take a good look at the room it looked cozy, clean and comfortable. The bed covering was a colorful Indian blanket Aaron had gotten in trade. Now, with the deerskin, fur side up, lying next to the bed, it was a very inviting room. Sera hoped it would influence Gideon on his decision to stay but either way, she wanted him to carry good memories of his sojourn with them. Gathering up the work tools that had been used, with a final look at the premises, she and the girls returned to the cottage. It was time to prepare supper, though what she would fix was beyond her imagination. When she stepped through the door the tantalizing aroma of boiled ham and beans made her mouth water. Aaron and Gideon were sitting at the table grinning at her pleasure in their surprise.

Sera couldn't control the urge to give each a huge hug of thanks. She and the girls were truly exhausted but feeling quite satisfied with the outcome of their labor. Gideon would be very surprised when he saw his sleeping quarters.

It had been a long busy day and appetites were rampant. Dinner was the most delicious Sera had ever tasted. At least, to her tired mind, it was. Even the girls were finishing their second helping. Sera glanced at Aaron, giving him a smile of thanks when he looked over at her. Even after all these years of marriage he still managed to spring surprises on her. The meal had been exactly what she had needed in her tired state. Heaven knows what she could have come up with at the last moment.

When she and the girls were about to rise from the table, Gideon insisted they remain seated. He would take charge of the cleanup. It would be a small token of his deep appreciation for their kindness to him, a complete stranger. He cleared the table, wiped it clean and placed the dishes in the metal pan. Dipping hot water from the water kettle over the fire, he used the lye soap, washed and dried each dish and placed it back on its shelf. Once everything was completed to his satisfaction, he sat back down with the family.

It had been a long day of travel for Gideon. It seemed ages since he had arrived at the family's door but it had only been this morning. Unable to hide the huge yawn behind his hand, Gideon apologized.

Sera signaled silently to Aaron that it was getting late and time to retire. She rose from the table, shooing the girls up to bed. She filled a jug with hot water and handed it to Gideon. "You may want to wash up a bit before you sleep. This will feel much more comforting than using cold water. She also handed him one of their spare hurricane lamps to light his way, and his new quarters. Giving a soft pat to his shoulder she walked him to the door, brushing a small kiss on his cheek as he exited. Gideon gave a smile of thanks and headed for the barn. It was late, the cool night air filled with the earthy scent of spring. Some of the stars shone so brightly, it seemed he could almost touch them.

He was dead tired, it seemed ages since he had left the birch grove this morning. On entering the barn he checked to see that Night was resting comfortably in his stall and was greeted with a snort acknowledging Gideon's presence. It always gave a tug to his heartstrings at the close bond they shared.

When Gideon opened the door and entered his room, he could only stand quietly for a moment at its miraculous change in appearance. From a plain, drab, dusty storage area, he was now looking at a place meant for rest and comfort. The lamp cast a warm glow on everything. After he had set the lantern on the polished chest, a small mirror that hung above reflected more light on the opposite wall, filling the room with a golden patina.

Pouring the hot water into the basin, Gideon stripped, washed, and then donned a clean shirt from his pack. Picking up the blue pouch that he had set aside, he opened one of the top chest drawers and placed it therein. His soiled clothing was folded and set on the floor in the corner.

Seeing nothing else that needed attention, he folded back the bedcovers, blew out the lantern and settled himself into bed. As soon as his head touched the pillow, he fell fast asleep.

Once again he found himself wandering through a deep forest. It was familiar now. He knew what to expect. He was not as tired and knew he could travel further than the last time. He heard the bark of a dog, and again sorrow brought the deep pain of loss.

Gideon slept like he hadn't in ages. When he awoke the next morning, it took a moment for him to realize exactly where he was. The cozy room looked just as inviting as it had last night when he went to bed. He lay for a moment recalling the warmth the family had shown him. He had been so lonesome and grateful for their companionship that, if he had been a puppy, he would have wagged his tail in joy. He felt a little embarrassed. Maybe his display of thankful emotion had looked childish. After all, he was seventeen now, too old to be acting like a kid. He could feel his face redden with remembrance.

Now, he must decide if he wanted to stay here, become part of their family. Normally, this would be an easy decision, but he had the feeling he should be someplace other than here. He truly WANTED to stay. A nagging restlessness inside simply would not allow it. He recalled his odd dream. The dog barking, the feelings it aroused in him. He knew for a fact this was not the first time he had experienced it. Whatever its significance, he needed to travel onward to try to discover its meaning.

Gideon sat upright swinging his feet to the floor. The deerskin was a nice comfort. No cold floor to give him the shivers, at least until he walked to his pack that sat on the chair. Hurriedly, he extracted clean clothing. He poured water into his hand and scrubbed his face, swiping his sleeved arm across it for a quick dry. He pulled on his trousers, then socks and boots. A look in the mirror, a hurried combing with his fingers and his hair looked presentable. He felt anxious about telling the family his decision, not wanting to appear ungrateful for all they had done for him. Pulling the door closed, he stopped to feed and water Night then proceeded through the barn and into the morning sunlight. It would be a beautiful spring day. New-sprouted greenery poked heads through the moist earth and the territorial song of mating red birds echoed through the farther pine forest. He could see a small fruit orchard beginning to leaf out. Turning his head, he spotted a pair of ducks on a distant pond that seemed intent on building their nest. In another direction he saw the remnants of last year's vegetable garden which soon would be dry enough for hoeing and replanting. This was a well-planned homestead, a place to be proud of. Someday he would build a place exactly like this. It was everything a family could desire. Aaron had provided everything humanly possible for a healthy, happy family to thrive.

Gideon reached the cottage giving a few raps on the door expecting a few moments' wait. The door was flung open immediately. The two girls grasped hold of each of his arms yanking him bodily into the room. Laughing and giggling with excited enthusiasm they couldn't contain their glee. The rich aroma of ham, eggs and fried potatoes was the most tempting he could imagine. It was a special treat to celebrate their meeting with Gideon. Sera had even made an apple cobbler. The serving plates were piled high and places were set, everything ready. The girls had been watching out the window, waiting for the first movement that he was on his way. They led him to his seat, and then seated themselves, waiting for their parents to join them. Aaron carried the jug of milk, Sera held a platter of buttered toast the girls had made over the open fire. They settled into their seats. All bowed their heads in a silent prayer of thanks. Breakfast was begun.

When everyone was comfortably full, the table cleared, dishes washed and stored, it was time for serious discussion. Aaron spoke first. "Well, son, what have you decided? You already know we have a great desire that you stay with us and become a permanent addition to our family." Aaron, Sera and the girls waited expectantly for Gideon's reply.

Gideon tried to figure what words to use to tell them he would not be remaining. He felt so ungrateful because of all the kindness they had shown. He felt right at home here. The family was everything that he would have wanted, as though they had been his own flesh and blood, but he just couldn't stay. The pressure to move on was too consuming, he wouldn't have a decent night's sleep if he didn't follow his instincts.

Nervously, he cleared his throat, the words firmly in mind and ready to be blurted out. "I can't stay." His face reddened as he paused. "There is such a nagging urge for me to continue onward that it's almost as though someone is pushing me with never a moment to forget or even try to think about something else, a constant itch that cannot be scratched. There is nothing I would desire more than to make a permanent home with you. The only thing I can add is that there seems to be a destination I am supposed to reach. Though where it is I cannot say. I only know that once I am there, I will have accomplished my duty." Gideon's eyes were red and tears ready to spill. With determined effort he controlled his emotions, straightened his shoulders, and waited uncomfortably for a reply.

Everyone sat as still as a field mouse, so disappointed that they couldn't think of a thing to say, everyone that is except Aaron. He watched Gideon, keenly aware that what had been said was the honest truth. There had to be a way out of this situation. He didn't want to lose this young man to an unknown destiny. He truly wanted him as part of the family.

Aaron was so deep in thought that Gideon became more upset, fearful that anger had turned the man against him. It was the last thing he wanted. He was on the verge of speaking when Aaron turned to him with a wide grin on his face.

"Son, how would you like to stay while I prepare for my trading trip, then you can travel north with me to the Winter Forest. Once there, we can rest a few days then continue onward. You'll learn a little about trading while heading in your desired direction. Would this be agreeable to you?" Aaron waited, hoping for an affirmative answer.

Gideon needed only a surprised moment to make his feelings evident. He leaped to his feet, grabbed Aaron's hand and shook it so enthusiastically that Aaron felt his teeth rattle. "Yes! Yes! That's perfect. I couldn't have come up with a better solution." Gideon was so ecstatic he could hardly contain himself. It felt as though a heavy weight had been lifted from his shoulders. He saw that everyone else seemed to feel the same way.

Aaron had an idea. While he readied for the trip, Gideon could ride to Mica's and make a trade. He broached the idea to Gideon, asking for his opinion. He knew that this would give the young man confidence. It would only be a half day's ride there and another back. Gideon agreed readily.

Sera packed food while Aaron searched the attic storage area for the ideal trade items, finally selecting two of the beaver coverlets. If the trade was good, both would be needed, if poor only one, or maybe no trade at all. He hoped for the best. It depended on what was available.

Gideon had Night saddled and ready, the beaver wrapped in skins tied to the saddle, the food pack slung over his shoulder. Following directions, he exited the property at the rear following the trail. As soon as he cleared the forest he kneed Night to a gallop. A little after noon they arrived at Mica's Trading Post. It was important he do well on this trade. Most of all, he wanted Aaron to have complete faith in his judgment. This would be the basis on what their future together would be.

Riding up to the wooden building he inspected it and its surroundings. It was quite old, the wood turned to a silver gray with age. The large glass window at the front was so dusty that the various articles behind could not be easily discerned. The porch sagged a bit but he could see the heavy wooden boards that braced it visible at the deck's edge. There were three steps that looked newly replaced.

He dismounted, led Night over and looped the reins securely around the wooden railing. He removed one of the beaver coverlets tossing it over his shoulder. Striding to the door he gave a sharp knock before entering. Pushing the door open, he stepped inside.

The place was a regular emporium with shelves lining every wall, an endless array of trade goods of various descriptions were exhibited to tempt patrons to purchase. Gideon was amazed at the assortment, from kitchen goods to fabrics, men's, women's and children's attire. Tools, dishes, pots, canned goods, flour, spices, candy, boots and shoes. The shelves were built as high as the roof with a ladder for reaching. He kept turning himself round and round looking at everything. As soon as he heard footsteps coming from the back room, he faced the grizzled old man who entered.

Mica looked to be one hundred years old but only because of the sun-lined wrinkles that wreathed his walnut-brown face. Sharp black eyes, bright with intelligent interest were focused on Gideon, assessing him and the internal person he might be. Mica was an excellent judge of character. He could tell by the way the person looked him in the eye if that person was honest or had something to hide. He liked the way the young lad stood tall with eye-to-eye contact and an open friendly face. He waited to hear what the young man would request.

"Mr. Mica, Aaron Hamlin sent me here to make him a trade. He needs a good horse. One that isn't too young or too old. It has to be sound and he doesn't want any walleyed troublemaker. I noticed you have a few in your corral. Are they for sale, can we take a look and see if you have anything we might want?" Gideon waited.

Mica seemed deep in thought as though trying to arrive at some important decision, a picture of intense concentration. When he seemingly solved the dilemma, the smile that broke across his face looked like sunshine through clouds. He took Gideon by the arm and led him from the cabin to the barn that sat at the rear of the property. "You have just solved a problem for me, young man. I got this animal in trade a month or so ago. It had a bad leg that the owner thought was serious, I gave another in exchange. By the time I discovered that it was only a stone deeply lodged in the hoof, the person had gone on his way." Mica pulled the barn door open and drew Gideon to one of the stalls.

Gideon couldn't believe his eyes. It was the handsomest mare he had ever seen. She stood as tall as Night and as deep-chested and strong muscled. They were a perfect match with the same glistening black coat, except for a white lightning bolt mark on her chest. She was just what he wanted. Now, if only he could arrive at a satisfactory deal with the old man, he knew Aaron would be well pleased.

Mica could see the expression on the lad's face, the strong yearning to possess the beautiful mare. He already knew he would trade. She was too good for any ordinary farm work. He had seen the stallion the young man owned, the pair was meant to be together. "Come along, my lad, we have some dealing to do. Tell me what you have to give."

Together they walked back to the cabin. Before entering Gideon grasped the second beaver coverlet and placed it over his shoulder with the first. The smooth fur seemed to caress his face as he followed Mica through the door. Once inside he faced Mica head-on.

"Sir, I know she is an expensive animal. These beaver bedcovers are prime skins. Sera, with her very own hands, stitched her hand-woven wool onto them to create these one-of-a-kind fur bed spreads. They'll wear like iron, keep a person warm as toast on the coldest wintry evening and give you bragging rights of having the most beautiful bed covers anywhere. If you decided to trade them, you know for a fact you would make out exceedingly well."

Gideon waited, hope showing so plainly on his face that Mica didn't have the heart to play the trading game with him by trying to up the ante. He truly wanted to rid himself of the animal. The feed and care she needed was more than he wanted to bother with. This was a very good deal for him. He would keep one of the covers, trade the other and still come out ahead of the deal. The furs were the most beautiful he had seen in a long while. He didn't realize that during the time he was thinking, Gideon had lost heart believing there would be no deal. Mica noticed that the poor kid almost had tears in his eyes and realized what his meditations had done.

"Son, you tell Aaron and Sera the trade suited me just fine. I'm happy the mare will have a good owner. Set a spell while I make out this trade bill as proof of ownership. Then we can have some lunch. You can put your horse in the barn for the night and bunk with me. It's supposed to rain later, I can feel it in my bones and they never lie. Maybe we can have a game of checkers, it's not often I get company but since you're a friend of the Hamlins I welcome you."

Gideon was so happy he could hardly sit still. "If you don't mind, Mr. Mica, I'll just take my horse to the barn now and get him settled. I'd like to see the mare again too, maybe get a little acquainted with her and make sure the two of them get along okay. I'll be back in a flash." Before Mica could reply, Gideon was out the door. Mica couldn't help grinning. He was well pleased having company for the evening. It got pretty lonesome sometimes. And he sure did love to play checkers. He finished filling out the paperwork and placed it on the counter near the candy jar, picking up a big can of beans on his way to the back kitchen. His cook stove was still hot but he added more wood anyway. Slapping the iron skillet on the stove he added some fatback to it. Shortly, the sizzle and aroma of pork filled the room. When it was nicely browned, he opened the can of beans and poured them in, sliding the skillet half off the heat so it would just simmer and not burn. He found the two tin plates, spoons and hardtack. His mouth was already filling with the expectation of good ol' pork and beans.

Gideon returned and placed his pack in the corner, he felt ravenous. Soon they were both sitting at the table digging enthusiastically into the steaming meal. The dried tack tasted wonderful as a bean scooper which softened it a bit. As soon as every bite had been eaten, the plates were scraped clean then washed at the pump which he had mounted inside at the sink instead of outdoors.

The checkers game set up, soon Mica and Gideon were in deep concentration. The challenge of the game was a welcome change for both. Gideon had played many times with his grandfather; this was a pleasant surprise to Mica, having the chance to play against such a clever opponent. It was close to midnight when they finally put the game away and went to their beds. Gideon didn't hear Mica's snores, he too slept soundly.

Gideon awoke to the smell of bacon and eggs. He rolled out of his bedding, pulling himself erect, feeling a little pull in his back from crouching over the checkerboard for so long the previous night. He had really enjoyed it, bringing back memories of his grandfather and the many evenings they dallied over the games. Mica had some of the same ingrained characteristics, patience, honesty and a kindly heart. It had been a wonderful evening. Gideon promised the next time he was at Aaron's he would come again. Mica had won over half the games and been declared champ, he was due a challenge.

Mica called Gideon to come eat. Half a dozen eggs each served with plenty of bacon and soda biscuits. Both were famished and downed the meal in record time. Afterward, they cleaned up leaving everything neat once again.

Gideon was anxious to be on his way. Aaron would be so pleased with the mare that he just couldn't wait to see the expression on his face. Mica walked to the barn with him. Once Gideon was mounted and had the mare on a lead ready to go, Mica grasped his booted ankle and looked up at him with a wistful expression. "You have a care, young fella. I liked your company and hope you get to visit me again. You give my regards to Aaron and his family, tell them I was glad to be able to help trade wise." Mica followed Gideon out the barn door. With a last wave he watched the young man ride away.

The morning was cool and fresh from last night's rain, the sun just beginning to peek over the eastern mountains. The horses were in a frisky mood wanting to run but it was a little too awkward with the mare on a lead. A comfortable gallop would have to suffice. He loved this weather. The air so clear and fresh he could see for miles. He almost felt like kicking up his heels just like the horses, pure exhilaration in being alive. The cool breeze against his face was so invigorating he could almost keep riding and not even stop for a rest at noontime. Not a good idea though. The horses would be too tired and so would he, common sense must prevail. He was no longer a reckless youth without a care for consequences.

Near noon Gideon found a nice place to rest and water the horses. He allowed them to graze on some of the sweet clover growing nearby while he stretched out in the shade and relaxed. What a handsome pair they were. He could imagine what their offspring would look like. Hopefully, his future would be tied to Aaron's family. He wanted family and friends to care about, it would be terrible to even think of a future without them.

Enough of this dallying, time to get moving again. Remounting, looping the lead over the pommel, he nudged Night into a gallop and they were on their way, anticipation foremost in Gideon's mind. After another brief respite, he could see the familiar tree line at the rear of the family's property in the distance. Entering the faint trail, he led the mare slowly through the maze of trees finally emerging into the clearing, the cottage visible in the near distance. He called a loud "HELLO."

The two girls scrambled out the door first, and then Aaron and Sera appeared on the front steps right behind them. When they saw what was following Night, they erupted in shouts of joy and welcome. When Gideon dropped from his saddle and handed the lead rope to Aaron, he watched the stunned incomprehension that flickered on his face.

"This is what you were able to trade for? Where in the world did Mica get such a beautiful animal? My God! Gideon, do you know what this can mean to us, to you?"

Aaron stood speechless. When he could overcome his amazement, he walked to the mare and gave her a thorough inspection. She was perfect. He rubbed her nose gently, letting her get to know his smell, that he was a gentle person. He sent Mina to the root cellar to get a few apples for both horses, a nice treat after the long ride. Sera was entranced, she had ridden often as a child, it was one of her most cherished memories, maybe she might well be able to once again. The thought thrilled her. She would love to teach the girls about the excitement they could experience atop a beautiful horse. They all stood, looking at and imagining what the future might hold.

The two girls were in love. They had never seen such a wonderful horse in their entire lives. They could hardly wait to pet, brush and pamper her. They wondered if Father would allow them to ride. It wouldn't hurt anything just around the property. They would have stood there forever if Sera hadn't called them to go with her to the house and ready the family meal.

Aaron and Gideon led the horses to the barn and tied them up while they emptied two of the stalls which held a few empty cider kegs, spare planks of lumber, two pitchforks, a spade, post digger, and a few extra posts into one. Now there were three usable stalls, Bell in one.

Aaron was excited, Gideon exhausted but both famished. They hurried to the meal that Sera had waiting for them. After everyone finished, both men sat before the fire and discussed how the next several days would be used. Aaron had an old saddle in the attic storage area he had gotten in trade. It had been years since he had checked its condition. In the morning he'd dig it out from under the other items and bring it downstairs. It might need oiling if the leather was dry. Also they would both need to ready themselves for the trading trip. Sera would gather the items she had made. The girls would add their little novelty creations they had assembled during the winter. Some were quite unique. A few handmade rag dolls and braided hair ties. Whatever Aaron got back in trade would belong to the daughter that made the traded item. They were always excited to see what their work had brought them.

Conversation came to a halt at the huge yawn Gideon displayed. It had been a very long day. It seemed ages ago since he had departed Mica's cabin. Embarrassed, he excused himself, stood, gave Aaron's hand a hearty shake, planted a kiss on Sera's cheek, called a "Goodnight" to the girls and exited the cottage. Bright starlight lit his way to the barn. In the semi-dark he passed the stalls and made his way to his room on the left. Through the open door at the barn's rear he could see nothing stirred outside. The sound of crickets, the echoing call of a toad to its mate at the far pond, filled the evening air. Wearily, he stripped off his clothes and fell into bed. Pulling the Indian blanket over himself, in a moment he was fast asleep. He wasn't aware of the slight noise from the old chest drawer. If he had heard, he probably would have thought it a small field mouse or shrew making mischief in their playful nightly romps.

The first thing Gideon heard on awakening was one of the horses nickering. It didn't sound like Night. He arose and pulled on his pants, slipping his feet into his boots without taking time to lace them. When he saw what the fuss was about, he couldn't help laughing. Both Mina and Nia, still in their nightclothes, were petting the horses, cooing over them as though they were babies. Night was perfectly content with the attention but the mare was unsure of what to make of the billowy clothing the girls were wearing. With both barn doors open, the morning breeze wafting through was creating havoc with the ribbons and lace. Gideon had to admit it was a very pretty picture; however, it wasn't good to have the mare become upset in her unknown surroundings. She needed to become accustomed to the new environment. He was about to explain when the girls, becoming aware of their attire, gave a yelp of embarrassment and fled to the sanctuary of their home knowing Mother would be ashamed if she knew they had displayed themselves in their nightgowns.

When they pushed open the door, she was already standing with her arms crossed and a frown on her face waiting for them. "What in the world were you two thinking? Since when do you go outside in your night clothing, knowing we have a guest in the barn, and expose yourself? Get yourselves upstairs right this minute, get dressed properly, and do not dawdle. I want you back here promptly. There are a few words I have to say to you two. Now get going." As the girls scurried away, Sera turned with a smile on her face. A good lesson for them, but she remembered when she was their age. It had always been action before thought. They were so much like her it was both a blessing and a curse. She would give them some extra housework to do as punishment.

Aaron had gone somewhere early this morning. She had heard him leave in the predawn hours. Sometimes it was just restlessness that made him go traipsing off to release some of his excess energy. By winter's end he could hardly sit still for any length of time, anxious to begin his trading again. She hoped when he grew older, time would settle him down a bit. He would be walking in any minute asking what was for breakfast, hungry as a bear after his brisk morning jaunt. When the girls returned neatly dressed, she scolded them again then set them to peeling and slicing potatoes and onions. This would be everyone's favorite breakfast. Selecting a deep, flat-bottomed pot, which was just the right size for this meal, she stir-fried crumbled sausage until brown. She added the sliced potatoes and onions, covering the pot so it would cook faster. Day-old bread was broken up and added to the mixture along with a dozen beaten eggs. A good dash of black pepper was the perfect seasoning. Everyone was partial to Sera's recipe, it was better than beef hash.

Aaron entered with a pail of fresh milk, Gideon right behind him. Still-warm milk was poured for everyone. Breakfast was begun with very little conversation. As soon as the meal was completed the men left the table. They had so much to ready for the trip. Aaron already had the old saddle oiled and ready to place on the mare.

Today Sera and the girls would have all their trade goods neatly packed. Extra food would be well wrapped, the kind that wouldn't spoil easily and traveled well. Cheese, hard-boiled eggs, salt pork. She fixed waterproof packets of corn meal and oats. A small sack of apples would be a welcome treat for as long as they lasted. Finally chores were completed.

The smoked ham Sera had put on to simmer was ready in time for supper. She fixed brown gravy and sliced the bread thick. Each person assembled their plate to their liking and Sera poured gravy over each sandwich. The men groaned in pleasure at the first bite. This would be their last home-cooked meal for quite a while.

There wasn't much conversation between the family that evening, just plans the two men were contemplating for next morning's departure. Soon the girls said their goodnights and headed upstairs to their beds, Gideon left soon after for his bunkroom in the barn, and Sera and Aaron settled themselves into bed. Aaron fell asleep immediately. Sera lay for a while, mentally checking if she had packed all the items she had created for Aaron to trade. At last, she too slept.

Before the sun even lightened the eastern sky Aaron and Gideon were putting last-minute items into their bundles. No heavy breakfast for them, preferably just porridge or cornmeal mush. It was always better to travel light as Aaron had learned years ago. Final hugs and kisses were given. With a last inspection that everything was securely tied behind the saddles, the men mounted. Waving a final goodbye they exited the property at the eastern edge of the forest, turning left in a northerly direction and following the trail along the base of Widows Mountain. It was a beautiful day to begin their journey.

The trail was not quite wide enough to ride side by side so Aaron took the lead. The mare handled so well it felt as though they had been lifelong partners. This was a huge thrill. He was so used to toting everything on his back during his trading sessions that having the luxury of riding felt impossibly indulgent, as though he had somehow shirked his duties. He was so busy with his mental musings the morning slipped away. They were almost past the area at the spring where Fila had disappeared when Aaron became aware that it was time to break for lunch. Aaron turned Lady, that was what he decided to call her, back a few paces and entered the clearing, Gideon followed close behind.

The two men rested, enjoying the thick ham sandwiches Sera had made. The horses nibbled at the sweet clover, nuzzling a cool drink of water from the spring. Aaron told Gideon how Fila had disappeared and his frantic search for her. How she had somehow assured him she was safe and unharmed. He told about Luther and how he had put Sera into a trance. The Relic and Fila's treasure chest were also mentioned. Aaron hadn't talked this much since he had been a youngster but he wanted Gideon to know everything that had happened recently to his family. On recollection, it had been quite a bit.

Gideon, in turn, revealed how his grandfather had found a Relic while searching for the bodies of his mother and grandmother, who had drowned in a flood. He told how years later, when he had returned home from work, he found his grandfather dead and their dog, Buddy, missing. The Relic had also disappeared.

The two men gazed at each other in astonishment. There were two things very similar in description, the dog and the Relic. As Gideon gave a detailed description of both, Aaron nodded in agreement. This was more than happenstance. Destiny seemed to have taken a hand in their meeting.

After the revelations, a stronger bond seemed to have formed between the two. They were meant to be more than friends. Gideon was aware that the internal urge that had nagged and prodded him onward since leaving his grandfather's home was no longer present. It had disappeared. He felt relief settle through his body like soft feathers floating on a breeze. He hadn't realized what a disquieting sensation it had been until now.

The two quietly repacked a few provisions, took a cooling drink from the spring and then remounted. They rode in silence the rest of the day, not speaking until finding a suitable campsite for the night. After the horses were unsaddled, brushed and fed, they settled in for a hot meal of ham and grits. They were comfortable in each other's presence. A few words sufficed for a "Goodnight, rest well." They fell asleep immediately.

Chapter Four

Fila and Alea had just finished cleaning the storage area, rearranging the items neatly. Most of the winter they had spent their time stitching and sewing, making things that Aaron would be able to trade. They expected to see him arrive at any time. This was just the time of year he got impatient with staying at home and anxious to be on the trail.

Friend was sitting nearby watching quietly, curiosity causing him to take note of every move they made. Sometimes they surprised him with a little treat of dried venison or a piece of hardtack. Whatever, he was ready to catch it if they tossed anything his way. He had gained some weight, his fur now smooth and shiny from the care they doted on him. He had never been so contented in his entire life. In return, he was a most impressive watch dog. A slight noise from outside and he barked his little head off, usually for naught. Today his ears caught a sound quite foreign from what he was used to hearing. Stiff legged, he strutted to the door, sniffing along the bottom to try and pick up a scent. The ruff on his back was upright, his tail standing straight up. The two girls were surprised to hear a growl echo through the cabin. This was not his usual reaction. A look of concern passed between them.

Peeking through the window, they could see no sign of anything moving in the vicinity. It was probably just a raccoon or other animal causing Friend's reaction. They went back to stacking and folding their handmade goods. Again the dog growled, this time more threateningly, his lips curling in a nasty snarl of anger. He remembered the scent, the hurt that he had gotten on his head from the man-smell lurking outside. He turned to look at his charges, the ones he was intended to protect. The danger was coming closer. He gave a sharp "YIP" and started scratching at the door to be let out. Alea obliged, and Friend darted through the opening and shot away toward the woods. Alea hoped he wouldn't run into a skunk.

Friend paused at the old oak tree. He had heard his master's voice clear as a bell. "Do not run directly into the forest, you must use stealth. Luther has arrived, as we knew he would. You must trick him into following you. There is a deadfall that you can lead him into. He will be injured. Hurry now, you will be successful. In two days company will arrive and they will take care of the rest."

Friend veered to the left of the forest trail, slipping through the underbrush so quietly that not even the birds were aware. He could hear the crushing of leaves and rustle of branches as Luther made his way toward the clearing. With perfect timing, the dog dashed in front of Luther causing the man to stop in mid-stride.

For a moment Luther was perplexed, the animal looked familiar. The dog had dropped to the ground and was lying there looking at him expectantly. When Luther took a step toward it, the dog backed up a little into the forest's edge wagging its tail expectantly. Luther was just about to pass it by when he stopped short with remembrance, this was the very same mutt that had been in the old man's home where he had found and taken the Relic. The association between Relic and dog caused Luther to completely lose every ounce of common sense. He wanted his Relic, of course the dog would lead him to it. Without pause he started following the animal into the forest. The many turns and twists were getting Luther confused, he had no idea where he was. The last thing he heard was the crash of timber and a wall of darkness falling over him.

Fila had just packed the last of their creations into a leather satchel. Alea was busy as usual concocting a new recipe for their supper. She had found her true calling as a great creator of new dishes, and very tasty they turned out to be. Fila was the perfect taste-tester, she adored trying new things, whether foods or adventurous activities, she was game for it all.

Their conversation this morning was centered on when they thought Aaron would arrive. They were so accustomed to his restless nature that they were positive he could not abide being home another week, especially with the weather being so unusually mild this early in the spring. They expected, at any time, to hear his voice calling a greeting. They were so involved in their guessing game, it was a while before they realized the loud excited barking of Friend was intruding. They both hurried to the window, expecting to see their vocal canine chasing a squirrel or rabbit. They were surprised to see two men on horseback trotting toward them. On a second visual inspection they could see one of the men was their father.

Friend was cavorting madly around the other rider, yelping his little head off with excitement. They had never seen him act so crazy. Their main attention though was focused on Aaron and the beautiful horse he rode. It looked almost a mirror image of the other rider's steed.

They couldn't wait to hear all the latest news. Fila took off with a leap, her long hair floating in the morning air, her face aglow with loving greetings. She reached down and lifted her skirts to gain a better running advantage. She was such a picture of grace and beauty that Gideon was struck dumb. All he could see was the vision of perfection that seemed to be racing toward him. He pulled Night to a halt, waiting expectantly for the dream creature to reach him.

Aaron was amazed at how Fila had matured, she was a young woman now. To his great pleasure she was still as impulsive as ever. He wore a proud grin as he slipped from the saddle to give her a huge bear hug. Alea was close behind to also collect the fatherly greeting. Animated conversation was carried on for several moments until Aaron became aware that Gideon was still on horseback waiting quietly to be introduced. When Aaron turned toward him, Gideon slid from the saddle and stood, reins in hand, waiting.

Introductions were made, Gideon bowing first to Alea, then to Fila. He couldn't take his eyes from her she was such a picture of loveliness. For the first time in his life, he was speechless.

Fila was also entranced. Gideon had beautiful sky-blue eyes, black curly hair and a very handsome face, not only that, he seemed deeply absorbed in watching her. She wondered if her hair was too mussed or mayhap, her face dirty. She couldn't remember being this concerned over her appearance before. She felt a funny current of shock jolt her, awaking an unrecognizable awareness of the intriguing young man. Suddenly, she felt awkward and surprisingly, a little shy. She wondered what in the world was happening, she was becoming embarrassed. Turning toward the cottage to hide her confusion, she bade the men settle their horses in the barn while she and Alea readied an early supper.

Before the men entered the cabin, Fila had taken a moment to make herself presentable. Once satisfied that she looked her best, she helped Alea prepare the food and set the table. As soon as the men returned and washed up, everyone sat to partake of the supper. Thank goodness Aaron was there to cover Gideon's awkwardness, he was all thumbs. Was this what happened when a young man became smitten, he wondered. If so, God help him.

Aaron noticed the interested look Gideon was giving Fila when her attention was directed elsewhere. He also saw the introspective look Fila had whenever her eyes rested on the young man. It was obvious the attraction each felt.

As soon as the meal ended Aaron drew Gideon aside, making an excuse to his daughters that they had to finish bedding the horses down for the night. Together, the two men exited the cabin, Friend following closely on their heels. Before anything progressed further between the two young people, Aaron wanted to have a talk with Gideon. In these times, it was common to make matrimonial arrangements quickly when there was a mutual attraction between two young adults. There were few opportunities since families lived so far from others who would be a suitable match. They headed for the barn in silence, both deep in thought.

Gideon had an idea why Aaron had made an excuse for their leaving so soon after supper. It was much too soon to speculate what the outcome might be for Fila and him. He just wanted to know if Aaron would give his consent if the attraction deepened and marriage became a serious objective. He wasn't about to rush into an early commitment without knowing if the feeling was mutual.

As for Aaron, this was his firstborn daughter. He would not allow a hasty decision when it could be just a matter of infatuation, which was fleeting. Here today, gone tomorrow as the old saying went. How to broach the subject to Gideon would be a touchy matter. He didn't want the young man to think he wouldn't make an admirable son-in-law. It was just that this was the first meeting of the two, and no matter how attracted they were to each other, it was too soon. In fact, the sooner he started on the trade route with Gideon, the better. He planned on leaving in a few days but didn't want to make it obvious he would be trying to hurry the leave-taking.

Not aware they had each arrived at similar conclusions, they both sat on stools facing each other, trying to find words to express their concerns. Gideon blurted, "Fila is a very beautiful girl and I would like your approval that we can keep steady company." At the same time Aaron spoke out, "I can see you are both attracted to each other, but I do not want you two to rush into anything,"

There was a moment of surprised silence then they both broke out in relieved laughter. The decision had been made, now any future for the couple would be up to Fila.

Arm in arm, they strolled back to the cabin, Gideon leaning down to give an occasional pat to Buddy's head. When they pushed through the door, Gideon called the dog by the name his grandfather had given him. Buddy acknowledged with a wag of his tail and sloppy lick on his hand.

The two girls were surprised at the dog's attraction to Gideon until Aaron filled them in on the connection. The drowning of Gideon's mother and grandmother, Calis, Gideon's grandfather, finding the Relic while searching for their remains. Finally, the theft of the image and disappearance of Buddy, now called Friend. It was quite a narration. When the tale ended, both girls were silent in retrospect. The connections between the two families were astonishing, a continuous link flowing from one to the other almost as though pre-ordained by Destiny. Fila felt a shiver run down her spine, she looked more intently at Gideon. Was it possible the Relic had brought them together? She had to concede that the attraction seemed mutual.

The hour was late. Gideon and Aaron would share the double bunk on the main floor. Fila and Alea climbed to their upstairs sleeping area, while Buddy curled into his bed near the fireplace. Soon sleep settled on the occupants, a few snores echoing from the deeply slumbering men.

Buddy had his ears up, nose actively scenting the air for a familiar unwanted presence that may, or may not, be in evidence. His instincts told him to be on guard.

The next morning fog misted the area so heavily not even the barn was visible. Aaron and Gideon decided to lay over another day. There was no rush to reach any destination. They spent the time sorting and repacking everything, adding more items the girls had made to the voluminous stack of trade goods.

Gideon was an excellent wood carver. In his spare time he created lifelike birds and animals, each about the size of a man's thumb and accurate in every detail. It was something he enjoyed doing to pass the time during lonely nights on the trail. He had learned the art from his grandfather, who would select a piece of wood, turn it this way and that until he could imagine the image hidden within, then proceed to carve away the unwanted outer layer until the little figure was revealed. It had always seemed like magic to Gideon until he realized that indeed, the shape of the wood always hinted at what was beneath. He was pleased to have something to contribute for trade.

The day passed quietly. After chores were completed Aaron and Gideon sat for a game of checkers. The girls played with Buddy trying to teach him tricks which, because of his exuberance, became an all-but-impossible task. Their sides hurt so much from laughter they had to call a halt to the challenge.

As evening drew nigh, supper had been eaten along with the custard pie Alea had made for dessert. They sat for a time before the fire, desultorily chatting about the trip and items the girls wanted in return for their trade goods. When the hour grew late, the girls departed for their beds and the men settled themselves for their last good sleep under a roof. Buddy was already curled up in his, exhausted from the hours of what he considered playtime.

Outside the fog was lifting, leaving tree limbs heavy with moisture-sparkled glints of moonlight that shifted dark to light with the passing clouds. The air was awash with the scent of damp rich earth. Silence settled heavily on the night air, not a breeze stirred, nor leaf, nor budded twig.

Deep within the forest a tumbled pile of deadfall moved a fraction and then lifted as an arm reached out and began pushing branches aside. Slowly a shoulder emerged, then the head of a man. At length, finally easing himself from beneath his wooden prison, Luther stood painfully upright. His body ached from two days' confinement and the nasty wound on his head throbbed like the beat of a drum. He could smell the blood that had dripped onto his clothing because he had been unable to wipe it away. He was not only stiff, he was furious. Reaching within the folds of his cloak he withdrew a small emerald cat. Holding it in the palm of his hand he muttered, "I bid you bring fire and food." He watched as the cool, beautiful gem turned deep crimson. A small tornado of vapor streamed from the figurine's mouth and swirled overhead, then settled into the pile of deadwood that had been Luther's jail. In moments a fire was crackling, generating welcome heat. Then from nowhere, a reed basket appeared on a nearby log. Luther limped over and sat, stretching his long legs out toward the welcome heat.

When morning dawned, Aaron and Gideon packed everything onto the horses and readied themselves to leave. A few quick bites of breakfast, hugs and waves goodbye, they mounted their steeds. Rather than exit where they had originally come in, they rode to the northern perimeter of the property and wended their way through the forest until they cleared the woods. In an hour's time they were well on their way.

Luther was long gone, headed back home hours ago after checking the cabin and barn. Too many people there for him to carry out his plans. His time would come, the Relic was his. The girl and the dog would be taken care of too, that was a promise…

Gideon knew they would not return until late fall. This was just fine with him. It would give him a chance to figure out how he would manage if Fila agreed to marry. There were so many things needed to set up a new home. All he had to trade were his carvings. What could he receive that was worthwhile for those little things? Granted, they were very lifelike images. He took pride in his workmanship. One thing his grandfather always told him: "Put forth your best effort, anything less would be shameful." It was good advice.

Aaron noticed the worried frown Gideon wore. He wondered if there was something he had said or done to cause the expression. Finally, not being able to stand the suspense, he decided the best way was to be forthright. "Say, Gideon, is something bothering you? You seem upset. I hope it isn't anything I've caused by word or deed."

Aaron was sensitive about others' feelings, he always tried to think before blurting out anything, sometimes unsuccessfully. Gideon was a straightforward type person, just the kind Aaron admired. He wouldn't, for the world, want to hurt the young man's feelings. Best to clear the air before the trouble festered.

Gideon came back from his musings with a start. He had been lost in reverie, not even noticing the trail they followed nor his companion. For a moment he reddened with embarrassment, and then a huge grin split his face. This man could be his future father-in-law, may as well tell him what he was worried about, maybe he would think of a solution. Gideon began to drop the worrisome load from his shoulders. The more he talked, the less problems seemed until at last, as he looked upon Aaron's smiling face, there were no problems at all.

Aaron just couldn't help grinning. He recalled when he had courted Sera. He had driven himself crazy wondering how he would provide for her. Time had taken care of everything. He had already found the property for his homestead. Once she had agreed to wed, he had built the cottage and furnished it with trade goods. He remembered planting seeds and tiny saplings acquired during his trading treks. Eventually the growth had provided them with everything needed. Sera had been happy and to this day, content. As Aaron related his experiences during courtship and marriage, Gideon began to relax. No sense worrying now, it wouldn't solve anything. He already felt better having the cleared the air between them. That evening they camped, fed and watered the horses then settled in for the night. In the morning they would arrive at the Indian encampment and have their first day of trading.

Daybreak arrived clear and cool. The trees were in leaf, a few spring wildflowers were visible peeking from sheltered glades. This was the time Aaron loved the best. Everything new and green, the rich smell of earth with dewdrops sparkling atop the sprouting grassland.

Splitting the remaining slices of a small loaf of Sera's wheat bread, the two men each added a hard-boiled egg and slice of cheese, folded the bread over all and proceeded to enjoy their morning's repast. A cool drink of water washed everything down. They were ready to hit the trail again.

Toward late afternoon, the smell of wood smoke told them they were nearing the Indian encampment. Aaron called a loud greeting to let them know visitors were approaching. One of the camp guards answered with a welcome. Soon they entered the central clearing of the village and proceeded to the chiefs' lodge. They dismounted, reins in hand, they waited for the chief to step from his tepee.

"Welcome, trader, we've been expecting you. Usually you come earlier in the spring. Blow the elk horn, Red Stag. Trader Aaron has come."

Soon it seemed every man, woman and child had gathered before the tepee to inspect the display of goods being laid out on the men's blankets. There were colorful braided belts, rag dolls and scarves made by Aaron's daughters. Woolen coverlets and vests from Sera, and of course the carved animals from Gideon. Skeins of wool that Sera had dyed in bright colors sat midst the array of items. These were cherished by the Indian women. They used their bone needles to stitch decorations onto the deer-hide apparel they created for their families.

People scattered to their homes gathering items, hoping theirs would be the offer accepted for their most desired object. It was a madhouse of activity. At last they were all congregated, politely waiting for their chief to make his selections.

Slowly, he walked around the displays picking up something to examine more closely, replacing it, going on to another interesting item. As they watched his posturing progress they discerned exactly where his interests lay. Their eyes turned as one to the area of the blanket where the young man had placed his small carved animals. Even as their chief made another circuit around the displays, they knew the carved images would belong to him before the day was over. He gave a nod letting them know their trading could begin.

Gideon was intrigued with all the goods he could see being offered. He was getting worried no one seemed interested in his carvings. He watched Aaron dicker and bargain, trying to get the best of a trade. Slowly the blankets emptied of some of their goods while quite a stack was accumulating in front of Aaron. Gideon was about to place his collection back in his pack when he felt a tug on his sleeve, it was Chief Badger letting Gideon know he was interested in a trade.

Badger inspected each little figurine. They looked so lifelike he felt he was holding their spirits in his hand. It gave him an eerie feeling these powerful images would aid him when he sought knowledge from his dreams. They would also be a source of intimidation to all who looked upon them. There were only a few he was interested in. His namesake, the Badger, was most important, then the Moose and Fish. Both would guarantee good hunting and fishing. He was very fond of smoked Salmon. Holding his three choices in his hand, he drew Gideon into his tepee and over to the woven baskets that held his wealth. Lifting the covers from each of the four that sat against the skin wall, he gestured to Gideon to make his choices, this must be a trade worthy of the carvings.

Gideon didn't know what to do. He stood gazing at the baskets, indecision plain on his face, what to pick? How much or many was he entitled to? Finally in desperation, he motioned to one of the baskets, signifying that was where he wished to make his selections, it looked to be mostly beaver skins.

The chief was satisfied this would be one of the best trades any chief had ever made. The spirit images he had acquired would be sung at group meetings and every special occasion where tribes gathered. He would be the chief most remembered in the tribe's songs of history. His chest swelled with pride just thinking about the prestige he had acquired. With a nod of acceptance to Gideon he walked outside. His wives began to arrange the items on a deerskin which would be rolled tightly into an easily toted bundle.

The chief meandered about the encampment showing his prizes. He watched as their eyes flickered with intimidation for an instant then was hidden. Yes! This was exactly the feeling he had wanted, the images were perfect.

Trading had come to an end. Tomorrow the people would celebrate with food and dancing. It would be a welcome break from the routine of everyday life. As for today, everyone was tired from all the dickering, which had lasted much longer than expected. Soon everyone had departed except Aaron and Gideon who set up their campsite near the edge of the woods, then retired to their bedrolls completely exhausted. They slept like babes until the playful shouts of children awoke them the next morning.

Pots were set over fires and soon the aroma of cooking filled the air. Target practice with arrow and lance became rowdy with laughter and teasing. Young male children had races and tag teams to see who was the swiftest. As guests of honor, Aaron and Gideon joined the competition, an occasion only given those held in high esteem. By the end of day everyone was tired, well fed, and had danced until they were breathless. Little by little people began straggling off to their beds until only those who had overindulged drinking the tribe's strong potion were left sleeping where they had fallen. It had been a memorable celebration for all.

The two departed the following morning. Chief Badger was most vociferous with his words of praise and thanks. With a final wave goodbye they turned their horses in a more northerly direction, Aaron using an unfamiliar route following directions given by Badger. The horses couldn't maneuver some of the trails he had previously traveled by foot. It would take about four days to reach the next trade site.

If everything went well, possibly they could return as early as September. Weather held fair. Each trade brought exceptionally nice prizes to bring home. As the warm days drifted by and summer leaves began to lose their bright green, the cool days of autumn arrived. A touch of brilliance here and there gave hint of the colorful splendor to come. The time had come to head for home. Each felt comfortable in the close friendship that had developed. Deep mutual respect and true affection was evident in their easy camaraderie. What better way for future father and son-in-law to become acquainted than a trading trip. A person's true nature would surface whether avarice, subterfuge or other low characteristic, truth would out.

As the two wended their way back to the Winter Forest, Aaron discussed the division of goods between the two households. What Gideon had traded was his; however, Aaron needed to divide his share between Sera and Fila. The girls would sort through to see what they had acquired in trade.

Through the woods, closer to Winter Forest, the horses could sense the journey's end. They rode past a burned-out deadfall and commented how odd the fire had not spread, probably caused by lightning strike and storm. Soon the forest brightened as trees thinned and the sunny glade was revealed. Buddy's warning bark could be heard as the cottage door swung open. Fila and Alea hurried to see what the commotion was all about. When they spotted the two men, it was a race to see who arrived first for Father's hugs. Gideon felt his heart flutter at the sight of Fila. As soon as she hugged Aaron she turned, a warm smile on her face as Gideon slid from the saddle. They hugged quickly, shy at the internal disquiet each was feeling. Gideon groaned. How could a person's heart beat so swiftly and not cause an attack? He felt he would drop at any moment from the pure ecstasy of having held her in his arms. Stepping away, gazing at her lovely face, the words slipped from him before he could stop himself. "Fila, would you do me the honor of becoming my betrothed?" He waited in silence for her reply. Instead Fila took him by the hand and led him over to Aaron. "Father, Gideon has something he wants to ask you. He has my permission to speak."

Gideon looked with affection at the man who would become his father-in-law. They had built a strong relationship over the past months and he had come to love him. He paused a moment to mentally form the words that would best express his desire. "Aaron, I would like your permission to court Fila. You and I have had many conversations on love, responsibility and commitment. I agree with everything you spoke about. I promise to devote my life to making her happy." The two stood quietly hand in hand, waiting for Aaron's reply.

"Nothing would give me greater pleasure. I have always worried about my daughters' futures, who they would marry, if the person they fell in love with would be a worthy husband to them. I have complete confidence you are everything I desire in a son-in-law, I give you my blessing." Aaron couldn't help grinning. "Now that we have this taken care of, let's get our packs into the cottage, take care of the horses and get something to eat. The day is waning and there are a lot of goods to be sorted and divided between the two households. We will all head home in two days. Sera will help plan the wedding."

They parted, each to their duties. The men hefted the packs into the cottage then turned to the barn to brush, feed and settle the horses for the night. An early supper was prepared. By the time the men returned and washed up, it was on the table. Stewed chicken with dumplings suited everyone just fine. For dessert a plate of molasses cookies was set out and they all helped themselves.

At last, all the goods were laid out on the cottage floor. Most of the trade goods were animal pelts, excellent to use for purchasing supplies at Mica's store. There were also silver trinkets, leather shirts and vests, winter moccasins lined with rabbit fur, several packets of pemmican, dried fruits, nuts and fat pounded into a flat nourishing cake. Gideon had managed to swap his eagle carving for a polished turtle shell. The same one Aaron had traded away to obtain the obsidian knife. Bone needles, quill combs, hollowed horns filled with honey and sealed with wax, carved wooden bowls. Beautifully woven grass mats pretty enough to be used as wall hangings. When everything was divided, the items were repacked for easy carrying.

Huge yawns from the men hinted that they wanted to get some much-needed sleep, time for bed. Buddy was let out for his nightly five-minute jaunt. When he returned he got his goodnight pat on the head then curled up in his bed. The girls headed upstairs, still talking about Fila's upcoming wedding and their excitement at soon seeing their mother and sisters again.

The fire slowly died down, the air cooled slightly just enough to make sleep more comfortable. The men emitted gentle snores or groans at sore muscles. As for the girls, they were still talking about Fila's wedding. Soon they too fell silent and drifted into their own pleasant dreams.

Aaron was the first to awaken. Giving a great stretch and yawn he sat up, swung his feet to the floor and stepped to the window. It looked to be the beginning of a beautiful day. He felt good knowing he would soon be home with Sera. He couldn't believe that summer had ended and the season now well into autumn. The only explanation was the company he had enjoyed, and to think the lad would become his son-in-law. If he had searched the world over he could not have found a better traveling companion. All in all, he was well satisfied with how everything had worked out.

Gideon awoke slowly. When he finally opened his eyes, he saw Aaron standing at the window, a pensive look on his face. When Aaron glanced aside and saw that Gideon had awakened, he gave him a huge grin. "Good morning, son. Do you feel as hungry as I? Let's wake the girls to start breakfast while we take care of the horses. I'll race you to see who dresses the quickest and gets out the door to the barn first."

Those words started a cyclone of activity. Two men hopping from foot to foot, trying to pull on pants, get their shirts on right side out, hollering for the girls to awaken. Gideon fell onto the cot, both feet stuck in one of the pant legs. Aaron's shirt was half inside-out, he had neglected to reverse one of his sleeves. Red-faced, Gideon was finally able to tuck in his shirt, put on socks and shoes and disappear into the barn to care for the horses with Aaron close behind, laughing his head off. If Fila had seen her sweetheart in this predicament, Gideon would have died of embarrassment.

After breakfast the two men took a stroll around the forest glade. It was a beautiful site surrounded by mature forest whose leaves were turning crimson and gold. Gray squirrels chattered at their approach, chipmunks raced into the underbrush. A red fox fading into the distant shadows at the far side, caused a commotion amidst a flock of noisy sparrows.

The morning sun lighting up the centuries-old oak tree in the center of the large clearing, seemed to accentuate the majesty of its beauty. Gideon turned to Aaron, a worried look on his face as he voiced his concerns about being a good husband to Fila, being able to provide for her.

Aaron turned to Gideon with a look of serenity on his face and looped his arm across Gideon's shoulders, giving a squeeze of comfort. "You have worked hard all your life, it won't be much different when you and Fila marry. I went through exactly the same feelings when I married Sera. It seems like too much to handle but honestly I promise, you will be thankful for all the days of your life. Near family is where you will always yearn to be whenever you are away. Your wife, your children and the home you provide will be your heaven, and maybe even sometimes your hell, but it will forever be where you will find peace in your heart and soul. You will never regret the choice you made." Aaron paused, filled with all the treasured memories of Sera and his beginnings. He knew it would be a little easier for Fila and Gideon, that was the way it should be, better for one's children, less struggle to make a decent life. He and Sera would help whenever possible. He looked at Gideon, his affection showing plain on his face. "You have a home now, son. People to love you and be there for you come hell or high water. Don't you ever forget it." Aaron turned away, taking a quick swipe across his eyes with his shirt sleeve. "Darn, must have a speck of dust in my eyes."

Gideon couldn't remember a time when he had felt so loved. His grandfather and he had been very close. Praise he had received in plenty when he did well, but it had been an undemonstrative relationship. He had dim memories of his mother holding him, singing to him. After her and granny's death, the physical closeness had disappeared. He knew Gaddy loved him, it was just not a verbal assurance but something taken for granted. He made a promise to himself, he would always tell his family every day that he loved them. One never knew when that person would be taken away without warning.

The clear call to breakfast echoed through the morning air, the two men, breaking stride, turned toward the cottage. They were famished and ready to tackle anything set before them. Breaking into a lope, then a full-out run, they raced to see who would be the fastest. Surprisingly Aaron was first, possibly because of the years of walking that had strengthened his leg muscles. They burst through the door huffing and panting, both grinning from ear to ear.

It was a happy get-together. The eggs, bacon, and griddle cakes disappeared in short order. Conversation flowed smoothly, mainly what to pack for the trip home. Everyone would be ready to leave tomorrow. Aaron and Gideon would make travois's to pull behind the horses. They would be light enough with everything distributed evenly between the two animals, even though they would be carrying double. Fila would ride behind Gideon, Alea behind Aaron. Buddy would be able to keep up easily, they would not be traveling overly fast.

Breakfast over, the men left to cut the saplings for the two carrying frames. They would stretch deer hide between the posts which would then be attached to a halter arranged over the horses' backs. It would be a sturdy structure to keep the goods safe during their trip. Fila and Alea sorted through the items to pack. They placed everything in a neat pile so the men could divide it as they chose.

Evening arrived, they were ready. After supper the odds and ends all neatly put away, the cottage left in the same neat condition it had been when Fila first arrived. Tomorrow's breakfast would be leftovers from today's supper. Soon everyone retired to their beds, exhausted from the day's activity. A few snores floated softly through the silence. Even Buddy was chasing something in his dreams, overly tired from keeping track of everyone's whereabouts.

At first light the horses saddled, travois's in place they were up and riding out from the frost-dappled clearing. Gideon had decided at the last moment to set Buddy atop his travois. There was a spot just right for him to cuddle up and watch the scenery go by. They had to take the northern egress for the horses to navigate through the trees. Once they were clear of the forest, a turn left and then a day's travel would take them to the westerly edge of the Winter Forest where the homeward trail would be easy to follow. The sun began to warm the autumn air, their breath no longer visible. Travel was as swift as the travois's would allow. The horses were kept at a fast walk and occasionally they dismounted to walk beside their mounts, easing their double burdens for a while. Noon arrived with only a short stop to water the horses. A quick bite of ham and cheese, then it was back on the trail. By evening they had reached the turnoff toward home.

Camp was set up, the horses relieved of their burdens. By the time supper was prepared and sleeping sites arranged, the full moon was casting enough light to see quite well. They sat comfortably around the fire pit sipping honey-sweetened tea, discussing the wedding plans and the traveling preacher. Aaron had learned from Sera last spring that one of the homesteads about ten miles west of Mica's would be welcoming a new addition to their family sometime in September. That meant the preacher would be performing a baptism. If luck was with them they would arrive home in time to send word they needed his services. At last conversation dwindled to a few words of goodnight. The two girls bundled up together. Aaron and Gideon checked the horses for the last time, also tucking Buddy into a spare blanket, and then they too retired. Stray clouds accumulated until the moon was darkened and sleep deepened. Not a leaf stirred except for a shadow standing at the edge of the clearing.

"Sleep well while you may, my time is coming and sooner than I imagined. You are making arrangements well to my liking. Have your wedding, make all your plans. I know you two will be alone at some time or other then that nasty little thief will be left to herself. How nice of you to make everything so easy for me. I need only watch and wait." Luther had to stop himself from howling with glee, only a muffled hiss escaped his lips.

It was loud enough for little ears, twitching in sleep, to catch the reverberation in the still night air. Loud enough, in fact, to set Buddy on his guard. His enemy was near. The little dog came to full attention, nose searching for the hated smell he remembered from his days living with the old man. At last he knew where the scent was wafting from. He turned his eyes to the forest's edge.....THERE HE WAS. With furiously loud barking the little dog leapt from his blanket and raced toward the shadowed image, rousing everyone from sleep. Just in time he remembered the hurtful thump he had received on his head the last time he had come in close contact with this enemy. He stopped short a few feet away from the menacing figure and sat.

Luther was furious with himself. He reached inside his cape and withdrew a vial of powder. Carefully easing off the stopper, he flung its contents in the direction of the mutt, at the same time turning and scuttling deeper into the surrounding woodland. Buddy, caught in mid-bark, inhaled the potion. He could feel his nose burn like fire. He started sneezing again and again until he almost couldn't catch his breath, his nemesis forgotten.

Luther, once he had gotten far enough away, couldn't control his laughter. The look on the mutt after he had inhaled the pepper was choice, good for many a hearty laugh later. They would have no idea what had caused the disturbance. He could have sent the mutt to doggy heaven but that would have warned them something was amiss. Better to let them think everything was just fine. Anyway, pepper was good to have at hand, worked nicely to distract an enemy. Luther was still chuckling as he wended his way homeward.

After everyone calmed down and saw there was nothing to be worried about, Fila wiped Buddy's nose and eyes. She couldn't see anything that caused his distress, possibly he had heard a forest creature and went to investigate, coming in contact with some plant that didn't agree with his system. She tucked him into his blanket and then retired to her own bed.

Soon everyone was again fast asleep, even Buddy, who sensed that any threat was long gone.

At the crack of dawn everyone hurriedly repacked, grabbed a quick bite to sustain them until lunch, and started on their way toward home. The weather held fair and cold, which made the trip easier. No rain to muddy up their travel. The day went well. Noon lunch was again light. When they made their stop that evening Fila and Alea peeled potatoes, sliced and diced onions and ham. Combining the mixtures they set the pot on a tripod over the fire. By the time the horses were fed, watered and bedded down and their own sleeping arrangements set up, dinner was ready. Sifting around the fireside, enjoying the hot meal put everyone in a talkative mood.

Aaron stated he was positive Lady was pregnant with a colt or foal. It would be a nice addition to the farm and a start to having several mounts. If a colt, he would geld it, not good planning to chance interbreeding. Conversation went from breeding to gardens, to preserving foods. Aaron couldn't believe how knowledgeable Fila and Alea were. He should have known they had learned at their mother's knee and knew all the methods of homemaking. Fila would make Gideon an excellent wife. Finally a few yawns later, they all headed for their beds, tired from the day's travel but sated with the tasty supper the girls had prepared.

During the night frost settled. If they had awakened to see the moon sparkling on the silvered branches all about them, they would have thought they were in a magical place. As it was, they were nestled down in their furs getting a well-deserved rest. At sunup, when the crystals melted at the first touch of warmth, another beautiful scene was admired through still-sleepy eyes. The reflection in the beads sent shimmering rainbows through branches, treetops and prominent evergreens whose beauty was now fully appreciated set against leafless limbs.

That morning, their final day of travel, they ate the last of the food knowing a skipped lunch would be no big loss since they planned on arriving early enough to still have daylight. Setting as fast a pace as the horses would tolerate, they made good time along the Widows Mountain trail. It felt good being in familiar territory again. They passed Luther's territory, not aware he was watching from behind the bramble barrier. He had a gleam of triumph in his eyes that would have caused them great concern had they seen him.

The sun was low on the horizon when they reached the entrance to the family home site. Just enough time to settle the horses in the barn, carry their possessions into the cottage, then catch up on all the news with Sera and the girls.

Mina and Nia were just heading back to the cottage from the barn when they saw the riders. With a whoop of joy that brought Sera hurrying to see what the noise was all about, the two raced to their father, dancing about until Lady became nervous with their activity. Aaron slid down, clasping both girls in a great bear hug that took their breath away. He swung them around in a dizzying spin, finally setting them again on their feet where they swayed for a moment with giddiness, laughing all the while. Sera came running toward the group, not sure who to reach for first, her daughters or Aaron. The matter was settled when they joined together, arms stretched around each other, words of love and greetings pouring forth in a burst of joy at their reunion. Fila noticed Gideon standing alone. She reached out to him, pulling him into the welcome warmth of family love. Sera reached out as did Aaron, Mina, Nia, and Alea. Truly, Gideon had arrived home at last.

Everyone finally settled down to getting things stashed away while Sera swung the pot over the fire to reheat stew. Gideon hurried to the barn toting his packs, leading Night, who needed a good grooming. After he had everything put away he started work on Night, who reveled in the attention. When Night was once more shining like silk, he gave him a generous helping of oats. Thinking to accomplish two things with one trip, he grabbed a bucket, a bar of lye soap, pulled a clean shirt and trousers from the chest drawer and headed for the pond. Once there he removed his soiled clothes and dove into the cold water. He scrubbed from head to toe. The tail end of his discarded shirt served as a towel, and then he donned his clean clothes. He felt like a new man. Wadding his soiled garments up he tucked them under his arm and headed for the spring to get a bucket of water for the horses. Once back at the barn, horses taken care of, he checked his room to make sure he had left everything neat. He slid the top drawer closed, thinking he must have left it open when he got his clean clothes. Satisfied, he headed for the cottage.

They were just sitting down to supper, dishes already filled with the tantalizing aroma of a good stew. Gideon took his seat, everyone else sat watching the door. Aaron spoke, "What is Fila taking so long at? We sent her to fetch you about ten minutes ago." He looked at Gideon, waiting for an answer.

Gideon sat in puzzlement for a moment, and then a grin spread across his face as he thought about his bath at the pond. "I bet she spotted me bathing and decided to take off from the area so I wouldn't become embarrassed. Let me go get her, we'll be right back." He arose from the table and headed out toward the barn. A quick search about the area showed no sign of her. Now he was getting nervous. "Fila, where are you? Fila, don't be shy, come out." Gideon waited for a response. Soon Aaron was beside him also calling. Everyone had spilled from the cottage searching the premises, even as far as the tree line. There was not a sign of Fila. She had disappeared. There was not a single place left to look. Aaron and Gideon had even gone into the forest without results.

Gideon had a terrible feeling of dread. Somehow he felt responsible, though how, he had not yet managed to figure out. He walked back to the barn, returned to his room, and sat down on the edge of his cot deep in thought. Something was nagging at him. There was something that had been out of sequence. He mentally returned again to the time of their arrival, sorted through everything that had occurred. Went back, step by step, through each subsequent action and reaction.

Quickly he stood, walked to the chest and pulled open the drawer. Fila had placed a dried flower on top of his shirts, probably thinking he would select a clean one when he returned to the barn, not aware he had taken one with him to the pond. The opposite corner of the drawer was bare. The blue suede pouch was gone.

He knew the natural reaction would have been for her to look inside after she held it and began to feel the warmth it emitted. That was what he had done. He remembered how cold he had felt after almost drowning. When looking into the emptiness, his wish, and what he had seen inside afterward. The icy fear returned with the memory. "My God! Fila, what words did you speak when you opened that pouch? Where are you now and how will I ever find you? There has to be something I can do to return you safely home."

Gideon could still hear the family calling Fila's name. He hurried to find Aaron, needed to tell him about the magic pouch and the dread he felt knowing the power it possessed. He drew Aaron aside and began his tale. He watched as his friend's face turned white as snow.

Aaron was upset. "Do you know how we can find her? There must be something we can do, we can't just stand here talking about it." At least he knew Luther had nothing to do with her disappearance, which would have been the last straw. Aaron placed his arm across Gideon's shoulders. He was a smidgeon taller and it felt quite comfortable giving consolation to the forlorn young man. He knew Gideon had nothing to do with Fila's absence. She had a habit of getting into predicaments. There had to be a way, however, to discover where his daughter was. "First I have to tell Sera and the girls what has happened. Then you and I need to sit down and decide what to do."

As they talked Aaron guided Gideon to the cottage, closely following him inside. When Sera saw their faces a look of dread settled on her countenance. She stepped to Aaron's side placing her hand on his arm. "What has happened? Where is Fila and why isn't she with you?" She gazed so intently at him, he could hardly utter the words she must hear.

"Sera, please stay calm, Fila has vanished because she mishandled something she should not have touched. Hopefully she is in no danger, however we have no idea where she has been sent, nor how we may contact her." Aaron almost stuttered with nervousness. Sera was like a mother bear when it came to protecting her children. They would never be too old for her to guard.

Sera's arms dropped to her sides, her pale face showing the intense concentration she was mustering. She seemed to be gazing inward, focusing on something the rest of them could not ascertain. The moments slipped away, her very being seemed to waver as though in a distant mirage. Aaron caught her just as her eyes closed and she began to fall, he carried her to their bed and placed her unconscious form thereon. She lay so quietly that he could not even discern her breathing. He knew what she was doing, had seen this happen previously when she was searching for information about a family member. How she managed to accomplish this he had no idea.

Aaron pulled a light cover over her still form, motioning the others away. Then he sat with them at the kitchen table quietly waiting, knowing she would return from her distant visit to wherever with, hopefully, a morsel of information. Mina swung the pot over the fire to heat water for tea. Sera always needed it when she returned from one of her spirit-trips. When the water was heated she prepared the tea. The stew for their supper sat forgotten. Mina put a small portion into a bowl for Buddy's supper and set it down for him to enjoy.

The hour grew late, still Sera remained in her trance. Aaron was becoming uneasy. He didn't recall her ever being in this state for this length of time. If this continued he would somehow bring her out of it. Stress began to show on everyone's faces.

A small sigh escaped from Sera's lips, Aaron hurried to her side. Clasping her cold hand in his he began to gently massage warmth into it, coaxing Sera back to consciousness. When her eyes fluttered open she seemed confused at first, then aware that she had returned home to her family. In a moment, she sat up, swung her feet to the floor and stood to face everyone.

"I have seen Fila. She is safe but confused about what has happened to her. She doesn't know where she is, unaware of how she got there. The last thing she recalls is placing a flower on the shirts in Gideon's chest. She noticed a pretty leather pouch and picked it up. It felt so warm in her hand, she opened it to see what was creating the heat. The next thing, darkness had engulfed her. When she opened her eyes, she was standing in a place she had never seen before. It was nighttime, she couldn't see what was outside the windows, afraid to open the door to look. When I left her I told her I could sense no evil thereabouts, she would be safe. I tried to look outside but the view was closed to me, as though I was somehow an intruder. I didn't feel anything threatening me, just a blockage to my spirit. I did try several times without success. Tomorrow, when it is full light, I will try again."

Sera was herself, worries about her daughter put to rest. Even though it was late she emptied the stew from the filled bowls back into the pot and placed it over the fire. No one was in the mood for sleep and everyone felt hungry. As soon as the stew was heated the bowls were refilled and they all sat to eat.

Gideon had a hard time getting the food down. He kept thinking about Fila, wondering if she had something to eat. Guilt sat heavily on his conscience. He had known how dangerous the pouch was. Why in the world had he left it where it could easily be found? It was his fault Fila had disappeared. If it took the rest of his life, he would find her. He dropped the spoon into his bowl. Impossible to force anything else down his throat else he would become ill. Pushing his seat back he stood, excused himself from the table and left. It was a dark night with just a sliver of moon, enough light so he could make his way to the barn and his room. He needed to be alone. Once inside he closed the door and sat on the edge of his cot, head in hands. His misery over what had happened to Fila the only thing he could think about. Finally exhausted, he let himself fall back onto the cot. Flipping part of the Indian coverlet over his extremities, in moments he was deeply asleep.

Old memories and pictures danced through his dreams. His grandfather Calis, mother Cassy and granny Nola, drifted through his fantasies. The scent of sage became so strong it woke Gideon with a start. He could still smell the aroma that seemed to permeate the entire room. Sitting up, he peered about trying to discern where the essence was coming from. His nose crinkled, trying to ascertain which direction. It seemed to be strongest in the corner where his old pack was sitting. He dropped his still-shod feet to the floor, stepped to the corner hefting the pack up and sitting it on the chest of drawers. Opening its flap he lifted out the tied oilcloth package. Once the ties were undone and wrapping unfolded, he saw the beautiful linen needlework within. This would be a wonderful wedding gift for Fila. She would be so proud having something that had been made by his granny. Carefully he refolded the precious items and placed them into one of the chest drawers. The next package he lifted out held a small tin cup with ancient lettering around its edge, a small blue stone and a miniature golden arrow. At the very bottom lay a black book. As he lifted it out, a current of sensation shot through his hand and up his arm almost causing him to lose his sense of balance. His eyes caught the title, "DESTINY" written in bold golden script. Now the memory came back to him of the day he was packing to leave his Gaddy's home, and the warning that seemed to come from his Granny Nola. "You may drink from the cup. *Do not open the book.*" Why was he awakened? He could still smell the sage, as though Granny was standing right next to him. "Please, Gran, help me. The woman I love is lost and all through my fault, I was careless." He stood in silence, hoping for a sign. A clear metallic note echoed throughout the bunkroom. He was prodded to reach for the tin cup and when it was clasped in his hand, he was urged to dip some water from the urn. As he held the dripping cup to his lips, the Black Book trembled with vibration. With his first sip the cover opened, a second sip and the pages turned and as he finished drinking, the book lay opened for him to read. Gideon placed the cup next to the book, being careful not to let any drops fall on its pages, which were yellowed with age and looked very fragile. He didn't want to touch it, something inside warned that it could be very dangerous. He still felt the presence of his grandmother, almost as though she was guiding him to have the proper respect and treatment of her mysterious volume. When Gideon felt confident enough to lean over and read whatever was displayed, he focused his eyes on the first sentence that caught his attention.

"And when they met, love fell upon them at first sight. An early marriage was not to be. Darkness came upon the lass, taking her from present to past where she remained for a time among happy memories not of her knowledge. All was not lost, for when her swain was told of her destination, he had only to follow the path."

When Gideon finished reading the passage, the pages fluttered together and the cover closed with a snap. "Wait, wait, I didn't get to reread it, I need to see it again, make sure I read everything correctly. Please, I'm not sure if I remember it right." His pleading came to naught. The book remained closed and locked with iron bands. He mentally repeated everything he had read and shortened the message into as few words as possible. "Love first sight, Delayed marriage, Go from present to past, Memories not hers, Follow the Path." All he had to do was figure out what it meant.

Dawn was near breaking when he finally lay down to catch a short nap. He needed to talk to Sera. He felt sure she would know what the message revealed. In minutes he was deep in a dreamless sleep. When he awoke several hours later the sun sat high and the morning was half gone.

He was still clad in yesterday's garments. He splashed water on his face, finger-combed his hair and hurried out the barn toward the cottage. The door opened before he could reach it, Aaron motioned him inside. Sera dished up a bowl of hot oatmeal for him. While Mina buttered a few slices of bread, Nia poured him a glass of milk. Everyone sat keeping him company while he ate. When finished, the girls cleared the table.

Sera and Aaron waited for Gideon to speak. It was obvious to them he was nervous about something and needed to talk. At last he felt confident enough to relate what had happened with the book without losing self-control. When he finished telling every bit that had happened, from the scent of sage to the final closing of the book, he felt relieved at having someone share his dilemma. The burden of worry lightened.

Sera had fallen silent, sure that there was an explanation somewhere midst the words and phrases revealed to Gideon. She was good at deciphering puzzles. According to the book, Fila would be gone only for a time now that Gideon had been given the knowledge of how to find her. The problem was how to figure out what the instructions were. Taking a piece of charcoal from the edge of the fire she wrote the message on the back of the door, making sure it was written word for word. Now she could ponder on it every time her eyes fell upon the writing. Someday she would be able to wash it off once Fila was safe home again. Until then, this would be a reminder to everyone to try and solve the mystery.

For now there was work to get done, animals to feed and water. The girls were sent to gather the eggs. Aaron and Gideon headed to the barn to take care of the horses and milk Bell, the cow. Aaron was told to also slaughter two chickens when he had time.

Sera made the beds, swept the floor and started to peel and dice vegetables for today's meal of chicken soup with dumplings. Often her eyes drifted to the writings on the door. The hidden message was there, she just had to find it.

By noon everyone had finished their chores and headed for the cottage. They straggled in, one by one, waiting until all were assembled before sitting down to lunch. Not a word was spoken. Each, in turn, seemed to focus their eyes on the door's message trying to fathom its meaning without success. When lunch was over they quietly left the cottage, each trying to find something to do to take their mind off their worry.

Gideon returned to his room. He replaced the book and cup in his pack. Sorted through his clothing, bundling the soiled laundry into one pile. He would get some soap from Sera and wash them himself. Tucking them under his arm he returned to the cottage, tapping on the door before entering.

Sera was sitting at the table she had already wiped clean, deep in thought. When she heard the door open and saw Gideon, it was as though a light went on in her mind. "That's it. I know what the riddle means. Gideon, you must return home. That's where Fila has been taken. The path you follow is the path you were on to get here. It was right there in front of us all the time." She bounced to her feet so excited she couldn't sit still. When she noticed the bundle of soiled clothing Gideon held, she hauled out the tin tub. "You will need clean things for your trip. Empty the cauldron into the tub for me, I'll get these washed right away and hung to dry. You leave tomorrow morning."

Gideon was struck dumb. How could he have been so stupid when the mystery was no mystery at all? Filled with the urge to rush away at that very moment, he realized Sera was right, tomorrow was soon enough. The thought of seeing Fila again filled him with such intense joy he could hardly contain himself. After pouring the water for Sera, he was out the door calling to Aaron and the girls.

Aaron came striding out from the barn, the girls running from the chicken coop. When they saw Gideon waving frantically from the front stoop, they hurried toward him, meeting him halfway he was in such a rush.

"Sera knows where Fila is. I leave for home in the morning. Hopefully I can arrive before heavy snow settles in. I wouldn't want her there by herself for the winter. She'll need firewood and food. I can trade for things in town. I still have some of my carvings." Gideon was out of breath trying to get everything said all at one time.

Aaron had a strained look on his face after hearing the news. He needed to be careful how he replied. There was no way in heaven he would allow Gideon and his daughter to be alone without the blessing of marriage. "Son, we'll have to travel together, Fila will need clothing and blankets. I'll also bring items to trade for staples to last the winter, we have no way of knowing what sort of weather will set in. It would be impossible for you to carry everything, don't you agree?" Aaron looked askance at his young friend.

Gideon hadn't even thought of those possibilities, it made sense. A huge grin split his face at the thought of the two of them traveling together again. He had really liked the companionship during the trading trek, he would enjoy Aaron's company once more. It was settled. They would be packed and ready to leave in the morning. The rest of the day dissolved into evening with everyone busy getting supplies ready. They all retired early, the men wanting to head out before dawn.

For a while Gideon lay awake thinking about Fila. It caused a curious sensation in the pit of his stomach, or maybe it was closer to where his heart was. Whatever the feeling, he knew for the rest of his life, the love he felt for her would forever make itself known deep within his very being. He drifted off to sleep, his lips forming a gentle smile.

When he awoke it was still dark. He could sense it must be at least 6 a.m., this time of year the sun wouldn't show until much later. He dressed warmly knowing he would need the extra protection from the cold, he prayed snow would hold off until they reached his grandfather's home near Umer. Taking a final look around his room, he couldn't see a thing he had missed. Hoisting the pack to his shoulder, he went to saddle Night and tie everything down securely; the last thing he needed was something getting lost on the way. He was just finishing up when Aaron arrived to ready Lady. Soon they led the horses outside and closed the barn door. They made their way to the cottage to have a quick bite to eat, and then say their goodbyes.

A light breakfast of oatmeal sufficed. Within minutes Aaron had hugged and kissed his wife and daughters. Gideon gave each a quick peck on the cheek and a softly voiced "Goodbye." The two men were out the door, mounted, and on their way. When they exited the property, they turned left. They planned on making a short side trip to Mica's trading post, which would only be a quarter mile out of their way. Although they had brought clothing for Fila, blankets would be needed for the coming winter and provisions to supply the home.

Mica was happy to welcome company, specially his best friend Aaron and the checker player lad. By the time all the selections had been made, there was quite a bundle. A little more than could be transported easily on just the two horses. "Hey, partners, don't worry. I have a dapple-gray, four-year-old mare you can use. Just bring her back in the spring when you return. The care and feed you give her will save me work and pay for her use." Aaron was happy with the agreement. He settled the bill due on the supplies and the two men secured everything to their new traveling companion. Within an hour they were back on the trail to Umer.

The next few days went easily. The weather held fair but cold. They had bought horse blankets for the animals' comfort at night and a good fire was nice to cozy up to each evening. They didn't bother with cooking, satisfied with just beans and hardtack. When they reached Gideon's place there would be time enough for all the fancy stuff.

On the fourth day a storm hit. The snow was so thick they had to make camp, couldn't see a foot in front of their faces. They found a grove of trees well protected from the wind that looked suitable. After unloading the horses they secured them leeward of the storm and covered each with a blanket. Once fed, they were set for the night.

As for Aaron and Gideon, there wasn't much chance of getting a fire lit. They both hunkered down near the horses hoping the animals' body heat would help keep them warm. It was a cold, miserable night. Toward dawn when the wind finally abated, they set a good fire to warm themselves and have something hot to eat. It was almost midday when they started out. The snow so deep they each took turns breaking a trail. They were lucky to have even traveled five miles by evening.

Gideon was a little nervous. They should have arrived at his home by now. With the deep snow it might take them another two days. If a new storm hit in the meantime, it could be much longer before they arrived safely. This was hard weather for man and beast. They needed to get someplace safe from the cold, which seemed to get icier with every passing hour. He had a sudden memory of a young widow sitting him down at the edge of her well to eat of the meal she brought him. It had been the day he left home. Her place was somewhere within a day's ride. In the morning they would head for her place. For now, they just had to make it through another cold night.

The temperature kept dropping and by morning had become so frigid that ice crystals began forming on their collars from the steam of their breath. Their feet and hands felt numb. It was becoming a dangerous life-or-death situation. They decided not to build a fire, it would take too long. Best to load the horses and get started. Gideon led the way with Night breaking a trail for Aaron and the other two horses. Within an hour he was so exhausted he had to let Aaron take the lead. For the remainder of the morning and into early afternoon they made small progress, relieving each other as often as necessary.

Gideon almost didn't recognize the frozen stream it was so snow drifted when they crossed. It was only a small patch of ice showing around the base of a branch that caught his eye and sent a shock of awareness through him. They had only to maneuver up the distant slope and the woman's cabin would be in sight. They could be there before dark.

Just the thought of reaching a safe destination gave them renewed vigor. Even the horses sensed a change in the men and strove harder to gain footing in the deepening snow. Slowly they ascended the hill, finally reaching the summit. Gideon did not see evidence of the cabin although drifts could be hiding it from view, nor could he scent a wood fire in the swirling wind. He was positive of his location, knew for sure the woman's place was near. He remembered his fast ride to cross the river before rainstorm raised the water level.

Step by step they strove to gain headway until finally they espied the top of a chimney projecting above a distant snow drift, though not a wisp of smoke wafted from its stack. With their objective in sight they strove mightily to overcome the last of the deep drifts, arriving finally at the cabins door.

"Hello, inside," Gideon called as he approached the door and gave a solid knock on its surface. Several more knocks and calls brought no answer from within. When he tried the latch, the door swung open easily revealing an empty abode with no evidence of its occupant. Gideon turned to Aaron, a quizzical look on his face. "She was fine when I last saw her. She even gave me a hot meal before sending me on my way. I wonder what has happened to her. Well! I'm sure she wouldn't mind us using her place to get out of the storm. I recall a small outbuilding we can use to stable the horses. Let's unpack here, then I'll help you get them settled and fed. In a short time we will be warm at least, and out of the cold."

They unburdened the animals, stored their belongings indoors, and led their mounts to the shed where it was dry and well protected from the wind. A few handfuls of oats, a good shake of the horse blankets to remove excess snow before covering each, and the three were cozily bedded down for the night.

Now it was Aaron and Gideon's turn to get warm and put some food under their belts. They hadn't had a decent meal in several days. At least now, out of the storm, they could prepare something hot. Soon a pot over the crackling fire was heating a few cans of beans and shaved ham. Another small pot packed with snow was set near the fire to heat for their tea fixings. As the small cabin warmed, the two men removed their outerwear and wet socks. Aaron produced two pair of woolen socks Sera had included in his pack. By now, they were both so drowsy that it took all their willpower to stay awake. If they hadn't been so famished, surely they would have slept, but the mouthwatering aroma tantalizing them could not be ignored.

Their bowls were filled, strong sweetened tea in oversized cups sitting near to hand, waiting to be lifted to cracked lips. They finished every morsel in the pot, and drank every drop of their tea.

Curling up in their blankets near the fire they drifted off into their first good night's sleep since leaving home. The fire died down to embers as they slept through the entire night getting their much deserved rest.

The two awoke to a cold, clear dawn so bright with sunlight it was blinding. The night winds had kicked the snow into high drifts that would be impossible to travel through. Both Aaron and Gideon were uncomfortable with the idea of not reaching Fila sooner. Nothing, however, could be done about the situation.

Aaron went to care for the horses while Gideon built up the fire to warm the cabin and start breakfast. He sorted through his packs to find a change of dry clothing, discovering the small pack containing his grandmother's keepsakes. He set the book and cup aside. The small blue stone remained resting next to the miniature golden arrow at the bottom of the pack. He had a feeling one of the items could be important, how he had this knowledge didn't concern him. Intuition told him a small measure of help was there before his eyes but which one to select? How was he to proceed after making his choice? Holding the blue stone in one hand, the arrow in the other, he pondered his dilemma. Finally in irritation, he voiced his confusion aloud. "How in tarnation am I to choose which of you two is the one?" He felt so ridiculous standing there like an idiot. "I might as well just put you away, what good are you?" As he moved to replace them back into the pack, he felt a strong vibration in the hand that held the arrow. He dropped the blue stone into the pack, and then concentrated on the golden arrow. It was quivering on the tips of his fingers, ready to soar off into flight. What was going on? How was this going to help him?

Just then Aaron entered the cabin. Before the door could be closed, the arrow shot from his hand, as though from a bow, soaring through the open door and away, a few quick golden flashes of sunlight highlighting its path as it disappeared from sight. Aaron was aware something had shimmered past him as he closed the door. He looked at Gideon standing as though in shock or surprise. "What's wrong, lad? You look as though you'd seen a ghost or something. Was there a bird trapped inside? Don't tell me you're afraid of them? A little thing like that can't hurt you."

Gideon shook his head in disbelief. "Aaron, if I told you what happened, you'd never believe me. Let's just say that life is full of surprises and leave it at that." He replaced everything and set the pack aside. The snow had melted in both of the pots. He added cornmeal and a few chunks of bacon to one. In the smaller pot he threw in a hearty pinch of tea leaves, pushing the container closer to the fire. The aroma of cornmeal mush and the scent of bacon made their mouths water. A few pieces of hardtack to dunk in the tea completed their banquet.

With nothing else to do and nowhere to go, they searched several drawers in the kitchen chest looking for something to do to occupy their time. Sure enough, there was an old carved checker set, something most people kept on hand to while away quiet evenings. They set up the game at the kitchen table, refilling their cups and making themselves comfortable. It was going to be a long time before they could continue on their way. Thankfully, they had shelter for themselves and their animals. Things could have turned out much differently.

Meanwhile, the arrow was being drawn like a magnet. Straight and true it flew through the icy morning air soaring over drifts, around and over treetops, skimming just above the snowy ground. At times it aimed straight up into the sky avoiding heavy branches laden with snow and every other impediment that might deter it from reaching its destination. Its golden shaft quivered from the force of its projection. Ever closer it drew to a small cottage and a frightened young woman stranded in a strange environment, who was wondering what had brought her there.

Chapter Five

Fila had caught a glimpse of Gideon heading for the pond. She knew he would need a clean change of clothing after bathing and so decided, on the spur of the moment, to leave a romantic memento for him to find. Pondering over what to give, she remembered the small dried flower she had from the past summer. Perfect. He would wonder where it could have come from. Scurrying up the attic steps she quickly retrieved the posy from where she had placed it in her favorite book, then raced down and out the door wanting to get to the barn before he discovered her intrusion into his room. From a distance she could see he was still out in the middle of the pond. Good. She had laughed a little at what he would feel when he saw her little token. If he enjoyed surprises as much as she, he would probably blush at her gift, then tuck it away someplace safe.

As soon as she entered his room, she planned to place it on his pillow. After thinking it over, however, it seemed like it would be too personal there. Not on top of the chest, he would notice it too quickly. Probably on top of his clean shirts would be a sensible spot. Sliding the drawer open, she placed the bud atop the folded clothing. As she was about to close the drawer she noticed the suede pouch lying in the opposite corner. She had never seen such a beautiful color in her entire life. It looked so soft, almost like velvet. She couldn't resist the temptation to caress the object once her fingers felt the smooth surface, she couldn't help but pick it up. Warmth radiating from its interior seemed to invite her investigation. Gently, she loosened the top closure and carefully pulled apart its opening, peering into the blackness within. Oh! It felt so cozily warm, just like a nice soft blanket to cuddle into. She could almost see something inside that looked to be a figure holding something. Bringing the pouch closer to her eyes, trying to decipher exactly what the figure was doing, she became so deeply absorbed that the next instant, when she looked up through darkness, she could see someone looking down at her. Puzzlement flashed across the face until shock turned it white as snow. SHE had been the person looking down at herself. How could this be? With that thought still echoing through her mind, the figure looking down vanished.

Fila sat in total darkness nested in a soft, warm closure without knowledge of where or how she had gotten there. She ran her hands along each side of the barrier and felt only a textured wall of some type of material unfamiliar to her. She tried pushing against the sides working her way around the entire circumference, without finding any entryway. A second try and still nothing. At last panic began to overcome her. "Oh! Please let me out. If I did anything wrong, I'm sorry. Tell me what you want, I'll do anything, just let me go home." Her pleadings were in vain. She began talking about anything that came to mind. "I just wanted to surprise Gideon with a flower and look what has happened to me. The color was so beautiful, almost the color of Gideon's' eyes.

A voice spoke softly from the darkness. "My poor child, don't be afraid, there is nothing here to harm you, I will see to that. So, you are the one my grandson has his heart set on. It's good I heard you use the name so dear to my heart. There is nothing I can do about releasing you from your capture, however I can arrange for you to be taken to a place where you will be safe. Sleep for now, when you awaken your confinement will be of a different sort. Take heed, it will not be forever. You have the mate to more than your heart. Only time will reveal the mystery of why."

Fila was suspended in silence, the name "Nola" swirling around in her mind. At least she knew the voice had been Gideon's grandmother's. It had given her immense relief from the fear that had overwhelmed her when she first found herself confined in the darkness. Now, the fear had returned. Not as intense, but still an uncomfortable feeling that seemed to grip her whole being. She did not like it. As a person who had always used action to counteract circumstances beyond her control she now felt as though she was frozen in limbo. The urge to leap, run, scream, or fight was held in tightly. Somehow she just knew if she did any of these things something dreadful would happen.

Time seemed to stretch into oblivion until at last Fila curled into a fetal position and drifted into sleep. Fragmented dreams slipped through her quiet world. She could see Gideon in a strange cabin with someone who resembled her father sitting at a table. The next scene was of a cottage in a far place unknown to her. As though floating in space, she saw a small town in the distance, beyond the town, farther away a mountain, and beyond the mountain a place that looked very much like the Winter Forest. She felt breathless with the vista spread before her. What was happening? Turning a little to her left she could see her family home clearly illuminated, her mother walking from the barn with a pail in her hand. It looked to be filled with fresh milk. Each scene was as clear as crystal, as though she was actually there in person. A little past her home she could see Mica's trading post. He was standing on the porch talking to a tall dark-haired man in a black cape. Mica seemed a little nervous and uncomfortable. Suddenly, the dark man turned and looked right at her, just as though he could actually see her. Fila found herself back in the darkness wide-awake, icy chills traveling down her spine. She gave a shiver and sat up, the image of the man clear in her memory, the fear she had felt still present.

Somehow the darkness was different. Though it was still black as pitch there was a current of air wafting across her face. She seemed to be sitting on something. She stroked her hand over a rough surface then, on her other side with her other hand. It was a bed. The covers carried the scent of sage which gave a measure of comfort to her.

Standing upright, she began to feel her way around until she encountered a wall. Then it was just a matter of inspecting the perimeters until she felt the outline of a closed shutter. Sliding the wooden latch back she swung the panels open to reveal a moonlit night. The sparkle of frost seemed the most beautiful sight she had ever seen. Sliding up the sash, she drew in a deep breath of the cold fresh air. Her spirits soared and her adventurous nature again took hold.

She was confident everything would be fine. At least she was out of the darkness. Come morning she would figure out where she was and then try to get back home again. That thought had only just emerged when she noticed clouds skidding across the moon's surface. A few random snowflakes floated through the window touching her cheek with a light kiss. As she watched, the few flakes turned into a flurry and the moon disappeared. Quickly she closed the window, and then turned to view the dim interior.

She could see the outline of firewood stacked against the far wall near a fireplace. When she had gathered kindling and used the flint and stone to set the flame, it wasn't long until a crackling fire was warming the room. Checking the cupboard she found a canning jar that held strips of dried venison. Lifting the metal clasp that held the glass lid in place, a rich spicy aroma made her mouth water. Removing a few pieces she closed the container, sat in a chair next to a table. The venison helped relieve her hunger pangs just enough to allow herself to relax and ponder the things she must accomplish before the storm hit full blast.

This was a pretty place. One that a caring woman had planned carefully to make cozy and snug. Not a single draft of wind entered around or under the door. Her husband must have been very handy at building. The table was nicely crafted with some fancy engraving around its edge. The backs of the four chairs were also carved with curlicue figures. Hard to ascertain exactly what they were, neither flowers nor decipherable lettering, but pretty nonetheless.

The fireplace was built of fieldstone and there were two shepherds' hooks holding pots. A tin sink set into a corner cupboard had a water pump mounted at one end, it would need priming. Good thing it was snowing, some melted snow would serve to get the thing working again. She'd have to remember to keep a jug of water always handy. She tried pumping the handle without success, just a lot of dry squeaks that made her grit her teeth. The other side of the sink provided a good working surface. She admired the tin flour bin sitting at its very end and flipped open its top finding it half-filled. She would check it later to see if it was usable.

She inspected the contents of two cupboards over the sink. Dishes, bowls, cups and tableware were stored neatly in the first. The other held three sealed stoneware containers stacked closely together marked "Oats," "Barley" and "Cornmeal." A smaller lidded glass jar held what looked to be tea leaves.

In the lower cabinet three huge glass-lidded jugs held an assortment of cured vegetables, cabbage, and pickles. Two gallon-sized tin containers, one labeled "Dried beans," the other "Lentils," sat side by side. Dried bunches of herbs, peppers, and sausage hung from the ceiling. The sausage was covered with green mold but she could smell the enticing aroma that made her mouth fill with anticipation of a first taste.

Everything was too well kept and provisioned to have been vacant for any extended length of time. Where were the people who lived here? Not a hint of abandonment nor hurried leave-taking was evident anywhere, not a single thing out of place. She expected, at any moment, the owners would walk in, see her as an unwelcome intruder, and boost her out the door. How could she explain to them she hadn't arrived of her own volition, she was brought to this strange home. The more she dwelled on the possible confrontation, the more nervous she became.

Finally, in desperation, she flung open the door and called loudly to anyone who would be within hearing. Hopefully, she awaited a reply without success. When the cold air began to make her shiver, she closed the door latching it securely. If the people came and found her, fate would decide what happened to her. She was much too tired to worry anymore tonight. Too tired to make a meal, too tired to do anything but return to the cot she had first found herself on.

Banking the fire so it wouldn't burn out during her rest, she made her way to the rear room and dropped onto the bed. Pulling the covers up to her neck she snuggled deeper into the warm comfort and felt herself beginning to drift into slumber. Deeper still she fell into the bottomless depths of sleep not to awaken until the storm-filled morning.

The fire's hot ashes kept nuggets of wood burning throughout the night keeping the frigid cold at bay. The windows frosted, the wind began to whistle outside the sturdy walls.

The first thing she heard on awakening was the wind, the second was the creak of roof timbers under the onslaught gale. In daylight she could see the cottage was well built of fieldstone with one interior wall constructed of thick knotty pine boards polished to a golden glow. The ceiling was only about seven feet tall which helped to keep the heat down where it was needed. On the wall next to the doorway a wooden peg was embedded next to a shelf that was empty of articles. A chest of drawers sat in the far corner and near the foot of the bed sat a pretty rocking chair, handy when removing shoes and socks. Everything looked as though it had been freshly cleaned. Not a speck of dust lay on furniture or floor. Someone kept a very neat home.

Slowly, Fila sat up stretching and yawning, she'd had a wonderful rest. Arising saw she had neglected to remove her shoes and had let her shod feet hang over the edge of the bed all night. She must have been exhausted to do something like that. Mother would have skinned her alive for being so thoughtless.

She remade the bed neatly, pulling the colorful quilt back into place over the two pillows. The room was not too small. She would have referred to it as cozy. She noticed a ceiling panel in the corner that gave access to an upper storage area. There was also a peg set into the wall about four feet beneath the panel, and another peg about a foot from the ceiling. She assumed it would come in handy for hanging articles of clothing or bundles of possessions. Since the ceiling was so low, they were all within easy reach. She really liked the wicker rocking chair. It had a padded seat and a pretty knitted afghan, just the right size to use as a lap cover, draped over the back.

Entering the main room she selected several pieces of kindling, poking them down into the hot ashes. As soon as the fire caught she added a few larger logs, placing them so the fire would build quickly into a warming blaze. Once she saw the wood catching nicely, she reached for a metal pot sitting at the edge of the hearth, intending to pack it with snow which, when melted, she would use to prime the pump.

As soon as she lifted the latch the door was torn from her hand and flung against the wall. The windblown snow so thick it blinded her, the drifts piled so high she could see nothing else. Bending against the driving wind she hurriedly scooped up as much snow as possible, set the pan inside the doorway, and then struggled to get the door closed against the turbulent gale. Pushing as hard as her strength would allow, she was at last able to secure the door and drop the latch into place.

The cold had invaded the cottage, she could see her breath with each gasp of icy air. All she wanted to do now was get the fire built into a hearty blaze and get the place warmed. Adding more wood she slowly succeeded in getting a good heating blaze started. The pan of snow had melted, there was enough water to prime the pump. She poured the liquid into the lever opening all the while working the handle up and down. Soon she heard the gurgle of rising water being pulled by suction up the pipe. When it gushed from the spout she kept pumping until it ran clear and then she filled the bucket to the brim with fresh clean water. She poured a portion of this into one of the iron pots and cleaned it thoroughly. Adding water to it, she swung it over the flames to heat. Returning to the pump, she again filled the bucket to the brim.

She felt so chilled she wondered if she would ever feel warm again, she needed a cup of hot tea. Using a small metal pot to heat the water in a few minutes she was sipping the warming liquid.

By the time she finished her tea, the water in the larger pot was starting to simmer. She needed something hearty to rebuild her strength. It seemed ages since she had eaten a decent meal. At least heat was returning to the chilled rooms.

She opened the barley, removed a generous scoop, and then set the container back in its niche. She also withdrew a portion of dried carrots, peas and parsnips from tins in the lower cabinet. These she dropped into the pot. Eyeing the herbs hanging overhead, she decided on the rosemary and parsley for flavor. When she was satisfied there was nothing else she cared to add, she gave a stir to the colorful mixture and retired to her seat at the table.

She needed something to do. It was disheartening to just sit with idle hands. It would be a while before her meal would be ready to eat. Maybe there was something in the bedroom chest that would keep her occupied. The silence was unbearable otherwise, she being so used to family about.

Looking into the bedroom she admired the three-drawer chest of maple. A matching maple-framed mirror hung on the wall above its polished surface. Someone had treasured and cared for its beautiful workmanship. Fila wondered if the man who had lived here had crafted the furniture himself. Sliding each drawer open she saw only a few woolen shirts, several long johns, extra knitted socks, and two pair of overalls. Not a single thing a woman would use.

There was nothing else in the room to examine. She inspected the placement of the wall pegs again. What an unusual position for clothes to hang. Why not evenly, all in a row? Pulling the chair over to the corner, she stepped up on it. The ceiling was too low for her to stand upright. Finally she gave a push upward on the ceiling panel, which immediately lifted and flipped back into the attic. Standing upright, she could see nothing in the pitch blackness, but she did notice the hinges at the edge of the panel. Reaching up she pulled the panel back into place and stepped back down to the floor. Now was not the time for an inspection. She needed a light of sorts and the oil lamp would serve just fine when she felt ready to explore.

The aroma of barley soup began to permeate the atmosphere. She knew it would be another hour before everything was cooked to perfection. Meantime, she would clean the lamp and find the oil to refill it. There was no reason to rush into anything, and she had all the time in the world. At least the excitement of suspense took away her boredom.

She washed the glass globe, trimmed the wick and refilled it with lantern oil from a container she found in the bottom corner of one of the cupboards. Double handles made it easier to carry after it had been filled with the weighty oil. She placed the lamp in the center of the table. It cast such a nice warm glow about the room. At least now she could close the inside shutters on the windows to keep out some of the frigid cold. It seemed the outside temperature would never stop dropping. Now she needn't feel the cold emanating from the glass windows in order to have light.

The soup was ready. After swinging the pot away from the heat, ladling some of the porridge into a bowl, she took a seat at the table. The first sip was heaven and she consumed every drop. Finally replete, she washed and put everything away.

Not able to contain her excitement, she took the lamp to the bedroom placing it on the shelf. Stepping onto the chair she placed a foot on the lower peg, grasped the top peg and pulled herself up into the attic. She reached back for the lamp to light the darkness.

At that same moment Gideon's dream deepened. He heard his grandmother as she scolded him. Calis and she had been busy weeding the vegetable garden while Gideon had been told to work on his letters and numbers. She had returned to the cottage to get a bucket of water. When she saw he was not at the table studying, she was just about to go look for him when she heard a thump from up in the attic. "You little billy goat, fie on you for being so stubborn. Get down here this minute or Gramps will tan your hide". Granny Nola stood, hands on hips waiting for Gideon to clamber down from the attic. "Let me see how much work you have done on your studies. You know if you don't get these lessons finished correctly your grandfather will not let you buy that colt you've been begging for. What will you do then when someone else buys it from under your very nose? Especially since you've been working and saving for so long." He wanted that colt very much but sometimes it was so hard to sit at the table studying when it was a beautiful early-summer day. He had gotten restless, knew he couldn't leave until he had finished and decided, just on the spur of the moment, to look in the attic for anything he could use when he brought his colt, Night, home at the end of the week. It was dark as pitch but enough of the sunlight that brightened the downstairs reflected into the attic, he could decipher what most articles were. He was positive he had caught the gleam of a shiny leather saddle at the far end of the enclosure. Just as he had been about to investigate, Granny's voice had shocked him to his very toes. Then Gideon became puzzled. He was no longer a young lad being scolded by Granny. He was an adult listening to his grandmother's voice relate something important to him. "What, Gram? I can't understand what you're saying. Who are you talking about?" The feeling of urgency in her voice made him anxious. In the next moment he saw the panel flip open and a head of dark hair emerge from the opening. Soon Fila clambered up into the attic, reaching back down to bring up an oil lamp which she placed on the surface of the flipped-back ceiling panel. The attic was bathed in its soft golden glow, every item stored clearly visible. He caught his breath at how beautiful she appeared with her long black hair almost to her waist, her delicate face. Those beautiful eyes of gray, which seemed to look into his very soul. He longed to take her in his arms and feel her warmth pressed against him. Although he reached out for her, it was only a mirage.

    For a moment Fila hesitated, as though she felt his presence. Then the feeling disappeared as she began to inspect numerous items placed around the edges of the slanted walls. There was an old leather-bound cedar chest, a cradle, high chair, and child's rocking chair. A few stuffed toys and a very old wooden dollhouse with miniature furniture arranged within its rooms. She saw the name CASSY stenciled on its door. All the pieces were handmade and beautiful.

She decided to inspect the contents of the chest. Maybe there was something she could sew or knit, something that would make the hours pass more quickly. Lifting the lid, the scent of lavender permeated the stuffy attic air. Several pretty dresses were folded neatly on one side of the interior, on the other were skeins of dyed wool in all colors of the rainbow. She saw various sizes of crochet and knitting needles. A large assortment of embroidery needles displayed in a heavy paper folder made her eyes light with anticipation of using them on delicate handwork. At the very bottom of the chest she found a generous stack of cotton and linen material. Probably saved from worn-out clothing or household goods. Selecting a pillowcase, she stuffed everything inside. Taking a last look about, she closed the chest and made her way back to the attic exit.

Leaning into the opening she placed the lamp on the shelf below, the filled pillowcase next to it. She then began to lower herself down into the room below. Placing her foot on the lower wall peg she reached for the higher peg to balance herself. The lower peg broke with a loud crack, tumbling her to the floor, causing her to hit her head on the chair and knock it over as she fell. She lay unconscious, her foot at an awkward angle.

There was a humming sound outside the cottage. It seemed to be circling round and round the building as though searching for something. Then, the sound stopped. In a moment a *Zzzzzing!* sounded loudly from up in the attic accompanied by a whistling noise that seemed to be coming closer.

If Fila had been aware, she would have been startled by a small golden object that seemed to be creating a whirlwind in the center of the bedroom. Faster and faster it spun until it looked to be a golden hurricane whirling about with something slowly coming into focus in its center. By the time the speed had diminished and the golden glow disappeared, a little, old, wrinkled woman was standing there trying to get her bearings, seemingly just a little dizzy from being in the vortex.

She tiptoed over to where Fila lay and gently placed her hand on the young woman's forehead. "Mmmmm! Cool to the touch, no fever. My dear, what has happened to you? Of course, I don't expect an answer from you in your condition. Ah! I see the broken peg lying on the floor, the open attic panel gives me to believe you have fallen. I'm not completely daft, even though I have reached a ripe old age. At first, when I left here, I felt quite lost in this other world. Now, of course, I'm quite happy. I can see my family anytime I please. Even talk to them sometimes, and would you believe, they sometimes answer. Of course, they just think they are talking to themselves. Well! There I go again, getting sidetracked. I must get you off this cold floor and you taken care of. GOLDIE...get over here. I want you to get this lass over onto the bed and this time, do not dawdle or I promise to melt you into a nugget."

The little golden arrow began its spin until the force was strong enough to lift Fila from the floor and deposit her onto the bed.

"Thank you, little friend, I promise to reward you for your effort, now go away but don't disappear, I want to know where to find you should the need arise."

The old woman inspected Fila carefully for injuries, finding only the sprained ankle and a nasty bump on the back of her head. She opened the pillowcase that had been sitting on the shelf and pulled out a length of heavy denim. From her pocket she removed a pair of scissors with which she snipped the material into a strip suitable for binding Fila's ankle. Then she went to the kitchen to prepare some herbal tea which would ward off any headache the lass might suffer. She also soaked and wrung out a cloth in witch hazel, which she had always used for that type of pain. The lass would be just fine. She had taken care of many neighbors when she had been here in her other life. They had always called for her when there was sickness in someone's family. She still held the knowledge from those days. Finally, with nothing else she could do for Fila at the moment, she rested in her rocker which she pulled closer to the bed. "My dear, you have a beautifully sweet face. I can see why my grandson fell in love with you. I have a feeling he will try to get here very soon."

Groggily, Fila opened her eyes, lost for a moment. She could see someone sitting next to the bed. An old-fashioned, kindly-looking woman who seemed to be dozing off. Fila closed her eyes trying to refocus herself and remember what had happened. When she opened her eyes, about to ask the woman a question, no one was there. Now she really felt confused. She was positive she had seen someone sitting in the empty rocker. Reaching her hand to touch a throbbing lump on her head she dislodged a damp cloth. She recalled her tumble and the impact with the chair. Swinging her legs to the side of the bed, she was about to stand when she noticed the snug wrapping around her ankle. At the same time she saw the opened pillowcase sitting at the end of the bed, a pair of scissors lying next to it. Rubbing her fingers across her forehead, she tried to remember binding her ankle. She must have been only half conscious when she did this, but how had she manage to close the ceiling panel? It was too painful to try to contemplate.

Dropping back to the bed she lay supine, the thought creeping into her mind that sleep would be a very good idea, maybe when she awoke the pain would be gone. Forcing herself to relax completely, she at last drifted into a deep dreamless sleep.

The old woman rocked gently, an occasional creak issuing from the old maple frame of her favorite chair. It had been years since she had enjoyed the comfort of being enfolded in its wooden arms. She had loved her chamomile tea sipped from her little dream cup, the book of Destiny resting on her lap opening for her perusal. She had read about her and Cassy's possible future demise in the flood, had been informed about the relic Calis would find when searching for their bodies. It had been a choice she was given. She had discussed the details with Cassy. Of course Calis had not been told, he would have forbidden it. The entire procedure had to do with Gideon. The book had shown both paths of her grandson's future.

After Cassy had borne Gideon she had never regained her strength. For each of the five years since his birth she had slowly faded like a rose at summer's end. It had been too much for her after her husband, Cyrus, and been killed in the mill accident, knowing Gideon had lost his wonderful father with never a chance of meeting the man who had awaited his birth with such intense longing.

Cassy felt she only had a limited time left, she could feel something growing inside her body, something that was already reaching to take her away. It had been beckoning her for years. She did feel, however, that her mother-in-law, Nola, had too much to live for but Nola had lost her son, Cyrus. There would be no more children welcomed into the family until Gideon married. That was the prize that would be handed to the family if the women were willing. They would also be given an after-gift but what it was would remain a mystery.

They had an entire year to reach a decision. At the end of that time, the fates would be casting the bones of change and a move would have to be made, one way or another.

The year had expired, a huge storm was forecast in Nola's book of Destiny. Their decision was firm, they had to be at a preordained site before the tempest arrived. The two women dressed in their Sunday best after making sure the cottage was neat and well stocked with provisions that Calis would be too upset to even think about. Holding hands, they arrived at the appointed place in plenty of time. In the distance they could see the mammoth black clouds advancing toward them, the haze of heavy downpours clear to their eyes. It was a 100-year storm that seemed to sweep them from the very face of the earth. After the storm passed, Calis eventually found their bodies and in turn, the promised Relic that would lead Gideon to his future destiny.

When Fila awoke she realized she had slept through the night. Her headache gone although, when she rubbed the lump on her head, it gave a twinge of pain. She had a vague memory of an old woman tending her but assumed it had been a figment of her imagination. Her ankle was a bit swollen. Rising from the bed she found that by placing most of her weight on her good foot, she could limp about quite nicely.

Hobbling into the main room she stoked the ashes adding more kindling and, as the fire built, heavier lengths of wood. Soon the sweet aroma of maplewood permeated the cottage. When the fire was once again a cheerful blaze she replaced the pot over the heat. Leftover barley soup would be just fine for breakfast.

Waiting for the soup to heat, she sat at the table trying to recall everything that had occurred the previous day. The only thing quite clear was her fall, everything else a hazy blur. Inspecting the wrapping around her ankle, she didn't remember placing it there, or even seeing that type of cloth among the assorted material she had stuffed in the pillowcase.

Instincts told her to check the pillowcase. Maybe she would find something that would help revive her memory. Favoring her sore ankle, she limped to the bedroom and retrieved the case and the scissors.

Back again at the table, she arranged the contents across the tabletop. Yes! There was the remnant of denim. She could see the snipped edge where the strip that bound her ankle had been removed. Inspecting the scissors, she was positive it had not been she who had cut the material. The scissors were fashioned for a left-handed person. She would have remembered the awkwardness and discomfort of a right-handed person trying to use them. Someone had been here. Her memory of the old woman returned, the image in the rocking chair as clear as a bell tone, the name "Nola" prominent in her recollections.

Fila pulled the pot away from the heat and filled a bowl with soup. She cleared a place at the table then sat in deep concentration. By the time she had reached a conclusion, she had consumed her soup and was gazing distractedly into the empty receptacle in front of her. The woman Nola had been there when she needed help, had somehow placed her on the bed and ministered to her needs and finally came recognition of the woman's voice. The very same voice that had consoled her when she had become trapped by the blue pouch. Fear and intimidation dropped from her shoulders. A huge sigh left Fila feeling lighthearted and a bit giddy with relief, the old woman was Gideon's grandmother.

Oh! If only she could talk to her, learn all about Gideon and the things he liked and disliked. His favorite meals, what he planned for the future. If he had a good temperament or, when angry, did he pout? She had such a hunger to learn everything about him it was driving her to distraction. Just thinking about him caused a tremor throughout her body and a shortness of breath. This must be what was called lovesick. She wondered if he felt the same about her.

Well! She couldn't just sit here when the soup pot had to be cleaned and readied for supper. The material needed sorting. Some to be used for embroidery, others sewed into a patchwork for making a marriage quilt which would hold memories for Gideon and, when she returned home to collect her salvaged material to add to it, her memories also. It would be something to treasure all their married lives.

If bustling about with a limp were possible, Fila certainly accomplished it. After everything was done to her satisfaction she returned to the bedroom to rest her foot and take a short nap. It had been tiring having to hobble about. A few days' time should see her ankle back to normal and her activities no longer curtailed. Softly, sleep crept through her busy mind closing doors on all the busy thoughts that tumbled through the passageways. When the deep breathing of slumber became audible, the old maple rocking chair began its gentle movement.

As Fila slept, Aaron and Gideon were preparing to leave the cabin they had taken shelter in. The snow had stopped. Above-freezing temperatures made travel possible once again. If things went well, they would reach Gideon's cottage that evening, or next day at the latest. The horses were anxious to be out in the open again and started off in a frisky mood. Soon however, they settled into a steady pace, making their way through the easiest passages between melting drifts.

Not a word was spoken by the two men, conversation having dwindled the past few days from lack of new topics to discuss. Their saving grace had been the checker board. Now, with open space and fresh air bringing back their usual lightheartedness, their grins flashed often when their glances met. They found their only discomfort was the harsh reflection of the sun off the snow that felt quite painful to their eyes.

Aaron called a halt and began searching through his saddle pack. When he handed over the odd-looking object with leather laces knotted at each side, Gideon was puzzled. "Here, put these snow shades on. Tie the thongs back of your head and position the carved wood so you can see through the slotted openings. This will protect us from becoming snow blind." Aaron tied his in place, Gideon followed suit making sure the laces were secure. When they continued onward Gideon had to admit his eyes felt much more comfortable. After a short time he completely forgot he was wearing them.

When they became hungry they stopped for only a short time. Just to dig something from the packs, give their horses a handful of oats then continue on their way making as good time as possible. They were determined to reach Fila before nightfall. Twilight was just dropping its curtain when they saw smoke from Gideon's cottage in the distance. There would be just enough light left to feed and settle the horses, and get everything indoors before dark.

Gideon led the way to the rear where the original log cabin had been made into a small storage building. Several stalls had also been sectioned off inside. Still solid after all these years, it would serve as housing for the horses. Night remembered, he went directly to his old spot. When the horses had been brushed and fed with blankets thrown over their backs they were settled for the night. Some of the packs were left in the shed. Hefting several others onto their shoulders, the two men made their way to the cottage door, giving a hard rap on it before pushing it open. Fila, startled, let out a brief yelp of surprise and hurled herself into her father's arms, her injured ankle forgotten. Dropping his packs to the floor, Aaron picked his daughter up in a bear hug. When he noticed the wrapped ankle, he walked to the chair and deposited her gently in her seat.

Fila was so overwhelmed she was speechless. All Gideon could do was stare at her with such a lovelorn look that Aaron burst out laughing. "Come now, my lad. I thought you were anxious to see my beautiful daughter. Why are you standing there? Isn't there something you wish to say to her? Speak up, or she will think you are not that happy to see her again." Aaron couldn't help but remember when he had felt the same way about Sera. Women made a man act ridiculous, at least that's what Aaron presumed. He remembered feeling like a jackass, struck dumb when words just could not come out. A little prodding always helped to get the mind working again.

Gideon's face flushed a rosy red as he tried to garner his composure. When he at last stepped to Fila's side to plant a kiss on her cheek she quickly turned her head, their lips met. The tremble in their bodies the kiss created was quite visible to Aaron. For a moment he forgot Fila was now a woman. The image of his little girl in this man's arms was almost more than a father's heart could bear. He turned away, not wanting them to see the pain etched on his face. His little girl was gone.

Gideon gave a cough of embarrassment. Fila, flushed, arose from her seat and walked without limping to the fireplace to stoke the fire and start preparing supper. Aaron busied himself sorting through the pack they had brought in. Gideon was standing at the window seemingly interested in something outside until he could bring his emotions under control. It had been an intense moment for everyone.

Next morning the weather was still clear. Preparations needed to be made for spending the winter. Gideon decided to take along Mica's gray mare when he rode to the village to obtain feed for the horses. If he could stock an extra week's worth into the work shed attached to the old cabin it would give them a little more security in case bad weather prevented him from getting to the village. As long as the weather held, he didn't mind the ride to buy several days' worth of feed at a time.

Aaron was cutting wood for the fire and stacking it near the old cabin. Fila was sorting out the extra clothing and blankets. The two men would be sleeping in the main room. She wanted them to be as comfortable as possible.

When Aaron saw Gideon preparing to leave he called for him to wait, he wanted to ride along. There might be staples they would need themselves. Hurriedly he saddled Lady and nudged her over to Gideon's side. "We need to make sure we have enough to tide us over should another bad storm hit. Is there a suitable trading post where we can buy extra supplies? I also need a whetstone to sharpen this axe, it's slow cutting with such a dull edge." They set off with as fast a pace as the snow would allow. Within an hour they had reached the village.

Aaron was surprised at the busy activity. The Umer Grist Mill was closed for the season but the lumber mill was cutting timber for new buildings. A small stone church sat at the crossroads in the center of town. Next to it was a rectory where three children were having a snowball fight. He could see a woman standing at the window watching. Farther down the street he could hear the ring of metal coming from the blacksmith's, which sat next to the barber shop. The very last building was Zena's Trading Post, their destination. The slush was crisscrossed with wagon tracks and hoof prints. Deep impressions of people's boots showed and also the impression where someone had taken a fall. "HEY, GID, IS THAT YOU? WHERE HAVE YOU BEEN ALL THIS TIME?" The loud, booming voice was heard by everyone within the village. Several hurrying people stopped in their tracks to see who the voice was calling to. When they saw Gideon nudging his mount over to the barrel-chested, black-bearded smithy, they called greetings to him, happy to see him back in the vicinity.

"Hey! Smitty. Glad to see you're still busy making those horseshoes. You look well. How's Verna and your two little ones? Guess they aren't so little anymore though, it's been a while since I left. By the way, this is my friend Aaron, a trader up northern way. We're here staying at Gramps' for the winter. We'll be stopping in now and then. Right now we need horse feed and some staples, any suggestions who has extra for sale?"

Smitty paused, a momentary frown crossing his forehead. "Sure, try the lumber mill. They took a load of hay as barter for some lumber last fall. They still have some as I recollect."

"Thanks, Smitty, appreciate that. Next time I'm in town I hope we have more time to catch up on news. For now, guess we better get movin' in case the weather turns. Take care, tell Verna hello and that I still remember her swell-tastin' peach cobbler." With a wave of his hand Gideon turned Night and headed for the sawmill, Aaron at his side. When they reached the mill they progressed to the rear where lumber was stacked inside the huge storage area.

Sliding from his saddle, Gideon tied the reins to a hitching post and strode to the open door. He saw from the corner of his eye that Aaron was heading in the same direction. As soon as they entered, the scent of hay filled his nose, he took a deep breath. He remembered his days of helping on many of the farms, earning money to buy Night. It was a warm reminiscence about Gramps and how he had encouraged him, loved him. All the stories he had learned at his knee, and the secure feeling he always had. Maybe someday he would have the same chance with children and grandchildren of his own. For a moment his thoughts dwelled upon Fila, her strength of character, courage, and tenderheartedness. Yes! He was determined to have the same sort of life he had been raised in. He had found his heart's mate.

The hay was stacked all the way to the ceiling on the opposite wall from the lumber. Every fall someone needed lumber and paid for it with a load of hay. By spring it was usually all sold. Gideon was almost positive it was a set deal in case people had need of extra. Sometimes to use as winter protection around the outside of their homes when temperatures fell far below zero.

Amos had inherited the mill after his father had died in an accident. A saw blade had broken and the metal piece had shot out like a bullet, his dad standing in harm's way. Amos was a softhearted guy, he had almost fallen apart when his wife had died in childbirth ten years ago. He had never remarried. He still took care of his mother and two younger sisters.

"Well! Look who's here. Son of a gun, Gid, you're a sight for sore eyes. Where've you been keeping yourself? I missed seeing you on that black horse of yours comin' and goin' to all them part-time jobs you took on. Everybody missed the help you used to give 'em. Will you be stayin' now you're back here at home? Sure was sorry to hear when your granddaddy passed on. Thought for sure you'd stick around and end up marrying one of the local gals. You know how Suzy always was makin' eyes at you when you came to town. She ended up marrying old man Zeke's son. You remember, the one who was always tryin' to pick a fight with you? He sure was jealous when you bought that horse, he sure wanted it for himself." Amos ran out of breath, took a big gulp of air about to proceed again.

"Hey, Amos, how are you, old buddy? You sure haven't changed since I've been gone, I see you're still busy with the mill. How are your mom and sisters? Last I was here your younger sister Lulu was seeing Gordy and they were planning to marry. Any little nieces or nephews for you to spoil?

"Gid, you won't believe this. Ma said Lulu can't marry 'til her older sister is wed. It just wouldn't look right. So Gordy is searchin' for a husband for Mary. Even though she's a good cook and can sew a blue streak, she's not considered very good-lookin', took too much after our dad. I can't see nothin' wrong with her myself. Last I spoke to Gordy, he had a good prospect up past Carltown. A widower with three little ones who is lookin' for someone to take over the responsibilities. Mary is goin' to meet him soon. It will be up to her, but Lulu is pushin' her to make the match. Better wed than dead as the old sayin' goes. So, what can I help you with friend?"

Gideon pointed to the baled hay. "How many can our three horses carry? I want extra in case I can't get here in bad weather. Otherwise, we'll ride in whenever we need to." Amos didn't want to overload the small dapple-gray mare. Two bales per horse would be plenty. He had good leather slings to rig each horse to tote one bale on each side, a comfortable balance they could carry for miles. The wide width of the slings also kept the rough hay from scraping against the horses' sides. "I'll fetch the slings. We'll have it set up in no time. If I was you, come back in a few days for another load. That way you won't be diggin' into your emergency surplus for the daily feed." Amos was headed for the work room as he was explaining, Aaron and Gideon close at his heels dickering about who wanted to pay. Aaron won. He stated it was his daughter they were there for, so it was his responsibility. After the two were married, then Gideon could have his chance.

While Amos took care of loading the horses, Aaron and Gideon went to the trading post for supplies. Flour, sugar, coffee, dried beans, lentils, peas. Home-canned tomatoes caught Gideon's eye and his mouth watered for their taste. Carefully, the jars were wrapped in burlap. A slab of bacon, two cured hams, and a packet of saltwater taffy completed their purchases. Everything was packed into a wood-handled crate. Gideon was quick to pay the bill before Aaron had a chance to argue again. They each grasped a handle and made their way back to the saw mill. After the crate sat safely on the dapple's back tied snugly between the two hay bales, the two men remounted, waved their goodbyes, and started home. The sun was high overhead. They looked forward to getting everything unloaded and stored safely away before evening.

Meanwhile, Fila had been busy cleaning. Not that the place was dirty, it was just something to do to occupy her time. She swept, polished, cleaned the pots, shook out the bedding, and finally rechecked the contents of the pillowcase where all the needlework was stored. Sitting at the table she inspected several pieces of unfinished embroidery that seemed to be a set of linen pillowcases. The needlework looked delicate, the flowered outlines were violets, her favorite flower. Several flowers had already been finished and looked so lifelike she placed them against her nose expecting to scent their sweet fragrance. Instead, the homey aroma of dried sage filled her nostrils making her feel as though warm arms were enfolding her in a comforting hug. Yes! She definitely wanted to finish these pillowcases.

Laying them out on the table she could see where letters had been outlined in the center of the violets. On one case the initials "GL" had already been embroidered. On the other case she could see the faint outline of the initials "FL" yet to be finished. She intended to complete them as they had been intended. The importance of the initials was obvious. Somehow, the creator had known about her and Gideon. This couldn't be a chance happening. She spoke aloud to the woman she intuitively knew was responsible.

"Granny Nola, you were the one who set the wheels in motion to draw your grandson, Gideon, and me together. How did you know? It feels as though a thread that led from the distant past to the future had been tied together at each end and the circle closed, leaving us nowhere to turn but toward each other. We seem meant by destiny to share our lives. Why? I ask. Is there a need in each that our unity is required by fate? Are we truly drawn to each other, is this a truth or figment ruling our minds? The thought frightens me that should there be a purpose, once the deed is accomplished, we may be forever lost to each other. How may I learn of the path that has led us here?" Fila felt tears gather and start to spill down her cheeks. The thought of Gideon as her very own, then losing him, was so hurtful she dropped her head on her arm and sobbed her heart out.

As Fila sat in misery a soft whisper sounded in her ear. "My child, you two would have drawn together no matter the circumstances. You and my grandson are truly meant to be as one. For the time being, I cannot tell you what the pressing need is for you to wed Gideon, the sooner it is accomplished, the better for all." Fila raised her head and looked around, it had been Granny Nola's voice.

All her life she had sensed another dimension that had hovered just out of her sight. Sometimes she felt another person's essence standing near, a person that seemed familiar to her. Possibly same relative that had passed away and stopped to link for a moment with her own spirit. She had finally accepted the shadowy encounters as just the acute sensitivity of her nature being receptive to departed souls. It did not frighten her in any way. It seemed to be her choice if she wished to acknowledge they were present. If she ignored them, they simply left.

Deep in thought, Fila almost missed the neigh of a horse, a signal the men had returned from the village and would be hungry. She didn't have time to use the deep iron pot so she hefted the big fryer over the heat, added a dab of lard, and mixed up a good-sized batch of cornmeal which she added to the pan, then covered. She sliced a generous amount of salami, dug out some of the dill and sweet pickles from their crocks, and pushed a smaller tin of water close to the fire for the honey-sweetened tea.

By the time Aaron and Gideon had settled the horses and toted everything inside the cottage, the cornbread was ready and the table set. Mugs of steaming tea sat by each plate. Fila cut the cornbread lengthwise through the middle to make the salami sandwiches. It was a simple meal but enjoyed by them all. When they finished and the table had been cleared, the many bundles they had brought inside were unpacked and stored neatly in their proper places. The bacon and hams hung from ceiling hooks away from the fires heat.

Gideon held one small packet behind his back. "Fila, take a guess what I brought you. You have three chances. If you choose right, you can have the packet right now. If all three guesses are wrong, you have to step outside while I hide it, but you can't search for it until tomorrow."

Fila adored surprises. Her gray eyes sparkled with amusement at the unexpected pleasure Gideon was giving her. "Mmmmmm, let me see, could it be a pretty apron, No? Well, how about a small bottle of rose water? Ohhhh! Wrong again. The only other thing I can think of might be a twist of peppermint candy?"

Gideon couldn't help grinning at the hopeful look on her face, then he pretended to frown for a moment to draw out the suspense a little longer. Finally, he extended the beribboned packet toward her, feeling a deep sense of pride at the joy he had given her.

Fila almost bubbled with happiness, her face so aglow it was hard to keep his eyes from showing the deep emotion he felt. Carefully she removed the dainty ribbon and peeled back the wrapping paper, being careful not to tear it. Tied inside a square of pretty cotton was a generous handful of taffy, each piece twisted in waxed paper. With a smile she extended her hand to Gideon to select the first piece, and then to her father. Lastly, she unwound the wrapping from her own and popped the sugary sweet in her mouth. All three stood grinning with pleasure, chewing like contented cattle working their cuds.

Fila found a canning jar in the cupboard and sealed the rest of the taffy inside, setting it on the bottom shelf so it would be noticeable each time she walked past. The only thing missing was her mother and sisters to make her day complete. "Father, did Mother pack my treasure chest in with my things? If so, I'm going to contact her as soon as we find it."

Aaron remembered they had left several packs in the shed. He drew on his coat and hurried out, Gideon right behind him. The packs were sitting atop of the hay, well away from being nibbled by curious horses. Aaron knew one of the packs held extra blankets, the other two were toted to the cottage for Fila's inspection. The treasure chest was sitting at the very bottom of the last pack she was searching through. Lifting it out, she placed the chest on the table and took a seat to be comfortable during her inspection of its contents.

She knew it was the hand mirror she wanted but it had been so long since she had placed everything inside, she wanted to familiarize herself once again with the precious collection. Aaron and Gideon looked on as she removed and placed each piece on the table. A heavy gold ring with symbols etched into it, a slender golden arrow, the silver-handled mirror, several small blue orbs, a dainty tin cup with fancy inscriptions about its rim, a small iron-bound book, and then possibly a dozen other items in odd shapes, colors and textures.

When Gideon saw the cup and book almost identical to the ones he possessed, he was so shocked he sat speechless, unable to fathom the implications. Would Fila think similar thoughts about what their future meant? Would they have had a choice in selecting their lifelong mates? Gideon could feel himself back away from the idea that their meeting had not been by chance at all. He did not like the idea that somehow he had been led like a lamb to slaughter, unknowing what lay in store.

When Fila glanced up, the expression she saw on Gideon's face was so cold and distant she almost felt she was gazing at a stranger. When he noticed Fila's puzzled look he realized his feelings were showing too plainly and forced a smile to hide his distaste of what seemed evident. "You have quite a collection in that chest. Where in the world did you find all those things?" Gideon looked searchingly into her eyes hoping to read a hidden message, or hear a logical reason for the disturbing collection she possessed. "Gideon, you know about the Relic I brought home. I guess I neglected to mention that after I placed the Relic in my old treasure chest for safekeeping, everything took on a different look and significance. These were things I had collected during my childhood. Before, I used to play with them, afterward I had a feeling that these could never be used as toys again. Somehow it caused me to grow up, take responsibilities seriously."

Fila watched Gideon closely, disturbed by the expression on his face and the cool look in his normally warm, expressive eyes. Her discomfort was so obvious it was beginning to make Gideon feel awkward. He arose from the table, making an excuse he needed a breath of fresh air, and hurried out the door making his way to where the horses were stabled.

Aaron waited a few moments after the door had closed then turned to inspect the table's display. He couldn't understand why Gideon seemed so upset. There was nothing he could see that would cause such a reaction. The abject misery Fila exhibited was enough to break his heart. What in the world had happened? He searched his daughter's face but somehow she had closed him out and drawn the hurt deep within herself. Now her countenance looked as cold and forbidding as had Gideon's. Aaron left the table, grabbed his and Gideon's outerwear and headed for the old cabin to try and have a serious talk with the young man who was breaking his daughter's heart.

Aaron's confrontation with Gideon failed dismally. The young man would not even comment about what had happened. He seemed so remote that Aaron sensed his thoughts were anywhere but here in the present. "Young man, I don't know what has happened that you could turn such a cold eye on my daughter. She has done nothing to merit your hardheartedness. I thought you truthful when you professed love for Fila. Love does not just disappear. Sometimes strife may blur its edges for a time or difficulties may make it seem that it is gone forever, but unless a mean disposition or cruel nature destroys it completely, the love is there. I think it is time for me to take Fila home. You must remain here. Search your heart and be guided by the feelings within."

Aaron returned to the cottage prepared to tell Fila to ready herself for the trek home. He was not surprised to see she was already repacking what had, seemingly moments ago, been unpacked. He could see the closed look on her face, her lips firmly pressed together in determination.

Fila had made up her mind. There would be no outcry from her, or condemnation when she said goodbye to Gideon. The hurt she felt deep inside seemed to have built an icy wall around her heart to protect her from further pain, not one tear would she shed. "Father, I would like to leave for home today. Can we be ready immediately? I can't bear the thought of remaining here another moment." She looked to Aaron, saw his nod of agreement and in that action knew everything was truly over.

Within the hour they were mounted and on their way. Travel, though not easy, did not pose a problem. It seemed impossible that just a few hours ago she had been thrilled with Gideon's surprise gift of taffy. She turned her head to hide the tears that blurred her vision. Enough of this, she was no longer a child. Her life would go on but, why did it have to hurt so much?

Aaron nudged his horse into a faster pace. He wanted to reach the cabin where he and Gideon had stayed during the worst of the snowstorm. With luck and the better conditions they should be there by nightfall.

The sky was darkening but reflection from the snow made it seem much earlier. The cabin was in sight. This time, however, a spiral of smoke drifted from the chimney and lighted windows guided them unnecessarily. When they arrived Aaron dismounted, leaving the horses waiting, while he rapped on the door.

The young woman swung the door wide about to beckon him inside when she noticed the rider on the other horse. "Bring your things inside then stable your horses in back. I have just finished supper with plenty left for you to fill your empty bellies."

Soon both were seated before the fire enjoying a hearty chicken and dumpling stew along with cups of sweetened tea. They had introduced themselves. The conversation was carried on mostly by the woman named Velda, who seemed starved for companionship. She said she had been away for the past month seeing her father laid to rest after a long illness. After her mother's farm is sold, which should be very soon, she would come here to live. It will be a welcome arrangement for both.

Supper over, things cleared away, it was time for bed. Fila and Aaron rolled into their blankets facing the fire while Velda retired to her bed. Soon the only thing heard was the crackle of burning wood and Aaron's deep snores, which Velda welcomed as a dear memory of her departed husband. She fell asleep immediately. Fila stared into the embers until her sight blurred, her thoughts numbed, her tears dried, and sleep at last dulled the strange ache that seemed to originate from the center of her chest.

As soon as dawn lightened the sky Aaron and Fila, thanking Velda for her hospitality, proceeded on their way. Their succeeding days of travel unimpeded by the light snow flurries. When they at last reached Mica's Trading Post they purchased a few supplies and told Mica they would return the mare in a few days after they had settled in.

Mica was pleased to see them but too polite to ask why Gideon was not with them. He could see by the look on Fila's face that something had upset their plans. "Tell Sera and the girls I'm looking forward to seeing them this spring to show them the new bonnets. They'll be mighty surprised at some of the new colors. You all take care, another storm is on the way and will probably hit by evening. Get yourselves home soon as possible, hear? And don't tarry, looks like it might be another bad one, these old bones of mine never lie." With a wave goodbye, Mica watched them ride toward home. The snow was just beginning as they rode the forest path and entered the familiar homestead. Dropping the packs at the cottage door, they continued to the barn to unsaddle the horses, curry and feed them, and settle them down for the night. When the chores were finished they hurried back to greet the family.

Aaron couldn't understand why no one was at the door to meet them. Smoke was visible wafting up from the chimney and he could see light within. Grasping their packs they pushed open the door dropping their burdens to the floor. The room was empty. "Sera, Mina, Nia, Alea? Where is everyone?" The silence throughout the home was frightening and a cold fear settled upon Aaron seeming to chill his very bones.

Fila climbed the attic stairs knowing, before she searched, they would not be there. She felt fear creep silently into her awareness that something was horribly wrong. Where could four people just disappear?

When Fila confronted Aaron she could see the same confirmation on his face. Aaron looked around the room, noticing that the fire was consuming the last of the wood. It had been a while since it had been replenished. He put a few more logs on to keep the fire going. He inspected the cook pot and saw the remains of lunch. It had a thin film of congealed fat over what looked to be soup. If it had been supper, it would have still been warm.

Night had settled in with a rising wind and blowing snow. It would be impossible to see farther than a few feet, impossible to begin a search in such weather. Aaron was so nervous he couldn't stop pacing, the inactivity driving him to distraction. Fila felt the same although she busied herself cleaning the dishes and utensils that still remained after the family's lunch. As she removed the remaining bread plate from the table, a piece of paper that had been tucked beneath dropped to the floor. Aaron seeing the flash of white, hurried to pick it up and lay it on the table near the lamp, his hands pressing out the folds that distorted the writing which looked unfamiliar to him. Fila, as soon as she saw it, recalled a similar note that had been left when her mother had been in a sleep-trance put upon her by the sorcerer Luther. With dread so great she almost felt ill, she leaned over to read the missive.

YOUR FAMILY IS TAKEN. YOU WILL NOT FIND THEM..... RETURN MY PROPERTY....I WILL RETURN YOUR FAMILY. THIS TIME YOU HAVE NO CHOICE IF YOU WISH TO SEE THEM AGAIN.

LUTHER

Chapter Six

Luther couldn't contain his glee over his accomplishment. He had the family. Of course the main one he had wanted was the brazen thief Fila. However, with the entire family now at his so-called "disposal," he was positive he would succeed at getting his precious Relic returned. There were so many opportunities he had missed because of her theft. She would be punished, there was no stopping him now. The view of the opal cave was fully displayed below him. He had been watching the woman and her children walking about in a seeming daze, wondering what had happened and how they had gotten into their strange environment. He had to stop himself from laughing aloud in case they spotted his lofty crow's nest high in the cave's dome. He could hear every word spoken, watch every move. There was no exit from the place except for the hidden stairwell that led down from his apothecary and it was an entrance into, not an egress out unless a lever was pulled before entering the cave. They could search the place from top to bottom and not escape.

Years ago he had stumbled on his caverns accidentally while searching for a rumored fountain of magic. A torrential rain storm had sprung without warning and he had taken refuge in the nearby cave. On exploration, it was everything he could ever desire as a reclusive home. Little by little, using old-fashioned magic and some hard work he had succeeded in turning it into a secretive retreat. How that little monster had gained access was still a mystery. Somehow a little of his magic must have weakened while guarding the entrance. Now, with the Relic gone he had to really be vigilant against intruders.

Finally tiring of his vigil, he stepped away from the ledge, passed through the hidden doorway into his sleeping room, and slid the stone panel closed behind him.

Rubbing his hands together with anticipation, he stoked up the fire and began to prepare a special mixture from his herbal collection that he sometimes used for drugging a subject. He flavored it with a slight hint of wintergreen then poured the mixture into a stone jug which he then sealed with a cork. He attached a tin cup to its handle with a leather thong which was long enough to allow the liquid to be poured and drunk without being detached. Before upending the cup over the jug's top, he quietly muttered a few unintelligible words of a binding spell as an added measure of protection. He would use every method possible to keep his captives under control.

His final action was to select a wooden tray, place bread, cheese, a bowl of winter apples and the jug of herbal water on it and depart through the hidden passageway once again. This time, however, he took a flight of steps to a lower level. Once at the small closet-like room at the bottom, he placed the tray on the floor and raised a trap door, sliding the tray through the opening. He quickly closed and locked the panel, pulling a cord that rang a bell on the other side of the wall. He hurried back up the steps to view the activity below from his hidden aerie. He almost felt like a bird of prey inspecting his victims.

Sera and the girls heard the delicate echo of the bell throughout the chamber. It took a moment for them to locate the source. The image of the laden tray created a mystery of how it had gotten there since the panel was completely disguised by various rocks and stones imbedded in the wall. A small golden bell suspended from a miniature metal rod protruding from the stony surface swayed gently above the proffered sustenance.

Although Sera couldn't account for the amount of time that had passed since their abduction, lack of hunger told her it had not been too many hours. They inspected the tray's contents with interest but did not partake of the offerings, however they did retrieve it from the floor and brought it to the area that contained essential furnishings of a makeshift household. Two full beds, a table and four chairs, one hurricane lamp and a tall bulky cabinet sitting against the wall completed the arrangement. They placed the tray on the table.

They were curious about the cabinet. Sera stepped over to open its single door, the sound of rushing water assaulted her ears and she realized it was a commode. She backed out of the enclosure and pulled the door closed behind her.

Sera knew she must act confidently to keep her daughters from becoming distraught but she had no idea what had happened nor how they had arrived at this strange place. One moment they had been clearing the table after lunch and the next, it had seemed as though something had swallowed them with one gigantic gulp and spit them out into space. When everything seemed to return to normal, they had found themselves sitting in a corner of the cave, looking windblown and totally disoriented.

The beauty of the cavern could not stay Sera's fears. True, the fiery sparkle of greens, reds, pinks imbedded in the milky haze of opals bedazzled the eye but did not allay the growing concern about how they would return home. One thing she was positive of, the scoundrel Luther was responsible for their dilemma. Somehow they must find a way out.

"Come, girls, we have a job to do. We must find a way out of this prison. Alea, you go the opposite way, search along the wall for any hint of an opening or hidden doorway. Nia, you go along with her and search closer to the floor. Mina, you and I will do the same. Remember, we must go slowly and do a thorough search. This furniture got in here somehow, we must find where."

The inspection was tiresome, the area quite vast, and the light from the hurricane lamp, though reflected tenfold by the iridescent walls and ceiling, was not quite bright enough to reveal any hidden outlines of passageways. Their disappointment was so disheartening the girls were close to tears. Sera, however, knew that somewhere there was an opening and she would find it.

At last exhaustion called a halt to the search. They returned to their corner and the table holding the tray, pangs of hunger now causing discomfort. Each of the four tin plates received an apple, a chunk of bread and piece of cheese. Bowing their heads in thanks, they commenced their meal, waiting until the very last to sip the cool water thirstily, each taking a turn filling the tin cup from the stone jug.

Within a few minutes they managed to stumble over to the beds and collapse onto them, sleep already dulling their senses as their heads touched their pillows. Sera was the last to succumb. She thought she saw something move high overhead in a jagged part of the cave's ceiling. Before she could focus on the area, she felt herself falling into the darkness of slumber, an odd sound echoing in her ears.

Above, Luther could control his laughter no longer, it rippled throughout the closed edifice bouncing off walls and ceiling, building into a crescendo that was almost deafening. Wiping the tears of glee from his face as he descended the steps, he pulled the lever that opened the hidden doorway and entered the cavern retrieving the tray.

Back upstairs he put the tray down and went to his bed. Soon he was fast asleep in the best rest he had had since his Relic was taken. Not a single dream disturbed his slumber.

The clear sound of the small golden bell pulled Sera from deep slumber. She couldn't remember having ever slept so soundly. The girls were still asleep. She lay quietly trying to remember what was nagging at her memory of last night. Something she had seen or heard. Her gaze traversed the high dome of the cave scanning the rough surfaces. The colors were spectacular. At least the lantern was still burning, though getting low on lamp oil. The slight flicker of the flame shifted the colors into a dizzying display except for a small area that was shadowed. She wondered why that section was different than the rest of the dome. She focused on that part of the ceiling, peering closely. It looked as though part of the wall bowed out below the cast shadow. She was still trying to discern the shape of the distortion when a slight movement at the edge of the outcropping caused her to freeze motionless. It was someone's head peering down, the rest of the person concealed behind the ledge of the stone balcony. "So! That's what the bulge was," she thought. "A hidden hidey hole to watch us like rats in a trap." Intuition told her to feign sleep. With eyelids half closed, she watched the mysterious person above.

Luther thought he may have added a bit too much potion to the water jug, the four were still deep in slumber. He spoke aloud, cursing himself for his carelessness. He was a little too anxious at finally having something to barter for the return of his treasure. It would be some time before they roused, might as well return to his living quarters and do a little conjuring.

He needed to keep a sharp eye out for Aaron. Wherever he had gone, chances are he would be returning home soon to read the note and make his way here. Luther's harsh laughter resounded throughout the cavern before finally fading away, causing an icy chill to creep up Sera's spine. Now she recognized who the person was who planned harm to her family. She made a silent promise. "By all the Fates, you have another surprise coming if you think you will get away with this plan you have devised. I swear I will find a way to defeat you, Luther. Don't forget what happened to you the first time you trifled with us."

Sera arose from the bed, careful not to disturb Nia, and made her way to where the tray was again sitting on the floor next to the far wall. "So, Luther," she whispered to herself. "You need to enter the cave to retrieve the tray and take it back to your quarters. At least I know of a weakness in your plans for us. Somehow, I will put this knowledge to good use. Sooner or later you will make a slight mistake and I will be sure to use it." Picking up the tray she carried it to the table and set it down, inspecting the breakfast items Luther had placed there.

The three girls awoke at almost the same time. Sera was sitting at the table so deeply in thought she didn't notice them until their soft voices disturbed her concentration. She had made several serious decisions that had to be carried out without the girls being aware. The first was the use of the doctored water. She had to allow the girls to drink or else Luther would know he was suspected and change his tactics. It was only a sleeping potion, no adverse effects had been evident except for drowsiness. As for herself, she would sip only enough to slake her thirst.

This morning oatmeal, a jug of milk, and four apples were displayed. The water was not present, a sure sign he wanted them thirsty by evening. Sera almost smiled at the hidden knowledge she was beginning to accumulate. "Come, girls, the cereal is still warm. Let us enjoy it along with the fresh milk, it will give us strength. We will save the apples for a midday snack." Enthusiastically they prepared their bowls and commenced eating, unaware that Luther had added something to the milk this morning to keep them a little off balance.

Luther still remembered how Sera had almost blinded him the time he had captured her spirit and tried to keep her under control. Somehow a spirit blade had appeared in her hand and he had lost his eyesight for several days because of the flash that had seemed to pierce his entire scalp. Never again would he even give an inch of leeway where Sera Hamlin was concerned. He was quite aware that she did not have magic powers like he possessed, but the mystery of her first escape still nettled him. He refused to concede that he had lost. There had to be a reason somewhere. Until he was assured it had not been anything that he had done wrong, it would continue to fester in his consciousness.

The family had finished their meal as he silently observed them from his high perch. Soon the effects from the potion would begin. This time they would be in a trance-like state that would allow him to question them without their having any memory of it when they awoke. He desperately wanted to find his Relic and this was one way of acquiring information without them being able to hide anything. All they knew would be revealed. He waited patiently for the signs that signaled they were ready. When he saw they were sitting upright in their seats, arms dropped to their sides, chins resting on their chests, he lingered only a few more moments before making his way down the stairwell.

Their breathing did not change when he touched his hand to each of their heads. Now he had at least part of an hour to ask questions to his heart's content. He thought he'd start with the mother. "Sera Hamlin, can you hear my voice? Nod if your answer is yes." He waited for the almost imperceptible dip of her head, and then continued. "Do you know where the Relic has been hidden? You may speak."

Haltingly, Sera answered, "Yes."

"Tell me where it has been taken to." Luther waited with bated breath.

Slowly, as though hesitant to answer, she replied, "The Winter Forest."

The burst of joy that Luther felt almost caused him to shout aloud. "Where in the Winter Forest has it been secreted?"

For a moment Sera seemed confused, and then replied, "In a secret niche."

Now Luther was beginning to grit his teeth, his impatience growing by leaps and bounds. "Where is the secret niche?"

Sera pondered the question, then answered, "In a wooden receptacle."

His voice rising several notches higher and a few decibels louder, "Where is the wooden receptacle?"

Without hesitation Sera replied, "In the Winter Forest."

Luther lost it completely, so angry all he could do was scream with rage. Not one word was recognizable spewing from his lips. If he had been able to pose the last question of "What part of the Winter Forest," he would have known about the ancient oak tree in the clearing. His face almost purple with fury he flung the contents from the table, so very tempted to strike Sera, he was almost beyond managing to control himself in time. It wouldn't do to mistreat his prisoners when he had information to glean from them.

When Sera and her daughters regained their awareness later the confusion they felt on viewing the strewn contents of the table scattered around the stone floor completely unnerved them. It was like waking from a dream and finding yourself in a strange place other than your own bed. No explanation was possible. Quietly, they cleared up the mess, picked up the broken pottery then just sat looking at the spilled milk that, for lack of cleaning cloths, they couldn't wipe up.

Back upstairs Luther tried to control his frustrations. "So close," he could feel he had been close to learning where the Relic was hidden. He wondered if he had made a mistake by choosing to question Sera first, but he sensed she had been completely truthful in her answers. It was somewhere in the Winter Forest, he just had to find the site.

Muttering to himself as he went about his various methods of concocting potions to use on his hostages, time passed without a second thought on his part about feeding them lunch or even, at the end of the day, what he would give them for supper. Tired at last when the hour became late, he munched on some fruit and cheese and then retired to bed. He fell asleep immediately completely confident that tomorrow would give him the answers he desired.

Meanwhile, in the Opal chamber below, Sera and the girls had each eaten their apple earlier in the day and were now quite hungry and thirsty. Although they had waited hopefully for lunch and then supper, they were now exhausted. The girls had finally fallen asleep. Sera, however, was still sitting at the table deep in thought. There had to be some way of deceiving

Luther into setting them free. She was aware that Alea knew where the Relic was hidden and if he questioned her, she could not help but reveal the hiding place. It was a nasty position to be in, it was then Sera began to formulate a plan.

Bringing every ounce of energy into play, she concentrated on Fila so deeply that she could feel herself drifting into a semi-conscious state. Nothing else was present except for the waves of electrical impulses that began flowing outward seeking communication with its counterpart. Sera at last reached a plain of sensory perception so totally complete she could feel the jolt when the connection was accomplished. Fila had been waiting for her.

"Mother, why has it taken you so long to get in touch with me? I have been trying for two days to reach you. When Father and I arrived and found the home empty and the note from Luther left under one of the plates, we were frantic. Dad went immediately to Luther's but found the place vacant, although there was evidence he had just recently been there. He could fine no footprints outside that led away, however the snow had been falling so heavily there was the possibility your tracks had already been covered. Tell me where you are, we will come as soon as possible." Fila's concentration remained steady, the stream of conversation continued.

"Daughter, you will never realize how happy I am to reach you. It was only a few moments ago I remembered what had happened the last time we had our run-in with Luther and how we had remedied the situation. However, this time it's a bit different. He has captured me body and spirit. I don't know if the same logic will apply. Do you think it possible? He has us in a secret cave under his domain. There is a hidden door in the stone wall he uses to bring us food after we have been safely drugged. There is also a small ledge balcony he uses to spy on us. We have searched every inch to find where the entrance is without success. It is too well disguised."

"Rest now, Mother, try to get some sleep. Give my sisters hope we now share. I will ask Relic what devices will be useful for getting you away from that dreadful man. The key I wear around my neck will give me mental access to our little friend who has become so important in this situation. Please don't worry, Mother, tomorrow I should be able to tell you what plans we can use to gain your freedom. For now, don't fret. Tell Nia to be ready in case we will be following the same procedure as last time. She was the catalyst that made it all happen. It was she who was given the knowledge of using the obsidian blade that obtained your freedom."

Sera felt herself regain normalcy, left with a feeling of complete relaxation that was quite pleasant. Making her way to the bed she shared with Nia, she curled up against her daughter's warmth and drifted asleep immediately. It seemed only moments later that the muted tones of the little bell brought her awake. The aroma of bacon also bringing the girls to full awareness that they were very hungry and something smelled delicious.

Apparently Luther regretted not feeding them well enough and was making up for yesterday's lack. A mound of bacon, scrambled eggs and thick slices of buttered bread was displayed on the tray that Sera placed on the table. This time four bowls, cups, a jug of cider, and four forks were also included. They were so thirsty they drank some cider first, and then filled their bowls with bacon and eggs. Sera used the remainder to make sandwiches for later in case Luther neglected to feed them. Once they were replete, sighs of satisfaction echoed through the gloom. Sera noticed the lamp had been refilled. At least they wouldn't have to be in darkness. She shivered at the idea of this huge cave without light. Then the thought began to create possibilities. She had an idea that might coincide nicely with the plans she and Fila would formulate. Life was beginning to seem much more interesting.

Luther did not make an appearance all that day. The family ate the sandwiches and drank the rest of the cider thankful there had been enough for their two meals. When at last fatigue set in they quietly went to their beds and settled in for the night. It seemed Luther had decided not to doctor their meal today since they had suffered no adverse effects from consuming the food and cider. Although Sera used her concentration she could not contact Fila. They slept until morning.

"Come, girls, let's play a game. Remember how we used to concentrate and try to guess what the other was thinking? It's been a while since we've tried and we were getting very good with our guessing game. Who wants to go first? Nia, how about you matched with Alea? You two were becoming quite adept at reading each other's thoughts."

Nia and Alea moved their chairs to face each other, not touching. "Think of something, Alea."

Nia watched as Alea closed her eyes and began to concentrate, and then she did likewise. Soon the deep breathing of each was very audible. Several minutes passed.

"It's Buddy. You're worried about him getting fed, right?" Nia gave a huge grin when she saw Alea's nod of assent. Then she, in turn, closed her eyes and concentrated, awaiting Alea's searching presence.

Instead, she found herself back in the family kitchen standing next to Fila and reading her thoughts as though they were having a serious conversation. "Do you think you can do this, Nia?" Fila asked in a concerned tone of voice. "This is the only way I think we can get everyone safely home again." She turned to look at Nia, as though they were truly standing next to each other.

Nia took a moment to answer, aware that the conversation was being carried on through their mental prowess. With a flash of recognition, she knew what the question was about, also knew what a clever plan Fila had devised. With a nod of agreement to Fila, she was immediately back in her chair opposite Alea, hearing her sister's gasp of surprise at the information she had mentally assimilated about Nia and Fila's meeting. They both turned to their mother, who gave a knowing smile, placed her finger to her lips for silence. Mina smiled, recognizing the signal of precaution to keep silent.

Not a single word was spoken aloud but now all knew of the arranged escape. They were thinking about the possibility of escape and the game they had just played, completely unaware that their early arising had angered Luther.

He liked the idea of ringing a bell to announce that a meal was waiting. He enjoyed watching them from his observation deck, seeing how a regular family shared food and conversation. It was such a strange ritual to him. He couldn't recall ever having had that sort of experience during his childhood, or at any time since, for that matter. Occasionally he had supped with strangers after his departure from home. Never did he recall anything other than the sound of utensils clinking against bowls or plates. Maybe he had intimidated them with the scowling face he usually wore, and that's why they weren't forthcoming with conversation. Whatever the reason, he sometimes experienced such a strange yearning while watching his detainees, it infuriated him, made him feel he was becoming weak natured and he couldn't afford for that to happen. Yet, he just couldn't refuse himself the vicarious pleasures he received.

Luther prepared a breakfast tray with buttered bread, hard boiled eggs, wedges of cheese, a plate of fried sausages, four apples and a pitcher of milk, all undoctored with any of his potions. He slid the tray through the opening near the cave's floor and then hurried up to his viewing platform. This was the best part of his day. He watched as Sera carried the tray back to the table and everyone began partaking of the morning meal. He was unaware that Sera had known about his spying since the second morning of their captivity, she had not told the girls of her discovery.

Tonight they would try to manage their escape. Until then, even if Luther had doctored the food, they would enjoy the breakfast. She detested the fact they had no privacy, Luther seemed like a lurking vulture waiting to pounce from high in the shadowy dome. Her only fear was the possibility he might eventually get his hands on Fila and discover where the Relic was hidden. Something told her that life would be much better for everyone without his recovering the little object.

After the meal was finished and the dishes restacked on the tray, Sera replaced it on the floor next to the wall where she had retrieved it from. They began to play a game of "Simon Says." It felt good to laugh together after so long a time. It seemed ages since they had been safely at home. Today they must act completely natural and not show any traces of nervousness or anxiety. Luther must be taken unaware when they made their move, with not a hint that anything out of the ordinary was about to occur. The day seemed to drag by, plodding along until it seemed twice the amount of hours had passed. It was almost time for Luther to bring their supper tray.

Sera was aware that Luther would again use one of his potions. She would hazard a guess it would be in either milk or cider instead of the food, he knew they usually drank the entire beverage but sometimes the food was not entirely consumed. He would not want to chance they were not completely under the influence of his concoctions. Hopefully, tonight would be their chance to escape. If not tonight, then it would have to be some other. She was determined not to sit and rusticate like an old saw stuck in a dusty corner. They awaited the sound of the bell.

Luther placed the tray and hurried up the stairway to view his "family," for that was the way he was beginning to think of them, his very own private brood. An intriguing display meant for his daily amusement. Who else could boast of such an accomplishment? He almost strutted like a peacock as he made his way to his secret perch. This time he even had a stool on which to sit comfortably while watching the actors on his very own stage.

"Remember, girls, take only tiny sips from the milk," Sera whispered. "And only a total of five, and then finally pretend you have drained your mugs."

The family continued their meal until every last morsel had been consumed. As Sera began stacking the dishes onto the tray, the girls went to their beds and curled up as though ready for sleep. Soon they looked to be deep in slumber. With a huge yawn Sera reached for the jug of milk accidentally brushing her arm against the lantern and sending it crashing to the floor. Darkness flooded the cavern.

Luther sat in silence listening for movement. A final noise as though Sera had brushed against the table, and then he heard the creak of a wooden bed. He was sure Sera had retired for the night, his potions already having their effect. Still, he wanted to be sure and delayed for another span of time. At last, feeling confident, he made his way down the stairs and pulled the lever that opened the door. The candle he carried only emphasized the blackness. As he stepped through the portal, a heavy object was swung with force against his head. He dropped to the floor without a sound, the candle rolling away, the flame extinguished.

"Hurry, girls, come to the sound of my voice immediately, we may only have a few minutes." Sera felt along the inside wall, her hand coming in contact with a metal handle. As her last daughter safely passed to climb the steps, Sera gave a strong tug on the lever and waited until the doorway was again sealed closed. With a grateful sigh she made her way to the dwelling above. The plan had worked, they were safe at last.

When they had gathered before the crackling fire in Luther's living room they were exhausted, the small amount of doctored milk they had drunk lulling them into sleep. They paired themselves into the two chairs, and the deerskin-covered settee, the heat of the fire bringing the first comfort they had enjoyed since being at home. They slept until morning.

Down in the cave Luther was just regaining consciousness and becoming aware of what had happened. He had been tricked. Stretched out on the cold floor his bones were starting to ache. Using every ounce of his energy he pulled himself upright and tried to make his way in the darkness to where he judged the table had been sitting. It took a while stumbling about until he stepped in the crunch of glass, the remnants of the lantern. He fumbled his way to one of the nearby chairs.

He was really in a fix now, he thought, trapped by his own creation. He wondered what they would do to him. Why hadn't he had the foresight to provide another entranceway in case of an emergency like this? Unless he could bargain with them to regain his freedom there was a likelihood he could very well die in this godforsaken tomb. Perhaps there was something he could trade. Something they would desire so much that they would release him. Of course, he would make a vow to them he would not retaliate for their deception. He almost choked at the thought of having to do that. Impossible, he must think of something else. Slumped in the chair deep in thought he had no idea that dawn had arrived.

Sera and her daughters had slept like hibernating bears. On awakening, Sera placed more wood on the fire and then searched for a pantry. Wandering through the cluttered living area then through the large shelved laboratory and into the sleeping room she discovered the doorway that led to the balcony. On a whim she stepped onto the viewing ledge and called down to her former captor. Through the darkness she heard his answering voice echo through the chamber.

"Just what do you intend to do with me now that you have turned the tables? At least I fed you and your daughters. I haven't eaten since yesterday and I'm hungry." Luther held his temper in check. It wouldn't do to antagonize the woman.

Sera considered the problem, she had no intention of using the cave entrance to retrieve the tray and get trapped like he was. She would wrap the food in a cloth and drop it down to him from the ledge. "Where is your pantry? I haven't seen any food storage cupboards."

Luther replied, "When you leave the balcony, the pantry is on the left side of the wall just before you enter my sleeping chamber. You'll see a wooden door with a lift-latch."

Sera turned without another word to Luther and, stepping through the archway, noticed the wooden door recessed a few feet back from the short passageway. The glow from the lantern she had placed on the bedroom chest was casting just enough light to illuminate the area. Retrieving the lantern, entering the larder, she was surprised to see a rather spacious and well-stocked pantry. Bins of potatoes, apples, carrots, parsnips and cabbages lined one entire wall. Hanging hooks held smoked hams, bacon, and cured sausages. The distinctive aroma of sauerkraut emanated from a huge crock, while the mouth-watering tang of dill made her yearn for the crisp crunch of a sour pickle. There were sealed and labeled crocks of oatmeal, cornmeal, flour, barley, honey and sugar. She spotted a container of rendered lard and near to it a smaller crock sitting by itself in a corner. She suspected it held a very important ingredient that every home needed. When she lifted an edge of the covering, the yeasty aroma made a smile light up her face. This was original yeast, propagated by using what was needed and then replacing a bit of the newly yeasted dough back in the crock.

Each time bread was baked, a small portion of the yeasted dough was added to the crock. This would keep the supply sufficient indefinitely. It was a very old recipe that needed to be carefully followed with each new batch of bread making. If anything happened to the yeast supply, the only alternative was to try and get a starter from some other family. If that was impossible, there would be no more bread baking. A family's yeast supply was treated like a precious possession, and that's exactly what it was. Sera had gotten her starter from her mother, and she from Sera's grandmother.

Sera opted for baking meat pies. She called the girls to help select the necessary ingredients. She picked up the lard crock and also scooped enough flour to make the pie crusts. The rest of the morning was spent baking.

After she had lowered food and cider to Luther, the four of them enjoyed the first good meal since leaving home. Once everything had been cleared away Sera sat, deep in thought, trying to figure out how she could leave for home with the girls and at the same time find a way to release Luther without him causing trouble for her. It was a dilemma. She would just have to study the problem until she found a safe solution. Until then, they were stuck here. Resting her head against the chair, Sera surveyed the large room, her eyes drifting across the huge fireplace to the utensils hung from hooks imbedded in the stone, then over to the heavy bookcase, and finally to the long table near the entrance passageway that was laden with such miscellany. Everything seemed fairly neat except for the table's display. She had not really paid much attention to anything after escaping from the cave. Now she had time to really examine Luther's domain. Her curiosity about the table's scattered odds and ends at last caused her to rise from her seat and meander over to inspect the mysterious objects. Trailing her hand idly over the unusual collection, she found herself drawn to a small carved image that seemed to beg for her attention. She closed her fingers around it.

The warmth generating from the delicately crafted feline seemed to infuse her entire body with a comforting glow. She drew the object close to her breast savoring the coziness it conveyed. It was the most beautiful deep green she had ever seen in her entire life. The contours of the cat were etched to perfection and although it seemed impossible, she felt a strange emotion rising within her being. What in the world was this strange little image doing to her she wondered. It's just an animal figurine. Beautiful, to be sure, but only an ornamental object. Something to dress up a corner of a shelf, or maybe a dresser top. She began to replace it on the table but before the action was completed she unknowingly tucked it into her dress pocket. She forgot about its existence completely, as though she had never laid eyes on it.

Unaware of what had just occurred, Sera continued perusing the table's artifacts, touching items here and there but taking no special interest in any single one. Finally, satisfied with her inspection she returned to her seat. After a few moments she began to doze and was soon deeply asleep.

The girls congregated around the fireplace quietly so as not to awaken Sera. The three sisters Alea, Nia and Mina talked about home, how much they missed their sister Fila and their dad. They wondered about Buddy, if he was still outside their home waiting to be let back indoors. They had just finished lunch when they had been taken. Poor little mutt might not even be alive out in that cold with no food or warm place to take shelter. They avoided each other's eyes, ashamed of the tears welling just below the surface. The last thing they needed was a crying fit. If wishes could come true, they hoped their pet had found a warm spot to stay and food to fill his empty tummy. They fell silent, absorbed in thoughts too dreary to speak aloud.

Sera, meanwhile, was just stirring from her nap. Fila was to contact her this morning and she could hardly wait to tell her they had managed to escape without help. It had worked out perfectly. At least now that Fila and Aaron were home they could find a way of releasing Luther while still keeping everyone safe from his nasty spells. She wondered why it was taking so long for Fila to make a mental connection. A fretful sense of unease began to settle uncomfortably over her heretofore restful mood. Aaron was not a man to dawdle when something so important was afoot. Unable to continue sitting, she rose from her seat and began pacing restlessly, not aware of the distressed expressions that began to appear on her daughters' faces. They knew when their mother was upset about something her pacing spoke louder than any words. Alea was just about to ask her mother what the trouble was when she saw a huge smile light up Sera's face.

"Come, girls, your father and sister should be here very soon. I have a feeling we will leave for home before nightfall. Let's straighten things up a bit." The words were no sooner spoken than the sound of footsteps could be heard entering the front entrance. Sera turned with a happy cry of greeting and threw herself into her husband's arms. Fila rushed to her sisters, everyone talking at once.

As soon as everyone calmed a bit, Aaron's face clouded with anger. "Where is that scoundrel Luther? This is the last time he will put my family at risk. I have decided to truss him up and tote him to the nearest town where they know what to do with troublemakers like him." Aaron waited, wondering where the culprit was hiding while everyone was here in the living quarters.

Sera calmed him at once. "Don't fret so, Aaron. Luther is securely trapped in the cavern he had planned to use for our confinement. There is no way he can escape. We can take our time planning what to do with him. Until then, sit down and warm yourselves by the fire while I fix you something to eat. You wouldn't believe what that man has stored in his pantry. There are enough provisions to feed an entire family for the winter." Sera hurried off to retrieve the remainder of the meat pies she had made earlier. There would be enough for both Fila and Aaron.

Later, Sera and Aaron discussed what to do with Luther. There was no way they could set him free. He could not be trusted to keep the promises he had made after Aaron had talked to him from the ledge. It was a dilemma. They could not leave him down in the cavern. Certainly, they did not want to stay here to feed him, they wanted to go home as soon as possible. Their animals had to be fed and cared for and Bell milked. For now, they could lower enough food to last Luther several days until they found a reasonable solution. That decided, Sera gathered a supply of edibles along with a small cask of cider. Aaron dropped it down for Luther to catch. A supply of lantern fuel and another lamp was also lowered. Once they saw light illuminating the cave, they were ready to leave.

No new snow had fallen. The trail Aaron and Fila had made was still passable. In a matter of hours they were within sight of home, their pace quickening with anticipation. Aaron had banked the fire just before leaving and now, adding a few more chunks of wood soon had it sending new warmth into the room. Buddy was wiggling about, wagging his tail with enthusiastic happiness, ecstatic that everyone was home again. It seemed ages since Sera and the girls had been abducted when actually it had only been five days.

Chapter Seven

The family settled into their regular routines. The girls swept, put misplaced items back in their places and straightened the contents on the wall shelves. Several rag rugs were taken outside and given a good shake then returned to their places, one in front of the fireplace hearth, and the other by the corner bed. After everything had been neatened to Sera's satisfaction she started a pot of stew.

The girls departed to the attic. There was so much they wanted to talk about. The problem about Luther was foremost on their minds. Somehow, they must find a way to protect themselves from him when he was released. The only thing Fila could think of was to return to the Winter Forest and ask the Relic what could be done. She fingered the golden key she wore. Each time she became conscious of it and held it in her grasp she could feel a tingle through her entire body, a connection to her absent mentor. She wondered if it would be possible to communicate over the distance by concentrating. She had never thought to try.

Hushing her sisters' conversations she closed her eyes trying to focus on the key. At first nothing happened, then in an instant she was deep in the quiet netherworld of mental fugue, lost in a gray swirling haze. She could make out shapes that she felt she could almost recognize and then they floated away on the mist. She was becoming a bit disoriented and fear began to threaten her composure. When she tried to pull herself back nothing happened. Now she could feel definite movement as currents of air wafted across her face. Her hair and clothes felt damp from the moisture, yet still, she moved onward. Fear subsided, serenity held sway as eventually she drifted downward and found herself standing next to the huge oak in the center of a foggy Winter Forest. Looking down at herself she seemed almost transparent. A small squirrel scampered nearby unaware of her presence. Confidently she opened the small door and inserted the key.

The key turned easily and the inside panel swung open. The Relic sat in a warm golden glow that made Fila feel as though she were basking in sunlight. She reached to take up the little figurine, however a sudden awareness told her it was not necessary. Silent words were exchanged, questions answered. Fila bowed her head in gratitude, finally relocking the panel and closing the small outer door. She felt herself flowing backward and with a snap of time found she was again sitting on the edge of her bed hearing the whispered conversation of her three sisters who thought she had nodded off to sleep. All she had to do now was figure out what the meaning of the solution could be. "As a leaf is carried on a tumbling stream so too will all things seek its level. Fear not, for such destiny has been decreed you shall play no part in. Each must find their way."

Fila returned to the kitchen to tell her parents the information she had been given. Both Sera and Aaron puzzled over the words, trying to analyze the meaning. Did it signify that they should abandon Luther to his own devices? Guiltily they avoided each other's eyes, afraid that too much would be evident about their individual wishes for that to be true, it felt like the right thing to do. However there was a nagging worry that if Luther did not find a way to escape, he would starve to death. They couldn't justify having that on their conscience.

In a short time they would be returning to Luther's. Until then they would ponder the meaning of the instructions, possibly find a hidden solution to their dilemma. With a sigh of relief that seemed to brighten each of their faces, they returned to their individual tasks—Sera, to add more ingredients to the stew, Aaron to tote more firewood in from outside, and the girls to do a little darning on several pairs of worn stockings. Buddy curled comfortably in front of the fire. It felt wonderful having everyone together again.

The next several days were spent currying the horses, cleaning the stables and getting things back into normally neat condition. Fresh eggs from the chickens were used to prepare a few custard pies, a favorite during the off-growing season.

All too soon it was time to return to Luther. This time Aaron saddled the horses and also took an axe which he intended to use to chop a path through the hedge barrier. It was ridiculous walking there because of not being able to get the horses into the compound.

It was decided only Sera and Aaron would go, with much argument from the girls. No need for the entire family traipsing over there. The girls could take care of Buddy in case they had to stay overnight. After final goodbyes they mounted and were on their way. Lady, though filling out with the new addition due in the spring, was happy to be on the road. The dapple-gray mare that would be returned to Mica in the spring was keeping pace.

When they reached the hedge barrier Aaron set to chopping the dry branches with vigor, slowly making progress widening a path through the thorny impasse. Sera used a crude makeshift rake to clear the cuttings away. After an hour's work it was wide enough for the horses to get through. Remounting, the two made their way to the rugged cavern in the near distance. Aaron decided to bring the animals indoors and tethered them just within the entryway.

Wasting no time they went directly to the pantry. Aaron found a burlap sack and they began filling it with sealed containers of food, apples, smoked sausages and a keg of cider. Food to last at least a week. Then they both stepped to the stony platform and called to Luther. They watched as he rose from one of the beds and made his way closer.

Even as they began to lower the food, Luther's tirade echoed through the vaulted ceiling, bounced from the walls, undiminished by any weakness they had presumed he might be feeling from inactivity. Aaron was at the point of exploding; the ungrateful cur could at least be thankful he wasn't being starved. He could feel his resentment rising at the loud angry words exploding from Luther's mouth. "If you don't close that trap of yours this instant you can go without food. I don't have to take this kind of treatment from a scoundrel like you who totally created this problem you now have by abducting my family and holding them prisoner." Aaron held the food-filled bag suspended over the semidarkness. Luther's white-moon face peering up seemed to float in midair. Aaron gritted his teeth in irritation. If he had his way there would be no food or drink until an apology was extended and reparations made for the nefarious deed. He knew though that Sera would never agree.

Luther reached out and caught the sack before it hit the stony floor. He would have liked throwing it back in Aaron's face, but he knew it would be a foolish way to display his rage. Eventually, he would gain his freedom and then he would have his revenge. If only he could figure a way to escape. There was a niggling, nudging discomfort that had recently started to invade his inner composure. Something that was trying to tell him a secret he should be aware of. If he waited long enough the information would surface and he could determine his actions. Well, he wasn't going anywhere, time seemed to drag and if he didn't get out of here soon he feared he would lose his sanity. Luther could feel his rage build once again. The day he had to depend on someone else to survive was long past. He had been a young lad filled with hope for a better life after leaving the two who had made his existence miserable. Things hadn't turned out the way he had hoped but he had learned. It was better to live alone, be accountable only to himself. The thing his life centered on now was not to find love or companionship like ordinary people strived for, but to use to his advantage all the magic, potions and spells he could devise. He LOVED some of the surprises that turned up unexpectedly. It piqued his weird sense of humor and gave him such intense pleasure that he could never imagine living another existence other than the one he had. For a moment a dark mood descended as he recalled his attempts to recover the Relic. No need to worry though, he knew where to go. It was hidden somewhere in the Winter Forest and he had no doubt that with a little encouragement extended to the right person, he would find his trophy again.

Above in Luther's living quarters Sera and Aaron were getting ready to return home. With a last look around to insure they had extinguished the oil lamp and left everything neatly in place, they led their mounts outside and headed for home. When they passed through the opening Aaron had chopped through the barrier, it looked as though new growth had mysteriously begun to reclose the passageway. By their next trip Aaron would need his axe again. Sera felt a shiver pass through her body as though an invisible phantom had paused for an instant before passing on. Aaron looked askance, wondering what could be causing his wife to look so uneasy. Sera nudged the dapple into a trot, then a gallop, Aaron close behind. She wanted to get away from here as quickly as possible. Something was in the wind, she could sense it approaching. She felt the farther she rode, the safer it would be. As for Aaron, his only thought was to get home.

When Sera glanced back for a last look at the hedge barrier it was already reclosed with thick thorny branches. There was something evil about the way the branches had writhed about while sealing the opening. It made her anxious about the next passage they must make through it within a week.

Meanwhile back at the cavern Luther, with a snap of his fingers, relit the candle he had retrieved from the floor where he had dropped it when Sera had escaped. Carefully he searched until he located the fallen lantern. Although the glass chimney was shattered there was still plenty of oil remaining. Touching the candle to the wick, he placed the lamp on the table and turned to the sack. Lifting it to the table he began to sort through the supplies. With each item he removed his anger grew until he was so filled with rage he had trouble controlling his actions. Gritting his teeth, he threw the half-emptied sack to the floor. There HAD to be a solution, he could almost see a faint image swirling and spinning in his subconscious mind. He tried to focus on it, slow its passage so he could pick up the faint message it seemed to imply. He began pacing, round and round he walked, sometimes pausing for a moment as though close to a solution. He could feel it was within reach. He paused by the large wooden structure that had offered privacy for the family's daily ablutions and became aware of the sound of fast-flowing water that had become an everyday familiarity to be ignored. Ahhh...now he recalled the work he had done and how the underground stream flowed downward into a deep pool that emptied through a low cavern, then outside to a waterfall. At last...his freedom was within reach. No need to rush off now. He would have something to eat first, and then seal some of the foodstuffs into one of the oiled cloths for protection. Maybe even a short nap before setting off on his escape. Better to be prepared for emergencies. After assembling the things he needed and eating lightly, remembering the old adage about going in the water too soon, he couldn't stand waiting longer. Tearing some strips from the bedding he looped one end about his waist securing the food pack to the other end. Now he was ready. He was able to just barely work his fingers under one edge of the wooden panel on the stand that had held the wash bowl. With great effort he strained until he felt a shift and sudden loosening of the wooden joints. The surface panel fell with a thud and he was looking down at the dark, swirling waters that tumbled down through the funnel-like tube. Just large enough for him to drop down into the torrent and be carried away to freedom.

Standing on a stool and holding the food pack above his head he paused for a moment, took a deep breath, and then stepped into the void. The water was icy cold. He could feel the smooth, worn sides rubbing against his clothing. A few times the opening narrowed and he felt like a cork popped from a bottle. He was feeling the desperate need for air. Just when he felt he could hold his breath no longer, he was airborne, plummeting into the depths of the lagoon. The weight of his clothing was a heavy drag on his efforts to reach the edge before being carried over the waterfall. At last he reached the safety of the rocks. Pulling himself onto a ledge he caught his breath. He had made it.

After a few minutes of clambering over the slippery obstacles, he exited the cavern and found himself standing on the upper edge of the waterfall. Now he could make his way home again. Cautiously he descended the embankment and once at the base surveyed the terrain to get his bearings. He headed for a cave entrance knowing it would have access to a path that led to the top of Widows Mountain. It took him several hours to reach the upper-level cave where he exited to follow the trail that crossed the summit. Eventually he reached the downward path and the trace that led near his compound.

Evening was drawing near when he reached the hedge barrier, so exhausted he could barely walk. With a few mumbled incantations the way was opened to him. He passed through on his way to his domicile turning once, before proceeding, to place an "Impasse spell" on the thorny barrier so none but he would ever again gain access. At last he had arrived home.

He was famished. The food pack he had previously tied to his waist had been soaked through and was inedible. Hurriedly he stoked the fire, pushing the water-filled pot over the flames. Once steam was visible, before placing dried vegetables and meats into the bubbling liquid, he ladled out water for tea.

Relaxing in his favorite chair, feet on a stool, head propped against the padded cushion, he savored the minty flavor of the beverage that sent a wave of warmth through his tired body. Soon he dozed off into a light slumber. The scent of the cooking food tickling his nostrils finally awakened him.

After finishing his meal, not even bothering to clear the dishes, he made his way to his bedroom dropping onto the welcoming softness of his bed, soon falling into a deep dreamless sleep.

Late the next morning after finishing chores he had set for himself, it was time to start plotting his strategy to recover the Relic. Spring was not many weeks away, the time he would make his way to the Winter Forest. He'd need one of his "Search Icons" to locate the hiding place. Pacing slowly around the long table that held his numerous collectibles of magical handiwork, he peered closely at each object searching for the perfect one. Something was missing, he couldn't quite place what it could be. For now, he focused on which item would be the best at finding the hidden cache. Fingers touching here and there, as he made his way around the wooden circumference, odd forms catching his attention, holding them a moment then replacing them with a dissatisfied grunt, he finally reached for a small, oddly shaped piece of chalcedony. As soon as he held it in his hand he could feel a shivery tingle infuse his entire body. This would serve his purpose perfectly. Although he didn't make a habit of talking to himself, the excitement of his discovery almost had him doing a jig, just stopping himself in time as he began to take the first dance step. Now all he need do is wait for time to pass. A few weeks would pass quickly.

Placing his selection on the shelf at the end of his bookcase where it would be easy to find, he selected a heavy tome of *Warlock History of Spells*, and retired to his favorite chair. The next weeks were spent brushing up on the best techniques for magical manipulation, the reading quite fascinating and very informative. He would be prepared for any undue disruptions.

The weeks dwindled away until the drip of snowmelt played a musical tune on the rocks surrounding his cavern, signaling the advent of spring.

When Sera and Aaron had returned to Luther's compound to provide him with additional provisions, their efforts to gain access through the barrier hedge were fruitless. Aaron spent great effort trying to hack through, but the only thing he accomplished was to exhaust himself. At last discouraged, they had returned home. The constant worry that Luther could be starving or dying would not let their consciences rest. Guilt sat so heavily that they both had trouble sleeping.

As spring blossomed, snowmelt began to dry enough that Aaron began to traverse the area finding families that had items they wanted to trade. Slowly he worked his way across Widows Mountain to the eastern side knowing there were a few Indian tribes who sometimes established seasonal settlements on the shores. They boiled the salty water to garner the dried granules remaining. Salt was a great trade commodity. Aaron often dealt with these tribes before beginning his yearly trading routes to the north.

It was during this visit that he discovered a clue that suggested Luther had somehow managed to escape from his detainment. Part of a food pack that he definitely remembered dropping to Luther was tangled in some rocks, which had prevented the bundle from being washed into the sea. With a huge feeling of relief the weight of guilt was immediately eased, he tore a sample from the strip placing it in his pack.

After completing the trading, he headed for home, anxious to tell Sera of his discovery. The mystery of Luther's escape uppermost in his mind. He wondered if there was a possibility that retaliation would be visited upon the family. "Great!" he muttered to himself. "Just get rid of feeling guilty and now we have to worry about Luther's revenge. That man is more trouble than he's worth. If I was a different kind of person we wouldn't be going through this aggravation," Aaron mumbled to himself as he made his way back home. He was almost tempted not to show Sera the evidence he had found, but secrets were something the two had never kept from each other.

Sera was busy finishing up some of her weaving for the trading trek when Aaron entered the cottage, placing the salt sack on the table. They would keep a portion for themselves before dividing the salt into numerous packets, thereby preventing any spillage during trade sessions. The odd expression on Aaron's face caused a moment of unease for Sera. She was aware that her husband only looked this way when he had upsetting news of some kind. Without waiting for him to open the conversation she asked bluntly, "Why the serious look and down-turned mouth, dear husband? Did something upset you, or are you just nervous about your upcoming trip?"

A sudden look of indecision flickered across Aaron's face momentarily, and then he reached into his pack and withdrew a ragged strip of material. Extending his hand to his wife he watched her expression change from puzzlement to relief, then concern. Reaching for the cloth, her fingers curling around the damp material, she voiced the quandary that overwhelmed her. "So! He's free. He's not a person to forget what I did to him, better though this fear than the weight of a guilty conscience because of his possible demise." Turning from her husband she placed the scrap into the fireplace and watched the steamy smoke rise. At last when all the moisture had evaporated, tiny licks of flame nibbled at the edges of the material until, with a sudden flare, it was annihilated.

Sera faced Aaron, a resolved expression on her face. "This is the last time I'm going to worry about Luther. All the trouble he has caused us, upsetting our lives, destroying our peace of mind, I will not have his name mentioned again." Sera turned resolutely to tasks at hand, determined to bring the family back to the comfort of safety they had previously enjoyed.

Aaron agreed with his wife's decision. For too long Luther had been a thorn in the family's existence. He stepped behind Sera and placed his arms around her still-firm body. Drawing her close, pressing his lips against the side of her neck, he planted a soft kiss then turned her to face him. "Sera, I worry about leaving you this time. I can't help thinking that Luther may seek some kind of revenge. I know you and the girls can't travel with me, but maybe we can find someone to stay and help with chores while I'm gone. The room in the barn that we fixed for Gideon is very suitable. I would feel much more at ease if I knew there was someone to protect you. Let me talk to Mica. Maybe he knows of someone who would like to earn extra money."

Sera could sense the deep concern Aaron was trying to hide. She, however, would never have a stranger here. Not with several nubile daughters who would be a constant temptation and a cause for maternal worry about their safety. Placing her hands on each side of her husband's face she pulled his head down and planted a firm kiss on his lips. "My dear, you know this would be a foolhardy action to take with two young marriageable daughters vying for attention and confirmation of their beauty. We'll be fine. I somehow feel that Luther has other important business to attend to and I don't think he wants to contend with trouble he would face should he try to recapture us." Sera gazed into her husband's eyes with such confidence that Aaron felt his trepidation ease slightly. She was correct about being worried about a stranger. On second thought, he wouldn't want someone lurking about watching his daughters either.

Aaron stepped away. He needed to get the sheep sheared, the wool bundled and placed in the barn where it would stay until Sera prepared it for spinning it into yarn. Then he must assemble articles the family had made for trading. He also had to take a ride to see Mica, take the dapple-gray back. He had a problem. Lady was going to foal any day. He couldn't use her this year. He hoped he could make a deal with Mica to either buy, trade or rent the dapple for use until autumn. If only he could think of something to trade. He left to take care of the shearing, his mind sorting through the bundles of trade goods stored in the attic, hoping to remember something worth the price of the dapple-gray.

As for Sera, there were myriad tasks to be completed in the next week before Aaron left. She called the girls to start collecting any items they wanted their father to take with him. This year there wouldn't be as many for trading, no thanks to Luther. For a moment she let herself dwell on the circumstances that caused the dearth of goods. Thankfully, the family was finally together. It had been a very strange year with dangerous events putting them at risk. They would still manage.

Everyone concentrated on getting ready. Aaron, once the shearing was finished, rode the dapple-gray to Mica's. He had an idea worth presenting to the old man. When he arrived at the trade post he hitched the mare to the rail and entered the store, a broad smile on his face. Mica was pleased to see his friend, aware there would be some serious dickering going on before the day ended. Mica grinned back, this was just what he loved about his business, never knowing what each day would bring.

"Pull up a chair, Aaron. I'll put the coffee to boil." Mica had a nonchalant attitude, the thought of an exciting day spent haggling with a good friend making him try to curb the show of intense pleasure he was feeling at this rare occurrence. This was what he lived for.

The two men settled at the table in the back room. Mica filled tin mugs with strong black coffee, placed cornbread and a tub of butter for them to enjoy while dickering, then sat himself across from Aaron. The sparkle in his eyes made Aaron suppress a grin of pleasure at the obvious glee Mica tried to subdue. Naturally, business wouldn't begin immediately. Talk of weather, family and neighbors came first. When the waiting game became too intense to bear, the serious discussions would begin.

"Well! Aaron, I can see you have something important to say to me. Let's start our game of checkers. We can enjoy both games we'll be playing." Mica gave a laugh at his joke. There was nothing he loved better than checkers and making deals. He had the best of both this afternoon. Mica removed the empty plate containing only crumbs and refilled the coffee mugs while Aaron set up the checker game. Finally, elbows on the table, both men relaxed while studying their prospective moves.

"I'd like to dicker for the dapple," Aaron muttered as he made his first move. Silence, as Mica decided strategy. "Sure, Bud. Make an offer, I'll consider it if it's tempting enough." He hid a grin knowing Aaron would mentally be sifting through items to add to the deal. Oh! How he loved the give and take of trading.

As the competition continued, Mica began to draw Aaron out on what would be offered for the mare. The thing was, he liked the lad a lot. Even considered him sort of adopted, that is if he'd wanted a son. The whole family had carved a niche in Mica's heart. Of course, it would be a cold day in Hades if he ever let on to them or anyone how tenderhearted he was. Just thinking about someone even guessing, made his blood run cold. It would be the ruin of him, and his pleasure doing business.

Back and forth, the conversation and checkers finally came to an end, Mica being the winner of three out of five games. Evening approaching, he invited Aaron to sleep over. Aaron accepted knowing Sera would not expect him home until morning, his usual time when going to Mica's in the afternoon.

Both men were satisfied with the bargain they had reached. Not only would Aaron swap some trade items from previous trips, but this year he would take a portion of Mica's store goods to trade at Indian camps. Canned goods would be an unusual treat for the tribes to experience, like tinned milk, or fruits. This was the first time Mica had given store goods to be traded elsewhere. Who knew what an exciting experiment this could be? Mica rubbed his hands together. He might be old, but he would never be bored with life. Not when he had a smart fella like Aaron for a neighbor.

For their supper Mica fixed fried, sliced potatoes with onions, a stick-to-the-ribs meal. Sliced cured sausage fed their taste for meat. After plates had been wiped clean with slabs of buttered bread, utensils were washed and returned to the cupboard. For dessert Mica fished out several apples from the oak barrel in his cellar. They were as fresh and crisp as when they had been carefully placed therein early last autumn. Each separated by tufts of clean straw to keep them from deteriorating.

The busy day had ended. Mica retired to his room. Aaron curled up under a wool blanket resting on a canvas-covered stack of other wool blankets. Soon harmonizing snores echoed through the nighttime air. The scurry of a field mouse inspecting the premises for edibles the only other sound.

Early morning Aaron was on his way, the promise to return to pick up Mica's trade goods on his day of departure the final seal to their bargain. He was well pleased. The dapple-gray mare was worth everything he had promised Mica.

When he arrived home Sera and his daughters were already packing, folding and getting items ready for his trek though it would be a few days before he was ready to leave. At least, having the mare would make his travel easier.

The day settled down to finishing chores, planting vegetables and pruning dead branches from some of the fruit trees. A few cedar shingles would have to be replaced on the roof before he left. Buddy followed him about most of the day, happy to have a romp outside with someone he loved watching his dance of joy. He was a little heavier being so well fed with table scraps but managed to keep muscles firm with outside exercise, either jumping through snow drifts in winter or chasing varmints from the garden.

Aaron had just returned to the barn when he heard an odd snort from Lady. He instantly knew what was happening, they had all been waiting anxiously for this day to arrive. He hurried to call Sera and the girls to watch the birth of their first addition to the family. Lady's foal, sired by Gideon's stallion, Night. They wondered if it would be a filly or a colt, not really caring which, either would be treasured.

It was an easy delivery. Lady cleaned the beautiful black colt, nuzzling him until he gained his shaky legs and was able to stand. Soon he was nursing greedily, safe and secure by his mother's side. Feeling comfortable it was now safe to leave the pair alone, the family returned to their various duties, each thinking of the wonderful advantages they would enjoy having possession of fine horses they had never expected to own.

The afternoon passed swiftly, everyone so involved getting as much accomplished as possible before dusk, that the horseman was already nearing the cottage before he was noticed. There was something familiar about the figure. In moments they recognized who the visitor was.

Gideon dismounted stiffly. He had been riding without stop since before dawn, the only thing pushing him onward so desperately had been the fear he could lose Fila forever to another man. Someone as beautiful as she would have suitors coming from miles away to seek her hand in marriage. He had realized as time had stretched into a boring, humdrum existence, that no matter how circumstances had arranged their meeting, he did not want to live without her. Even the thought of her in the arms of some other man drove sleep away and caused his appetite to virtually disappear. He looked haggard, had lost weight, and had an unhealthy pallor to his complexion. The term "love sick" suited his appearance aptly.

As for Fila, she too had lost a little weight and her color, though pale, could have been mistaken for lack of sun, normal enough for long winter days. As she came around the corner of the cottage she stopped short at the sight of the black horse standing quietly, Gideon's figure momentarily out of sight behind the stallion. With a gasp of surprise she recognized Night, and for a moment was stricken with fear that something had happened to the rider. She stepped forward, reaching out to stroke the flanks of the steed. At the same moment Gideon stepped forward, grasped the outstretched hand and drew Fila into his arms.

With a shivery sigh Fila pressed herself against the only man she would ever love. It was foreordained and truly meant to be.

Once the excitement had abated and everyone had gotten reacquainted, supper was prepared and for the first time in, it seemed ages, they all sat to enjoy their meal and the enthusiastic conversation that held sway. Once the meal was finished and the table cleared, serious plans began. It was the wedding that Gideon and Fila wanted to have accomplished as soon as possible. The time they had spent apart had been almost more than either could bear.

Fila would wear her mother's wedding dress. Gideon, a new pair of homespun wool trousers and vest he had brought with him, and a white cotton shirt. Sera took time to clip Gideon's hair so he would look neat. Aaron rode to Mica's and had him contact the preacher who was in the vicinity on his yearly spring rounds. The wedding was set for the following Saturday, only four days away but still plenty of time to get everything ready.

Aaron slaughtered a pig and hung it high in the barn for the meat to age a bit. He dug the fire pit where it would be slow baked for an entire day on a spit that everyone would take turns tending. Sera and her daughters began baking pies and bread loaves. Time passed in a fever of activity. Saturday morning dawned bright with the possibility of a beautiful day, chores were completed early and everyone prepared for the soon-to-arrive guests and preacher. The girls Mina and Nia were taking turns turning the handle on the spit.

Aaron was in the barn with Gideon. The room had been freshly cleaned. Newly laundered bedding, fresh towels, and polished chest made the room bright and cozy. Ready for the newlyweds' bridal night. Gideon was so nervous he almost stuttered when Aaron began asking questions about the young man's experience with intimate matters. When Aaron realized how limited Gideon's knowledge was, he gently explained how patience and tenderness would be most important to begin a marriage. Satisfied that the young man would now know how to act, he gave a friendly pat on the back of his soon-to-be son-in-law. "Don't worry, son, almost every man on this earth will, at one time or another, go through this ritual. I was every bit as nervous as you."

In the cottage Sera was helping Fila dress and fix her hair. Alea was tying a velvet ribbon around a bouquet of wild violets that Fila would hold while the wedding vows were spoken. Fila was quite calm. She knew this was exactly what she wanted. Sera had already explained what to expect on her wedding night. For some reason, possibly because she was so confident in Gideon's gentle nature, she was not afraid. In fact, there was a feeling of excited anticipation hovering in the back of her mind.

The sounds of horse-drawn buggies, cheerful voices raised in friendly greetings could be heard in the yard. Sera and Alea went outside to welcome the guests. Gideon emerged from the barn with Aaron close at his side. Aaron entered the cottage to fetch Fila while everyone arranged themselves in a semicircle facing the front porch. Gideon faced the preacher, whose back was toward the cottage door.

When Gideon saw Fila step daintily into the sunlight, the sweet scent of the violets adding a never-to-be-forgotten memory to this auspicious day, he thought his heart would melt. This was his beloved he would cherish all his lifelong days.

Aaron placed his daughter's hand in the hand of the man who would now be her caregiver. For a moment the twinge of loss, his daughter now passed to another's care was hurtful, all the memories of her childhood tumbling through his mind almost caused him to thrust her behind him, keep her from this stranger who would take her away. Then realization dawned, he placed her hand onto the young man's strong, work-hardened palm.

Love, honor, the words echoed through the silence bringing tears to the women and stern expressions to the men. It seemed, too quickly the service was over.

The day was filled with laughter and contentment, good food, gossip and games for the children. As the day drifted toward lateness, people gathered to bid their goodbyes. It was time for Fila to depart to the barn and ready herself for bed while Aaron kept Gideon busy with last-minute distractions to ease the young man's obvious nervousness. At last, with final goodnights to the family, Gideon made his way to the barn and the cozy nest that had been prepared for the newlyweds.

Soft light filtered from around the edges of the closed door to the tack room. Hesitantly, with a gentle knock and a moment's pause, Gideon pushed the door open. Fila was sound asleep.

Sitting in the chair, elbows in knees, he looked about the cozy room that had been so welcoming to him. Was it really almost two years since he first met Aaron on that day he had ridden in on Night, lost in dreams and reveries? From a young man without family he now had a new wife and warm loving in-laws who had made him feel whole-heartedly welcomed.

He looked at Fila's sleeping countenance, feeling such a sudden rush of protectiveness and overpowering love he felt his breath catch for a moment. Could he take care of her the way her father had, make a decent living so she never need go without the little luxuries women seemed so pleased with?

With a huge sigh he leaned back, resting his head against the chair's headboard. He liked watching Fila, she seemed in such a deep sleep that he didn't have the heart to awaken her. Maybe he'd just rest here for a while so as not to disturb her, it had been such a long day and she must be exhausted.

Soon Gideon was sound asleep, the occasional movement of the animals in the stalls unheard. He didn't observe the restless movements of his new bride nor hear mumbled words that occasionally slipped from her lips. One of the words was "Luther."

Chapter 8

Luther had a good feeling about finally getting his hands on his Relic—it had been too long out of his hands. There was a sense of unease knowing it was hidden somewhere not readily available to him.

He watched Fila as she slept in the dream world he had induced. She would not waken until he called her. It was the best he could do to keep her from the mental connections she had with her mother. He had learned his lesson well the time he had abducted Sera. He remembered the sear of the hot blaze from the obsidian knife that had singed his eyelids and blinded him for several days when Sera had thwarted him. How she had accomplished it was still a mystery to him but he was aware that it had been some type of collusion on the part of the women. It made him uneasy not knowing exactly how they had succeeded putting him in such a precarious position. He would take no chances this time. Not one iota of latitude would he allow.

As for Fila, she was in a faraway place with Buddy at her side. She found herself walking a path not easily traveled. They walked for the remainder of the day.

Eventually, evening drawing near, she came upon a clear tumbling brook that meandered close to the edge of a nearby forest where they stopped to rest a moment. While sipping her fill of the cool, sweet water Fila inspected the surrounding area. Just inside the tree line she discovered the faint outline of wooden logs. Her spirits lifted and a smile began to form at the upturned corners of her lips.

Luther wondered what she could be smiling at. He had a nervous feeling something could go wrong. He pulled the chalcedony from his cape, passing it back and forth across her unconscious form. Not a single vibration that anything was amiss. Yet, he was aware of a strange, almost imperceptible pulsation that felt very much like a heartbeat. It definitely was not Fila's.

Luther swung the kettle over the fire for water to heat, and then wandered to his apothecary to find a particular herb that would make Fila more receptive to his Domination Spell. He simply felt an impediment was somehow blocking him from total control, it was making him agitated. Slowly, lingering at each promising-looking vial of liquid, or jar of powdered herb, Luther navigated each shelf. Either not satisfied with the qualities, or the power of each prescriptive he investigated. He was not aware of passing time, so absorbed was he in finding the perfect solution to his dilemma.

In her dream Fila was inside a cabin. It was so dark she could see only the sun's path that lighted part of the room through the door she had left ajar when entering. She turned aside and opened the shutters on the window, then closed the door latching it securely. Inspecting the room she had an immediate feeling of comfort. There was a cobblestone fireplace with two chairs sitting nearby. One, a light-colored cane rocker, the other a sturdy high-backed chair with a cushioned seat. Both well-used and comfortable looking. There was a rough-hewn ladder near the far corner of the room resting against the upper half-floor of the attic. She caught a glimpse of some items stacked at the edge.

Fila poured some water into one of the iron kettles hanging from the shepherd's hook and swung it over the wood she had so carefully laid. With a flick of her wrist, she used her little blue orb to ignite the fire. She found some strangely scented tea leaves that urged her to sample their brew. This she did. What a strange feeling, just as though she were two people. The watcher and the one watched. She saw herself deeply asleep on a strange bed. She saw a dark shape bending over her. What was the shadow doing? It looked like a cup in his hand. He lifted her head and soon, no matter how she tried to resist, she was drawn inside the sleeping figure of herself. Darkness closed about her....

Luther had checked on Fila just in time. How it had happened he couldn't begin to guess but somehow she was beginning to counteract the spell he had put upon her. He was sure he had followed every step. What was wrong with him? Maybe he had missed something? He searched his massive collection of books to find the one that contained the spell he had used. He couldn't afford to be slipshod. His mission was too important for him to mess up by being careless. He found the missive, located the passage and carefully perused each line and word. He began to feel a heavy weight descend upon his entire psyche. Something was very, very wrong. He had followed the instructions to the letter, his memory accurate. All he could do now was keep watch so Fila didn't regain consciousness.

Fila could hear Luther talking to himself. It sounded so far away that she didn't know if it was she who was distant or he. The only thing she was sure of was, she was trapped, held in a state of immobility that was driving her to distraction. She thought if she could concentrate long enough she would pull free of the invisible bonds that held her so closely. Just as she felt herself at the brink of freedom, she was slammed back into the dark ties of bondage and dreams.

Luther was confident she was completely under his control. A powerful "Sleepwalking Dream" spell would allow her to travel with him to the Winter Forest, unaware of her passage. This was a perfect morning to start the trek. A soft whisper in Fila's ear and they stepped from Luther's cavernous home. When they reached the barrier hedge Luther opened a pathway through the brambles which closed immediately once they were on the opposite side. Drawing a narrow silken ribbon from his cloak, he fastened one end about her wrist, the other around his. For a moment a silver spark shimmered along the length from him to her, and then it disappeared.

As they traveled to their destination Luther was at times puzzled by the poses Fila sometimes exhibited. She would bend and extended her hand outward, other times she seemed to be talking to someone at her side, a smile curving her lips almost as though there was an invisible companion keeping step with them. It made Luther very uncomfortable. He didn't believe in ghosts so the only thing he deduced was that his spell might be raising shadowy specters in her imagination. Anything was possible but it was something he would not worry himself about.

They made excellent time the first three days. So good in fact that he expected to arrive at the forest late the next day. The weather had been sunny and mild with, luckily, not even the threat of rain. The trail had been dry and easily traveled. They camped for their last evening just off the edge of the trail. Luther fed Fila first then gave her his canister of water to drink her fill. When she was curled near the fire fast asleep, he himself ate and then dozed, he felt unsure about allowing himself a decent night's rest.

"Oh! Well!" he muttered to himself, tonight was the last on the trail. Tomorrow he would see his success at recovering his Relic. He recalled when he had first located it in the village of Umer and the deceased old man who had once been the owner. Everything that had happened since that day seemed foreordained, too weird to contemplate. The Relic was his, it belonged to him, would always be in his possession as long as he had breath in his body. He needed it, the why of it he didn't even want to contemplate.

When he opened his eyes again it was morning, he had slept the night through. He gave a nudge to Fila and when she opened her eyes, he pressed a chunk of cheese into her hand and a piece of buttered bread. Dreamily she consumed the food and when he offered her water she drank it thirstily. She dropped a piece of cheese and a bit of bread on the ground. Careless, he thought, inedible now. Let some wild animal enjoy the tidbit. Rising, he pulled her to her feet, the ribbon stretched between them they continued onward to their destination. Luther expected to arrive before dusk.

Meanwhile, Fila, caught in the dreaming spell Luther had put on her, was treading a path that seemed familiar to her, Buddy prancing along at her side. She could still taste the bread and cheese she had eaten, dropping a remnant to her little pet. For a moment she couldn't remember where the food had appeared from and with a shrug of her shoulders decided it really didn't matter as long as they weren't hungry. She wondered where she was traveling to. A strange sensation numbed the edges of her mind, she felt like a ghost floating above the earth. An invisible tug at her wrist reminded her how she never felt alone and it had nothing to do with

Buddy....

The sun was settling low on the horizon when Luther stopped Fila for a moment before entering the forest. He wound most of the ribbon about his hand until only a short span separated the two of them. He didn't want Fila straying off the path and breaking the bond. Not at this time when success was within reach. Before nightfall he would have the Relic in his possession.

With Fila in the lead they made their way into the dusky tree-lined trail. Fila quickened her pace, excitement building as recognition dawned at the unexpected sight and smell of the forest. This was her special place. She remembered the cozy cabin set in the center of the clearing. Her special tree holding the secret she was destined to guard. Her hand reached to caress the golden key which hung about her neck. Everything became clear to her, even the reason why the shadowy presence dogged her footsteps was revealed.

Fila heard a familiar voice whispering instructions to her. Telling her what to expect when Luther made his demands. She must obey his every request. Above all, she need not be fearful of any consequences. Fila couldn't help but feel just a little apprehensive, even though she now knew every action would be guided by the Relic. For a moment a shiver traveled up her spine and she felt the hair at the back of her neck raise slightly.

Luther felt a cool breath of air waft against his cheek. Searching the closely knitted branches lining the edge of the path he hoped it was but a wayward breeze that had found a way through the forest. Still, he felt the beginning of a knot forming in the pit of his stomach. His muscles were so tensed that the strain was causing an ache to work its way through his shoulders. Even his neck was becoming stiff. Hunching his shoulders and turning his head in awkward positions to relieve the pressure he heard his neck bones creaking in protest. Muttering to himself about "Not being old enough to be suffering this kind of discomfort" Luther stayed only a few steps behind Fila, making sure she stayed on the pathway.

Unexpectedly, the forest ended and they were standing at the edge of the clearing seeing the sun dropping behind the tree tops and shadows beginning to form at the far reaches of the glen. The cabin stood starkly outlined against the quickly fading light. It was much too late now to accomplish anything further this evening.

Guiding Fila toward the cabin Luther pushed open the door and led her inside. After seating her in one of the chairs and using a little of his magic, the fire was soon sending warmth throughout the room chasing away the spring chill.

Now completely attuned to the present situation, Fila pretended to be dozing. She watched through half-closed eyes, every move Luther made. There was a darkness that seemed to surround his form, a shifting shadow that seemed part of his essence. This was someone she did not want to be in the same vicinity of. "Oh! Please be there when I need you tomorrow," she whispered to the Relic hoping her words were heard.

Luther was first to awaken in the dark before dawn. He had positioned himself in front of the door and though the floor had felt hard as stone, he had slept soundly enough in fits and spurts to do what needed to be done today to recapture his lost prize. "Never," he murmured to himself, "will I ever allow the Relic out of my possession again." All this time he had felt vulnerable to outside influences. He detested the feeling of helplessness that overcame him at odd moments when, without warning, a deep sense of depression dropped like a leaden weight upon his shoulders. When that occurred it felt as though doom itself loomed so closely that he could feel its cold breath upon the back of his neck. He never knew what caused the things that had been happening to him but he felt having the Relic back in his grasp would make his world feel normal again.

When aware that he was still resting on the hard floor, he managed to arise stiffly and make his way to the fireplace to stoke the embers and heat water for tea and porridge. He would need strength, he thought, to accomplish his deed.

Fila awoke to whispered words floating in the predawn darkness. She was aware that Luther was muttering to himself in the far corner of the room. She, at least, had enjoyed a good night's rest on the corner cot. She did, however, feel very nervous about Luther recovering the Relic. When her fingers twined around the key hanging at her neck a quiet peace descended upon her. Swinging her feet to the floor she arose and barefoot, she made her way to the fireplace where Luther, his back turned, was too busy to notice her approach. When he turned he gasped aloud in shock at her unexpected presence.

The sight of Luther, paralyzed momentarily with stunned surprise, caused Fila to burst out laughing. "You," she stuttered, "look SO funny," more laughter, "for someone who is," laughter echoed loudly, "supposed to be such," the laughter crashed against the walls and bounced from the ceiling, "a monster."

Fila could not control herself. She seemed to be standing back, watching the drama unfold. She wondered if this delirium was caused by nervousness or possibly a scene created by the Relic. She was convulsed with mirth yet her hidden self was coolly observing Luther's reaction.

He looked as pale as winter moonlight on midnight snow. Frozen in mid-motion, reaching for a ladle, he couldn't move a muscle. Never in his entire life had he ever been the subject of ridicule or laughter. The more he tried to break free of his invisible bonds, the tighter he seemed to be constrained. Rage was building within with nowhere to vent. Fila watched, hearing her laughter roaring and echoing throughout the cabin. At last Luther succumbed to the internal stress inundating his entire system. A low moan escaped from his compressed lips, his eyes rolled back into his head and he fell to the floor like a limp burlap sack emptied of its contents.

The laughter stopped abruptly, the overwhelming silence like a heavy weight settling over the room. The sound of the crackling fire made itself known, the bubble of boiling water could be heard quite clearly. Fila's ears were still echoing from the reverberations that had seemed to almost deafen her. She stepped to Luther's prone figure not knowing what she would find.

He lay stretched out on his back, arms flung wide, legs spread-eagled. The slight rise and fall of his chest the only sign he was alive, his skin so pale he looked like a ghost. Fila reached for his hand closing her fingers around the pale flesh. It felt quite warm. When she felt the strong pulse in his wrist she heaved a sigh of relief that he had not been seriously harmed. She felt a stirring of pity begin someplace deep within, this she did not need. Hurriedly she dropped his hand at his side and stepped away.

What could she have been thinking? He had abducted her on her wedding day. She had no room in her heart for pity for this creature. For a moment her mind dwelled on what Gideon must be going through, what her parents and sisters were planning, knowing they would do everything in their power to find her. Right now she couldn't dawdle around guessing what might happen. She had to go to the old tree where the Relic was hidden and find out what she should do about Luther.

The sky was just beginning to lighten in the eastern sky as she made her way to the gnarled old tree where the Relic was ensconced. It seemed ages since she had placed it there. She stood silently for a moment before the wooden sentinel. Then, pressing a spot that opened the hidden panel, she inserted her key and the secret of the inner niche was revealed. The Relic sat on its pedestal seeming, for a moment, as dark and silent as the old tree wood that surrounded the opening.

Fila felt a stirring of the air about her head, the scent of burnt ashes stung her nostrils and her eyes began to water from acrid fumes that seemed to originate out of nowhere. For a moment she felt a sense of panic as though she stood on the brink of a dangerous precipice ready to be catapulted into empty space. The feeling passed immediately as recognition was projected into her consciousness. Waves of serenity inundated her until she was suspended in a cocoon of sleep.

Luther, suspended in limbo, was desperately trying to find his way. Whispers began to circle about his head like vultures over a dead carcass; he could not distinguish or make sense of the words and phrases that bombarded his senses. At last everything began to string itself out like written passages from a long-lost tome.

"You have meddled in my affairs for the final time Luther, now feel what your life would have been like as an ordinary man. This Dream Curse is yours Luther, awaken."

Luther awoke in his own bed feeling dizzy. Turning his head he noticed two young women standing at his bedside, one with a wet cloth in her hand. At the same time he became aware his face felt damp, the coolness very refreshing.

"Are you feeling a little better, Luther?" the taller of the two asked.

He recognized Fila, who had recently been married. His eyes turned to Alea as he responded. "Whatever has been affecting me seems to have passed." He could actually feel strength flowing back into his body as he began to swing his feet over the edge of his bed feeling embarrassed.

Alea smiled at his discomfort. "When you didn't appear for dinner as promised we came immediately to see what was wrong. We searched the rooms until we came upon you stretched out on your bed in a faint. I wouldn't be surprised if perhaps you were just hungry. Did you skip lunch to save your appetite for our home-cooked meal?" Alea laughed at the expression on Luther's face, knowing that was exactly what he had done.

"Come along, Luther, we have our horses waiting," Fila said. "You can ride double with Alea. We'll be home before dinner gets cold." They each grasped one of his hands and pulled him to his feet, tugging him through the rooms and out the door. Soon they were taking a shortcut between the two properties. When they arrived at Aaron's cottage Gideon was just exiting the doorway eager to unsaddle the mounts and get everyone settled at the table. With a friendly backslap of greeting to Luther's shoulder, he urged them toward the door while he led the horses to the barn.

The entire family was present. Luther thoroughly enjoyed the dinner. Sera had stuffed and roasted two chickens. Mashed potatoes with gravy, creamed peas, early leaf lettuce with cider vinegar dressing, and soda biscuits slathered with fresh creamery butter completed the meal. Apple cobbler was served for dessert.

While the dishes were washed and the kitchen neatened the three men sat before the fire enjoying lively conversation, laughing at jokes, feeling the warm comfort of each other's presence while waiting for the women to join them.

The hours drifted toward evening until Luther rose, gave a stretch, and stated he was ready to head for home. "Take my horse, Night," Gideon offered. "Just turn him loose once you're home. He'll make his way back here quick as a wink."

"Thanks, Gid. I appreciate it," Luther replied as they made their way to the barn to saddle the stallion. With a friendly wave of farewell, Luther rode away.

In the next instant he found himself lying on his bed seeming to hear the last words of a friendly conversation drift away. He was alone, although why he was expecting someone else to be there was a mystery.

He felt a strange yearning lodged somewhere inside his chest, a strange almost painful emotion he had never felt before. He wished it would go away.

His first and only taste of family devotion and friendship would forever haunt him, a permanent part of him, a feeling he would try to ignore for the remainder of his life.

Chapter Nine

After the girls departed to their beds upstairs, Gideon and Fila to their privacy in the barn's remodeled storage room, Sera and Aaron sat for a while before the slowly dying fire. Sera looked at her husband noticing the traces of gray at his temples, his still-youthful sun-browned face so dear to her. They had been married twenty years ago this spring. It didn't seem that long a time. The years had passed so swiftly with raising her daughters and now, impossible to comprehend, a new son-in-law to help Aaron on his yearly trading missions. Her life was so full, so complete. She couldn't contemplate a better life other than the one she had.

Aaron noticed the thoughtful, serene expression on Sera's face. His eyes traced the outline of the curve of her cheek, the soft contour of her lips, and her still-black hair with only a minimal threading of gray throughout. Although it seemed impossible, he loved her more than the day they wed. Oh! They had their occasional disagreements but it had never progressed to hurtful words of anger. Somehow Sera had a knack of calming tempers down, either with words of plain old common sense or a trick of distraction that caused a person to momentarily forget their bone of contention. It made for a peaceful home-life, wholehearted laughter with the comfort of a close-knit family sharing the same type of disposition, and mutual concern about the well-being of each family member. Never, while growing into manhood, had he ever expected to find a wife of her worth when he reached marrying age, or have such gentle daughters. They, of course, had learned at their mother's knee.

Sera delicately covered a yawn, glancing at Aaron to see if he felt ready for bed. She caught his contemplative expression and couldn't help smiling back at him. "Come along, sweetheart," she said as she grasped his hand and pulled him to his feet. "Morning will be here too soon, time to get some well-deserved rest." Aaron placed his arm around Sera's softly rounded body and drew her close to his chest. Her clear gray eyes gazed at him with tenderness as their lips joined in a loving kiss. She could feel Aaron's heart beating strongly against her breasts. With a sigh she clasped her arms about his neck surrendering to his loving embrace.

Bright morning sunlight highlighted every piece of furniture in the room. Sera awoke with a start from a deep dreamless sleep. The patch of sunlight warming the bed had awakened her. Aaron was dozing lightly, enjoying the extra few winks before beginning his busy day. Slipping on her robe she rekindled the fire, swinging the iron pot over the mounting flames. While the water came to a boil she hurriedly dressed. Running her bone comb through her hair she pulled it back and secured it with a braided twist of dyed wool. A quick look in the mirror to see that she was presentable, she turned to start breakfast. It would be porridge this morning with slices of crisp bacon on toasted bread.

Aaron stretched heartily and arose to pull on his trousers, boots and shirt. When he reached the barn he saw Gideon had already finished milking and was on his way to the cottage and Fila had already gathered the eggs and was on her way to help her mother with breakfast. The two met at the door with another morning kiss. By the time they walked in, her sisters were tumbling down the attic steps ready to lend a helping hand.

It was a happy morning. Plans were made for the duties each would accomplish. Gideon would ride to Mica's to pick up additional supplies. Sera and the girls would finish packing. Aaron would select items from the attic storage to use in trade. It would be a busy day.

By afternoon with most of the chores finished, Alea was up in the attic inspecting the rag dolls Mina and Nia had made, making sure the stitching was tight and the faces drawn neatly. It was only a show on her part knowing her sisters were waiting for words of praise for the workmanship. Not wanting to keep them in suspense too long, she couldn't help but smile at their anticipation. "These are absolutely beautiful," she said, examining the tiny stitches on the firmly stuffed bodies of the little girl and boy dolls. "You've chosen nice colors for the clothing too." The girl doll wore a white cotton dress decorated with tiny pink polka dots that Mina had spent so much time creating by dipping a sharpened stick into beet juice to make the pretty pattern of miniature spots. A matching bonnet completed the outfit.

The boy doll wore brown homespun trousers. Brown suspenders decorated his white shirt. Nia had needled a multitude of dark threads through the crown, clipping the protruding ends to create hair. Alea smiled at Nia's imaginative creation. It was quite good for a twelve-year-old and she told Nia so, watching the glow of pride her words had brought forth on her sister's face. "I'm sure Father will bring you both something very special in trade for all your hard work." The two young sisters exchanged grins of expectant anticipation; it would be a long wait until his return from trading. They scurried downstairs to tell their mother what Alea had said and show her the dolls.

Alea decided to neaten last winter's clothing, which was piled in a corner basket. It would all be laundered in early summer and then packed away with dried lavender, ready for the first onset of cold weather. At least folded it would take up less space and it would only take a short time to do.

Halfway through the pile, she felt a slightly weighted lopsidedness in one of her mothers' woolen dresses when she held the garment up to fold. Searching the pockets she felt a small hard object her fingers fumbled to grasp. It felt so cool and smooth she couldn't imagine what it could be. Drawing it forth she couldn't take her eyes from it. Oh! The color of it, the most wondrous green ever imaginable. The smooth contours so delicately wrought, the image seemed almost alive. She peered into the verdant depths of the feline, feeling herself being slowly drawn into its interior until, at the last moment, she found herself listening to a quiet rumble that emanated from all around her. The sound mesmerized her until she could no longer stand upright, then her body folded gently downward and curled up falling fast asleep, the emerald cat clutched tightly in her fist.

Dreams held her tightly, though not fearfully. The resonating sound swirling about her was very comforting, thwarting any feelings of danger that might lurk at the edges of her mind. She felt pampered, loved and admired for her beauty. She stretched luxuriously and felt sleek muscles ripple under her flesh. Her hearing was so acute she could hear the whisper of the breeze outside the window. Her nose twitched catching the scent of meat simmering down in the kitchen. She stretched out her hand and felt her nails rake the wooden floor beneath her. She felt like digging them in to get a good hold.

Alea opened her eyes finding she was recumbent on the attic floor, a small figurine clutched tightly in her hand. "What in the world happened?" she murmured. "Did I fall asleep?" She had no memory of making herself comfortable on the floor when there was a perfectly nice bed of her own to nap on. Confusedly she opened her hand seeing the catlike figurine she had held so tightly. Rising from the floor she secreted the image under her pillow, forgetting about it the moment it was out of sight. Hurriedly she finished folding the clothing giving the pile a final pat when the last article was placed neatly on top. With a last glance about she descended the stairs, not quite sure why she was feeling so restless but aware of a new perspective of life.

Sera was searching through the cupboard trying to decide what to fix for supper when Alea appeared suddenly at her elbow. "Oh! You startled me," Sera exclaimed with a quick smile at her daughter in forgiveness. "I didn't hear you come down. Did you finish whatever it was you were doing up there?"

Alea encircled her mother with a warm hug. "Did I ever tell you what a wonderful mother you are? I know I'm not very demonstrative and seldom speak out about my feelings, but I just felt like letting you know how much I love you."

Sera tilted her head back to look at her second-eldest daughter, a misty glow in her eyes. Giving a firm hug, she reached to grasp Alea's hands in her own. "My dear child, I realize the love you hold for me but I must admit, nothing touches the heart more than hearing a loved one speak words of endearment. You have done this since you were a youngster. Thank you, my dear, your words were a gentle reminder to me that I must also voice my feelings more often. I too love you with all my heart." Sera gave a final squeeze to her daughter's hands and a light caress to her cheek before turning attention again to the cupboard. Soon their heads were close together discussing recipes for the evening meal.

Everyone returned within minutes of each other, work for the day finished. Aaron and Gideon were discussing their trading trip which would begin in a few days. Fila, Mina, and Nia bringing in the early leaf lettuce which would be served at supper with sugared cider vinegar as a salad dressing. When supper was over with dishes washed and put away, Gideon and Fila departed to their quarters and the three girls up to their sleeping area, Sera and Aaron to sit for a while before the banked fire to discuss the day's accomplishments and tomorrow's plans.

In the attic the girls were settling down for the night. The deep breathing of Mina and Nia signified they were asleep. Alea, still wakeful, tried to find a more comfortable position. Sliding her hand under her pillow to plump it a bit she felt something cool touch her skin. With a jerk she pulled her hand away quickly, a moment of panic almost making her cry out. As she lay tensely afraid to move, wondering what could be hiding in her bed so near to her head, a gentle resonance began to emanate from all around her. It was such a pleasant contented sound. It made her feel so drowsy she fell into a suspended state of euphoria, drifting in undulating waves of vibration.

A soft voice began to speak to her. "Listen closely, Alea. I have plans that you and Fila must implement, it is the next stage of Destiny. You must follow these instructions faithfully at the ending of the seventh day."

Alea slept soundly, awaking the next morning with the instructions still echoing in her mind. She knew what she'd like to do, ask her father if she could go with him as far as the Winter Forest. However, there was not a chance he would allow that. She'd just have to slip away on her own to complete the mission. That would be something that would really frighten her. She felt the hair stand up at the nape of her neck just thinking about being on the trail alone. She was trapped with no way out. She had better start making plans immediately, push her fears deep inside to be forgotten—slim chance of that happening.

The next morning as Aaron and Gideon were preparing to leave, Fila and Sera were anxiously checking the food pouches, adding last-minute items they had prepared on arising. Biscuits were still warm, sausages folded into each one. Chunks of cheese in a linen cloth, fall apples, the best from the cellar barrel, all placed in two pokes which would hang from the saddle horns. The two horses, Night and Apple, were anxious to go, nervously tossing their heads, hooves doing a tattoo on the new spring shoots of grass growing near the cottage steps.

"Goodbye, Sera, if you need any help send word to Mica. He'll lend his handyman. I think though everything that could be done has been taken care of. The new wool is waiting for you, Gideon made sure it was nicely cleaned and ready for you to spin. We will be back as soon as all the goods have been traded, hopefully in early fall." Aaron gave his wife a final hug, pressing a quick last kiss on her trembling lips. Goodbyes were always so painful not knowing what fate would bring. Sera made it a point not to cry but it was so difficult watching Aaron ride away, not to return for such a long time.

Fila and Gideon were not doing quite as well. The newlyweds were so enthralled with their newfound bliss that it was a struggle for both to retain their composure. The pain of separation was already making itself felt. At least Gid had the satisfaction of knowing Fila, now his wife, would be waiting for him. He held her closely nuzzling her neck, whispering the words of love he was too bashful to say aloud. When Aaron mounted the mare, Fila gave a last hug and kiss to her husband pushing him away, the sheen of tears glistening in her eyes. "Stay safe," were the only words she could choke out, afraid she would burst into sobs.

"You too," Gideon managed to gruffly reply, his throat feeling tight with emotion. "I love you, sweetheart"

They watched until the horsemen were out of sight. Sera knew she had to find something for everyone to do immediately or there would be too many teary eyes. She sent Mina and Nia to weed the garden; Fila and Alea had already disappeared. As for herself, sewing was always a good way to keep her mind occupied for the remainder of the morning.

Alea and Fila were deep in a serious discussion. Alea had decided to tell her sister what had happened and the warning issued. They decided the only reasonable course to take was to tell their mother what had occurred then the two could make plans to leave for the Winter Forest immediately.

Sera was not happy. Bad enough the men had just gone off until autumn, now her two daughters were caught up in a scheme that didn't make much sense to her. Alea tried to explain that although things seemed ordinary something was very wrong. Looking at her two eldest daughters she felt impelled to allow them to follow their instincts.

There were still leftover biscuits and sausages, apples and cheese. Packs were readied, clothes changed for easy traveling. Boots exchanged for slippers. A quick hug and the two slipped away before the younger girls returned to prod and pester for answers. Time was wasting, the first of the seven days had begun, who knew what troubles they would encounter before they reached their objective. They made it to the trail without being spotted by their younger sisters. Setting off at a strong pace that would take them a fair distance each day before dusk set in. They set cold camps, not taking time to search for firewood. Their packed food was stretched to the limit, the last of it eaten on the morning of the fourth day. They weren't worried knowing there would be ample provisions at the cabin.

That evening, making their way along the narrow trail through the woods, both were exhausted. They looked forward to enjoying a good night's rest in a bed. The ground had felt exceptionally hard during their nightly sleeps. Maybe because they were older and not as easily adaptable.

Entering the clearing, the moon was just emerging over the pines illuminating the clearing. The cabin was a welcome sight; they hurried their steps anxious to be inside and sitting before a warm fire with something to eat. While water heated for tea they selected hardtack with a few strips of dried venison for their supper. A shared pint jar of elderberries would serve as dessert. Tomorrow, after receiving instructions from the Relic, they would prepare a suitable hot meal and enjoy a few days of relaxation. As for the remainder of the evening, after savoring a last cup of hot herb tea the two made themselves comfortable on the bed, drifting off to sleep almost immediately. Neither was prone to tossing and turning so both slept deeply.

Bright sunshine awoke Fila. Quietly she slipped from her side of the bed being careful not to awaken Alea. She heated water, added a generous scoop of cornmeal and a handful of dried currants. While that cooked she filled a bowl with whole-wheat flour, mixed in a little salt then added just enough water to make a dry dough. Rolling portions into egg-sized balls which she flattened into very thin rounds she placed these on an iron griddle that had been heating on the fire. These Indian pan cakes would be spread with preserves to be eaten as dessert or wrapped around fried bacon or other cooked meats and enjoyed as lunch or supper. By the time the food was ready Alea had risen, set the table and straightened the bedding.

"Do you have the emerald cat?" Fila asked as they made their way to the old oak. It was late morning, a little cool with a light breeze ruffling the tree tops. The sun, warming the newly sprouting greenery and damp earth beneath, made the air redolent with the scent of spring.

Alea pushed her hand deep into her pocket feeling the smooth cool surface of the little icon. She felt a shiver run down her spine creating goose flesh along her arms. She could actually feel the little hairs on her skin raise. "What in the world is happening?" she replied. "We only have to find out what to do with this cat image and I have the oddest feeling about this figurine. I can feel you're getting premonitions."

Fila stopped. Raising her head she looked over the surrounding area, then farther out toward the edge of the forest, then finally toward the old tree which stood alone in all its ancient mystery. She didn't truly sense any danger, yet there was a disquieting feeling. "You're right, Alea, I think something extraordinary is going to happen and I'll be relieved when the entire thing is over."

When Fila reached for the key that hung around her neck it was gone, along with the delicate chain. Looking down she saw a tiny gleam deep within the drifted leaves of last fall. Reaching within she withdrew her missing necklace. The key, however, was not attached. Search as she could, it was gone.

Fila tried to make contact with the Relic without success. The mental connection she had always felt was absent. Even pressing the knot that should open the wooden access did not work. "Can you think of anything else you were told in your dream, Alea? Anything that could explain what is happening?

Alea pondered a moment. "No! Not a thing. Only that I was to take the image to the Winter Forest. I think we should remain here until the seventh night, Fila. Maybe something will happen that will help solve the dilemma. There is nothing else we can possibly do for now."

For a moment Fila's thoughts, turned inward, caused a frown to work its way across her forehead then, decision reached, her face cleared and she spoke in agreement. "That sounds exactly right, my dear sister, something is happening that's beyond our conception and I have the feeling it's necessary we face it together. Day after tomorrow is the seventh. It's not that long a wait for the outcome of this impasse."

Making their way back to the cabin both felt uneasy, as though there was some type of spirit hovering about waiting for the right moment to pounce. Alea felt a little more secure than Fila. Having the emerald feline seemed to give her a small degree of comfort though for the life of her, she couldn't imagine why.

The next two days passed uneventfully. They occupied their time doing a thorough cleaning of the cabin. The windows sparkled, the wooden floor was bright again, all the rugs had been beaten and aired, so even the air inside smelled fresh. Now, all they had to do was wait for evening. The seventh day had arrived.

They ate an early supper, though neither had much of an appetite. After everything was put back in place they fixed tea, sitting together before the fire, watching twilight creep through the clearing after the sun disappeared behind the trees. Silently, expectantly, they waited, not knowing what would happen or even if anything would happen. The windows darkened and night descended. They were both fast asleep.

It must have been midnight. If there had been a grandfather clock it surely would have been striking the time. A dark shadowy figure hovered outside, seeming to wait for the final strike of the chime.

As the last tone echoed through the room the cabin door opened. The figure moved to the two women noting the deep breathing, the eye movement that suggested dream sleep. A harsh laugh sounded but the women did not waken. A voice began a litany of words. "It is my time once again, my beauties. What shall I do with you? I am stronger than I have ever been, my power has multiplied tenfold." Again laughter sounded, this time sounding smug and well content. The figure leaned over the two slumbering figures contemplating their features, admiring their beauty, yet there was a touch of something malignant shifting behind the artificial smile. Suddenly, with a sharp snap of his fingers, the sleepers were awake.

Both Fila and Alea took a moment to get their bearings, still feeling the fingers of sleep that had held them so tightly in dreams. They were not aware of the figure that stood so closely, it seemed just a shadow cast by the flickering flames of the still-burning fire though surely, the momentary mirage was created by the figure itself. When the two realized there was someone standing before them, the old spell that had been cast by the Relic was shattered and a new spell was about to unfold.

Luther was holding the Emerald Cat. His gloating laugh sounded again. "I have won at last. Soon I will have the Relic in my possession, nothing can stop me. You two will take a seat and remain in place until I return." With a last glance to assure the two were spellbound in their chairs, Luther exited and hurried to the fated meeting with his Relic. When he was positioned in front of the oak tree, a light tap on the panel with the Emerald Feline opened it. Another tap on the inside access and his long-sought icon was revealed. "You have managed to evade my spell," the Relic stated calmly. "Are you positive you wish to have me in your possession once again? The situation will be much different than when you last owned my image and my powers. You see, I also have been given an unexpected gift. Are you truly willing to accept me and all that I now represent without knowledge of the changes that have occurred?" The Relic waited silently for a response.

Luther was in turmoil, not really sure what to do. He did want his icon back, but not knowing the new circumstances gave him pause. He wanted everything exactly the way it had been without surprises or unexplained glitches. He tried to peer into the Relic's mystical aura without success; it was like looking at a blank wall. Anxiety began to build. He was beginning to feel a trap slowly closing about him. Hurriedly he stepped back wanting more space between him and an unseen threat that loomed, he felt, just out of sight. What to do, he thought, I want my Icon. Should I take the chance, ignore this menace I feel, simply take the image and flee as quickly as possible? Luther was in a quandary. Making a split-second decision he reached out, grasped the Icon and fled. After only a few paces he came to a complete halt. Not a thing had happened. No bolt from the blue, nothing that made him feel threatened. Clasping the Relic tightly in his fist he felt impervious to any assault that could have been dealt him. HE HAD DONE IT. The Relic was his, never to leave his possession again.

He would make sure of that.

Making his way back to the cabin he tried to decide what to do with the two young women. He never wanted to set eyes on them again. Fila had started the entire mess when she had taken his Icon. At least he had put an "Impasse" spell on the hedge barrier and was protected from any further intrusions. While his mind sorted through options he could implement, he pushed open the door and made his way over to stand before the women. Fila and Alea were just as he had left them, immobile in their chairs. When he approached them with the Icon still clasped in his hand, they calmly arose from their seats and stood facing him, speaking not one word, nor showing any signs of animation. Luther was stunned that they were able to move, and then his temper erupted. "What secrets have you two discovered that you can thwart my spells?" Luther asked angrily. "Don't think you can play some clever trick to fool me into believing I have become powerless, it won't work. I am much stronger than anything you could ever imagine. Sit yourselves down immediately before I place permanent ties that will bind you to me and my bidding forever. The only thing giving me pause is that I couldn't bear the sight of the two of you every day." The two young women were reseated, not quite understanding why they had no control over what was happening to them. They would have rather stayed upright and confronted Luther. Yet, they felt no fear of what might come down on their heads by way of a curse from the man they detested with all their heart and soul. Their eyes focused on the Relic Luther held so tightly. "Patience," it seemed to be saying to them, "all will be resolved in due time."

Luther slowly began to back out of the cabin, fearful of turning away from the two sisters though what it was he feared he couldn't fathom. Once he cleared the doorway he sprinted off toward the forest with the Relic clutched possessively, his flight from an unseen threat he sensed but could not see. When he reached the tree line he turned to view the clearing, fully expecting to see a phantom figure trailing close behind ready to tear the Icon from his grasp. The area was ghostly moonlit with nary a cricket nor toad singing in the deadened night. Luther could feel a tiny pulse begin to beat against his palm where the Relic was pressed so tightly. Ignoring the dread that seemed to intensify with each contraction he scurried through the trees, ducking swaying branches, feeling bruises rise on his legs from protruding limbs that attempted to delay his progress. By the time he exited the forest he felt as though he had survived the tortuous passage by the skin of his teeth. He wondered why he felt so vulnerable, his capture of the Icon should have enhanced his powers. Slowly the realization set in that his hand was becoming quite numb from clutching the Relic so tightly. Opening the leather pouch that was fastened at his waist he tucked the image inside, making sure the thongs were securely tied. Then, turning toward the trail, he set as fast a pace as he could manage without collapsing from fatigue. He planned on completing the trip home within three days and indeed, it was accomplished.

Fila and Alea were more than halfway home by that time. They had camped each night with a warming fire, partaking of meals they prepared from food they had packed. When they settled themselves down for their last evening on the trail, Fila began talking about the Relic and Luther. "Do you remember, Alea, when I first brought the Relic home, when I told how I was led to take it? It was an impulse I had no control over, I don't think there was a possibility I could have refused its possession. Now that I recall how it all evolved I truly believe it could have been the Relic that possessed me, rather than the opposite. We are not thieves, yet even Mother was led to take that Emerald Cat. Without the Cat Luther could not have gained access to the Icon. I have always felt the Relic was my friend but what if I'm wrong? What if everything so far has been a trick of some sort and we are being led into a trap? I wish there was someone that we could tell what has occurred and get their opinion." Fila looked to her sister, watching the various changes of expressions flickering across her face, at last settling into one of anxiety.

"I understand how you feel. I've been having the same premonitions and doubts about all the unusual experiences our entire family has gone through. Our very ordinary lives erupted into too many strange occurrences. Some pleasant like you meeting Gideon, others just plain weird. Luther's intrusions have been the worst. It feels like everything is tied together somehow but for the life of me, I cannot find the connection. If we could only locate the thread that began it all we could unravel the complete mystery." Alea sat quietly, contemplating the various mishaps that had been visited upon them. For the remainder of the evening neither spoke another word about their misgivings. There would be time enough once they arrived home. Fila thought it would be interesting to learn what their mother thought; while Alea regretted that their father and Gideon had already left on their trading trip. It would seem a long, long time until the men returned in the autumn. A sense of deep unease descended upon the young women, each well aware of the other's feelings. It would be a restless night for both and a vast relief when they arrived home on the morrow and discussed their fears with their mother.

Meanwhile, Luther placed the Relic back on the table where it had been before Fila had taken it. With a sigh of relief he also replaced the Emerald Cat. At last his possessions were back where they belonged. From this moment forward he would never have to set eyes on that crude, irritating, Hamlin family again. He had his privacy once more, never to be disturbed by anyone. It would now be impossible for them to gain access through the bramble barrier not only because of the thorns, but the "Impasse" spell he had cast would prevent even an animal getting through. He could relax in comfort to begin his search once more through his books of magic for other objects he considered worthy of his effort to attain. It was exciting perusing each page, never knowing when he would by chance stumble upon something so rare and intriguing that it would take him on another quest. Just imagining the scene gave him a tingle down his spine, the hunt and acquisition was the sport that made his life worthwhile. With a flick of his wrist he sent a miniature whirlwind spinning amongst the articles displayed for his inspection. Within moments every speck of dust had been removed. Now the sparkly gleam of gold and gems were much more attractive to his eye. It pleased him immensely to have his prizes on display for the constant reminder of his cleverness. Each item had its individual use in casting spells, or conjuring images to frighten, lure or repel, create illness or gargantuan strength, generate fruitfulness or famine. The range was so extensive that he had listed them in a ledger with their strengths carefully documented. He was a wealthy man having all these "Treasures" to do his bidding. Whatever he wished, he could attain.

The remainder of the evening was spent enjoying a hot meal then off to bed to recuperate his strength; the days on the trail had exhausted him. As he began to drift off to sleep he sensed for a moment something missing, however fatigue overcame him and soon he became lost in a dream-world search that held him pleasantly captive for the entire night. When he awoke refreshed in the predawn hours, he had forgotten the momentary sense of loss he had experienced. Ah! He breathed deeply, home at last. The thought that he had the entire day to enjoy without the concern of making a recovery of one of his prized possessions, seemed too luxurious for mortal words to describe.

After partaking of an exceptionally tasty breakfast, he meandered lazily past the shelves of books he had collected over the years carefully inspecting each, looking for any editions he had not yet perused. Idly brushing his fingers over the leather-bound spines, he waited expectantly for the slight tingle that would signal a book he had not yet marked as read. Eventually he found three, and of those he selected only one. Settling himself comfortably in his favorite chair before the fire, which was successfully chasing the chill from the previously unheated room, he opened the heavy tome and began to read.

The words leapt out at him as a cat would pounce upon a mouse. "And it came to pass that the comfort the Seeker felt was as flimsy as a leaf before a gale. Knowing not, he dwelt in the surety that he had succeeded, ignoring the secret twinges that tried to warn him of his error." Luther began to feel a definite sense of unease. What sort of book was this? He wondered aloud. Flipping to the front cover he read the title he had ignored, *Secrets of the Two Books of Destiny*. This was not what he wanted to read about, he was searching for unusual occurrences or events that had been caused or changed by something substantial, like his Relic or other items he had collected. Snapping the volume closed, he thoughtfully replaced it back on the shelf choosing another. Returning to his chair he settled himself once again and soon became lost in his search for new collectables. By evening he was still engrossed in the hunt.

Chapter Ten

Aaron and Gideon were in trouble. Gone only a week, they were just at the beginning of their trade route when Aaron's mare, Apple, went lame. They decided Aaron should ride Gideon's mount to the Indian encampment, make arrangements for the use of one of the tepees to store the goods that Night carried. He would return to Gideon, transfer Apple's burden onto Night, and then together the two men could make their way to the Indian camp. Twilight was descending when at last they arrived at their destination, both feeling tired and depressed. As soon as the horses were settled for the night in a makeshift corral, they were invited to join several tribe members for an evening meal of venison stew. After the meal was over plans were made to open the first trading session early the next morning. They would remain until the mare was able to carry her burden, hopefully within a few weeks' time.

In the meantime runners were sent to other tribes with the news of the traders' visit. Within a few days groups began to arrive with goods to swap or sell outright. Aaron was surprised. He had never considered having a rendezvous trading arrangement. It turned into a celebration with games of archery, marriage pacts, feasting and gambling. Although it was too early for bounty from the tribes' gardens, venison, grouse, and fish were abundant. Prizes were given to the person bringing in the largest trophy of each.

The days passed busily and still the trading continued, Aaron and Gideon deciding to remain right where they were. The goods Mica had contributed were swapped for quality beaver pelts. The elaborate dolls that Nia and Mina created traded for deer-hide vests decorated with colorful quills and fringes. Gideon's artful carvings were gone within the first week, garnering items he thought Fila would use and enjoy.

As some tribal members departed for their distant homes, others arrived daily from even farther away until the time came when all the goods brought had been depleted. Even some items that had been taken in trade had been swapped for better. It was time for the two men to pack up and head for home. What a surprise it would be for the women when they arrived so unexpectedly, toting so many valuable items. Mica was sure to be ecstatic when he saw the prime pelts which would more than pay for the dapple mare.

The gray mare was in fine fettle, Night prancing alongside as Aaron and Gideon made their way home. They had put on a little weight during their stay with the tribe. This would be the first time in years that Aaron would arrive home so early. Turning to Gideon he asked, "Are you planning on homesteading here, near us? It's so early in the summer that we could have a cottage built on the far side of the property before cold weather set in. A perfect spot would be on the northwest site. Have you and Fila discussed this at all? I'm not pressing you into making a decision, it's just I know Sera would be so happy to have you both nearby, 'specially for when you two start a family." Aaron paused, feeling his throat close up just thinking of the possibility of not having one of his daughters close by where he could help in case of an emergency, or danger. Fila still seemed like his little girl even though she was now a married woman. He wondered if every father went through this turmoil when a daughter wed. He turned to Gideon expectantly, waiting and hoping for the reply that would ease his heartache.

"Truthfully, Aaron, we haven't even had a chance to discuss this. You know I have a very nice home near the village of Umer that my grandfather left me. It's not wise if I leave it uninhabited. You recall it's well built of fieldstone and not too far from the village. I have the feeling that Fila would get to love it there. The people are very friendly and know me well from all the odd jobs I did when I was a kid trying to earn money to buy my horse, Night. I can earn extra money working at the sawmill. It will be a very good life for us and Fila wouldn't be left alone for long periods of time. She would meet other women to enjoy all the things females like to do when they get together, but I promise to leave it up to her. If she decides she would rather stay, I can make other arrangements regarding my house." Gideon fell silent. He loved Fila enough to abide by her wishes but hoped with all his heart she would decide to move with him to his childhood home. There was something so hurtful about selling a once-happy home to strangers. He knew that if this happened he would regret it for the remainder of his life and always have the memory of his loss.

The two continued their ride in silence. Aaron, for the very first time, realizing how lonely it must have been for Sera all these years when he had been away on his trade routes. He had always assumed that the children would keep her company. How wrong that had been. What sort of adult conversation could she have ever enjoyed just chatting with the children? In all this time she had never voiced one single word of discontent. He recalled how eager and excited she always was at his return. How she sometimes talked a mile a minute, bursting with energy. Now he realized she was thirsting for the company of an adult, needing the confirmation she was still viable in the grown-up world. God! He was such an ignorant husband. He loved her to distraction, how could he have put her through this misery? He imagined all the days, weeks and months of stifled monotony she had tolerated. He could have gotten a job with Mica. Maybe the pay wouldn't have been much but at least he would have been home as often as he liked. Their needs were simple, they could manage quite well without this trading trek every year.

Aaron and Gideon didn't notice the other's serious expression. Each had a very important subject to discuss with their wife and each was anxious about their spouse's reaction. There were big changes forecast for the imminent future. Gideon felt that Fila would like to stay for her mother's sake.

The following days spent on the trail homeward passed uneventfully. The weather held clear and warm. The horses, even though burdened with the new goods, felt frisky being out on the trail again. Apple especially, since her injury had healed. When they at last reached the homestead, the horses picked up their pace sensing release from their burdens and a good feed. The two men felt the same. Anxious to bathe, eat a good home-cooked meal, and look forward to their wives' company.

Buddy had let the women know the men had returned. He was running circles around the horsemen, yipping with joy. Sera and Fila stood on the porch watching the advancing figures while the three girls, Alea leading the way, raced toward the men trying to be the first to get a hug from their father. Gideon only had eyes for Fila. His eyes traveling down her trim figure and proud stance, her long hair pulled back from her beautiful face, a warm smile welcoming her husband home. His heart seemed to lodge itself high in his throat. He couldn't have spoken a single word if his life had depended on it. She was his love, the reason for every happiness now and until his last breath on earth. Whatever he could do to complete her life and fill it with contentment, he would. For a moment the memory of his grandfather's home caused a pang of loss, then he put it away. His only concern was of Fila. She was his future and he hers. Sliding from his horse he gathered her into his arms, at last being able to speak words of love. "I'm home," he whispered pulling her close.

When Fila looked into her husband's eyes, saw the expression on his face, she was immediately aware that something of importance had occurred. "I can see you're upset, did you and Father have a disagreement?" Glancing over at Aaron she could see he was distraught but did not look angry. Gideon shook his head. Fila gave a thankful sigh of relief, whatever the problem at least it had nothing to do with how the two men got along. Pressing a warm kiss to her husband's lips she drew him into the cottage, Aaron and the rest of the family following close at their heels.

Questions were foremost, Sera first to ask, "What happened? This is only the beginning of July, you never get home before autumn. Was there trouble with some of the tribes, or sickness amongst them that you felt it unwise to stay?" Inspecting her husband for any signs of illness she could see he looked very hale and even a little heavier. "Aaron, do not keep me in suspense one moment longer. I want to know." Sera stood with her arms crossed, a frown beginning to tighten her brow.

Aaron, with a happy grin on his face, pulled her over near the table, sat her down and took a seat opposite her. He began to explain everything that had occurred, starting with Apple's lameness. While the tale was unfolding Fila put on the kettle for tea and began to make sandwiches with the fresh-baked bread her mother had made that morning. Gideon occasionally added a word or two until their adventurous story was concluded.

For a moment there was complete silence until the full meaning of what had occurred, the unexpected consequences that unfolded simply because of Apple's injury, was made clear. Never again, need Aaron be absent for so many months. The worry each felt for the other during those long empty days, the loneliness, and the ache that began to build at the first lost sight of the beloved, only to ease at last when they once again came into view.

Sera bent her head trying to hide her tears of happiness. Aaron gently took her chin, lifted her face, and then with his thumb carefully brushed them away. "Sweetheart, I should have been more considerate. I don't know why I never thought of a different system of trading. All those months, in all those years that I wasted traveling. I promise you it is finished. From now on it will only be a few months in late spring that I'll be gone." Aaron drew Sera to her feet and pulled her close to his heart pressing a kiss to the top of her head. A deep feeling of release seemed to swell within, as though a heavy burden had been lifted from his shoulders. He had never, until now, realized how much he had dreaded leaving his family each year for such a long period of time. Life would be so much easier now. His loneliness had unknowingly weighted his very soul each time he'd had to leave.

Fila placed the food on the table, everyone taking their seats. It was nice having the family all together. She noticed that Gideon was sitting quietly seeming to be in deep thought. He looked over at her then quickly down as though he didn't want her to read any expression on his face, inside he was in turmoil. He had seen the pleasure Fila had exhibited having her family around her. Could he truly ask her to give this up and go with him to his family home? He dreaded she could very well refuse; he couldn't blame her if she did. This was a wonderfully warm, loving household; they had welcomed him as though he had been a long-lost relative. He loved them, the last thing he wanted to do was cause hurt. They were his family now too. He wondered if he should even pose the question of leaving to Fila. If only there was some way to solve this dilemma. Then, as though summoned, the thought surfaced that he did indeed have a place to go. It was sitting in a drawer in their room in the barn. He lifted his head with a smile. Fila saw it, her lips turned up in a grin of pure pleasure. With a sigh of relief she heard her stomach give a growl of hunger, the food looked wonderful after all. She helped herself to the other half sandwich and refilled her glass with milk.

The remainder of the day was spent sorting through some of the goods, separating Mica's fur pelts and a few other items that would be taken to him on the morrow. Mina and Nia were overcome with happiness at the two prettily decorated deerskin vests they received for their two dolls. There were copper bowls showing the indentation of the pounding tool, winter boots that reached almost to the knees lined with fur, moccasins, woven reed baskets and mats, purses decorated with dyed quills, rabbit-fur capes, braided ropes of deerskin. It would take several days to decide what they would keep and which goods would be turned over to Mica to trade for them. He always received a commission.

After the evening meal Gideon and Fila retired to their room in the barn, the three girls to the attic, Aaron and Sera to their corner bed. Too tired to carry on conversations, all in the cottage were soon fast asleep. As for Gideon and Fila, they were sitting respectively on the bed and nearby chair, discussing the day's events. Gideon was itching to open his Book of Destiny and try to discover a solution to his problem. Better if Fila would feel tired and fall asleep, he didn't want her to know what was bothering him.

Fila sensed Gideon was edgy. He kept glancing toward the chest of drawers as though something there was upsetting him. Finally, she could stand it no longer. "Gideon, what is wrong with you tonight, you're as nervous as a mouse listening for a cat. Please, honey, I can feel trouble in the air, we cannot start our marriage with secrets. You must tell me." Fila watched as her husband's face showed first uncertainty, then anxiety, and at last resignation. He leaned over, taking her hand in his and began to speak.

"My one desire is to make you happy, Fila. I want to make a home for us. A place where one day we can welcome our grandchildren who will come visit. I wasn't going to tell you my feelings because I know how much you love your family and would want to stay with them, but I also think you should know how I feel too. You know my grandfather's house. It's well built, near the village where there is plenty of work that I can make a good living at. There are other young women who would welcome you as a friend. You would have a full happy life there with me. If you desire to live here with your parents, I will accept and make a home for us. Aaron has already said he will help build our own house nearby." Gideon arose, stepped to the chest and opened the top drawer, withdrawing his black book. He carried it to Fila and placed it in her lap.

She had never really looked at the book before, it was so similar to hers they could almost have been twins. Somehow, she knew it was different. A wafting scent of sage began to wrap itself around her. She recognized it was from the old woman she had seen in Gideon's home. His grandmother, Nola was her name. A deep sense of unease began to creep up her spine causing the hairs at the nape of her neck to stand upright.

"Gideon, put this book back immediately. This is not for me to see, any more than you should see into my own Book of Destiny. Somehow they are intertwined but I know not how. Please, now. Then I will tell you what I feel we should do."

Fila watched as Gideon replaced the book and closed the drawer, returning to sit next to her on the edge of the bed. Taking his hand she began to caress it as she put her feelings into words she hoped he would be happy to hear. "I do love my family, but my heart is yours until my very last breath. I like your grandfather's house, it will be a good home for us and our future family. We'll tell my parents tomorrow and get ready to leave."

Fila slept poorly, thinking of how her parents would take the news of their leaving. She knew deep in her heart, this was the right thing to do. She sensed that Gideon needed to establish his own home and provide what was necessary for their success. He would have stayed just to please her. That would have been the very worst thing for a happy marriage. He would have always felt her father was responsible for their well-being instead of being able to take pride in. his own accomplishments.

When the early sun began to lighten the eastern sky Fila arose. Giving a nudge to her husband while she pulled on her moccasins, she leaned over his dozing figure to plant a kiss on his brow. "Wake up, sleepy head, this is going to be a busy day. Before doing anything else we should tell my parents of our decision during breakfast while everyone is present, then questions can be answered before we begin packing." With a quick toss the bedding was thrown back and Gideon grasped Fila about her waist flinging her to the bed and tickling her until tears of laughter left her breathless. Evading his clutch she sprang for the door, flung it open and raced down the path, Gideon in close pursuit. It only took a moment for him to realize he was in his long johns—the chase was not to be. Fila gave him a merry wave as he turned back to the barn. She continued on to the cottage to help her mother prepare breakfast.

Breakfast was almost over when Fila spoke of the decision Gideon and she had made. For a moment not a word was uttered, as though the magnitude of the decision was too much to grasp, then quiet questions were asked about when they planned to leave, and what help could be offered.

Aaron had expected this. He had become well acquainted with Gideon, knew the pride he possessed and what he wanted to accomplish to make his marriage a happy, stable relationship. He didn't blame him. He had felt the same when he and Sera had wed. It was an ingrained trait in most men of ambition. Aaron put his arm around Sera pulling her against his side, knowing the contact would help give her the strength to contain her tears. Alea, Mina and Nia crowded about their elder sister trying not to let disappointment spoil the last of the precious time they would have together, knowing a memory was best treasured if a smile could be recalled instead of sadness.

By midmorning they were ready to leave. Night had been saddled, side bags packed with goods and a generous bundle fastened behind the saddle completed his load. Aaron had given Fila Apple, who was also well laden although not overly so. Aaron would ride Lady with them as far as Mica's, where he intended to drop off some of the trade goods. Sera had packed food for the trip. They would reach Mica's by evening, camp there overnight, and then continue on their way in the early morning. In about five days, weather permitting, they should arrive at the cottage near Umer.

The next morning, long before sunup, Gideon and Fila were on their way. "I remember dreaming of your grandmother after I had been transported to her home after looking into that blue suede pouch," Fila said with a smile. "I had fallen and hurt myself climbing from the attic. It was such a strange lifelike occurrence. I even sensed you in the attic but of course it was all my imagination. It seemed so real, her sitting in her rocking chair next to the bed, I could smell the scent of sage so clearly. I instantly liked her, and she me."

Gideon turned a quizzical expression on his face. "I dreamt about you in the attic, saw you poking your head up through the trap door. I felt I was actually there."

They both fell silent contemplating the eerie events that had drawn them together. Maybe someday they would discover the mystery of why. For now, the only thing that mattered was that they were together and on their way to a new life in Umer. Slowly, they became aware of the sound of hoof beats growing louder with each passing second. Pulling their mounts to a halt they waited for the first sight of the rider to come into view.

Aaron had Lady at a full run. When he saw them he let out a yell of greeting, racing full tilt until he reached their side and pulled back on the reins. Lady snorted, breathing rapidly, her sides quivering from exertion. "Thank goodness I caught you before you had ridden too far, Sera would have nailed my hide to the barn. I forgot to give you this. I don't know what it is, she just said to tell you to be careful because it's breakable." Aaron extended the wrapped and snugly bound package to Fila, who then slipped it into the large leather pouch hanging from her saddle. It had felt soft to the touch. She assumed her mother may have insulated it with sheep's wool.

With a smile lighting her face, Fila felt a burst of happiness at the chance of enjoying a few last minutes with her father, it had seemed there was never enough time to say goodbye. Nudging Apple closer she leaned over and placed a kiss on Aaron's sun-browned cheek. "I'm happy you brought the package, Daddy, so we have these few extra minutes. I promise to write as soon as we get settled."

Aaron gave a tug to one of her shiny tresses. "I'll ride every week to Mica's watching for that letter, honey. We know you'll be well taken care of, you're in good hands. We liked Gideon from the first moment we met him. We'll just need to know you're both well and everything's okay with you two. Get along with you now, if I'm too late getting back home you know your mother will have my head." Aaron watched as the two turned their horses, gave a final wave of farewell, and continued on their way.

He'd ride Lady a little slower on the way home, even stop at Mica's for lunch and a quick game of checkers. He drew in a deep breath of fresh air thinking, as he often did when enjoying such a beautiful day, life was perfectly wonderful, he couldn't wish for anything better. By noon he had reached the trading post.

After turning Lady into the corral he made his way to the front door calling Mica to get out the checkerboard. The back room was empty, he was surprised his friend was nowhere in sight. Thinking Mica must be in the barn he hurried out to lend a hand with any chores his friend needed doing. When he discovered that the barn was also empty he began to get seriously worried. Mica would not ride off without tacking a note to the door telling when he would return. Walking around to the back of the barn he saw Mica's horse standing quietly next to a crumpled figure on the ground.

"My God! Mica, are you all right?" Aaron knelt at the old man's side checking for signs of injury, not seeing any indication of bruising or broken bones. Hurrying to the water trough he soaked his bandana and then returned to the unconscious man to wipe his feverish brow and place the cool wetness against the back of Mica's neck. Impatient with the unresponsiveness he gathered his friend into his muscular arms, carried him back inside the trading post and placed him on the bed.

When Mica regained consciousness he, at first, wasn't aware of what had happened. Then, as his mind cleared, he recalled the sudden bout of dizziness that had felled him like a pole axe. He was too old to feel embarrassment but for the very first time, he felt a secret twinge of fear that seemed to take root in the very center of his being. He had to acknowledge the fact that he was growing old. He watched Aaron busily fixing tea, filling a heavy mug, then setting it on the table next to the bed and helping him sit so he could drink the hot liquid. He peered into Aaron's eyes intently, searching for some sign that would tell him his feelings about the man were correct. What was quite obvious to Mica was that Aaron had a true concern about his well-being, an open honesty that couldn't possibly be misunderstood. He relaxed against the bed pillow, confident his intuition about the younger man was as right as rain on a spring day. He felt better already. Sipping at the hot tea, Mica reached a decision that had long been forthcoming; it was time for him to put his final decisions in order before he kicked the bucket. He hated the thought that his time was now limited. No longer could he add the possible years ahead and say he had plenty of time to accomplish all that he desired. His decision made he sat up, swinging his legs off the bed, and placed his feet on the floor. Aaron stood close by ready to lend a helping hand. With a final swallow, he handed the empty cup to Aaron and carefully stood upright. When no indication of dizziness was felt he leaned over, pulled open the top drawer in the bedside table and withdrew a sheet of writing paper. He already had a pencil stub he carried in his shirt pocket. Making his way to the kitchen table he sat, placed the blank paper in front of himself and began to write in the clear precise penmanship he had learned at the Christian school on the Indian reservation that had been his childhood home.

Aaron busied himself washing out the mugs, looking out the window at the scenic surroundings of forest, fields of meadowland, white-capped mountains in the misty distance, the deep blue of the sky with not a cloud in sight. He realized Sera would wonder if anything important could be keeping him. He smiled to himself knowing she never counted on his speedy return anytime he was visiting Mica. She knew how much they enjoyed their checker games. When he at last turned from his reverie he saw that Mica was just sealing an envelope, the missive he had worked on so diligently had been completed. Mica handed it to Aaron, who noticed it was addressed to him.

"What's going on, Mica, what do you want me to do with this?" Aaron had a puzzled expression on his face wondering why in the world Mica would give him a sealed envelope?

Mica was enjoying every moment of the mystery that had his friend stymied. "I have written my last will and testament. It's up to you to see that my final wishes are carried out to the letter, other than that, there's not a single thing for you to do. Now, how about that game of checkers we were going to play as soon as you came back from your rush to catch up with your daughter?" The words were barely uttered before the checkerboard was set up and each was contemplating their first move. Ah! they each thought, this time I will beat the britches off him.

The afternoon passed pleasantly, each winning two games. It was getting too late to begin a fifth. Aaron knew he should start for home; it would be dark before he arrived. He would let Lady have her head once night set in, she would find her way quite easily.

With a wave goodbye Aaron, confident that Mica was back to normal after his fainting spell, turned Lady toward home. It was not yet twilight, sun still hovering above the distant tree tops, eastern sky already a deep violet slowly making its way toward the westerly setting sun. It was too cool for mosquitoes so thankfully the ride home would be pleasant. Aaron nudged Lady into a gallop making good time while he could still sight any rabbit holes that could cause her injury. They still had miles to ride when darkness enveloped them. Now Lady would use her sense of smell to avoid holes and her instincts to guide them unerringly as she slowed to a walk. The sound of crickets, the hoot of an owl and the song of toads were the sweet music accompanying them as they wended their way through the night. This was the latest Aaron had ever arrived home. When he entered the homestead site he could see a lighted window in the distance which gave him a warm feeling of welcome. Riding Lady into the barn he unsaddled her, trying to give her a good brushing while Blacky, her colt, nuzzled her happily. It was the first time they had been separated for this length of time. Satisfied nothing else needed attending, Aaron made his way to the cottage, tired and happy with how his day had turned out. He really loved that old man. He remembered the envelope he had placed in his shirt pocket. Removing it, he glanced briefly at his name scribbled across its surface before placing it on the kitchen table.

Undressing, then snuffing out the lamp Sera had placed in the window, Aaron clambered into bed pressing himself against the warmth of Sera's back, flinging an arm across her recumbent form. Soon soft muffled snores sounded in Sera's wakeful ear. Now she could truly fall asleep, no longer listening for a distant sound that would signify her husband's safe return home. Soon, she also was fast asleep.

Meanwhile, out in the barn a shadowy figure was searching the room that Gideon had used. Not a single item remained in the emptied drawers of the chest, nor anyplace throughout. There was, however, an essence that seemed to permeate the room's atmosphere. A lingering scent that almost made the figure drool in anticipation of his acquisition. He knew where to find the new treasure that had been described in his *Path of Discovery* book. The herb sage was linked to its creation many centuries ago and was also instrumental in keeping the magic alive and potent. Who would have believed that leather would survive after all those years and not disintegrate or turn to dust? It was a very rare find and he would have it, regardless of how far he had to travel or how long it would take. He felt a very slight pang of disappointment, but not too much. The thrill of excitement at planning his new quest, the challenge of the search, the danger of being caught, the pure excitement of finally laying his hands on the very prize that led him into unknown peril, was more precious than he could even explain to himself. Ah! The hunt had begun.

Slipping out of the barn Luther made his way off the premises, through the forest, and back to his cavern home. In a few days' time his plans would solidify. For now he must gather together the things he would need to prepare himself for his journey. In substance, he must change everything about himself, make himself into a completely different person. No one must suspect he was anything other than who he would portray. It meant the difference between success and failure.

The hour was late, time to bed. Making himself comfortable, pulling the bedding partly over his shoulders and finding that perfect place on the pillow to rest his head, Luther closed his eyes letting the curtain of sleep slowly descend over his idly meandering thoughts. He sank deeply into the oblivion of darkness.

Early sunrise found Luther busily searching, packing, concocting potions and preparing what he would need. He would make a trip to the trading post tomorrow to purchase a horse and a burro, and then leave the following day after assuming his disguise. On second thought, it would be good to try it out on Mica, see if he was recognized. His anticipation was boundless. This would be another exciting quest. He could feel it in his bones. His plans were perfect.

Chapter Eleven

Fila and Gideon were within hours of reaching their new home well before sundown. It would give them a chance to make up their bed, open windows, sweep out the floors and have a decent meal sitting at a table instead of hunkered down on the ground. "I can hardly wait to see the place again," Fila murmured to herself, recalling the intense pleasure she had felt being in Granny's home. The old woman still seemed so real. Even now, knowing the bump on her head had probably caused her hallucinations, she could picture the old woman in the rocking chair. Fila smiled to herself. She must have been really dizzy to imagine it moving.

Gideon looked over at his wife seeing the sweet smile curving her lips, crinkling the laugh lines at the corners of her eyes. If he lived to be one hundred he would never know how he had become so lucky. He was about to pull Night over to her side when he realized they had reached the crest of a hill and could see the town in the near distance with their new homestead only a few miles away. "Look, Fila, we're almost there. If you like we could head for town first to get supplies." Gideon could almost read Fila's mind, knew she would want to get home first. Tomorrow would be soon enough for shopping and introductions to his friends. He grinned at her response.

"Truthfully, Gid, I think I'd rather get home first. It's going to take a while to make it presentable. As soon as we get there you unload the horses, then brush and feed them. I want a clean bed to sleep in, a bath and a hot meal. If you stoke the fire to heat the water while I make the bed, then I'll do the sweeping while you fill the bathing tub. After I bathe, I'll prepare supper while you bathe. Then we can both enjoy a good meal, get a restful night's sleep and make our plans in the morning."

Gideon's grin looked a mile wide. This was his wife. A get-up-and-go type of gal who suited him to a "T." Life was so pleasant when two worked together as one. Following Fila's plans, by day's end they were sitting cozily in front of the banked fire, a final cup of tea in hand, well sated with Fila's tasty meal. They were bathed, the home clean and neat, except for the bundles they had brought with them which they'd sort through in the morning.

When Fila's yawns started Gideon mimicking her, it was time for bed. Extinguishing the lamp they quickly undressed in the dark. Gideon picked the bedside next to the wall, which pleased Fila since she was always an earlier riser. A final kiss good night, the exhaustion from their travels and exertions on arrival at their home provided them a deep, dreamless, refreshing sleep in their soft, clean bed.

Tomorrow would be another busy day. There were provisions to purchase, trading to do and Gideon had a huge surprise in store for Fila. He had made arrangements when last he had been here, when he had been so fearful someone else might win her hand in marriage instead of him. It had been a gesture to bring him good luck and he couldn't help thinking that it possibly had.

Morning, bright sunshine peeking through the eastern window, Fila had breakfast halfway prepared. Pan bread, bacon, fried potatoes and onions. Gideon awoke to the aroma of his favorite start to his day. Hurriedly dressing, a quick wash to his face and hands, a brush through his hair, he was ready to eat. Today he would keep Fila busy in town for most of the day. His black curly hair still glistening with water, his sky-blue eyes sparkling with secret pleasure, Fila couldn't help admiring her husband's good looks. He seemed very pleased with himself this morning. She gave him a quizzical look, then one of her generous smiles that lit up her entire face. She adored him. What more could she ever want in life but this man who had stolen her heart. It would be quite obvious to anyone who looked at them they were definitely still newlyweds.

After breakfast was finished, table and dishes cleared, washed and put away, they readied themselves to travel to Umer. The horses were well rested and anxious to be on the road again not toting a burden as they had been. It was less than an hour's ride at a leisurely pace over a hill, down a swale across another low mesa-type hill and then into the outskirts of the village. As they began to meet others hurrying to get supplies or visit friends, Gideon began introducing his new bride to his friends. Fila couldn't remember a single name to connect to a specific person. "Don't worry about it, hon," Gideon said with a grin, seeing the little worry frown between her eyebrows. "They only have your name to remember, they don't expect you to remember everyone on your very first visit. Before we stop at Zena's I want you to meet Smitty's wife, Verna.. I have some business to take care of at the sawmill and will only be gone just long enough for you to take a cup of tea with her and get to know their two kids. You'll like them, and Verna knows everyone around here, even some in Carltown. That's a village a few days' ride west of here. Of course, if you'd rather go to the mill with me that's fine too but the place is dusty and really noisy." Gideon had his fingers crossed she would opt for teatime and she did.

After introductions, waiting until he saw the two women comfortably engaged in conversation, Gideon excused himself and headed for the mill. This would be a tricky maneuver to instigate but he had the utmost confidence in his pal Amos, the smartest man he knew.

Amos had seen Gideon ride into town with the young woman at his side. He had immediately called his helpers to load the various items onto his wagon, sending the two seasoned handymen to take it to Gideon's cottage and assemble everything in the place Gideon had selected. It would be a close call with the young bride anxious to get back home and finish unpacking. When Gideon arrived the wagon was just moving out of sight at the end of the road.

"Thanks, Amos, I appreciate this and owe you a big one." Gideon couldn't help grinning at his friend. Just the thought of the look on Fila's face when she entered their home and saw what was sitting there, all ready and waiting for the touch of her hand, made him feel like kicking up his heels and dancing a jig. "Do I owe you anything?"

"Nope! We pretty well evened up on what was due the last time you were here. Didn't have any trouble getting the thing and since it wasn't assembled, it didn't take up very much space. It was kept out of sight, but you know how rumors get around. I think probably the whole town knows what your bride is getting for her wedding gift. It made a few of the ladies pretty jealous and some of the men were coming in huffing about me not hiding the thing better. Fact is, I got two orders out and expect the shipment later this summer. Guess some fellas weren't getting much sleep what with their wives burnin' their ears off asking why they couldn't have one too. Have to say it's sure been good for my business what with everyone stopping in to look at the assembly catalog that was sent with your shipment."

For a while the two friends caught up on all their news until finally Gideon left to fetch Fila. They would spend several more hours at the trading post getting supplies and visiting with Zena and his wife, Ella, who was the town's mid-wife and women's health care and family sickness expert. The man at the barber shop took care of everything else, like tooth extractions, sewing gashes up or general injury stuff. Fila had said she wanted to meet Ella. It suited Gideon just fine, the more time they spent, the more sure he would feel about getting home late enough so his surprise wasn't spoiled.

By the time their visiting was over and shopping completed it was late afternoon. Gideon had seen Amos' wagon return and knew it was safe to head for home. It was a leisurely ride. He and Fila felt a new closeness that had slowly built during their very first appearance as a couple at the places they had attended that day. The serious discussions they had over supplies, heads together inspecting the various items, agreeing on what to spend their money on. It was a distinctly different feeling of unity.

When they reached home Gideon dismounted, helped Fila down and placed several light packages in her hands while he grabbed a few others and commented, "Let's get this stuff inside then you can start supper while I tend the horses." He hurried to open the door for her, standing aside as she entered.

Fila had only stepped a few feet into the room when she gave a gasp of surprise, then a high-pitched yelp of delight. "Gideon, how did you manage this? Dropping the packs to the floor she flung her arms about her husband kissing every inch of his face. Still not satisfied that she was expressing enough gratitude, she at last grasped him by his ears and proceeded to kiss his mouth until he gasped for breath. By now his face was quite red and truthfully, he was sure he felt a few drops of perspiration on his forehead. He still had hold of the packages, too overcome to even notice.

When finally Gideon placed his bundles on the table they both stood in front of the brand-spanking-new iron cook range, admiring the fine attributes it contained. It had a large water reservoir built onto its side which, when kept filled, would provide all their hot water, there were six cooking areas, a warming shelf at the top of the rear panel, and a baking chamber. Amos' helpers had set the range on the left side of the fireplace, chiseling out one of the stones in the wall to accommodate the stove vent pipe. The water reservoir had been filled, the fire laid, ready to be lit. Everything ready for the young couple to begin preparing a meal as soon as the surface became hot enough for cooking.

Taking embers from the fireplace Gideon placed them carefully around the stacked wood and watched the flame take hold. Latching the door they could see through the isinglass windows in the door the fire begin to build. The scent of heating metal, the warmth beginning to circulate through the room, the young couple was absorbed in the excitement of watching what was happening. When a slight swirl of smoke began to circulate through the room Gideon realized the vent lever was closed and hurried to open it.

A few hours later Fila was cooking their supper. She browned beef in the iron fry pan adding some onions, cornbread was baking in the oven, and a pan of potatoes was slowly browning in the second oven. When they finally sat down to table both were famished. However, as a new start to their life here in their own home, they bowed their heads and gave thanks for all the good things the day had brought. It would be a habit they would adhere to for the rest of their married life.

When at last they had eaten their fill, cleared the table and washed the dishes with the hot water from the range reservoir, they sat with a final cup of tea before bedtime. When they climbed into their bed Gideon pulled Fila close to his heart. Soon they were fast asleep. The activities of the day finally overcoming their youthful exuberance.

The next morning began with Fila preparing breakfast on her new range. She would need some new pots with flat bottoms. The ones used for the fireplace were round and not suited. With a light heart she set the table, filled the mugs with hot tea and called Gideon. He strode into the room finishing tucking his shirt into his trousers, lifted her into his arms and then tossed her over his shoulder. Carrying her out the door he deposited her next to himself placing an arm about her waist. "Look, Fila. Have you ever seen such a beautiful sunrise? The sky all rosy gold with those puffy clouds floating past picking up the reflections?" Gideon breathed in a huge lungful of the fresh dewy air. The scent of wild violets growing nearby, the call of a meadowlark floating on the morning breeze made the morning so perfect that Gideon couldn't find the words to express his profound pleasure at standing here next to the woman he loved. Fila admired the beauty for a few moments then, realizing breakfast was getting cold, drew Gideon back into their home and sat him down at the table. With a warm smile she filled his plate with the bacon, eggs and leftover potatoes from yesterday's supper. He had to admit, nothing had ever tasted so good.

The morning was spent sorting through articles and finding places suitable for them. When at last the cupboard had been restocked, clothing folded into the chest Gideon had brought down from the attic, and all the miscellaneous items from home put away including her treasure chest, the only item left was the round padded package that her father had hurried to bring her. It was sitting on the shelf awaiting her attention. Fila didn't feel like hurrying. She prepared tea, baked corn muffins and then sat with Gideon at the table discussing where they would plant their garden. Carrots, potatoes, cabbage, cucumbers for pickles and relish. They could get apples, pears and peaches from neighbors until they could harvest their own. Gideon had found dozens of canning jars in the attic. He planned to add a pantry and an extra room to the home which they would need when children arrived. For a moment he caught his breath at the thought of fatherhood and the responsibilities it would present. Maybe, just in case, he would start on the additions this spring. It was always nice to have extra space. For now, getting some fruit tree saplings planted would be smart. He finished his tea and muffins, saying he would return before supper. A quick kiss on Fila's cheek, then selecting some of his trade goods to dicker with, he filled a satchel and left.

Fila watched him ride away. This was the first time she had been alone since their arrival. Expectantly, she waited. Although there was the faint hint of sage lingering in the room nothing out of the ordinary occurred. A twinge of disappointment made her frown for a moment. What had she expected? Did she really think Granny Nola was going to appear out of the blue, sit in the rocking chair and have a chatty conversation with her new granddaughter-in-law? Still, there was a quiet peace throughout the cottage. She could almost picture the old woman busily tatting lacy doilies or antimacassars for her husband to rest his head against when he sat in his favorite chair.

Fila became aware of a thread of unease that seemed to distort the atmosphere in the room, like a small ripple disturbing the glassy surface of a lake in the predawn hours before the sun's heat stirred the cool air into breezes. Trying to distract herself from the discomforting chill that was edging its way up her spine, she reached for the bundled package her father had given her. Untying the ribbon, unwinding the layered wool, the mystery was revealed. The gazing Globe sat before her, its swirling mists drawing her eyes to search the depths of its secrets. She remembered what an important place it had occupied with her family when she had been at the Winter Forest. She wondered why her mother felt it necessary she have it. She realized her mother's intuition was not to be reckoned with, maybe there was a need for her to keep the Globe. She was about to place it up on the cupboard shelf out of danger of being accidentally broken when she noticed a vague, shadowy figure beginning to emerge from the depths of the mist. Sitting back against the chair she concentrated on the slowly developing image.

How strange, she had no idea who this person could be, knowing without doubt that she had never set eyes on him before. His black hair hung to his shoulders meeting the edges of his full black beard and moustache which covered most of his features. Part of a heavy gold chain holding a strangely shaped cross resting on his chest, was barely visible beneath the growth. A pair of thick-lensed glasses perched on the bridge of his nose. He was garbed completely in black and toted a black leather satchel.

For a while Fila watched the stranger as he rode his tall rangy-looking sorrel horse following a trail that looked vaguely familiar. She tried to recall the location, without success. The image slowly began to disintegrate until only drifting mists remained. She felt curious as to why she had been given this view of a complete stranger for such a short length of time. Wondering whether it portrayed an event of any significance, she carefully placed the Globe on the highest shelf.

When she realized the position of the sun, she couldn't believe it was so late in the afternoon. Where had all the time gone? She could have sworn that Gideon had ridden away only moments ago, impossible she had wasted so much time sitting at the table.

Adding more wood to the stove, measuring out flour, adding an egg, salt, and cold water, she made dough. Rolled it flat, then again jellyroll style. She sliced it into wide noodles, unrolled each and hung them all to dry on a broomstick balanced across two chair backs. She pared, sliced and diced vegetables and a large onion into the water-filled pot, added a dollop of chicken fat for extra flavor, then a good dash of salt and pepper. Placing the lid atop, she busied herself with the rest of the preparations.

When Gideon arrived home he brushed Night, then fed and watered both horses. Placing the young fruit saplings temporarily in a loose patch of soil he spaded up, he soaked them with water to prevent the roots from drying. Tomorrow they would select where the beginnings of their new orchard would be planted, also staking out where the vegetable garden would be established. So many things to do in a short length of time. He thought of the cottage addition, building a barn, putting up a corral, things he could begin after the garden had been planted. All together it seemed overwhelming but taking one project at a time, doing it right, it would all be accomplished. Oh! Not everything this year or, maybe, even the next, but he could picture it in his mind, a real homestead, something to pass on to his children and grandchildren. A thing of beauty to remember him by.

The aroma of vegetable soup made his mouth water with expectation. Fila had the table set with a plate of homemade biscuits, bowls filled with steaming, brothy vegetables and noodles. Dusk was descending. The oil lamp, chimney clean and bright, sat in the center of the table casting its golden glow on Fila's smiling face, her gleaming black hair. Gideon felt such a powerful burst of love and pride in her beauty, wisdom and abilities to make their place a welcoming home that he was overcome with emotion. She was truly his to have and hold from this day forward. Bowing their heads they said their prayer of thanks for all they had been given that day. Fila was about to mention the vision she had seen in the Globe but before she could utter the first word, some instinct told her it would be best to keep silent. It had been a disturbing scene revealing nothing other than the strangeness of the man and the uneasy aura that seemed to saturate the very depths of the mist itself. The span of time that had elapsed while she had been gazing into the orb was also upsetting to her. Where could those hours have disappeared? Surely, not with her just sitting at the table? She recalled the familiarity of the trail the stranger traveled. That was when the memory of the distinct scent of the surrounding vegetation came back to her. Now she felt truly mystified. How could this be? Concentrating on what she had experienced while standing at the edge of the trail viewing the subject, she remembered the feeling of a light breeze through her hair and the warmth of the afternoon sun.

Gideon's voice disrupted her reveries. Supper was over, the table had been cleared and she found herself standing at the window gazing at the descending twilight. "What did you say, honey? I was admiring the very last colors of sunset." Fila turned to her husband, a slight smile tweaking the corners of her lips, still not completely in the present.

"I said it's a beautiful evening, let's take a walk before nightfall and get a feeling for where we want our plantings to go." Gideon reached for Fila's hand, drawing her toward him and placing a kiss in her palm. Tugging her toward the door they stepped outside into the cool duskiness of day's end. "I love this special time. Once, years ago, a man came to visit my grandfather, Calis. He had traveled half the year to return home from a place as far west as a person could go. He said the one thing he missed most of all was twilight. Out west, at the end of day, nighttime just sort of drops down like a curtain with no in-between. I couldn't imagine ending a day like that, it's just too quick."

Fila thought about what Gideon had said. Sometimes twilight lasted a while. It was a quiet, restful time when shapes and colors sort of blended together leaving soft outlines and muted shadings at the very edge of night. Then the fireflies appeared flitting about, flashing lights that youngsters have always tried to catch. A little too early in the season for them now though.

Hand in hand they meandered over and around the grounds finally selecting the place that would be ideal for their orchard. She thought too, of all the fruit plantings her father had collected over the years, eventually they'd get cuttings from all their berry bushes. It would be nice having a parcel set aside, separate from the orchard and vegetable garden.

With a burst of energy Fila took off running for their house, Gideon close behind having a hard time catching up to her. They both stopped a few steps short of their front door, neither one feeling too much out of breath. For a while they sat, side by side, on the steps watching the rise of a full moon. It was one of those enchanting evenings when everything looked like a beautifully painted scene, picture perfect in every way. When the crickets began to sing and the mosquitoes bite, it was time to go inside.

Fila followed their nightly ritual and prepared tea. They sat quietly, discussing the day's events, sipping their hot, honeyed beverage. That's when Fila decided to tell Gideon about the gazing Globe and what she had seen and experienced earlier. They both agreed it was unusual; however, there didn't seem to be any reason to worry. They dismissed it, readying themselves for bed.

Mica sold the sorrel for a good price. The buyer had been clever at bargaining but it took more than a Bible-thumper to beat Mica at making a nice profit for himself, at least with strangers. When it came to neighbors though, he felt a bit differently about making money off them. Although the preacher had seemed friendly enough, something about the man had rubbed him the wrong way, he couldn't exactly put his finger on what it was. Maybe it had been that queer gleam in the fellow's eyes when he had first walked into the Post talking about finding a good horse. It was as though he had been laughing at a good joke, putting one over on old Mica. Huh! That would be the day. He'd been around when that fella had still been in dappers, or whatever those darn things were called. Mica could still see the stranger in the distance as he kneed his mount into a gallop, sure seemed bent on getting somewhere in a hurry. Not at all like the regular traveling minister who made the circuit each spring. There were always new babes to baptize, or dearly departed, buried since his last visit, needing some prayers said over their resting places so that the bereaved felt better, and of course new unions to bless and make legal in the eyes of God.

Mica swept out the store, straightening some of the merchandise and wiping the counter off where flour, sugar, tobacco residue had a habit of accumulating from the customers' purchases. He wanted to have everything finished early, feed the stock, get the eggs from his prized layers before Aaron arrived to spend the day playing checkers and inspecting for any repairs that needed fixing around the Post. Since then Mica had decided to leave it to him in his will. There wasn't another person who deserved it more. Maybe, if Mica was lucky, he'd even spend the night. It wasn't often they got a chance just sit, talk and enjoy their favorite game.

When Aaron rode up an hour later Mica was waiting for him at the corral. Lady was unsaddled and turned loose in the enclosure, a good sign Aaron wouldn't head for home 'til morning. The two men made their way to the post, stopping only a moment for Mica to show his friend the new rooster he had acquired, the old one having met his demise by a fox. The henhouse needed a little extra fence work to keep the critter out. It took only a short time for Aaron to do the repairs, making sure it was secure against another intrusion.

When at last the two were sitting at the table, savoring a cup of Mica's strong, sugared coffee, Aaron learned about the new preacher who had purchased the sorrel stallion. He was slightly disappointed, having been contemplating purchasing the animal, however, on second thought, it would be wiser to have Lady bred once again with Gideon's handsome black sire, Night. Maybe next spring plans could be made to visit them in Umer.

The checker game began, proceeding through the rest of the day with only short interventions for Mica to take care of customers who always commented about the beautiful black mare in Mica's corral, which was not for sale. At suppertime Mica fixed cornbread and baked beans mixed with onions and chunks of ham. He had opened one jar of spiced peaches from the half dozen he had taken in trade from Mrs. Perkinson last year when she had run out of sugar during canning season. They were the best darn peaches either had ever tasted.

Early the next morning, after enjoying a hearty breakfast, Aaron departed for home. It was a beautiful morning, the sun just peeking over the distant mountain. However, bright red colors, spread across the horizon, signaled a storm before day's end. He arrived at the homestead well before noon, having given Lady a good run for a few miles before letting her walk the remainder of the distance to cool down. She was his pride and joy. It would be nice when Blacky was old enough to ride. What a beauty he had turned out to be, the spittin' image of Gideon's stallion.

After giving her a good brushing she was turned loose in the corral. He could see the three girls weeding the vegetable garden, Buddy trying to get their attention for a little play time. It looked like it would be a good growing season, leaf lettuce was already being cut every day for supper.

Sera was busy spinning wool into skeins of yarn and, as usual when spending a lot of time in the procedure, became so self-absorbed that she lost track of her surroundings, not even aware he was there until he gave a slight cough to attract her attention.

"Did you notice the sky, Sera? Looks like we may be in for a storm later on. I made sure everything was secure at Mica's before I left. We had a good time yesterday and, as usual, he won most of the games, he always takes a while before making that next move. Guess maybe I'm more impatient and don't think on it enough. Makes him happy though when he comes out ahead on the games. He's a good old guy, runs into some weird characters though. He was telling me about some strange-acting preacher who came past yesterday, not too long before I got there, he bought that sorrel that I had been thinking on. Mica said it gave him the willies just looking into the man's eyes, but he got a good price for the horse, couldn't fault the man's lack of bargaining power. He sure couldn't stop himself laughing over it, got me to laughing too." Aaron finally ran out of steam.

Sera smiled, always amazed at her usually quiet husband when he became enthused about something that had happened and everything came spilling out like water from a tipped bucket. He probably wouldn't run more than a dozen words together for the rest of the day. Taking a few steps toward him she planted a robust kiss on his lips, giving a firm hug at the same time. The lopsided grin on his face at her actions only made her smile more. He was such a loveable guy, ever pleased at her displays of affection, as though he had been given an unexpected gift. This, of course, made her want to see his reactions quite often.

Putting the spinning aside for the day, she began lunch preparations. Calling the girls from their weeding they took their places at the table, Buddy curling up beneath to garner any dropped morsels. She relayed the tidbits of news Aaron had told her, also mentioning the chickens should be put in the henhouse and miscellaneous outdoor items placed in the barn before the storm arrived. When the table was cleared, everyone went to their respective chores.

Late afternoon, before the wind began to strengthen considerably, Aaron secured the outbuildings. They watched uneasily as the sky turned a dirty green, the slashing rain driven horizontally as the wind intensified. A heavy rumble could be heard advancing in their direction, and then an eerie, whistling noise began as even the heavy timbers in the cottage began to tremble and then shake.

Aaron gathered his family close together under the steps that led to the attic, everyone sitting on the floor, arms entwined, heads bowed, waiting with dread for whatever would happen next.

It seemed only seconds later that they were surrounded by felled timbers, tumbled logs and debris which had them securely hemmed in on all sides of the five- by eight-foot area where they had taken sanctuary. Part of the upper roof and floor were gone giving them a glimpse of the leaden sky. Too shocked to say a word, complete silence reigned until the soft sobbing of Mina and Nia could be heard, along with reassuring words of comfort from Alea. Sera was in a numbed state of disbelief, hugging Buddy closely to her breast with one arm, while clasping her husband tightly around his waist with the other. Aaron, feeling ill with dread, thought only of how to get his family safely out of their tight confinement. He could see patches of the darkening outdoors visible through some of the fallen timbers, leading him to believe that the entire log structure of their home had been destroyed. It was a blow almost more than he could bear. Putting Sera's arm aside he was able to stand almost upright at the opposite end of their enclosure. Surveying the lay of the tossed timbers he tried to find a pivot point where he could move one piece in order to move another. They all seemed wedged together in a tight mass. If he didn't find a way out they would die in this wooden prison. He felt panic settle in, his heart beating rapidly and his breathing beginning to quicken. Leaning against the one remaining wall he made himself calm down; this would not help his family one bit if he lost control.

Twilight was descending, the last streaks of evening sky filling the small space he had a view of. There was room enough for each to stretch out with their heads at opposite ends of the enclosure, the three girls at one, the parents at the other. They had to be careful moving so they wouldn't kick someone accidentally during the night. Eventually they slept.

Morning brought them awake. One by one, each felt hunger pangs and the thirst for something to drink. The only saving factor was the cool weather which prevented them from being too warm and needing water. Once again Aaron tried to move part of the wreckage to free his family, without success. The morning dragged on, each aware they were probably facing their last days together. Finally they sat quietly as Sera told about her childhood and how, meeting Aaron, she knew immediately he was the man she wished to wed. She told the girls about their birth, how thrilled their father had been when he held them in his arms.

Aaron relayed how he had built the home and collected all the growing things he thought a family would love. He told how Sera was the sweetest, most beautiful woman he had ever seen and had sworn to do everything right to make her love him, had promised himself he would never give her cause to regret their marriage. He had kept that promise. Sera was about to continue her musings when a heavy thwack sounded against the logs they were half leaning against. Another, then a second, a third

Aaron knew what that signified and bellowed a loud, "HERE...WE'RE IN HERE." The thunking, thwacking continued until the shiny blade of an axe carved its way through a section of log. Slowly it sliced its way to the bottom leaving a three-foot swathe in its wake. Then it started chopping another path downward about four feet away. A familiar voice yelled, "STAND SIDE," as a heavy mallet sent the logs in the three- by four-foot section tumbling hither and yon. A bowlegged pair of legs were visible standing near the opening.

"Well! Git yourself out of that mess, I ain't got all day. When I saw that darn twister headed in your direction I couldn't keep sittin' on my rear, could I? It's a mess all right. But don't you worry, everything's gonna be just fine." Mica was grinning ear to ear, happy to see his friends were alive and well. One by one he helped them exit the enclosure until all were standing in the late-morning sunlight, thankful to a good friend who had saved their lives.

For the first time Aaron got a good look at the destruction to the property. The cottage was totaled, the barn's roof gone and he didn't see Lady or Blacky anywhere. A sick feeling started in the pit of his stomach and began to travel upward, making him grit his teeth to keep from screaming out his rage and despair. In the distance he could see the wreckage that passed from the garden, to the berry shrubs, to the orchard and then into and beyond the forest. All the work, all the years it had taken to make this parcel and cottage a place to be proud of. A place, whenever he was away, was pictured in his mind as "HOME," a place waiting for his return to wife and children. Suddenly, the loss was more than he could bear and he turned, walking quickly away, so no one would see the tears that threatened to spill showing weakness that he was only a man who may never be able to replace what had been lost. Finally, straightening his shoulders, he turned to the family who meant more to him than any worldly possessions. "Come along, let's check out the barn. See what we can salvage from the part still standing."

Mica followed closely at their heels, too distraught to say a word. This was a terrible blow for his friend. Almost more damage than he could comprehend ever putting to rights again. He knew his friend could manage temporarily, but what of the gals? They had to have a roof over their heads. They were the closest thing he had to family since he had been a young lad, there had to be something he could do to help. Slowly thoughts, words, ideas seemed to combine into a very sensible remedy. He knew Aaron would not accept anything that even hinted at charity.

"Hey! Aaron, we can help each other out if Sera and the girls would be agreeable to it and if it's okay with you. Remember how I was always fussin' about getting stuff straightened up a bit at the Post? And, for sure you can't say as I'm the best housekeeper you ever seen. How about if Sera and the girls stayed at the Post, took care of the customers and sort of curried the place a bit? I could stay here with you to lend a hand. We could have things pretty well in order before winter's cold. By then I'd be happy with bein' back in my fixed-up place, and the gals would be happy back here in theirs. I might be old but I'm still mighty handy with tools."

Aaron had a thoughtful expression on his face as he contemplated the intriguing idea Mica had come up with. It might very well work. Thinking about the possibilities of what could be accomplished in the next five months, before November's snow, seemed to ease a huge burden from his shoulders. A wide grin split Aaron's face from ear to ear. "You're on, Mica, if Sera and the girls are agreeable to it. Sounds like a big solution to some of my problems. Well! Sera, girls, what's your decision? Do you think you can tolerate staying at and taking care of Mica's Post for the next five months?"

Aaron could see at a glance what the girls thought. Their faces had lit up like the rising sun peeking over the tree tops. Just inspecting all the stuff would seem like a treat. Sera, one eyebrow lifting a bit signifying a moment of pondering, gave her assent.

Suddenly there were smiles from the girls, the tension eased from Aaron's face, a grin from Mica showed his pleasure in helping his friend, and Sera? Well, Sera had every confidence in her husband that they would eventually all be together once more, it didn't matter about material things. The fear she had felt at the possibility of her children and husband dying had frightened her more than she would ever admit. All that she cared about was at her side this very moment. House, buildings, possessions were secondary. After all, what were they without the people who gave them life?

While Sera and the girls waited outside the damaged barn, the two men climbed their way over timbers to the section where part of the roof was intact. Aaron felt this was the beginning of a streak of luck. The refurbished room that Gideon had used was in amazingly good shape.

The window was unbroken and although rain had gained access where the other section of roof was missing, it was livable.

Decisions had to be made about buying provisions, getting Sera and the girls over to the Post, and fixing the roof of the barn so the two men would be out of bad weather during the rebuilding of the cottage. Aaron decided to first make a search for the two horses, which would be sorely needed. Mica went with him riding his old mule, Gus, in one direction, while Aaron went in another.

When Aaron discovered hoof prints leading into the forest he followed their trail. As the growth became thicker and ground cover more matted the prints were spaced closer together indicating a walking pattern. He knew it was only a matter of time until he found them, his only prayer was that they were uninjured. A soft nicker sounded from his left which surprised him. The two must have circled back, making their way toward home. Pushing through branches and thatchy underbrush he spotted a shiny, black head turned in his direction. Lady, recognizing his scent, began to make her way toward him, Blacky following closely behind. Aaron hadn't realized how anxious he had been until he saw his horses alive and uninjured. How easy it had been for him to take things for granted. God forbid that he could have lost his family, home, everything in just a single day. Why hadn't he gathered the family and run for the root cellar? Just because they had never experienced a storm like this before didn't mean it couldn't have happened.

Mica was already back at the barn replacing the downed poles around the corral. He was almost finished when Aaron rode up on Lady. After the two horses were fed and the water trough upended and refilled, the two men used Gus to pull timbers out from the barn. It was mid-afternoon when they finished.

Sera and the girls headed for the Post. Sera and Nia would ride Lady, Alea and Mina on Gus, with Blacky trailing on a halter. They would make decent time and arrive well before dusk. In the morning Alea would bring Gus back to the men. Mica told Sera about the black book under the counter that gave the selling prices of everything. It was his running inventory of buying and selling, and how to keep track of profits or loss. "You take whatever you need, Sera. Just make sure the chickens are fed.

Use what eggs you want and sell the rest, or if you want, bake stuff and make yourself a profit on selling the goods. Whatever suits your fancy will suit me just fine."

After Sera rode off with the girls, Aaron and Mica went to the root cellar to search for something to eat, finally deciding on a few jars of peaches, a half-dozen apples, and a tin of dry biscuits. It would suffice until tomorrow when Alea brought supplies.

After eating, they aired out the bedding, soaked up the rain water on the floor near where the door to the bunkroom had been blown open, and then gave a vigorous sweeping to the room. It would be quite livable for the time they would be there together. The two eyed the bed realizing it would not suit either one to sleep beside another man. With a single idea in mind, they each grabbed an end of the mattress and placed it on the floor. The sheepskin rug next to the bed was placed atop the bed frame, and then the bedding was evenly divided between the two resting places. With satisfied grins they were both content with their new arrangement, each needing their space, but willing to share the living quarters.

The next morning brought clear skies and a good day for working on the barn roof. Mica hefted the timber up to Aaron, one at a time, who then nailed it securely before reaching for the next. They were just about ready to break for lunch when Alea called a good morning to them. She was riding Lady, leading Gus, who was also pulling a cart.

Dismounting she led Lady to the corral and turned her loose. She unfastened Gus' harness letting him in also.

There were quite a few food packages. A dozen carefully wrapped eggs, two freshly baked loaves of bread, a container of yeast, a five-pound sack of cornmeal, salt, pepper, two roasted chickens, and a mouthwatering apple pie. A jar of honey, an assortment of dishes, utensils, soap, towels, and miscellaneous items Sera thought the men would find useful. Aaron and Mica were like kids at a penny candy bowl.

After everything was unloaded, the cart hitched to Lady, who for a moment didn't fancy the squeaky thing following so closely, and then calmly settled into the traces. Alea left to return to the Post feeling satisfied that the two men had enough provisions to last for a while. Her mom would feel better and not worry herself sick.

By the end of the day half the roof was finished. Thankfully, it was not a very large barn; however, it suited the needs of the family. If things worked out the way Aaron planned he would eventually add an addition. That is, if he could breed Lady a few times with Gideon's stallion. Too soon to dwell on that though, he needed to get everything repaired that had been damaged by the tornado.

They worked hard finally finishing the barn roof. It was late, almost twilight but at least if they got rain they would be warm and dry with a decent place to wait out any nasty weather.

A pot of water was beginning to steam for tea while the two men were finishing off the remainder of one of the chickens Alea had brought. A slice of apple pie topped off their meal nicely. Mica had to admit Sera was a great cook.

After a last swallow of tea, cups and dishes washed, set on the chest and covered with a clean cloth, the two men, tired but happy with their day's labor, retired for the evening.

Soon the soft rumble of snores floated through the cozy room, signifying a hard day's labor well spent with hopefully, another good day tomorrow.

When Aaron awoke, the aroma of the breakfast Mica was preparing started his day off with a grin. "Mica, you'd make some woman a very happy wife. What time did you get up? Usually I'm up before the sun. I can't believe a man as old as you can rise and shine this early after all the work you did yesterday. Do you have some kind of magic brew to give you all that energy?" Aaron pulled on his trousers, his stockings, and then laced up his work boots leaving his shirt until after he ate. A quick trip outside to the commode, then to wash up at the spring, and he was back just as Mica set the food on the table.

"I like cooking, Aaron, hope you don't mind, lessen you'd rather do it? I just figured that with a wife, she did it all and spoiled the pants off you. I can't abide burnt food. I'm dang good in the kitchen department, as you already know from all the checker games you laid over to play." Mica dug into the eggs and sausage with relish. "If you happen to notice, I took a look at your smokehouse and picked up a few things. Good thing you built it half in the ground, saved a lot of good vittles from being lifted away by the storm."

Aaron hadn't even thought to look. He had been too absorbed with what to do about the cottage and the barn. Suddenly, things didn't seem quite so depressing, maybe there was more untouched by the storm than met the eye. Within the next half hour they were ready to get to work and by the tail-end of the day the double doors repaired and hung, and the miscellaneous debris cleared from the yard. Tomorrow they would start on the cottage, which, from the looks of it, would take most of the year to rebuild.

It was a good kind of tired they felt that evening as they sat after supper, one in the chair, the other on the bunk, discussing what they wanted to attempt on the morrow. Logically, they would try to pull away and stack any useable logs. Those too damaged would be used for firewood. Once the area was cleared around the site, they could figure the best way to start raising the outer walls and cutting new logs for replacement. Right now, it was a complete disaster with only the one wall still standing, which, since Mica's axe job on it, would also need repair. It seemed almost too much for two men, one old and one middle-aged, to tackle but it had to be done and well before the hard cold set in next autumn.

When they finally called it a day and retired for the night, Aaron had a hard time falling asleep. He missed Sera and the girls, wondered how they were managing their new responsibilities at the Trading Post. Looking at the work still to be done here, it would seem a very long, lonely summer without them. When he eventually dozed off he dreamt of hearth, home and family, happily together once again.

Meanwhile Sera, the three girls and Buddy were doing very well. Word had traveled the gossip circuit about the young mother and her three daughters tending the place for Mica and the delicious array of bread, pies and baked goods set out for sale. Curiosity naturally brought people in to see what all the talk was about. Once there, a need to search for various supplies, plus a small purchase of just a bit of the tasty-looking displays kept people lingering, and therefore spending more money. Mica was in for a very pleasant surprise with the profits that were accumulating. Shelves were neatly arranged, floor scrubbed, counter polished, and even the front window that had cost Mica a pretty penny was shining clear and bright so everyone had a good view of the neatly arranged merchandise. Alea was exceptionally happy. Sera kept a close eye on the newly developing romance between her daughter and a young man named Jake who was quite smitten with Alea's charms. She had to admit, he was a nice-looking, clean-cut young man but looks weren't everything. Anyway, she was just getting used to the idea that Fila was now a married woman with her own home to care for. It was much too soon to even think about losing another daughter. Hopefully the glow would fade in a few weeks. At that very moment she noticed Alea leaning over the counter talking earnestly to Jake. A customer standing nearby seemed to have an ear cocked to the conversation. Sera hurried over, the two so engrossed they didn't even notice her. "Alea, I need some help, give me a hand in the back room for a moment, would you?" Sera paused near the doorway waiting for the intimate exchange between the young couple to cease. When Alea noticed her mother waiting for her, she spoke a few words to the young man, who unhurriedly turned away, giving a friendly smile to Sera as he departed.

"What were you two talking about? That woman standing next to you seemed very interested in what was being said. I certainly hope he was being respectful to you. After all, he is a complete stranger. It does not look proper for a young lady to be leaning over a counter with her chest pushed up from leaning on her arms, making a spectacle of herself. From now on when you are speaking to someone stand up straight, do not hunch over like an old woman." Sera was feeling a little put out and wanted her daughter to comport herself in a ladylike manner.

"I'm sorry, Mother, I was so interested in what Jake was talking about I didn't realize what I was doing. He is very enthused about starting his own business. He has his own delivery wagon and has even brought goods here to the Post from Carltown. He said it's a few days' ride past Umer, where Fila lives. He knows Gideon from when they were kids and saw each other sometimes when his father had business at the sawmill. He said next time he's in town he'd like to talk to you, let you see what kind of fellow he is. Honest, Mother, you'll really like him. He's hardworking, honest and I really think he'll make something of himself. Would you speak to him next time he's here?"

Sera was at a loss for words. This had gone much farther than she had thought possible, if they were already discussing his future plans. Maybe she was just a little nervous and overreacting. That must be it. Just a bit off center, what with Aaron off getting their home back together. Fila gone away, chances of seeing her again soon, very slim. Suddenly Sera felt old. Soon all her daughters would be married and gone away. She would be an old granny, she could almost feel her hairs turning white this very minute. With her mind focused on the distant future she didn't notice Alea waiting for her reply.

"Mother, what in the world are you thinking about? You look so worried, are you okay? You're not angry at me are you? Oh! Please tell me you're not. I promise to act like a lady from now on. Mother? Come sit down for a minute, are you dizzy? Oh! Please answer me, you're scaring me." Alea's eyes were brimming with unshed tears.

Sera had been so intently mesmerized in her musings it took several seconds to realize Alea had been pleading with her. With a start she came to full attention seeing how upset her daughter had become. "Oh! I'm fine, honey, just thinking about growing old I guess. Actually that's a long way off. Yes! I'd love to speak to your friend Jake and learn a little about him and his family. Next time he's in town we'll sit down to a nice lunch and get acquainted. He can see you were well brought up, that's why he's so interested." Sera realized the more she protested, the more Alea would be interested in Jake. She was not ready to see a new romance bloom so soon after Fila's marriage. Better to meet the young man, get to know him. She wondered if she was being too strict.

Sera spent the remainder of the day baking while the three girls tended the counter. At suppertime the Post was closed for the night and the family retired to the back rooms. It already had a woman's touch that brightened it considerably. The two younger girls had made curtains for the two windows. The floor had been scrubbed, table and chest nicely polished. The oil-lamp chimneys now sparkling clean, cast a nice glow giving a homey atmosphere that had previously been lacking. It no longer looked like a bachelor's quarters. They all worked hard to make the place feel like home but there was no comparison. The memory of their destroyed dwelling, fruit trees and gardens cast a pall over them at times. When that happened Sera found tasks for all to become occupied with. Soon Mica wouldn't recognize the place. Sera couldn't help smiling a bit at what his reaction would be. Men were sometimes odd creatures trying to act uncaring while secretly being quite impressed, too leery of not being seen as manly. Of course it really depended on how secure a fellow felt about himself. Some, like Aaron, never worried about what people thought of him. He was always confident of doing the right thing and if not sure, never afraid to ask another's advice.

In the middle of the night Buddy began to bark. Alea had brought him back with her when she returned with the empty wagon, worried that the two men would be too busy to care for him. Sera arose, checked the store, looked outside at the moonlit yard, and out toward the corral. Everything was quiet and serene. Still Buddy was not to be silenced. "What's the matter, Bud? Come here, little guy, let me pet you. Are you lonesome for home? Did you hear something outside? That's okay, Buddy, you're a good boy." Buddy would not settle down, he ran to the door, waiting to be let outside. As soon as Sera opened it, he dashed away into the night. Sera watched as he disappeared from view, heading away from the Post, racing as fast as his little legs could carry him. Maybe he was after a rabbit, Sera thought. He'd be all tuckered out when he returned in the morning. Returning to bed she was soon fast asleep. The girls hadn't even stirred at the ruckus, too tired to even open their eyes.

In the morning they watched and waited for Buddy to make an appearance. Anxious, the girls found excuses to check the barn and surrounding area thinking their pet had been injured. Night came, still they hoped and watched. When the following morning showed no sign of him, they thought their worst fears had been realized. Somehow, somewhere, their little pet had been badly hurt or killed by an animal. With heavy hearts they went about their chores finding little to make them smile or distract them from the feeling of loss they experienced. This had been their very first pet. So different from a favorite chicken or lamb. They had never realized how much love could be felt for a furry little dog who seemed to understand every word spoken to him. He had been so much fun to play with. Teaching him tricks, being amazed at how smart he was when he learned so quickly. He had become a part of the family. Each in turn, shed secret tears of loss, regret for an imagined slight they had given when he had wanted petting, or even sometimes ignoring him when he wanted to play. If they had it to do over they would act differently, if only he would come back so they had another chance to be good to him.

Still, the days passed and their friend did not reappear.

The sound of his master's voice awoke Buddy from a sound sleep. It seemed ages since he had been at the cabin in the Winter Forest guarding against the danger of the Seeker. Once again he was instructed about hampering the Seeker's plot. Somewhere in his mind was the distant memory of being selected from a small, specially bred litter of pups endowed with extraordinary abilities and perceptions. This was ages ago. All his litter mates had been sent to various places throughout the world to keep guard over their Master's precious artifacts, keeping track of where they were.

The very essence of his Master resided in his specially created Relic. Whenever one of the items, anywhere, was in danger of being taken, the Master sent one of his dog soldiers against those who would try to acquire and use any of those precious collectibles for unsavory purposes. Never should the artifacts be gathered into one place; however, it seemed the Seeker had that purpose in mind. Buddy was aware that the man would be very upset when he returned home from this present search.

After the door was opened by his mistress, Buddy picked up the correct direction of the scent he was supposed to follow, the freshest being the one leaving, not arriving. The scent of the horse the Seeker was riding would be followed as though it were a prized bone being waved in front of his nose. Buddy settled into a comfortable lope that would not tire him too soon. He had been bred for fortitude, patience, loyalty and a keen perception for what was occurring around him. The trail wasn't that fresh but strong enough to follow easily.

Through the remainder of that night, until near noon the next day, the miles passed beneath the loping paws until it was time to lie down to rest. After sleeping the afternoon away then getting a drink from a nearby stream, he tried unsuccessfully to find food. At twilight he continued his journey, his hunger forgotten for the present. All night until noon the following day he traveled, and then rested until night roused him on once again. He took a wide circuit to pass the Seeker unseen and reach the place where he was to bide his time. He knew he would have food and rest, be ready to face the challenge when the man made his move.

Hungry and exhausted he slowly made his way to the cottage door, scratching at it to get the inhabitants' attention. After several tries the door opened. "Buddy....what are you doing here? How did you get here?" Fila looked outside, expecting to see some of the family making their way to the door, disappointed when no one was there. She bent over and picked the dusty little dog up into her arms hugging him close to her breast. "You poor thing, you must be thirsty. You look as though you've been on your own for a while. Oh! I hope nothing is wrong at home, I can't imagine what could have happened." A spasm of fear quivered through her, making her slightly lightheaded. A sick feeling began in her stomach making her nauseated.

Setting the dog down she filled a bowl from the water pitcher and while Buddy slaked his thirst, she filled another with a portion of eggs and potatoes left from breakfast. Taking a seat, she watched as every bite was consumed. Afterward she washed the bowl and placed it in a corner of the room beside the water dish. Then she took the dog outside to the new barn Gideon and his friends had raised the previous week. Using one of the curry brushes she gave her pet a good grooming ridding him of dust, burrs and hair knots. When they returned to the cottage, he curled up on the cozy bed Fila made for him and fell fast asleep. He wouldn't awaken until the next day.

When Gideon returned late that afternoon he was surprised and worried to see his friend Buddy fast asleep in the corner near the new iron stove, sleeping so soundly he was unaware of Gideon's presence. Fila told her husband how ragged the dog had looked. She was worried that something was wrong with the family, otherwise why would Bud have left a good home? Nothing Gideon could say would ease her worry. "Let's wait a few days and see what happens. Maybe Aaron is on the way here and Buddy just got too excited to wait for him. I'm sure Sera was anxious for news on how we were doing and sent him to find out. If he doesn't show by tomorrow or the day after, I promise you I'll ride there and find out for you." Gideon watched Fila intently. She hadn't been feeling too well lately what with having a nervous stomach and sometimes even getting sick. He thought it was a change in the weather but usually, by afternoon, she felt better. It was a mystery to him. The next time he was in town he'd ask Ella, who was known for her knowledge about sicknesses and how to remedy them.

After supper was over they sat outside watching the sunset. Life was good. Gideon had been finding work once again with friends and neighbors, their garden was growing nicely, and the young saplings of apple, pear, cherry and peach had taken well in the section they had designated as their orchard. Fila had planted flowers around the cottage. Hollyhocks and columbine, yellow daisies and lemon verbena. Her herb patch held mint, sage, mustard, dill, and a few he didn't recognize. The ladies exchanged slips, as Fila called them. Little twigs of growing things to be planted. Food had never tasted so good with the seasonings Fila added.

When they retired later, Buddy was still deeply asleep. Soon Gideon's snores made Fila feel lonely lying awake until darkness began to fade a bit into the gray before dawn. She couldn't help worrying about the family. If only she knew they were all right. She was just beginning to drift off into a light doze when with a jolt, she sat upright, suddenly remembering what her father had last given her before riding away. The wrapped bundle she had opened then placed on the highest shelf for safety.

Carefully, so as not to awaken Gideon, she slipped from bed and made her way to the kitchen. Lighting the lamp she stood on tiptoe, retrieved the Globe then stepped to the table. Sitting in front of it she looked into the depths of its swirling mists.

She recognized the family barn but couldn't understand why her father was sleeping there next to Mica from the Trading Post. Lady and Blacky were not there, but an old mule was in their stall. Her father looked healthy and tanned, seemed to be sleeping peacefully. After a few moments the scene changed. She saw a strange room with her mother and Nia fast asleep on a cot. Against the wall a wide pallet had been made on top of a thick layer of straw. Alea and Mina were curled up, also deeply asleep. Fila felt troubled with the pictures she had observed. Why wasn't her family together? What could have happened to make them separate? Yet! They slept peacefully, untroubled. She would have Gideon ask about town tomorrow, perhaps someone had been over that way and would have heard news. Just as she was reaching for the Globe to replace it on the shelf, the mists parted once again revealing a bearded man, one arm out-flung at his side, lying on his back sound asleep with a strange gold cross resting against his chest. For a moment his eyes opened. She almost thought he could see her, then the mists closed about him and all was drifting fog. Thoughtfully she replaced the Globe back up on its high shelf.

It was almost dawn when Fila returned to bed, however she was still unable to sleep because of the oddly disturbing scenes she had seen. In a short time, knowing Gideon would soon awaken, she arose, dressed herself and returned to the kitchen to begin breakfast preparations.

After Gideon left promising to try and get information for her, she felt too tired to even think about working in the garden so, making herself comfortable in the rocking chair, she began to doze, soon falling into a deep sleep. It was at this time the dark stranger made his appearance at her door, rapping sharply to get the inhabitants' attention without, however, any success. Luther was looking at the changes made since the last time he had visited the premises. Odd that he had been guided here to obtain another treasure. This time a Blue Leather Pouch would be added to his collection. From what he had read, when used in the correct way it was an ideal item to have when an escape was needed.

When no reply was forthcoming from his repeated knockings he tried the door. It had been latched securely. Turning away in disappointment that there would be a further delay in his acquisition, he returned to his horse, mounted him and leading the burro rode away toward town. Actually, there was plenty of time and no reason to rush. He'd find a place to stay, visit the preacher and townspeople, and make acquaintances. Eventually he'd have a perfect opportunity to gain admittance once again to that old man's property. He wondered who lived there now. Maybe some distant relative had been notified of the death and found the place quite a prize. Whoever it was had done a lot of work to improve the property. He liked the addition of the orchard farther out, the garden was doing well too. Although he was not a domestic-type person, he still admired well-planned designs. Someday, when those trees were full grown, it would be quite a sight. He did enjoy fruit. Anything that pertained to his own satisfaction was of interest.

Arriving in town he asked about rooms for let, finding a place not far from the old stone church. Mrs. Ivy, a widow woman, showed him the upstairs front bedroom, stating that supper was included in the rent and was served to all four boarders at seven each evening. If you were late, you were out of luck. It was also up to him to feed and care for his animals himself. She was not responsible for their upkeep. He was lucky she was only charging a small fee for their shelter.

After unsaddling his horse and removing his belongings from the burro, he fed and watered them. Then gathering his pack he retired to his room where at least, it was clean. He stretched out on the bed and was soon comfortably asleep.

The afternoon waned. He awoke early evening, making it downstairs just in time for supper, which was, he had to admit, quite tasty. At least he wouldn't have to scrounge for a decent meal. Returning to his room, he spent the remainder of the evening reading his book. Even though he was in the process of acquisition, he was always on the prowl for new artifacts to add to his collection. The pleasure it gave him was beyond measure. At last, the hour growing late, Luther felt the urge for sleep finally overcome him. He laid the cross aside, undressed and finding a comfortable spot, pulled the covers up to his shoulders, his beard resting atop. The potion he had taken while creating his disguise had done a spectacular job of growing his hair and beard but he couldn't abide the feel of it against his skin. It drove him mad with its scratchy feeling. He'd be happy when this was over and he was back home in the security of his impenetrable cavern.

When Gideon heard the rumor about a tornado that had passed near his wife's home he knew she would want to return there as quickly as possible, the worry would be more than she could endure. He had also spoken to Ella. The joy he felt about the possible pregnancy was unbounded. A baby, what would Fila say when he told her? For sure he didn't want her traveling in this condition. He was almost tempted not to tell her about the storm but then, if someone mentioned it to her, how could he explain his secretive evasion? No! That would not be right, he had to tell her and let her make the decision herself.

When he arrived home about midday Fila had just awakened from her slumber. Embarrassed that she had slept so long and had nothing prepared for her husband's lunch she hurriedly brought out bread, cheese and some leftover breakfast ham, setting it on the table in front of Gideon along with a mug of milk. Sitting opposite him, she nibbled on a piece of bread, not relishing the look of food or the thought of eating at the moment.

As he ate Gideon relayed the information he had gleaned from a few of his friends. He was surprised when Fila only smiled when hearing about the tornado that had been sighted near her home. He mentioned the odd-looking preacher man who had rented a room at Mrs. Ivy's. Everyone was speculating about when he would be showing up at people's homes asking for donations. He sure didn't look like any of the revivalists that usually visited.

When Gideon finished eating Fila placed freshly brewed mugs of tea for them after clearing the table. That's when he felt comfortable about telling her his most important news. "I stopped at Ms. Ella's before coming home. She asked about you, how you were feeling. When I mentioned you had been experiencing an upset stomach almost every day she asked if you felt well otherwise. I could tell she was a little excited. She asked if your, um, chest felt a little tender. After I told her everything I could think of she grinned a mile wide and said, 'Son, you tell that sweetheart of yours to come and see me when she gets the chance. I expect you two will be stockin' up on a pile of baby stuff before the end of the year.' Well, honey, you could have knocked me over with a feather. I'm so excited I don't know how to calm myself. I just want to head for the highest hill and yell the news to everyone."

He watched the expression on Fila's face change from showing interest into a look of surprise as realization dawned she was going to be a mother. A new soft look seemed to settle over her entire countenance.

He saw her hand press gently against her stomach in a protective gesture for the precious burden carried there. The joy on her face must have matched that which shone on his own. Then, motherhood took charge.

"Gideon, we have a lot to do before our child is born. I need to start making the things to care for our baby, soft cloths to wrap its bottom, warm clothing for cold weather. Oh! I must speak to Ms. Ella about everything I need to have ready, and make a list so I won't miss anything important." For a moment Fila looked slightly intimidated, and then her adventurous nature took hold with a passion. This was going to be a thrill of a lifetime, a burst of exhilaration lodged within her very soul.

Gideon stepped around the table, grasped Fila's hand pulling her up and into his arms. She fit so perfectly in his embrace. He looked down at the face of his beloved, knowing that she now carried a symbol of their love safely in her body. "Whatever you wish I'll do, sweetheart, we have plenty of time before our baby's birth. Everything that must be done will be accomplished, I promise."

Chapter Twelve

Aaron and Mica had been doing well on extracting the felled logs from inside the ruined cottage. Most of the three walls would need to be rebuilt, a new attic reconstructed and a new roof. All of Aaron's trade goods had been lost to the storm. A devastating blow that Aaron still could not fully fathom. There would be so many things needing replacing. They were now reaching part of the structure near the stairway, which luckily had not been damaged. Aaron was about to hitch Gus to another log when the glint of something shiny caught his eye. When he sought the location of the distraction he was stunned to see his precious obsidian knife imbedded in a felled timber. Thinking the cutting edge must have been shattered during the storm, he nevertheless attempted to remove it without success.

Standing there, he contemplated the idea of snapping it off at the hasp, yet hesitated because he had admired it so much and didn't want to see it disintegrate completely, he was startled to hear a humming sound begin to reverberate from the extended hasp. When he stepped back in surprise the sound diminished slightly. Taking a step forward to see what could be causing the unusual effect, the humming increased. He stopped in his tracks, the sound was steady and monotonous. Testing his theory several times moving forward then away, he realized it was like a game, high tone if you're close, low if you're not. After various tries he was guided to a corner section that had not yet been completely cleared. Hitching Gus to the shattered log, it was pulled away from the half wall that remained, and tugged into the yard. All that was left in the corner was a pile of debris, broken dishes, and pieces of his favorite chair and various items of clothing. The humming had peaked and had become almost painful to hear. Searching beneath the clutter his hand came in contact with something that seemed to bind itself to his palm. When he withdrew his hand from the rubble, the noise stopped abruptly. The Relic, undamaged, was now clutched in his fingers.

Mica wandered into the half-cleared remains wondering why his friend was standing so quietly inspecting something he had in his hand. Curiosity sent him over to inspect. "So, what's going on, Aaron, you find something important? Anything I can help you with?" Mica reached out and lifted the crude piece of wood so quickly from Aaron's hand that he was already peering at it before Aaron even reacted. "Um, what in the world did you find? The workmanship is the crudest I've seen since I was a kid and tried whittling. Is this something that belongs to one of the girls?" Mica turned the object round and round checking the shape, looking at the rude features. Totally disinterested, but curious as to why Aaron was so attracted to it.

Aaron was holding his breath. Waiting for he knew not what, but expecting something to happen. As moments passed and nothing extraordinary occurred, he slowly expelled the air and resumed normal breathing. Reaching out he gently lifted the Relic from Mica's hand and slipped it into his shirt. He wasn't taking any chances.

"Yes! In fact it is, Mica. Fila found it quite a long while ago and for some unexplained reason became very attached to it. I think she feels it brings her and the family good fortune. At least that's what I have experienced. We've had some very unusual occurrences since it's been in her possession. The last I heard, she had taken it up to the Winter Forest and put it in a special place to keep it safe. I have no idea how it came to be here but surely that tornado is to blame." Distracted, without thinking, Aaron reached out for the obsidian knife, which slid easily and undamaged into his hand. When the realization sank in that he was somehow holding his unbroken treasure, not realizing how it had gotten there, he could only feel an overwhelming surge of thankfulness that it was undamaged. This artifact was worth its weight in gold. He knew that once the cottage had been rebuilt he would once again set out on his trading journey. By the time he returned, he'd be able to replace everything that had been lost in the storm. When Mica saw the wide grin stretch across his friend's face, he knew everything was somehow going to be just fine. For a moment he had been worried. Aaron had looked so disoriented and lost. Seemed that the wooden carving and of course that beautiful knife had finally pulled him out of the doldrums. He had watched his friend wander around over there for a while and thought the lad had lost his senses for a minute.

"Hey! How's about we have some lunch, old buddy? I'm starved. You in the mood for some beans and ham? I'll fix some pan bread to go with it." Mica made his way to the barn, Aaron trailing after his friend. By the time the food was ready Aaron was his old self, calm and settled. After eating, their work continued, clearing the remainder of the rubble from the cottage. Tomorrow they would begin rebuilding, fitting the logs that were reusable. Trussing for the roof, sawing boards for the attic floor, making cedar shingles. Stones had to be replaced on the chimney. Thankfully, Aaron had a stack of seasoned logs he had intended using for enlarging the barn.

That evening, back in their room in the barn, Aaron sat looking at the Relic he had placed on the chest earlier that day, wondering what in the world he was going to do with it. The thought of being responsible for its safekeeping was unsettling. Actually, he associated it with Fila since it seemed more in the nature of a feminine possession. Like someone, long ago, had carved it for a beloved daughter, a little doll-like plaything that would keep a girl-child amused. There wasn't a thing that was pretty about it and he wondered what could ever keep a child attracted to it. Mica, watching the fleeting expressions on his friend's face, contemplated the strange carving and wondered what could be causing Aaron's fascination with it. Whoever had made it was not a talented craftsman. Yet, he had to admit, something about the thing drew a person to examine it, hold it, turn it around in their hands and try to find what the mystery was that seemed to exude from every gouge, crevice and indentation on the surface of the dark wood. Mica felt the hairs begin to rise on the back of his neck and turned away from attraction that seemed to draw him into deep reverie. He shook off the feeling, deciding to take a walk outside while there was still twilight.

"Hey! Aaron, want to take a walk around the area before bedtime, relax a little and get a breath of air before hitting the hay?" Mica waited a moment and when a reply wasn't forthcoming turned and left the barn. A snort from Gus let him know his passage had been noted.

Walking farther out toward the pond he saw something moving toward him in the distance, and then the sound of a bell growing louder as a cow came trotting toward him. In her wake were several sheep, one seemingly quite attached to the bovine. He hurried back to the corral and once the animals were inside, latched the gate. Maybe he and Aaron could make a search of the area. The chickens and pigs had scattered, would be nice if they could locate a few. The song of a few toads and crickets began their nightly serenade along with the hum of mosquitoes. Time to get to bed, be ready for another big day tomorrow. Aaron was already asleep on his pallet when Mica doused the lantern and crawled into bed.

Aaron awoke to the sound of rain early the next morning. He could feel the dampness in the air. Stoking the small cook stove he added a few chunks of wood and placed a small pot on one of the lids adding a measure of water to it, a good day to have a hot bowl of cornmeal mush. A little of yesterday's ham added for flavor would sure hit the spot. While the water came to a boil he went to feed Gus, stopping in surprise when he saw Bell and several sheep in the corral. "Come on in here, Bell. Heyah, come, girl." As soon as she entered he put her in one of the stalls. A young lamb followed close at her heels. When it nuzzled at Bell's filled udder, Aaron couldn't help grinning. Poor little thing must have lost her dam in the storm, at least it had served both of them well, had kept her alive and relieved Bell the misery of not being milked. He'd seen stranger things in life.

Hefting one of the buckets Aaron soon had it half filled with milk, not milking Bell dry, but leaving some for the lamb. By the time he went to prepare breakfast Mica was already stirring the cornmeal and bits of ham into the boiling water.

"Well, son, from the look and feel of the weather, seems we'll be having a day of rest." Mica had an expectant look, waiting for Aaron's comment, then continued, "For sure, on a rainy day like this, it would just be a lot of slipping and sliding in the mud. Anyway we could use a day off."

Aaron agreed, knowing what Mica was thinking. They had toiled hard clearing the cottage and also parts of the surrounding area where it hampered their progress. A rest would suit both just fine.

After breakfast, miscellaneous chores having been taken care of around the barn, Mica took out the checkerboard, setting it up on the end of the cot. Aaron sat on his pallet, Mica in the chair. It worked out just fine, though not as comfortable as sitting at a table would have been. Mugs of steamy honeyed tea, setting on the milk stool next to them, were sipped leisurely between checker moves, refilled often from the simmering pot on the woodstove. It was a cozy, comfortable morning with the sound of rain making it feel even more so. Eventually the day drifted lazily away. The checker game, discussions about what the next day's project would be, how Aaron would like to ride up to see Sera but didn't want to use Gus because the mule was working hard enough towing logs.

After supper Aaron removed the Relic and obsidian knife from the chest drawer where he had placed them for safekeeping, the beautifully quilled leather knife sheath missing. He inspected every inch of the gleaming blade for damage. Mica moved in closer admiring the workmanship and deep glow reflecting off the blade. "Where did you pick this up, Aaron? I've heard about this stuff but have never seen it. There's an old folks tale about hell's fire creating a wondrous material more beautiful than the most precious black pearl, more lustrous than moon glow at midnight on a glassy lake. It's supposed to have magical powers. Can I hold it?"

Aaron carefully placed the blade in Mica's hand, at the same time showing him the thin scar on his palm that he had received because of his careless handling of it several years ago. Cautiously, Mica began to caress the wide flat surface of the blade, fingers rubbing against the deep ebony gleam of obsidian. The friction created a high, clear, delicate bell tone which sounded throughout the room. He stopped immediately, afraid the vibration would shatter the precious material. "I just had to try, Aaron. Part of that old story was if you rubbed the blade a certain way it would sing to you about secrets of long ago." Both felt a trifle nervous at finding out an old tale was actually true. The knowledge sat quite uncomfortably on their shoulders, making them wary of the beautiful artifact. Aaron placed the blade in an old woolen sock, then back in the chest drawer along with the Relic. He didn't feel he wanted to learn anything about old secrets from long ago. It sounded too…he tried to think of the right word to express the feeling he had…frightful, that was it. He didn't think he would ever feel the same about owning the thing. Until now it had been a subject of pride but after what Mica had shown him, he felt very uncomfortable having it in his possession. For good or evil, how could he ever know? Better to trade it off as soon as possible, yet, he suddenly recalled the time Sera had been held captive by that scoundrel Luther. It had been the blade that had helped her escape. Now he felt in a quandary about what to do.

Later, after the two men had retired for the night, Aaron still lay wakeful. His entire world had turned upside-down with the storm. His wife and daughters were on their own while he tried to rebuild their home. This was so different than being on his trading expeditions where he had the knowledge he was garnering a livelihood. He felt completely helpless with no other place to turn, stuck here until he could bring the family back where they belonged and then once again he could seek the means for his family's survival.

Too soon it was morning. Aaron dragged himself out of bed, dressed, and went to wash up. He milked Bell, turned the animals out to pasture, cleaned out the stall, and then returned to prepare breakfast and as usual, thankfully, Mica had taken care of that.

After eating, the work on rebuilding the cottage began. Eventually, the knife and Relic were both almost completely forgotten. That summer and into the first days of autumn, the work continued, except on Sundays when Sera came to visit bringing her fresh-baked bread along with any supplies she thought they would need. With each visit she could see the progress made along with a few changes that Aaron incorporated into a newer design. A room addition would also be added as their bedroom.

One Sunday near the end of September, Sera brought news that Aaron was not pleased to hear. A young fellow named Jake had been courting Alea. They were planning to marry in October. "Who is this young fella, Sera? How long has this been going on? I turn my back and suddenly I'm losing another daughter to some young buck too young to know what he's getting into. No wedding until I meet him and his family too. I won't have Alea tied to some worthless mutt who's not worth a pinch of salt. We were lucky with Gideon, he's a prize for any young woman, but who's this Jake anyway? Where does he live? How is he planning on supporting a family?" Aaron was starting to wind down. Sera waited patiently until her husband ran out of questions.

"He is well known and well liked, Aaron, a hardworking young man. His parents are Matt and Eva Wells from Gully, which is off the beaten path halfway between here and Umer. He owns a wagon which he uses to deliver goods to the Post among other places. I've met his folks, who made a special trip to meet Alea. They were quite taken with her and gave their approval to Jake. They know it's your decision for the marriage. Jake is friends with Gideon, they met when they were kids. I like him very much. He will be here later this evening to meet with you and will stay overnight. You will have a chance to look him over. Trust me, my dear. They are a perfect couple and will be happy together."

Aaron did trust his wife, it was just so soon... It seemed Alea was too young but on recollection, she was seventeen and the right age to wed. It felt like the family was falling apart, little bits and pieces disappearing into dust. He couldn't believe his little girl would never again live under his protection, gone before the cottage was even completed.

Silent for a few moments after considering how quickly the years seemed to pass, he nodded his assent. "Plan the wedding, Sera. We'll be finished here before the end of October, this is where our daughter will wed. I'll hurry the best I can on making another kitchen table, benches and two full-sized beds, one which will be for Mina and Nia in the attic, but you will have to purchase new dishes and other household items. In the spring I'll be going on my trade route again." Aaron felt uncomfortable about buying on credit but this time it couldn't be helped.

When Sera returned to the Post that evening Alea couldn't control her excitement at learning the ceremony would soon be performed at her parents' home. At last she and Jake could begin to make their own plans. They would live with his parents until their home could be built, since Jake's business was doing so nicely. How different it would feel living near

Gully town, being able to shop anytime she pleased or visit new friends. It wouldn't really be that far from her parents' place, just a few days' ride. She'd even be able to see Fila once in a while. Suddenly the overwhelming difference in what her new life as a married woman would be was more than she could comprehend. She realized how separated her family had been in their secluded domicile. The solitude she had experienced her entire life had seemed quite normal, at least until she had lived here at the Post. There was an entire busy world going on all around her and she had missed it.

Sera began to plan. Slowly she assembled items for her household, ordered a few things from the catalog that Mica kept on the counter and began to list the things that needed doing for the wedding. Each time Jake came to town with deliveries for the Post, he had offered to take Sera's purchases out to Aaron. That gave the two men a chance to get acquainted. They had taken an immediate liking to each other, maybe because Jake was much like Aaron when he had been a young man.

As October dwindled away there were only a few days left before the ceremony. The cottage had been rebuilt, refurnished, and restocked, waiting for the return of Sera and the girls, who arrived early Thursday morning riding in Jake's wagon along with the last of the supplies, and Lady and Blacky trailing behind on a lead. After the wagon was emptied Jake gave Alea a last kiss and left immediately. He would not see her again until the wedding on Saturday morning even though he would sleep in the barn bunkroom the night before. That's where they would spend their wedding night on Saturday.

After the supplies were put away, Sera inspected her new home. It was much like it had been before the storm except the fireplace was no longer used for cooking. A new cook range stood against one of the new walls, a flue pipe vented into the stone chimney in which a number of hooks were embedded holding various pots and pans. Aaron had even made a standing cabinet with doors, which stood in the area where they had taken shelter during the storm. Everything needed for managing a kitchen was contained within. Shelves holding dishes, linens, utensils, canned goods. Their new bedroom was built behind the fireplace, so its heat would warm the room during winter's cold. The access was on the corner wall next to the new cabinet.

She had enjoyed her stay at the Post meeting people, making friends. Mostly she had enjoyed making money. Her baked goods had brought in enough to restock the cottage and even pay part of the new cook range. She never would have believed it. Aaron had been amazed and, she had to admit, very proud of her accomplishment. She had even surprised herself and now, she could look forward to the marriage with peace of mind.

The remainder of the day she finished sewing the last seam on Alea's wedding dress, simple white cotton with a form-fitting bodice, full skirt, and little buttons down the back to the waist. Sera had added a delicate ruffle of lace around the scoop neckline. When finished she carefully folded the dress into clean sheeting and placed it atop the wall cabinet safely out of the way. Then it was time to prepare supper. It had seemed a long day. Everyone went to bed early knowing there was much to accomplish on the morrow. Friday morning dawned clear and cool. Waking the family she had breakfast already on the table, it was going to be a busy day and she wanted an early start. Aaron left immediately to complete his final chores for the party.

Sera started on making the wedding cake while Alea and her sisters began the food preparations to feed about twenty guests for the wedding party. If more came there would still be plenty. Alea and Jake planned to leave Sunday morning with Jake's parents. They would live with them until the building of their own house was completed in the spring. Sera was well pleased with both her daughters' selections of men. They were honest, hardworking individuals with good morals and tender hearts. They would have happy lives and good memories to share when they grew old together. Sera had hoped to see Fila at the wedding but Jake had brought news that she was expecting. If the weather permitted at the time, she would like to be there when the baby arrived.

Thinking about Fila becoming a mother was quite a stretch of her imagination until she realized she herself would become a grandmother. It didn't seem possible. After placing the cake in the oven she walked to the small mirror on the wall in the bedroom to see if she looked grandmotherly. Her hair was still dark but, was that a few gray hairs or only the cast of light from the window? Sera turned away, too much to do today for silly foolishness like this.

Sleeping arrangements had been made for after the wedding. Jake's parents would spend Saturday night up in the girls' attic room, their two sons sleeping on the floor on pallets in the kitchen with Aaron. As for Mina and Nia, they would sleep in the bedroom with her. The arrangements were suitable with everyone. The bunk room was ready for the newlyweds even though Jake would be sleeping there tonight. Sera would send him supper when he arrived. Sunday morning they would be leaving, along with Jake's parents, for their home in Gully.

By the end of the day everything was ready. The house looked nice, the table set up outside ready for the platters of food. Aaron had put together a few extra benches. Mica, much to their surprise, would play the new fiddle he had ordered from the catalog. The weather was cool but from the looks of the sunset it would be a nice day for the wedding.

That evening at supper the family realized this would be their last meal together. Alea, although thrilled about her marriage, was struck with the realization of the huge change there would be in her life. No more laughing and teasing her sisters at bedtime, or planning surprises for their mother and dad on special occasions. Having those private girl talks about things only a sister would understand and the giddy, giggling bouts over nothing at all, tears streaming down cheeks in unchecked merriment. Looking at her mother, she thought of all the duties she took care of without complaint, and she hoped she could do as well. She noticed a trace of sadness in her mother's eyes, realized she herself was feeling a sense of loss. "I'll miss you all very much. I promise to visit as often as I can, it's only a few days' ride. Maybe sometimes the girls can come stay a while after we get in our own home, you too, Mother. It would be so nice." Alea felt her throat tighten as tears began to well up and then, helplessly, she burst into sobs completely overcome with emotion. She felt overwhelmed, wondering if she was making a mistake by marrying Jake but then realizing that she truly adored him. How could she be so mixed up, feeling both fear and anticipation? she asked herself.

Sera took Alea by the hand and led her into the bedroom, closing the door firmly behind them. "Come over here, honey. Take a seat on the bed. It's time we had another heart-to-heart talk."

Alea dabbed at her eyes, hiccupping as muffled sobs refused to subside. Sera waited patiently. When Alea had calmed herself Sera began to speak. "If you have any doubts about marrying Jake tell me. Even when the preacher stands before you asking you to repeat the marriage vows, it is not too late to change your mind." Alea only sat silently, waiting for her mother to continue. "I don't believe there has ever been a bride or groom who did not wonder, even momentarily, if they were making a mistake. You can be sure that Jake will be searching his heart also. It's a big change having the responsibility of managing your own lives after living under your parents' guidance all these years. You both, however, have experience in seeing how your parents coped. That will help you in some of your decision making. You love Jake dearly, it's very plain to see, and he you. Both of you are levelheaded, have the same upbringing, so therefore are similar in what you expect from life. You will have a good marriage, go to it with confidence. You are loved by Aaron and me, by your sisters, by Jake and most likely, already by his family. In my heart I feel you will be very happy and Jake will be a good husband to you." Sera sat, hoping her daughter would feel less nervous, more sure of herself

Alea realized she truly did wish to marry Jake, it was only the feeling of loss for her family that was upsetting her. A sense of calmness enveloped her mind realizing that her family would still be here if she ever felt she needed them. She was still part of them and they of her, still a daughter, a sister. That would never change even though she would carry a different name. The brightness of Alea's smile eased Sera's heart.

The last evening before the wedding passed quietly, the satisfaction of knowing that everything was ready for the morrow gave peace of mind and therefore, contentment. The girls departed to their upstairs room while Sera and Aaron remained sitting before the banked fire enjoying a last cup of tea. Sera liked the two new chairs Aaron had made. She planned to make feather cushions for the seat and back of each. Something to busy herself with after the wedding weekend was over. It would take time to get used to having only the two younger girls at home. She must remember to find duties to keep them busy.

Hearing a muted snore from Aaron she arose, gently removed the emptied cup from his fingers and placed it, along with hers, on the table.

Turning toward him for a moment, she studied his face noticing the sprinkling of gray at his hairline, the laugh wrinkles at the outer edges of his eyes, the slight softening of the strong jaw line she had always admired. After all these years he was still her beloved. The light caress of her fingers on his cheek awoke Aaron. He saw the tender look on her face and wondered what had put it there.

"Come along, dear husband of mine, it is well past the time we should be abed, tomorrow will be a very busy day." Sera grasped Aaron's hand and tugged him to his feet pulling him toward their bedroom. With a huge yawn he followed willingly and soon, nestled together, she tucked against him, he with his arm curved over her body, both were sound asleep. The comfort of each other's presence an aphrodisiac for peaceful rest.

Saturday dawned clear and sunny. The family was up and already taking care of last-minute chores when the preacher arrived. He went to have his pre-marriage talk with Jake, who was already dressed and waiting for breakfast to be brought to him. The conversation was just ending when Mina brought in the food and told Preacher Jim that the family was waiting for him. She walked with him to the cottage.

After breakfast Sera put on a pot of beans with bacon, it would simmer all morning. A cured ham, potato salad, biscuits, baked bread, and stuffed cabbage sat on the extra table in the corner. The two-layer wedding cake in the center. The cabbage dish would be put in the oven to reheat just before the ceremony began. A keg of apple cider was already tapped. Everything was ready, work finished. Sera went to dress while the preacher took Alea aside for their private conversation, after which he went outside to sit with Aaron, who felt slightly depressed about losing another daughter, realizing there would be the loss of two more daughters in the years ahead. At least, he mused, there should be plenty to offset his loss once grandchildren began to arrive. Just thinking about miniature images of his children made him smile. Preacher Jim smiled in return, happy to see his friend's mood lighten. He had seen plenty of tears at these gatherings. Whether wedding or funeral, it seemed to unleash a font of emotion. He remembered when he had first joined the ministry he'd had a hard time at services keeping his own tears in check. It would have been unconscionable to be blubbering in front of people who depended upon him for strength. He almost laughed aloud recalling the first funeral he had officiated. Not that the funeral was funny, not at all. It was just he'd had to pretend to have a coughing fit as an excuse for the tears streaming down his face. The attendees had been so concerned for his welfare they had stopped crying in order to assist him, which in turn had helped him gain control of himself.

Sounds of singing could be heard in the distance and soon a group of people emerged from the forest trail. Jake's family, brothers Lew and Tom Wells, parents Matthew and Eva, followed closely by a half dozen neighbors from the area and then Mica, the very last of the group.

Once the horses were taken care of the guests gathered in a half circle facing the cottage door. Jake and the preacher had taken their places, Jake's parents and brothers beside him. Opposite him were Sera and her two daughters Mina and Nia. When Aaron exited the cottage with Alea on his arm conversation ceased. The ceremony began as soon as Aaron took his place next to his wife, leaving Alea standing next to Jake.

"We are gathered together to witness this union..." Preacher Jim spoke the familiar words as Jake and Alea gave their vows of commitment. When the plain gold ring had been placed on the bride's finger and the veil lifted for her to receive the first kiss from her husband, the gathering burst into applause and shouts of congratulation. Mica reached for his fiddle and began to play while the women hurried to bring the food to the tables. Some of the guests brought bedrolls and would stay the night sleeping under the stars. Others lived close enough to reach home within an hour or so.

When, much later, Alea and Jake retired to their bunkroom, they were serenaded with an old-fashioned shivaree, much to their startled surprise and delight. A final tribute to their marriage. Everything had been perfect. The weather, the food, Mica's gracious gift of music which had everyone either dancing or tapping their feet.

When at last the newlyweds fell asleep it was with happy anticipation of the future days and years they would share together, the warm memories they would recount to their sons, daughters and God willing, to their grandchildren.

Sera and Aaron arose early, wanting to provide breakfast for the remaining guests who would get an early start for home. Food was reheated. Beans with bacon, ham, scrambled eggs plus the remainder of the bread and biscuits, plenty for everyone who chose to stay a bit longer and postpone the chores awaiting them at home. It was still early dawn when the last guests departed with shouts of good luck, safe journey. Happy for the respite from their daily monotony, leaving with the anticipation of arriving at their own homes.

After hugs, kisses, handshakes, and well wishes Jake and his family went outside giving Alea private time to say her farewells. Although a bit teary eyed with emotion at the imminent separation, all went well with Sera, Aaron and their two daughters until the group disappeared into the forest trail on their way to Gully town.

For a while, the cleaning, sweeping, remaking the beds, raking litter from the yard and then washing dishes helped fill the hours for Sera. Then it was out to the barn to strip the bunk bed. However, no other cleaning was needed, the room was still as fresh as when waiting for the newlyweds. Sera, bedding wadded up in her arms, took a final glance around the room, ready to turn and walk out. Instead she dropped the bedding onto the chair and sat on the edge of the bed, loath leaving the room, at least for a while. She remembered the glow on Alea's face that morning, the love and happiness she felt for her husband there for all to witness. As for herself, the pride and pleasure in knowing it was a match well made gave her deep satisfaction. But the pain, little pieces of herself being pulled from her very soul. The loss of a beloved face etched so clearly in her mind. Not to see, to speak, to touch, to soothe. Only to miss in such a ferocious way, knowing time would never heal, nor somehow manage to fill that gaping empty space. It was there for her to live with, deal with, try to ignore. Regardless what she did, when she least expected it the pain would erupt once more reminding her of her loss.

Dry eyed, Sera walked to the chest to make sure nothing had been left behind. Pulling out the top drawer she saw a folded paper tucked in the corner. Reaching in, opening it, she brought it closer to the light from the window to read.

Dear Mother, Jake is still sleeping, so I'm taking time to write this note to you, knowing you will be doing exactly what you just did. I have never taken the time to thank you, Mom, for all the things you did for me. I don't mean for just my wedding, I mean my whole life. On this, my first morning as a wife, I realize all the responsibilities you had and how you tried to teach me and my sisters the right and wrong things that can make or break a person. Thanks to you, I am not afraid of what lies ahead and, Mom, if I ever have any questions a woman should know about, you will be the one I'll ask, even if I have to ride two days to get there. I love you, Mom.

Your devoted daughter,
Alea Hamlin Wells

Sera stood holding the note to her breast, tears finally making a path down her cheeks as she said a silent thank you to the thoughtful young woman who had made her feel so loved. She still felt the pain of separation but somehow it didn't seem so hurtful, so permanent. Thinking of the horses they had, how easy it would be to visit once in a while, Sera actually began to smile.

When she returned to the cottage she had dried her tears promising herself not to dwell on the absence of her daughters, but to concentrate on making life as happy as possible. It wouldn't be difficult. Mina and Nia were at the same age the older two had been when they were feeling the pangs of becoming adults. All the questions would begin. The curiosity about physical changes would happen to Mina very soon, possibly before spring arrived. It was always a milestone for them to discover they had become a woman capable of bearing a child. The thought of grandchildren filling the days of her old age lifted her spirits even more. By the time she walked through the door Aaron was surprised at the bright glow in her beautiful gray eyes, although a slight trace of redness remained from tears she had shed. Rising from his chair he took her in his arms and held her closely, knowing she felt the loss just as he.

The remainder of that day and several more was spent gathering the last of the vegetables from the garden. Cabbages washed and shredded for sauerkraut, late apples garnered from the few remaining trees the storm hadn't destroyed, the apples sliced and dried for winter use. A few squash and pumpkins, some sliced, threaded on twine and hung to dry. Pumpkin cooked and canned, seeds saved for next year's garden. The final cleanup accomplished before the first winter snowfall.

When all was finished Aaron saddled up for a trip to Mica's for supplies. He led Blacky to carry part of the load home. Salt, sugar, flour, molasses, another case of Mason jars to finish canning the pumpkin. Cornmeal, liniment, tea. The list was extensive, partly because of the losses they had sustained during the storm. So many staples had vanished into the vortex.

The visit with Mica was short, the sky looking threateningly heavy with dark clouds. As soon as everything had been loaded onto the two horses Aaron said his farewells, promising to return on the next decent day to spend some time with his old friend and play a few games of checkers. With a last wave goodbye, Aaron headed home. Providence was with him, arriving at the forest trail just as the first heavy snowflakes began to fall. He unloaded the horses near the front door, placing each bundle near the new cabinet where it would be convenient to sort and store. By the time the horses and Bell were taken care of, settled for the night, and Aaron was taking his coat off inside the cottage, the snow was falling so heavily that not even the barn was visible. Winter had arrived.

Time seemed limitless. Sera and the girls began cutting and stitching odds and ends of clothing, remnants for a new quilt. While Aaron decided to try his hand at carving. He had observed Gideon when he searched a chunk of wood, looking for the hidden image he could reveal with his knife. Aaron decided that although he couldn't detect any vision in the piece of wood he chose, he would let nature take its course and just carve away. Wood chips would help fuel the cook range. He placed the chunk on a stool, pulled up another to sit on, and began to whittle away. The clean scent of cedar filled the room with the freshness of a rainy day in the woods. Much of the succeeding days would pass thusly until one day in November when Sera told Aaron it was time she went to visit Fila. The snow was heavy but she would stop over to visit Alea before continuing on. Each stage would only be about a two-day ride. He would remain here with the girls. She was adamant about going and quite capable of taking care of herself. Aaron knew he could not dissuade his wife when she had set her mind to something. Preparations were made, Lady saddled with pack attached, prancing about knowing she would be off and away. On the day she had specified, Sera departed. Aaron and the girls watched as she rode away.

Chapter Thirteen

Luther was enjoying his respite in Umer. He hadn't dwelt on his desire to appropriate the item he coveted so much, feeling it would be available any time he chose to make his move. Maybe he was getting old. He liked his room, the view of the town and the people below doing their errands, stopping to converse with each other when on their way to various destinations. He liked not having to prepare his own meals or shop for staples. In short, he felt utterly entertained just sitting at his window viewing all the activities below. He had been here all year putting on a few pounds from consuming Miss Ivy's delectable suppers and even, occasionally, her tasty desserts. It was almost mid-November. He knew he should complete his mission and return to his dwelling, but it was so interesting being a voyeur, or bluntly, the town's peeping tom. One of the best surprises he had experienced was finding out that the brat Fila had married the person who had possession of the artifact he intended to take. Odd how destiny worked its wiles. He had even seen the ratty dog that had bitten him the last time he had been here retrieving the old wooden Relic from that dead man. That was one thing he'd have to be wary of, he had no intention of feeling those sharp little teeth in his flesh again. Maybe that was one of the reasons he had been stalling about snatching that Blue Pouch, just finding excuses, postponing the inevitable. Well, it was time for him to make his move. He wanted to get home, he had waited too long as it was. There would be provisions to get at the post, things to prepare before the hard cold set in.

As luck would have it he spotted Fila, looking as big as a moose, walking with her husband, who apparently was quite popular with the townspeople. This was a perfect time for him to retrieve the artifact and be on his way. Quickly packing his possessions he hurried to where he had boarded his horse and mule. He saddled up, secured the packs to their backs and within the hour he was on his way to take possession of the artifact.

As he rode through the village, women nodded to him and the men tipped their caps to the strange preacher who had remained a mystery to everyone since the day he had arrived. Not very friendly, he had never made an effort to become acquainted with the townspeople. Any person who had questioned him had been told he was ill and needed a rest before traveling on. Eventually he had been accepted as an oddity and ignored, which had suited Luther just fine. As he rode past Fila she was momentarily taken aback at his strange dress, the hairy visage he presented. For a moment she thought she recognized him from somewhere and tried to recall why he seemed so threatening. Putting the thought aside she grasped Gideon's arm as they continued on to their destination, a visit with Ella, the village medicine woman and midwife.

When Luther neared the stone dwelling he tied his sorrel to a nearby post while warily surveying the area, watching for the mangy cur that had left scars on his ankle. Feeling a bit braver he made his way to the door and, in case someone had noticed, although he couldn't imagine who since the vicinity seemed deserted, gave a sharp knock. Lifting the latch, he entered and pulled the door closed behind him.

Buddy had heard all the outside activity. At first he anticipated the return of his mistress and master but then, a familiar scent wafted through the miniature crack beneath the door. All the old animosity returned. The memory of his old master lying so quietly, this human entering the home taking something that wasn't his. The nasty hit on his head, the trouble this human had caused people he wanted to protect. He was waiting for the door to open so he could sink his teeth into this human. This was what he had been waiting for all this time, the chance to punish this human for all the evil things he had done. He remembered how he had trailed him from the post where his mistress and her young had been staying.

As he readied himself for the assault, it seemed an invisible pressure was applied to his shoulders forcing him to remain against the wall near the opening door, his presence hidden by a long winter cape suspended from a wall peg, its length sufficient to hide him from the Seeker's eyes. He watched in silence as his enemy entered the room pulling the door closed behind him.

Luther was immensely pleased. Not a sign of the mangy creature, good. Now to look, find, and then depart as quickly as possible. He noticed the changes since he had last been here. Cook range, table and chairs, two comfortable seats near the fireplace. Moving on toward the bedroom he saw a sizable rag rug next to the bed. Nice touch, no feet touching a cold floor when arising. A good idea for his own place. Finally turning to the chest, he began to pull out drawers and inspect the contents.

By the time he began searching the last drawer he was on the verge of desperation when a glimpse of blue in a back corner caught his eye. Gently he withdrew the soft, beautiful leather Pouch. The first thing he noticed was the stitched scrollwork around its top edge. "When in need, reach within my well. Do not drink too deeply." I wonder what a well has to do with this artifact, Luther thought, inspecting the stitching closely, thinking there could possibly be some sign or image that would solve the mystery. Time enough when I get back home. For now, I must make sure everything looks normal again, and then I'm off and away.

When Luther exited the cottage Buddy was still secreted beneath the draped cape, held immobile while waiting for his enemy to depart. He felt frustrated at not being able to move nor make a sound. It was a relief when the sound of the horse's hooves faded into silence and he was able to move and sound his warning even though there was nobody to hear.

Chapter Fourteen

By the time Fila and Gideon returned later that afternoon, Buddy had forgotten the entire episode and was curled fast asleep near the cook range. Nothing looked disturbed, the two had no inkling that an intruder had been violating their privacy. Preparations began for supper while Gid put away the purchases they had made. Numerous soft cloths for diapering, a nicely carved cradle that had been traded at Zena's during the summer and saved for them as a surprise. These were the final items Fila needed for the baby's arrival sometime in mid-November. First babies were said to be very unpredictable but they were ready. Fila would not be traveling to town until after the birth. Even then, it would be a while before taking the new babe out in the cold winter weather.

Several mornings later Gideon watched as Fila stubbornly made the bed, refusing any assistance from him. The early darkness of the winter morning made it seem more like midnight than their usual rising time of six. Fila was so uncomfortable with the girth of her midsection, it was even hard for her to breathe. He was afraid to be gone for any length of time. His nerves were frayed, his sleep broken with every turn and groan that Fila emitted during the night. He wanted his wife back, sleeping peacefully at his side. Her discomfort was more than he could bear and it made him feel guilty for what she was going through.

They sat before the fireplace after finishing breakfast, Fila stitching on a flannel blanket for the baby, Gideon reading a town community paper printed by the church. Weddings, births, deaths, new arrivals to town. Recipes, remedies, livestock for sale. It was how everyone kept up with all the town gossip. Any news was told to the preacher, it was all printed out for everyone to read. It was nice sometimes seeing your name in print. Nasty gossip was never set to paper. It would have been beneath the dignity of the church.

Fila had dozed off. Gideon carefully removed the needle from her opened fingers, folding the flannel neatly and inserting the needle in a conspicuous spot in the material so it could be spotted easily and not cause injury.

It had turned into a bright sunny morning. Not much snow had fallen in the previous days so although everything was blanketed with white, it was not overly deep. Gideon thought of taking Night out for a ride but then, glancing at Fila sleeping so peacefully, he did not want to awaken her. She had been so tired lately.

The neighing of Night and an answering nicker caught Gid's attention. He peered out the window seeing a bundled figure atop a black horse making their way to the cottage. Hurriedly pulling on his coat he slipped out the door closing it quietly behind him.

The animal looked familiar but he couldn't recognize the rider until the scarf was flung back and Sera's face, aglow with a huge smile, was revealed. "I finally made it in time," Sera gloated. "I stopped to visit with Alea and Jake for a few days. They are doing quite well staying with Matt and Eva until their home is built next spring. I have all kinds of news for Fila. I wanted to be here for the birthing. I knew she would welcome my help." Sera slid from Lady, Gideon there to help her down and lead her indoors where Fila was still comfortably sound asleep in her chair. Gid watched as Sera gently began to caress Fila's hand placing a kiss on her cheek. It would have been a quiet awakening if Buddy had not voiced his welcome in a very vociferous way. Fila awoke with a start, fully believing she was dreaming when she saw her mother standing before her. The ruckus Buddy created made her realize she was indeed awake and her mother was here.

Even with her unwieldy girth Fila seemed to spring from the chair and encircle Sera with, as closely as she could, a warm hug and deeply thankful words of welcome. "Oh! Mother, you're here, I thought I must be dreaming. This is so wonderful, you can't imagine how worried I've been since I've grown so big. Some have said I gained too much weight. I have a hard time sleeping or even walking. My back aches all the time and I wish I could get this all over with. I don't think I will ever look normal again." Fila almost cried tears of joy feeling the worry lift from her shoulders. Her mother had borne four children and would know exactly what to do when the delivery started. Not that she didn't trust Ella, who had been midwife to almost every youngster around, but it felt so much less fearsome having her mother present, a familiar face filled with love to help her through a trying time.

While the two women were busy Gideon unsaddled Lady, brushed and fed her, staying with her until she acquainted herself with her new surroundings. Once satisfied she would be comfortable, he returned to the cottage bringing Sera's pack with him.

Sera would sleep with Fila. He would make a pallet in the kitchen where he would enjoy a good night's sleep. He didn't want to seem selfish knowing Sera would now be the one waking when Fila groaned, but looking forward to a restful night pleased him immensely.

That night, surprisingly, Fila slept like a babe. Sera, tired from the travel, also slept well. The only one who didn't was Gideon, who kept hearing paws moving in doggie dreams, or little woofs of doggie chases. When those noises finally ceased, Gideon couldn't believe his ears when Buddy began to actually snore. Oh! It wasn't LOUD snores, but soft little wuffle-snorts that would stop dead for a moment, until he thought the little guy had died, then start up once again, giving Gideon a deep sense of relief that Buddy was still alive. The ups and downs of emotional worry at last put Gideon into dreamland. He awoke the next morning to the sound of Sera scrambling eggs while Fila still slept peacefully, having finally relinquished her duties to her mother.

"Good morning, Gideon. Did you sleep well? You look a little peaked this morning. Not worrying about Fila are you? Just relax, son, everything will be just fine now that I'm here. I just couldn't tolerate the idea of some stranger caring for Fila when I've been through this four times and have all this experience. I understand the midwife, Ella, has been assisting deliveries for many years, I'm sure she won't mind having me there to help." Sera paused to add some chopped ham to the egg mixture before pouring it into the iron skillet. The sizzle warned Sera to slide the pan slightly off the hottest section of the range top. Another pan held the potato-onion mixture. "It's nice you invested in this new cook stove. It'll be a lot easier on Fila than using the fireplace with those hooks and heavy pots. Aaron put one in our place after the tornado took most of our home. We still use our fireplace to help heat in cold weather but it's so much easier cooking now. Sure has spoilt me having this modern convenience. You're a good husband, Gideon, a lot like my Aaron in more ways than one. I had a feeling about you the very first time you came riding up to our home. Who would have believed that later you'd be married to my daughter and fathering my first grandchild. You'll probably be running into Jake, your new brother-in-law, from time to time. It's nice you two know and respect each other. Alea made a beautiful bride, I was sorry you and Fila couldn't be at the wedding. Likely you two families will get to visit each other once in a while seeing it's only a two-day ride. Those two sisters will be having plenty to compare and talk about to each other. 'Specially when both have children. I suspect Alea will be expecting before the year is out."

Gideon was already sitting at table having his eggs and potatoes when Fila appeared nicely dressed and groomed, ready to face the day. She had slept well and it showed on her smiling face. Having her mother here had seemed to dissipate all her worries about the coming delivery. She felt relaxed and surprisingly, not so uncomfortable with the bulk she carried. Of course it helped having Mother prepare breakfast, a load off her own feet so to speak.

The next several days passed pleasantly, Fila getting plenty of rest, Gideon trying to keep out from underfoot while preparations were made for the birthing which was expected at any time. The waiting seemed interminable.

In the middle of the night of the fifth day that Sera had taken up temporary residence, Fila awoke in misery. Waves of pressure and a feeling of wetness under her hips had built into actual discomfort. Arising from the bed she padded barefoot to where Gideon was sleeping heavily. Giving several shakes to his shoulder she at last nudged him awake. "It's time. Go fetch Ella."

Sera, hearing the commotion, arose and dressed. She pulled off the bedding, replacing it with several layers of clean flannel and a final sheet of cotton. Soft cloths were folded and ready. The fire was stoked in the range with several pots of water heating. Wash cloths and soap handy, Fila was undressed and given a clean gown to wear after being washed, rinsed and dried, fresh and clean for the newborn's arrival. Sera knew cleanliness was a given for survival of both mother and babe.

By the time Ella arrived she could see that Fila would not deliver before mid-morning. The hours passed between short naps, waves of pressure, sips of Ella's special tea, and Fila trying to push baby closer to birth until, at last, little Cal Larson greeted the world with his first cries. Named after his grandfather Calis, he would be his father's pride and his mother's joy.

Sera stayed on until Fila felt capable of caring for her family and home again. The days had passed so quickly that it was six weeks later and well into the new year when Fila saw her mother off and on her way. It had worked out well for travel, January thaw had set in. With luck Sera would be home before the next snowstorm. Stopping at Alea and Jake's with news of their nephew's birth, Alea was ready to leave immediately for a visit with her sister but common sense prevailed and she opted to wait until spring. On the second morning Sera continued her journey home. Anxious to see Aaron and her two daughters, wondering how they had managed with her being away for so long.

When Aaron looked out the window and saw the horse making its way toward the barn through the heavy snow he couldn't contain his elation. It was Sera. "Girls, get down here, your mother's home. Put your coats on, it's too cold to be running outside without them." The two scurried down the attic stairs grabbing coats from pegs and flinging themselves out the door, following in Aaron's footsteps.

Sera was just dismounting when the three crowded in. Aaron untied the packs, handing them off to the girls, and then clasped his wife in a bear hug that took her breath away. "Off with you, sweetheart, into the house with the girls. I'll take care of Lady."

The mare was nuzzling her colt, Blacky, over the stall wall, contented to be home again. Even Bell was tossing her head with excitement seeing her friend. Aaron finished the unsaddling, brushing and feeding and then, after making sure everything was secured from the storm he hurried to the cottage to learn the news of their new grandchild.

It was late, supper over, Mina and Nia preparing for bed as Sera and Aaron sat before the fire contemplating the change made in their lives having a grandchild. There would be visits in the summer, family gatherings here at the cottage occasionally, so much to look forward to.

As conversation drifted into silence Sera began to doze. Aaron pulled her to her feet and led her into their bedroom. Exhausted from her journey he helped her don her flannel nightgown and then tucked her into bed. Oh! how he had missed her, and it had seemed that nighttime had been the worst. During the day he had been able to keep busy, keep his mind occupied with helping the girls, caring for the animals. Anything to fill the hours Sera was absent. But the nights? There had been too many. He didn't like sleeping alone. He always felt comforted if he awoke and heard her light breathing, or felt her warmth when it was exceptionally cold and he could curl against her to fall asleep once more. She was so much a part of him that he could not bear the thought of ever existing without her. At last Aaron fell asleep. Deeply, soundly, the best rest since Sera had left, his love once again at his side.

There occurred a change in their lives. Almost, it seemed, in the very atmosphere that surrounded them. A calmness, a tranquility settled over the family. The new grandchild played a major part in the contentment that filled their hearts. It was no longer just this place, this home, this single family that was important. Their daughters would be stretching the bloodline, bearing new members who would multiply into the future. It was almost overwhelming thinking about it when for years it had been only the survival of those living here in this cottage.

Eventually, Mica turned the Post over to Aaron, extra living quarters added for Aaron and Sera, who cared for Mica until his death. The two daughters Mina and Nia eventually married and decided there was plenty of room for two families to live at their parents' site. Another cottage was built at the far side of the area. The one remaining question? Luther.

Finale

After Buddy barked his heart out after the intrusion of Luther with no one to hear, Luther smugly rode away on his sorrel, even removing the pack from the burro and turning it loose so he wouldn't have to be bothered feeding the animal. It followed for a short time but then, seeing a barn behind the cottage and catching the scent of hay, he ambled in that direction loitering about until he was later found by Gideon.

Luther was happy to be on his way home at last. He had enjoyed the interlude at the rooming house, the food satisfying, his voyeurisms a pleasant pastime. But people were a bore. Nothing exciting ever happened unless somebody died, and then everyone congregated like a bunch of nesting hens clucking away at nothing. It would be a long time before he cared to venture forth among people. Only to search, looking for those elusive treasures that would add power to his realm.

November snow was adding a little trouble traveling but it wasn't too difficult. On his third day, camped inside the wood line well beyond the trail, he saw a bundled rider on a black mare traveling in the direction he had just come from. Odd for someone to be out in this weather, he thought, not realizing it was Sera on her way to Fila's. For a moment curiosity piqued, then with a shrug of his shoulders he continued to consume his supper. Probably just someone going into Gully town, which he had just passed.

The next morning, rising early, he was on his way once more. He passed Mica's Trade Post without stopping, and by noon was on the trail that led to his own territory.

Turning into the path then exiting the trees, he pulled his horse to a stop, a feeling of panic almost stopping his breath. The bramble hedge was no longer there, not one twig or vine remained to protect his property. The entire area was as barren as when he had first discovered the place. Dropping from the saddle he tugged the horse toward the cave entrance that gaped wide open, no door to stop trespassers. Pulling his pack from the sorrel he whacked its rump sending it galloping away, later to be found by Aaron, who, not locating any owners, gratefully kept it.

When Luther entered his home he stood in shock at the sight before him. Every artifact, book, piece not secured, had vanished. The only things remaining? The heavy wooden furniture. Not even a speck of dust seemed to be present. It was as though something had siphoned it all away.

Sitting at the edge of the hearth he thought of all the travels, the searches he had completed, all for naught. Not a single artifact remained. But wait, he thought, he had just acquired one, that mysterious Blue Pouch. Opening his pack he shoved his hand in feeling for the soft leather he remembered. There, he had it. Holding it he inspected the scroll writing around the edges, once again reading "When in need, reach within my well. Do not drink too deeply." It did not make sense to him. Running his hand along the scrollwork he noticed several strands of the silk caught in some of the letters. Carefully he removed them. Ah! he thought, better. "When in need, reach within my well. Do not delve too deeply."

He could feel the heat in the leather warming his hands, it felt comforting as he pressed it against his cold skin. Tempted, he opened the pouch trying to see what was creating it. All he could see was darkness. Slipping his hand inside he felt a quick shock and then the darkness gathered him into its fold....